Swifty

OTHER KIT ANDREWS BOOKS
BY ROBERT W. CALLIS

1. KEMMERER
2. HANGING ROCK
3. BUCKSKIN CROSSING
4. SKELETON CANYON
5. THE NIGHT HAWK
6. ABOVE THE TIMBERLINE
7. THE REUNION

OTHER HISTORICAL FICTION
BY ROBERT W. CALLIS

1. THE HORSE HOLDER

I hope you enjoyed this book and thank you for reading it.

ROBERT W. CALLIS

Swifty

Robert Callis

SWIFTY

iUniverse books may be ordered through booksellers or by contacting:

iUniverse
1663 Liberty Drive
Bloomington, IN 47403
www.iuniverse.com
1-800-Authors (1-800-288-4677)

ISBN: 978-1-6632-0203-1 (sc)
ISBN: 978-1-6632-0204-8 (e)

Library of Congress Control Number: 2020909614

Print information available on the last page.

iUniverse rev. date: 05/26/2020

FOREWORD

This story is dedicated to Gary Carlson, my best friend from junior high school, until his death in 2005 at age 62. When I started writing, I created a character called Swifty Olson. I based that character on my friend Gary. Growing up I was a shy, skinny kid who didn't have an adventurous bone in my body. Gary was the exact opposite. He lived for excitement and adventure and went out of his way to seek it out. He dragged me along with him and made me see the world as he saw it. He and I had adventures I have never forgotten but have conveniently omitted from everyday conversation. He forced me to take chances, get in trouble, and deal with the consequences.

We were best men at each other's weddings. But, after that, we drifted apart due to pressure from others and the circumstances of creating families and a life.

To this day I regret not keeping in close touch. When Gary died, he had become a respected retired teacher, a successful farmer and cattleman, and a well-known local historian. He discovered a graveyard of Mormons on his property who died on their trek to Utah while wintering on the Illinois side of the Mississippi River. His research on the subject got him an invitation to speak at Brigham Young

University in Provo, Utah, and an invitation as an honored guest to the dedication of the new Mormon Tabernacle in Nauvoo, Illinois. Gary experimented with living in balance with nature. He built an early environmentally sound earth house, raised free range chickens, and was a strong advocate for a safe environment.

I remember him most as a young free spirit, eagerly looking forward to the next adventure life held for him. I think of Gary often when I am writing and feel the creation of the character Swifty Olson keeps Gary's wild and untamed spirit alive.

CHAPTER ONE

It had been a long day, and Kit was tired. He turned off the television set after watching the evening news and headed to his bedroom. He wasn't sure why he persisted in watching the news. It was 99% opinion and 1% news. The opinions were pretty much off-the-wall liberal thoughts he found both unrealistic and ridiculous. He headed into his bedroom, pausing only to check the monitors of the on-line security cameras. The old refurbished two- story building that housed his business, Rocky Mountain Searchers, was quiet and empty of any activity. He undressed and slipped into bed, looking forward to a good night's sleep. He fell asleep minutes after his head hit the pillow.

Kit's sleep was rudely interrupted by the ringing of his bedside phone. He sat up and looked at the clock on the nightstand.

"2:45 in the morning?" thought Kit. "Who in the hell calls someone at 2:45 A.M."

He grabbed the phone receiver from its stand and peered at the tiny screen.

"Unknown caller," read the screen.

"Crap," said Kit as he slid out of bed and hit the talk button on the phone.

"Who the hell is this?" growled an unhappy and still sleepy Kit.

"Did I wake the poor tenderfoot from his beauty rest?" responded a tinny voice from the phone.

Kit knew immediately it was his partner and good friend Swifty Olson. He was surprised because, while Swifty was very unconventional and unpredictable, calling Kit in the middle of the night was a first, even for Swifty.

"It's the middle of the damn night, Swifty," said Kit. "What the hell can be so important it can't wait till morning?"

There was a pause from the other end of the line. A pause on the phone was so not like Swifty. Now Kit was fully awake and alert.

"I need to see you. Can I come up?" asked Swifty.

"Where the hell are you?" said a still grumpy Kit.

"Outside, in my truck," responded Swifty.

"Come on up," snorted Kit. "I'll unlock the stairway door."

Swifty's response was a click as he hung up his phone.

Kit got up, threw on a shirt and some jeans and went to the control panel on the bedroom wall. He hit the switch that unlocked the stairway door. Then he went into his small kitchen and had turned on the coffee maker when the apartment's front door swung open and Swifty stepped inside the living room.

Kit grabbed two mugs from the cupboard and waited for the coffee machine to do its thing. When the light went on, he poured two mugs of hot black coffee. Then he added cream and sugar to his mug and nothing to Swifty's. He picked up the mugs and walked over to the living room where Swifty was sitting on one of the old leather chairs. Kit handed him the mug of black coffee and sat down on a matching chair just across from where Swifty was sitting.

Neither man spoke as they sipped their coffee. After about four sips, Swifty put his mug down on the coffee table and looked across at Kit.

"I need some time off," said Swifty.

"You woke me up at 2:30 in the morning to tell me that?" said an incredulous Kit.

Instead of the usual smartass retort Swifty was famous for, he remained silent. Kit knew something serious was up, and he calmly waited for Swifty to tell him what was going on.

"I just got a call from my sister," said Swifty. "She asked me to come home for a funeral."

"Sister? You've got a sister?" asked Kit. "How come I never heard of her before?"

Swifty looked at Kit like he was an addled child. He slowly shook his head in disbelief. Then he spoke.

"I got a brother too. Would you like a complete family inventory and history?" retorted Swifty.

Kit tried unsuccessfully to hide a grin. This was better. This was more like the Swifty he knew well, who took no crap from anyone, including Kit.

"Look smart guy," said Kit. "You've never told me a word about your family. Whenever I brought up the subject, you changed the channel. Now you tell me you got a call from a sister I never heard of and barge in here at 2:30 in the morning. What the hell is going on?"

Swifty looked intently at his friend. Again, instead of a smartass retort, he remained silent as if he was thinking about what he was going to say before he said it. This was a trait that was completely foreign to the Swifty Olson Kit knew.

Swifty reached down and grabbed his mug of coffee. He took a long drink from it and sat it back on the coffee table. Then he looked up at Kit.

"I need some time off," said Swifty. "Like I said before you interrupted me. My sister Melanie called me just before I called you. I haven't seen or talked to her since I graduated from high school and left the ranch to enlist in the army."

Kit wanted to ask why she called and realized Swifty was upset and the smart thing to do was to shut up and wait for him to tell his story in his way and in his own good time. So, he kept quiet and waited for Swifty to continue with his story.

Swifty took another swig of his coffee and sat in front of Kit, silently staring at an imaginary spot on the floor in front of him. After a couple of minutes, he looked up directly at Kit.

"I know we've been through a lot together and make no mistake, you are the best friend I have in the world," said Swifty. "I know I've never shared much about my life with you, but it ain't because I don't trust you. I do. It's just that my life up till recently never seemed to amount to anything I thought anyone would want to hear about. Most of my life up until I hooked up with you has been pretty forgettable."

Swifty paused and took another swig of his coffee. "You do make a good cup of coffee, Kit. I don't know how you can do that and then put all that crap in and drink it."

"By crap, I assume you are talking about cream and sugar?" asked Kit.

"Yeah. What I said. Crap," retorted Swifty.

Kit sipped on his coffee and waited. Swifty rarely talked much and when he did it, Kit knew it was best to stay quiet and not interrupt or distract him.

Swifty put his coffee cup down on the table and sat back in his chair. "This is a long tale of bullshit. You sure you're up for this?" he asked.

Kit glanced at his watch. "It's three in the morning. I'm pretty sure my appointment book is clear," he said.

Swifty grabbed his coffee cup and looked down into it. "I think I could use something in my coffee after all," he said.

"You want cream, sugar, honey, or what?" asked Kit.

"Whiskey," replied Swifty.

"Whiskey it is," said Kit, and he got out of his chair and went over to a cupboard and opened it. After glancing at the contents, he grabbed a bottle of good bourbon, brought it over and sat it on the coffee table in front of Swifty.

Swifty grabbed the bottle, opened it, and poured a good dose in his coffee cup. He recapped the bottle and set it on the coffee table. Then he picked up the cup and took a hearty swig. "That's more like it," said Swifty. Then he sat back in his chair, holding the coffee cup in his right hand, he paused for a moment, then he began telling Kit his life's story in what can only be described as frontier shorthand.

"I grew up on a small ranch just southwest of Cody, Wyoming," Swifty began. "I have an older brother named Bradley or Brad. He's four years older than me. I also got a younger sister. Her name is Melanie. She's four years younger than me. My mom's name is Janet. My old man's name is Eldon. Eldon Olson."

"The funeral my sister asked me to come home for is for my old man."

Swifty paused as if to take a breath or collect his thoughts. After a bit he continued with his story. "My old man was a grade A asshole. He was mean, ungrateful, and nothing I or my brother and sister ever did was good enough. I grew up being yelled at from sunup to sunset. There were a few times I mouthed off, and I got the shit slapped out of me for daring to defy him. My old man didn't believe in spare the rod. He believed in using a stiff rod and having a backup rod in case the first one got busted over my ass. My mom was a good woman, but she knew her place and she kept her mouth shut," said Swifty.

He paused and took another swig of his bourbon-coffee concoction and continued with his story. "My father was a miserable excuse for a human being, and he treated all of us the same, poorly. When my older brother Brad graduated from high school, the next morning he was gone, along with his stuff. Since then he's never called, written, texted, or telegraphed any of us. I got no idea if he's even still alive. He just wanted out of that hell hole and the sooner the better," said Swifty.

"When I graduated from high school, I packed my few things, hitched a ride into town and took a bus to Casper where I immediately enlisted in the army. Since that day I have never been back to the ranch. I send my mom a card on Christmas and her birthday, but I put no return address on it. I just put the whole damn thing out of my mind and moved on with my life," said Swifty.

"You never heard from anyone in your family since you left?" asked Kit.

"Never," replied Swifty. "Never talked to any of my family until tonight when my sister called."

"How did she know your number?" asked Kit.

"She got it from my Aunt Judy," said Swifty. "Judy was my best friend growing up. She snuck me candy when I was little, and money when I got older. I sent her birthday and Christmas cards, and I included my address and my cell phone number."

"Why did you confide in your aunt?" asked Kit.

"My aunt Judy always treated me well and I knew I could trust her," said Swifty. "She married a good guy, and they've done well. She was the only one who would stand up to my damn father."

"She stood up to your father?" asked Kit.

"She wasn't afraid of him and I think he was secretly afraid of her," said Swifty as a small grin overtook his face.

"Do you have any other family beside the ones you've mentioned?" asked Kit.

"Just my Aunt Judy and her husband," said Swifty. "She's my mother's sister." He took a long swig of bourbon laced coffee and sat back in his chair. "My grandmother died when I was young, and my grandfather died in Vietnam. They had one child, my asshole father."

Kit thought about what Swifty had told him and took a sip of his coffee. When he was finished, he set the cup down on the coffee table. "So, what's your plan?" he asked Swifty.

"I've thrown some stuff in a bag and will drive up to Cody. I can stay at the ranch with my mom and sister until the funeral and then come home," said Swifty.

"Why is your sister living with your mom?" asked Kit.

"She got divorced a few months ago and was staying with my folks until she could find a job," said Swifty.

"Does she have any kids?" asked Kit.

"No, she don't," said Swifty. "Thank God for that."

"So, when's the funeral?" asked Kit. "I'll need to get the word out so we can show up to support you."

"No. No, absolutely not," said Swifty tersely. "This is strictly something I need to do for my mom. I don't plan to stay there one more second than absolutely necessary, and I sure as hell don't want my friends to have anything to do with a funeral for my asshole father."

"How about just me?" asked a puzzled Kit.

"You show your face at the funeral, I'll shoot it off," snarled Swifty. "I told you. This is private and the less any of my friends ever hear about it the better."

"All right," said Kit. "I'll stay away, but I think you're being pigheaded and stupid about this. Friends are the ones who show up when you're in trouble and need help."

"I ain't in trouble, and I sure as hell don't need no help," Swifty almost shouted.

A silent pause followed, interrupted only by Kit picking up his coffee cup and taking another sip from it. Swifty just stared at the floor as he slowly cooled off.

"I'm sorry, Kit," said Swifty. "You didn't deserve that. I'm just pissed off about the whole thing. I don't want to go to a funeral for a father I hated. I'm goin', but I'm not staying one second more than absolutely necessary."

"Nothing to be sorry about," said Kit. "He might have been an asshole, but he was still your dad. Besides, after the ceremony, and he's in the ground and everybody's gone, you can take a moment and piss on his grave."

Swifty laughed. Kit joined in.

"So, you're leaving tomorrow and when will you be back?" asked Kit.

"The funeral is in four days," replied Swifty. "I should be back here at the end of five days."

"If you're not back in five days, I'll come looking for you," said Kit.

"If you do that, be sure to check out every bar and whorehouse between here and Cody," replied a grinning Swifty.

Kit looked straight in his friend's eyes. What he saw there was a mixture of grief and determination. "I'll stay here and mind the store, but if anything, and I mean anything bad happens, I expect a call."

Then Kit grabbed a pad of paper and a pen and handed it to Swifty.

"What's this for?" asked Swifty.

"Write down your mom's name, your sister's name, the address of the ranch, and their ranch land line phone number," replied Kit.

"Why should I do that?" said a puzzled Swifty.

"If you do need help, I don't want to be wasting time looking up details I might need to come up there and save your worthless ass," said a grinning Kit.

"All right," said a reluctant Swifty, "But you gotta promise me you'll stay away unless I do call."

"I promise. Scouts honor," said Kit with a fake serious look on his face, as he held up two fingers.

"Asshole," said Swifty as he began writing the details Kit requested down on the paper. When he was done, he tore off the page and handed it to Kit.

"Satisfied, Mom?" said Swifty in a sarcastic tone.

"It'll have to do for now," replied a suddenly serious Kit.

Swifty finished his coffee, stood up, and the two friends shook hands. Two seconds later Swifty was out the door and gone into the night.

CHAPTER TWO

Sunrise found Swifty north of Kemmerer on Route 189 heading to Jackson. He was about forty-five minutes from Jackson and about an hour south of Yellowstone National Park. Swifty had already partially packed his truck before his visit to Kit and was on the road as soon as he reached his pickup.

He wasn't looking forward to this trip as he hated funerals in general. He disliked having to explain to people where he had been for over fourteen years and felt almost no remorse over the death of his father. He knew he was returning to the ranch for his mother. The one good thought he had was that his mother's life had improved considerably with the death of his asshole father. Why she had stayed with him over all these years had always been a mystery to Swifty.

He stopped for lunch in Jackson at a small café that wasn't overrun with tourists and was soon driving into Yellowstone National Park. Even Swifty had to admit the views in the park were magnificent. The park was an amazing place, full of natural wonders unlike any others in the world. As usual in the summertime, the traffic in the park was heavy and progress was slow. Rather than fight it, Swifty decided to go with the flow and enjoy the scenery.

Finally, he was exiting from the east entrance to the park. A roadside sign announced he was fifty-three miles from Cody.

Over an hour later Swifty pulled into the outskirts of the west end of Cody. The buildings and businesses he saw were unfamiliar. When he left Cody, there had been nothing there but sagebrush and prairie grass. After a short distance he came to the junction for Wyoming Highway 291. He turned onto the familiar road and headed southwest. The road curved around to the left as it began to follow the Shoshone River. There were more homes and small ranchettes on both sides of the highway. He passed two new subdivisions on the east side of the road that had not existed when he lived on the ranch. He drove slowly, taking in the sights along the two-lane blacktop road. He saw more familiar landmarks, some of which were homes and small ranches and some of which were natural rock formations and cuts in the rocks. Mountains formed a barrier on the west side of the river, and he knew they would continue almost until he reached the ranch. The highway was about forty miles long and it ended in what had been a tiny settlement with the almost forgotten name of Valley. The valley was created by the Absaroka Range of mountains. Nothing remained of the town, not even a tombstone. But where the settlement had been now stood the entrance to his family ranch. The old wooden gate was wide open. It had been open every day of his life when he lived on the ranch. A weather-beaten wooden sign about the size of a license plate declared it to be the BR Ranch. The black paint on the old wood was barely visible. When he was a young boy, he had asked his father why the ranch was called the BR ranch and the only response he got from his father was, "It ain't important." It was the BR Ranch when he was born, and it was still the BR Ranch after his father's death.

Kit turned his truck into the entrance to the ranch and kept his speed down to about fifteen miles an hour as he scanned both sides of the road, looking for familiar signs from his youth.

Even driving slowly Swifty managed to send off a rooster tail of dust behind him. It was like a dirty grey cloud, announcing his arrival. He cleared a small rise, and there was the ranch house and outbuildings. He had not seen any cattle on either side of the road as he had driven in, but he could see cattle grazing on grass in the low hills behind the ranch buildings and down toward the river.

Usually when one arrives at a home where the recent death of a family member has occurred, the mood of everyone is dark and somber. Not here. As Swifty pulled into the yard in front of the ranch house, the screen door swung open and his mother, his sister, and two yapping dogs spilled out onto the front porch. Swifty got out of the truck and his mother swept into his arms and kissed him on the cheek. She hung on as if her youngest son was a life preserver and she had just jumped off the Titanic. Swifty kissed his mother back and had no sooner released her from his arms when his sister almost knocked him over as she leaped into his arms and hugged him like the long-lost brother he was.

Soon they all untangled, and the two women led Swifty up onto the porch and into the low, one-story ranch house. Before Swifty had a chance to catch his breath, he had been escorted into the dining room and placed in front of an ancient wooden chair at the head of the old long planked oak dining table.

"I thought you would be here around noon since you were driving from Kemmerer," his mother said. "Melanie made a fresh batch of chili and kept it on the stove until you got here."

Swifty grinned at his mother and sister and took the pot of chili his sister held out for him. He filled a large bowl and then grabbed some crackers from a tin on the table. His mother poured a large glass of ice water and put it in front of him. Swifty spent the next hour eating chili and washing it down with ice water and listening to his mother and sister trying to bring him up to speed. Swifty did what he had learned to do best since he left home. He listened carefully.

After lunch was over and his mother and sister were cleaning up the dishes, Swifty went out to the truck and brought his bag into the house. He stopped in the kitchen. "Same room?" he asked.

Both the women laughed, and his mother said, "Yes," and she pointed the way as if she thought he might not remember.

Swifty made his way down the familiar hallway and pushed open the door to his old room. He stopped and looked around. The room was unchanged from the day he walked out of it and left to join the army. He had shared the room with his brother Bradley, until Bradley graduated from high school and left, never to return. The small bedroom was dominated by the set of bunk beds. Being the youngest son, he got the top bunk. When Brad left after graduation, Swifty moved down to the lower bunk. Swifty tossed his bag on the bunk and sat in the one old wooden chair in the room. It was in front of what had served as a desk for both boys growing up. 2 by 4 wooden pine planks on top of stacked concrete blocks. There were no pictures on the wall, just a couple of faded colored posters for the Cody Rodeo.

Swifty and his mother and sister spent the afternoon on the front porch, drinking iced tea and "visiting" as had been the custom in their family for years. Swifty mostly listened and only spoke when he was forced to by his mother and sister. Even when he spoke, he was careful with his words, not wanting to reveal too much about his past life, but relishing hearing the stories of what had happened to his sister, his mother, and the ranch.

Tired from a lack of sleep the night before, he said good night to his mother and sister and was soon fast asleep in his old bed in his old room.

Swifty awoke to the smell of coffee and bacon frying. He showered and dressed and joined his mother in the kitchen. He looked around for his sister. His mother noticed and said, "Mel is still asleep." Kit nodded his understanding and accepted a hot cup of coffee from his mother and sat at the old table. His mother handed him a plate of scrambled eggs, bacon, and sourdough toast. Swifty quickly dug into his breakfast. His mother sat across from him with a cup of coffee, and after he polished off his breakfast, she asked him a question.

"How long are you here for?" asked his mother.

"I plan to stay until the funeral and go back the next day," replied Swifty.

"It'll be good to have you here," said his mother. "You're welcome to stay longer. Both Mel and I would love to have you stay."

"I have this thing called a job, Mom," said Swifty. "Kit would get a little upset if I didn't show up for work."

"I understand," said his mother. "It's just I have some decisions to make and would like to hear what you might have to say about them."

"You mean things like picking out a casket or songs for the funeral?" asked Swifty.

"No, Son. I mean about what to do with the ranch," she said.

"The ranch? What about the ranch?" asked a puzzled Swifty.

His mother took a sip of coffee and set her cup back on the table. Then she looked directly into her son's eyes.

"We've just been hanging on like most small ranchers around here," she said. "Now, with your father gone, I'm not sure how I am going to be able to run the ranch without some help and I just don't have the money to hire help."

"I understand, Mom," said Swifty. "I know how hard it was when I lived here as a kid. I'd like to tell you I'd come home and run the ranch, but I have a job with a good future. I like what I do and I'm doing all right financially. Maybe I could give you some money to help you out with the ranch?"

"I don't want your charity or your money, Swifty," said his mom.

"I wasn't trying to insult you, Mother. If I did, I apologize," said Swifty softly"

"I'm not insulted, Son. I'm just trying to decide what to do?" replied his mother.

"What is there you need to decide about?" asked Swifty.

"We have someone interested in buying the ranch," said his mother. "They've been interested in buying it for almost a year."

"Who's interested in the ranch?" asked Swifty. He didn't know much about the current real estate market around Cody, but he didn't think small, run down ranches were in big demand.

"Your father was approached by the fellow who manages the Haystack Ranch that adjoins our ranch to the east," said his mother. "He came out here several times and tried to talk to your father, but Eldon wasn't interested. The last time the man was here, Eldon practically threw him off the place after he threatened him and told him never to come back."

"When was this?" asked Swifty.

"I think it was about two months ago, but I could be off a week or so," answered his mother.

"Who was here from the Haystack Ranch?" asked Swifty.

"It was Randy Smith. He's the foreman of the Haystack Ranch. He came after you left. I think he's been there for about six or seven years," responded his mother.

"Did Dad ever mention how much the Haystack folks were offering for your ranch?" asked Swifty.

"No, he never did. He barely told me what it was all about. When I asked questions, Eldon told me it didn't mean nothing and it was none of my business anyway," his mother replied in a very soft voice.

"So, you don't know what the offer was?" asked Swifty.

"No, I don't," replied his mother.

"It's been awhile, and I am sorry to admit, I don't even remember how big your ranch is," said Swifty.

"Let me get the ranch book," said his mother.

She rose from the table and disappeared into a small room which served as the ranch office. She reappeared with a thick book where the covers could be separated, and pages added. She placed the heavy book in front of Swifty after he moved his empty plate away.

"Thanks, Mom," said Swifty. He flipped open the cover and proceeded to skim through the old ledger. He found copies of tax returns, bills, livestock records, and finally, he found a copy of the most recent real estate tax bill for the ranch. He studied the deed, checked a few other documents and then closed the ledger.

"It appears the ranch consists of seven hundred and twenty deeded acres with water rights, and at last count, seven hundred leased BLM acres. Does that sound about right?" asked Swifty.

"That sounds right," replied his mother.

Swifty got out his phone and activated the internet. He did a quick search on the current value of Wyoming pastureland and came up with a figure of $450 an acre. Water rights were a plus. At $450 an acre for 720 acres, the total was about $324,000. Not chump change, but not enough for an older woman to retire on.

"Is there any debt on the land, Mom?" asked Swifty.

"No, Son. There is no debt on the land. Your grandfather bought the ranch in the late nineteen fifties. When he came back from the Vietnam War, he paid off the mortgage. There has been no debt on the land since then."

Swifty reopened the ledger book and paged through

it until he found the deed and bill of sale for the ranch in 1957. The 720 acres was sold for $50 an acre for a total of $36,000. Swifty closed the ledger and moved it aside on the old dining table.

Swifty looked across the table at his mother. Her hair was turning grey, but her blue eyes were bright. Her skin was somewhat weathered, but she looked fit and healthy.

"Maybe you should give this Smith guy a call and see what he has to offer," said Swifty.

"I got a call from him right after he heard about your dad's passing, and he said he'd be at the funeral and would be available to talk if I was so inclined," said Swifty's mother.

"I know the Haystack Ranch is big and it adjoins our ranch on the east side," said Swifty. "Do you happen to know how big the Haystack Ranch is?"

"I have no idea, Son," replied his mother.

Swifty opened his iPhone and did a data search on the Haystack Ranch. After only four minutes he had his answer. At one time, the Haystack Ranch was over two hundred and fifty thousand acres. Over the years and a couple of owners, some of the ranch had been sold off and the ranch now consisted of about one hundred and fifty thousand acres. Almost all of it appeared to be irrigated with water rights. The BR Ranch was small potatoes in comparison, but it did border the Haystack Ranch and it did have good water rights. The more Swifty thought about it, the more it appeared as if the Haystack Ranch was trying to grow again. Lots of small ranches in the Cody area were struggling and were likely targets to be bought up on the cheap by a big outfit like the Haystack.

Swifty closed the ranch book and slid it across the table

to his mother. After a couple minutes of thought, he spoke to his mother. "I think I'll go into Cody to the sheriff's office," said Swifty.

"The Sheriff's office? Why would you want to go there?" asked his mother.

"I'd like to get a copy of the accident report," said Swifty.

"Whatever for?" asked his mother.

"Eldon was a lot of things, but he was not a reckless driver," said Swifty. "He rarely drove that old Dodge over forty miles an hour. I'm curious what the report says. It might give me answers to a few unanswered questions I have."

"Will you be home for supper?" asked his mother.

"Wouldn't miss it for the world," said Swifty with a grin. "Being a bachelor has one real drawback and it's a lack of good home cooking."

He hugged his mother and soon he was driving past the gate of the BR Ranch and headed back into Cody.

CHAPTER THREE

In less than half an hour Swifty was parking in front of the sheriff's office in Cody. The county building housing the sheriff's office and jail was a squat one-story brick and metal building that was located about two blocks off the main drag in Cody. He pulled open one of the double doors and entered the lobby. A woman he did not recognize but seemed somehow familiar sat at a front desk. Swifty stepped up to the desk and the woman looked up from typing on a computer.

Before Swifty could say a word, she was out of her chair and swept around the desk toward him. "My god, if it ain't old Swifty Olson back from the dead and buried," she squealed. The next thing Swifty knew she had wrapped her arms around him and was hugging him like an anaconda squeezing its prey.

When Swifty finally extracted himself from her grasp, he pushed himself slightly away from her and glanced at the nametag on her uniform shirt. Swifty smiled at her and said, "Melinda Gates. I thought you were probably in Hollywood by now, starring in big time motion pictures."

Melinda blushed and smacked Swifty on the arm. "Same old Swifty. You always were full of BS, even in high school. And it's Melinda Swanson now," she said as she held up her left hand and waggled her small diamond ring in Swifty's face.

"My, my, how times have changed," said Swifty.

"Where the hell have you been for the past fourteen years?" asked Melinda.

"Fourteen years? Has it been that long?" asked Swifty with a look of mock surprise on his face.

"You know damn well it's been fourteen years," said Melinda. "You weren't at the five-year reunion and then you missed the ten-year reunion. I asked your mom, and she said she had no idea where you were. Nobody had heard from you."

"I was kind of busy," said a grinning Swifty. "Did you know the world is full of unattached females, some of them almost as good lookin' as you."

"Good lord, you are still full of crap, Swifty Olson," said Melinda, but she was smiling when she said it. Then she looked somewhat serious and said, "What brings you home and to the sheriff's office?"

"My dad," said Swifty. "My sister called and let me know dad had died, so I came home for the funeral."

"That was sad," said Melinda. "Seems folks get older around here they seem to get in more accidents, but most of them aren't fatal like your dad."

"Well," said Swifty. "He's why I'm here. If it's possible, I'd like to get a copy of the accident report on my dad."

"I don't see why not," said Melinda. "Have a seat in front of my desk, and I'll see if I can pull it up."

Swifty took a seat, and Melinda retreated to her desk and soon was punching keys on her computer. Two minutes later, Swifty heard a humming noise behind Melinda and then a printer began spitting out printed pages. Melinda retrieved about five pages and handed them to Swifty.

"How long are you in town for?" asked Melinda.

"About five days," replied Swifty. "The funeral is in four days, and I plan to head back home the day after."

"Where's home?" asked Melinda.

"Kemmerer," said Swifty.

"What do you do in Kemmerer?" asked Melinda.

"I work for a company there," replied Swifty. He dug out his wallet, extracted a slightly worn business card and handed it to Melinda.

"Rocky Mountain Searchers," read Melinda out loud. "I think I've heard of them. Don't they find missing people and stuff like that?"

"You hit it on the head," said Swifty. "That's what we do."

As Swifty turned to leave, Melinda put a hand on his arm. "A lot of us, including old friends of yours, get together on Friday nights at a local bar called the Calaboose. You should come. I know a lot of folks would like to see you. Especially now that we know you're not dead," she added with a laugh.

"I'll try to make it," said Swifty and three minutes later he was out the door and in his truck. He started the engine and drove to a nearby parking lot. He parked his truck in a shaded corner of the lot and shut off the engine. Then he pulled out the accident report on his father and began to read.

Ten minutes later he had read the report twice. The conclusion of the report was an accidental death in a traffic accident involving only his father. Knowing how slow and tedious a driver his father had been seemed to contradict what he read in the report's finding. The report included the conclusion his father was driving too fast for conditions, lost control in a curve, and drove off an embankment. The report seemed routine but knowing how slow his dad always drove and how well his old man knew that road seemed out of place with the report. Swifty started the truck and checked the accident location in the report. Then he headed out back towards the ranch and Highway 291.

Swifty drove at a normal pace and when he got close to the location of the accident, he slowed down, allowing a pickup truck behind him to pass. When he reached the accident site, he found a place nearby to pull off the road and parked the truck. He walked back to the site. The road curved away from the river at the location of the accident. Swifty walked the area four times, each time he moved slower than the last time. He could just make out where the tires of the truck disturbed the dirt and gravel on the side of the road where his dad's truck had run out of road and gone airborne. He was puzzled why there were no marks indicating the brakes had been applied and no ruts as he would have expected from the breaking wheels. Swifty pulled out his cell phone and took photos of the tracks he could see and then headed back into Cody.

Once he was back in Cody, he headed for the sheriff's impound lot. Swifty assumed he would find his dad's truck there. The sheriff's office stored abandoned, towed, and wrecked vehicles in an old fenced in lot out on the north edge of town. His memory was correct. The lot was still there and was about half full of vehicles of all kinds and ages, most of them junkers and wrecks. No one was there at the lot and the gate was padlocked.

Swifty parked his truck and walked up to the gate. It was a simple ranch gate of metal bars. He climbed over the gate and walked into the impound lot. He immediately saw his dad's old truck. It was partially crushed and was laying on its side. Most of the glass was broken out and the roof of the cab was almost flattened. He looked inside the cab and he could see some dark stains, but he had no idea if the stains were blood from his father or who knows what had accumulated over the years. The old Dodge was almost new when Swifty left home fourteen years ago.

Because the truck was resting on its side, Swifty had easy access to the undercarriage of the old Dodge. After about ten minutes he found something unexpected. He reached out with his hand and grasped the broken brake line. Upon careful examination, Swifty could see the brake line was severed with a straight, almost precision-like cut. It was not torn or ragged like he would have expected. Swifty pulled out his iPhone and took several pictures of the broken brake line, being careful to take shots from several different angles. Then he put his phone back in his pocket and made his way to the impound lot gate. He quickly climbed over the gate and got in his truck. Then he looked at his watch. He had been in the lot less than fifteen minutes and not a single vehicle or pedestrian had passed by the impound lot.

Swifty sat back in the driver's seat of his truck and thought as he stared out the windshield at the impound lot. He sat there for fifteen more minutes and was undisturbed by any passing vehicles or pedestrians. He realized the lot was not manned and anyone could have entered it like he did and cut the brake line on his dad's Dodge. But why? Going into the lot to try to steal some salvage parts from the Dodge made sense. Going in to cut the brake line and doing nothing else did not make any sense.

Swifty felt the hair on the back of his neck rise. Something was off. Something was not right. His only conclusion was someone cut his dad's brake line when it was parked in Cody. When his dad drove back to the ranch, the brake worked a couple of times and each time brake fluid was pumped out of the reservoir until it was empty. When his dad pressed on the brake on the fatal curve, nothing had happened, and the truck had gone into the curve too fast and ran off the road and then off the cliff. Swifty had never been fond of his father, but sitting there in his truck, he closed his eyes and imagined the surprise, shock and then horror his dad must have felt when the brakes failed and his efforts to stay on the road failed and he and the Dodge were airborne until it crashed and killed him.

Swifty felt remorse for his dad's terrible death and then he felt a growing feeling of anger. Someone had murdered his father. He had no idea who did it, or why they did it, but he was determined to find out. He opened his eyes, looked around and saw no activity. He started the truck and headed back into Cody.

CHAPTER FOUR

Swifty drove back to the ranch. He felt both numb and angry and realized he was driving about seventy on a two-lane highway with a forty-five mile per hour speed limit. He slowed down and tried to get his emotions and his feelings under control.

When he reached the site of where his father had run off the road and crashed, he pulled the truck off the road and sat there, staring at the spot where his father had died. Then he remembered Big Dave's advice to Kit so long ago.

"Look for what don't belong."'

Swifty got out of the truck and slowly walked from the road to edge of the drop off to the river. Then he retraced his steps back to the truck. He got down on his knees and stared at the path from the road to the edge of the cliff that had been the last path his father had taken on this earth. Then he stood and went to the drop off and turned and faced the direction his father would have been coming from on the highway. The turn in the road was sharp and would have required braking for any make of car or truck. Forty miles an hour is a lot faster than it might seem, especially if when you went to hit the brakes to slow down, nothing happened. By the time your brain determined the brakes were gone, it could easily be too late to negotiate the curve and centrifugal force would have taken over and directed the path of the brakeless old Dodge.

Swifty got back in his truck and pulled out the sheriff's department accident report. He read it carefully as he looked straight at the spot where his father's old Dodge went over the edge of the cliff. He needed to slow down his emotions and think this over carefully.

First, the time of day. According to the report, a deputy was called out about 6:15 P.M. by a neighbor. The neighbor was a hobby rancher. A guy who had a few acres of land on the river and had some livestock. According to the report, the farmer raised angora goats. He was out feeding his goats when he heard a crash. He hiked over to the crash site and when he found the wrecked truck and body, he ran back to his goat ranch and called the sheriff's office. He estimated he heard the crash about 4:45 P.M. It took the hobby rancher about half an hour to walk to the crash site, find the crash, and return to his ranch to make the call. That seemed about right to Swifty.

Second, the weather. Swifty got on his iPhone and did a weather history search for Cody for the date of the accident. The weather report reflected things as clear and dry at the time of the crash.

Third, witnesses to the crash. According to the report there were none. Only the hobby rancher heard the crash, even though sound travels a long way at altitude. So, no witnesses.

Fourth of all, why was his father on the road at that time of day and who would know it? Swifty made a note to himself to ask his mother why his father had gone that day.

Swifty started the engine and then headed back towards Cody. After he had gone a mile, he stopped and turned the truck around. Then he drove back towards the accident site, pushing the accelerator until he was doing slightly above forty miles an hour. When he approached the tight curve, he resisted the instinct to apply the brakes and tried to make the turn. At the last second, he slammed on the brakes and brought the pickup truck to a stop. Swifty got out of the truck and walked to the front. His front tires were only about three feet from the edge of the cliff.

Swifty stood there for a minute, staring down where his father's Dodge had crashed. He was about twenty some years younger than his father, had better reflexes, and he knew what was about to happen ahead of time. He turned and walked back to his truck. As he headed back to the ranch, he was positive someone had murdered his father by tampering with the brakes. If he could figure out why someone had wanted to kill his father, he could likely figure out who.

When he drove up to the ranch house, he saw his mother and sister in the distance working on some fencing. He got out of the truck and hurried down the pasture to where his mom and sister were struggling with a fence post.

"Need some help?" asked Swifty as he approached the two women.

His mother looked happy to see him. His sister looked relieved.

Swifty analyzed the task and trotted back to his truck. He quickly returned with a pair of leather work gloves and a small tool bag. Twenty minutes later the old post had been replaced with a new one and the barbed wire had been properly strung and attached. The trio moved down the fence line and spent another two hours replacing three more badly rusted fence posts and rewired them.

When they finished the third fence post, Swifty's mother and sister headed for the house, and he loaded tools, fence posts, and wire in his pickup and drove to the tool shed where he unloaded and stored them. Then he drove to the house and went inside.

He opened the front door to the smells of something good being prepared in the kitchen invaded his nose. Swifty stuck his head in the kitchen only to be smacked on the arm by a long wooden spoon wielded by his mother.

"Stay out of my kitchen until you have cleaned all the fence mending dirt off you," she commanded. Swifty obeyed and quickly showered and changed into clean jeans and a denim shirt. Dinner was an excellent goulash with fried potatoes and green beans. Swifty had two helpings. At dinner, he remembered to ask his mother where his father had gone that day and why. She thought about his question but was unsure of why her husband had gone to Cody that day.

"He hardly ever told me anything and he sure as hell was not about to tell me why he was going to town," she said. "Your dad didn't confide in me about much."

"Did he go into Cody on certain days of the week?" asked Swifty.

"No, I don't think so," replied his mother. "Your dad would just get a notion, and then he'd get in his old Dodge and drive out the gate."

When dinner was over, Swifty offered to help clean up,

but he was shooed out of the kitchen by his mother and sister.

Swifty went into the living room and settled into his father's old leather recliner. He elevated his legs and then pulled out his iPhone. He had five messages from Kit. When he pulled them up, they were all basically the same. "Where are you? How are you? What are the plans for the funeral? Why the hell haven't you responded to my emails? When the hell are you coming back to Kemmerer?"

Swifty had to restrain himself from laughing out loud. Sometimes Kit was a good friend. Sometimes he was a good boss. This time he was acting like a good mother. Swifty wrote a short, yet terse reply that tried to answer Kit's questions in the fewest words possible. He smiled as he hit send.

Then he started thinking about his father's murder. He decided he needed to go back to the sheriff's office, find the deputy who investigated the crash, tell him what he had found, and show him the pictures he had taken of the cut brake lines. He wasn't a cop. The sheriff's office had jurisdiction and should be the ones leading an investigation into his father's murder.

Then Swifty began to think about a motive. Why would someone kill his father and make it look like an accident? Whoever did it must have been waiting for an opportunity to cut his brake line. This person would have to see his old man drive into Cody, follow him, and then wait for an opportunity to slide under the old Dodge and cut the line. It couldn't have taken the killer more than three minutes total. His father was a grade A asshole and probably had pissed off at least half the people in Park County. Cody was the county seat and probably 75% of the folks who lived there disliked his father. But disliking someone because they were an asshole was hardly a motive to kill them. When people disliked you, they avoided you, and they ignored you. They talked about you when you weren't around and never had anything good to say about you to anyone. None of that added up to a motive to kill someone.

Then Swifty remembered something Kit had once told him.

"Always look for the money first."

Most crimes involved money. One person had it. Another guy wanted it. In his experience in the military, Swifty had learned the hard way that sometimes hatred had nothing to do with money. Sometimes people just plain didn't like you, or anything about you. He had run afoul of a few guys in the army who were not fond of him. Most of them didn't wish him well, but their dislike generally stopped there. No one had rolled a live grenade into his sleeping quarters during his twelve years in the army. He had gotten into plenty of altercations and some had ended up in very physical fist fights. But, other than some bumps and bruises, they had generally ended there.

Swifty decided to try to stop thinking about a motive and do something else with his mind. He pulled up an e-book he had purchased online and started to read it. The book was about Geronimo, the Apache warrior, written by some guy he had never heard of and co-authored by Mike Leach, a college head football coach. Swifty liked Leach who was a very colorful guy who liked pirates. More importantly to Swifty, Leach was born and raised in Cody, Wyoming. Swifty fell asleep in his chair.

He awoke about three in the morning. He got up and went to his old bedroom and slipped into bed. He was sound asleep in minutes.

Swifty was up at dawn and dressed and out the door. He fed the cattle and horses hay and grain and then returned to the ranch house. His mother was up and making breakfast when he breezed in the front door.

"Something smells darn good," said Swifty.

"Scrambled eggs, bacon, and sourdough toast," replied his mother without missing a beat in her cooking. "Coffee is ready."

Swifty poured himself a cup of coffee and took a sip. It was strong coffee, black and hot. He took a seat at the table and sipped his coffee as he watched his mother finish up her cooking. Soon, Swifty had a large pile of scrambled eggs, bacon, and toast with strawberry jam on his plate. He immediately dived into the hot breakfast. When he was finished, he took his dishes to the sink, cleaned them off and rinsed them and put them on the sideboard. Then he went to a cupboard, found what he was looking for and returned to the table with a pencil and a small pad of paper.

His mother had joined him at the table and looked puzzled at the paper and pencil. "Are you taking notes?" she asked.

"In a matter of speaking," replied Swifty.

"Notes of what?" asked his mother.

"Actually, it's a list," said Swifty.

"A list of what?" she asked.

"It's kind of a to do list, Mom. I still have some questions about dad's death, and I find if I make a list of things, I work on each item until I can check it off the list. When I run out of items, I'm done," responded Swifty.

"So, you're headed back into Cody?" she asked.

"I am, but I'll be back before supper," said a smiling Swifty.

"Don't forget the funeral is the day after tomorrow," she reminded him.

"It's on my list," said Swifty and he rose from his chair and headed out the door.

"It better be!" she said to his retreating backside.

Swifty climbed into his pickup and headed down the lane to the highway. He had questions and he wanted answers. Like he had learned from Big Dave, "start at the beginning."

CHAPTER FIVE

Swifty arrived in Cody about 6:30 AM. He drove to the sheriff's office and parked in front. As he walked in the front door, he saw a young male deputy he did not recognize sitting at Melinda's desk.

Swifty walked up to the desk and greeted the deputy. "Hi, is Melinda working today?" he asked.

The deputy looked up from his paperwork and replied, "She's on today, but she don't clock in till eight."

"Is it all right if I just sit here and wait for her?" asked Swifty.

"Help yourself," said the disinterested deputy. "It's a free country."

Swifty found a chair by the wall next to the front door and checked his iPhone for messages. There were a few worthless solicitations and a short text from Kit.

"When you're done with whatever the hell you're messing around in, get your worthless hide back to Kemmerer."

Swifty grinned. He knew Kit was not happy with him gone and Kit not knowing what was happening, but this was Swifty's private family business. He felt perfectly capable of getting that business taken care of all by himself.

Swifty glanced at his watch. Melinda wasn't due to

arrive for over an hour. He got to his feet, told the deputy he'd be back and headed out the door. Once out of the sheriff's office, he walked down the street until he came to a small coffee shop. He went in, ordered a large black coffee and paid for it. He took his coffee with him and walked across the street to a pocket park. He sat on a bench which gave him a good view of the building housing the sheriff's department.

Swifty sat back on his bench, sipped his coffee, and watched the small world of Cody pass by in front of him. At first traffic was minimal, but as the time passed, the traffic on the road increased. At about ten minutes till eight, he saw four different vehicles pull into the employee parking lot on the side of the sheriff's office and park. The occupants all wore deputy uniforms, two men and two women. They entered the side door of the building and disappeared inside. Swifty finished his coffee and then got to his feet and walked across the street to his destination. By the time he entered the sheriff's office, Melinda was seated at her desk.

Melinda looked up, surprise on her face. "What in the wide world of sports are you doing here at eight in the morning, Swifty Olson?" she said.

Swifty smiled and said, "I'd like to talk to the deputy who investigated my father's crash. Is he around this morning?"

"Let me check," replied Melinda. She began pecking on keys on her computer and after a few seconds she looked up at Swifty with a grin. "You're in luck, Dandy Don Hillman just checked in. He's back in the ready room. I'll call him for you."

"Dandy Don?" asked a puzzled Swifty.

"You'll know why when you see him in person," smirked Melinda. She got on the phone spoke softly into the receiver and after a short pause, she spoke again. Then she hung up the phone. "He'll be right out," she said. "Apparently my call interrupted his coffee break."

"But you said he just came on duty?" said Swifty.

"You catch on fast for a country boy," said Melinda. "Why do you think he has the nickname Dandy? Did you consider my offer to show up at the Calaboose Friday night?"

"I'll wait to pass judgement," responded Swifty. "And, I plan to stop by Friday night."

"Good for you," said Melinda. "You won't be sorry."

Kit grinned and walked back to his chair, taking a seat as he waited for the deputy with the strange nickname of Dandy.

It was a full twelve minutes before Dandy Don Hillman made his appearance in the lobby of the sheriff's office. Dandy Don was about five foot eight inches tall, wearing cowboy boots. He was young, maybe twenty-five or twenty-six, and every piece of brass was polished to a high gloss, including his belt buckle. His pressed uniform pants had a razor-sharp edge to them, and the overhead lights flashed off his highly polished boots. He looked like he fell out of a recruiting poster for the Italian Air Force.

Kit stood as Dandy Don walked up to him.

"Mr. Olson?" said Dandy Don.

"That'd be me," said Swifty.

"Please follow me to my office," said Dandy Don and he turned on his heel and walked quickly back down a hall before turning through an open door to a small room with a table and three chairs.

"Please have a seat," said Dandy Don.

Kit took a seat and Dandy Don did as well.

"What can I assist you with, Mr. Olson?" inquired Dandy Don.

"I understand you were the investigating officer in the accident involving my late father, Eldon Olson," said Swifty.

"Why yes, yes I was," said a somewhat surprised Dandy Don.

"I read your report, and I have a few questions for you," said Swifty.

"Of course," said Dandy Don. "Anything to help a bereaved relative."

"Were you the only officer on the scene of the accident," asked Swifty.

"Yes, I was on patrol alone when the call came in," replied Dandy Don. "The accident was reported by a neighboring rancher."

"Did you call in a forensic team, Deputy?" asked Swifty.

Dandy Don frowned. "Why no, I didn't," he replied. "It looked like a one car accident pure and simple to me. Older man in an old truck. Probably took the corner too fast and failed to make the turn."

"If that were so, why were there no skid marks?" asked Swifty.

"Skid marks?" responded Dandy Don.

"You know, skid marks. The things a vehicle's tires make when you slam on the brakes to slow a truck to avoid an accident," replied Swifty.

"I don't recall seeing any skid marks," said Dandy Don after he paused for a moment to try to remember what he had seen.

"That's probably because there were none," said Swifty. "Not on the pavement, not on the gravel on the side of the road, and not in the grassy ground all the way out to the edge of the cliff."

Dandy Don looked puzzled. "No skid marks?" he said, still looking puzzled.

"No skid marks," said Swifty. Then he turned on his iPhone and flipped to photos and after finding the shots he took off the ground at the site, he slid the phone across the table to Dandy Don. "There are no skid marks anywhere," said Swifty.

"It could have rained and washed them away," said Dandy Don.

"I checked with the weather site," responded Swifty. "The weather was dry. No rain, no snow, and probably not even any spit."

"Maybe the driver just fell asleep and missed the turn?" offered Dandy Don.

"My dad drove that road every day for over forty years," said Swifty. "It seems unlikely."

"Maybe he had been drinking and fell asleep," said Dandy Don.

"Did the coroner do a blood alcohol test on my dad?" asked Swifty.

"I don't know," said Dandy Don. "That's not part of my job."

"Did you climb down the ravine and check to make sure my dad was dead?" asked Swifty.

"Ahh, no. No, I didn't," replied Dandy Don. The deputy looked surprised and uncertain. He paused for a minute and then he responded. "I could see the body of the deceased was half in and half out of the truck and I could see no signs of life. I called in for the coroner and he arrived about half an hour later and declared your father dead at the scene."

"So, you left the body for the coroner to examine," said Swifty.

"Yes. Yes, I did." Said Dandy Don.

"Did you climb down and examine the wreck?" asked Swifty.

"No. No, I didn't," said the deputy. "I stayed at the scene until the wrecker arrived and didn't leave until he had winched the old Dodge out of the ravine and left to take it to the impound lot."

"Did you examine the truck after it arrived at the impound lot?" asked Swifty.

"No. Why would I do that?" asked the now very nervous deputy.

"To check for any possible mechanical reasons for the crash," said Swifty.

Dandy Don had no reply. He put both his hands flat on the table and looked across at Swifty. "I did my job. I did what I'm supposed to do. Your old man got killed because he was careless."

"Maybe so, maybe not," said Swifty who sat back in his chair, as relaxed as if he was sitting in a bar having a drink after a hard day's work.

"If you've got a problem, I suggest you take it up with the sheriff," said a now upset deputy.

"I think I will," said Swifty. "Is the sheriff in his office?"

"I got no idea," retorted Dandy Don. "I ain't his social secretary. You want to talk to the sheriff, haul your butt out front and ask Melinda."

"I think I'll do just that," said a smiling Swifty. "Thank you for your time, Deputy." With that Swifty rose from his chair and walked out of the room and back up to the lobby.

By the time Swifty had reached the lobby, Dandy Don had disappeared into the bowels of the sheriff's office. He strode up to Melinda's desk and stood in front of her.

Melinda looked up, as though surprised to see him so soon. "Problem?" she asked.

"I need to see the Sheriff," said Kit calmly.

"Bad idea, Cowboy," she said. "He's an even bigger asshole than Dandy Don."

"Nevertheless, I need to speak to him," said Swifty.

"O.K., but it's your funeral," said Melinda as she picked up her phone. After a couple of seconds, she spoke softly into the receiver and then hung it up. "The Sheriff says for you to wait out here and he'll see you when he has some time."

"Any idea of when he might have some time?" asked Swifty.

"Nope. That's his way of blowing you off," said Melinda. "If you're still here in an hour, he will probably talk to you."

Kit shrugged his shoulders and went over to a hardbacked chair and sat down. After fifteen minutes had passed, he slid down in his chair and pulled his cowboy hat down over his eyes. To anyone in the reception area, he looked as though he was taking a nap.

CHAPTER SIX

Swifty's eyes were closed, but he was not sleeping. He listened carefully to everything said within his earshot. The longer he appeared to be asleep, the more conversation he was able to pick up, and people in the reception area seemed to forget about his presence. In the army he had learned a sleeping man soon became part of the furniture unless he was snoring or doing something that was disruptive to the people around him. He picked up on some petty office gossip, some disagreements, and some outright arguments.

After about an hour and a half, he heard boots on the thin carpet approaching his chair. Rather than open his eyes, Swifty continued to feign sleep. He heard someone clear his throat and then a loud bass voice called out his name. +

"Mr. Olson?" said the sheriff.

Swifty opened his eyes and swung out of the chair and up onto his feet. Standing before him was the sheriff of Park County. The sheriff was about five foot eight inches tall, weighed more than he should, and was wearing a freshly pressed uniform with a large star pinned on the uniform shirt that sparkled in the fluorescent overhead lights.

"Yes sir," replied a now wide awake Swifty. "My friends call me Swifty."

"Follow me," commanded the sheriff. Swifty noted the sheriff had not offered to shake hands. Not a good sign.

Swifty followed the shorter sheriff down a hall to the back of the complex to a large custom-made wooden door. A burnished bronze sign on the door announced the interior as the office of the sheriff of Park County, Wyoming. The sheriff opened the door and walked through it. Swifty followed him into the large office. The office was paneled in fake wood and had bookshelves full of large three ring binders full of official looking papers. Swifty doubted the sheriff had even opened any of them. On the walls were numerous framed photos of the sheriff with local dignitaries, and a few famous people who had found themselves in Cody at some time or another, probably by accident.

After the sheriff was seated at his overly large wooden desk in a large leather swivel chair that sort of comically dwarfed his rotund body, he looked up at Swifty and asked, "Why are you here?" Not, how are you, what can I do for you, do you need something or any of the usual pleasantries one might expect from a politician.

Swifty leaned forward in the chair he had taken in front of the sheriff's desk. He noticed his chair and the companion chair next to him were significantly shorter than the sheriff's chair. Cheap intimidation at its best he thought.

Before answering the sheriff, Swifty took a moment to view the various plaques and awards mounted on the wall behind the sheriff's desk.

"Pretty impressive number of awards, Sheriff," said Swifty.

The sheriff paused, as if interrupted in his planned canned speech about what he was sure was some kind of complaint against his department by a smart mouthed punk who had left Cody as soon as he had graduated from high school and never returned. Swifty's compliment had caught him by surprise.

"Just as few things I've picked up doing my duty as a sworn peace officer in the great state of Wyoming," said the bemused sheriff.

"You have a good reputation as a county sheriff," said Swifty.

"Thank you," said the somewhat surprised sheriff. "Now, what is it I can help you with, Mr. Olson."

"As I am sure you are aware, my father Eldon Olson was killed in a car accident," said Swifty.

"I am aware of the death of your father. It was a damn shame," said the sheriff. "You have my sympathy. Please convey my sympathy to your mother."

"Thank you, Sheriff. I'll be sure to pass that on to my mother," said Swifty. Then Swifty reached inside his jeans jacket and pulled out the small folder where he had stashed his notes and his copy of the accident report. He laid the small file on the edge of the sheriff's huge desk.

"I have a few questions about the accident investigation I was unable to clear up with your deputy," said Swifty.

"What questions?" asked the sheriff.

"First of all, your deputy did not go down into the gully to determine if my father was dead," said Swifty. "Second of all, your deputy did not go down into the gully to examine my father's wrecked truck."

Swifty paused for a moment for those two issues to sink

in with the sheriff. "And thirdly, I examined the wreck in the county impound lot and discovered something interesting about the truck's brake line."

The sheriff's face was suddenly flushed with anger. "You made unauthorized entry into my impound lot?" he practically shouted, ignoring the first two questions entirely.

"I did," said a suddenly stern-looking Swifty. "I did so and found the brake lines had been cut with a sharp object." Swifty pulled out his cell phone and found the pictures of the sharply cut brake line and turned the phone so the sheriff could see the pictures.

"And just what in the hell do you think that picture proves?" roared the now outraged sheriff.

"It tells me someone cut my dad's brake line knowing he would run out of brake fluid before he got home on a winding road next to a steep embankment," said a defiant Swifty.

The sheriff paused and tried to hold back his anger and at the same time digesting the pictures he had just been shown. "Did you become a lawyer when you left Cody years ago?" he asked.

"Nope. I joined the army," said Swifty.

"Well, here in the real world of law and order, your pictures, however damn pretty they are, would be inadmissible in a court of law. You illegally entered county restricted property and allegedly took photos of the broken brake line. You have no proof the line was cut. You could have cut the line in the impound lot which is unmanned, and then taken your pictures," the sheriff practically shouted at Swifty.

The sheriff paused, as if to get himself under control.

Then he lowered his voice when he continued. "Your old man was an asshole and a pain in the ass. I doubt he had a single friend in Park County. He was a lousy rancher and a worthless human being. He got killed because he was a careless driver, not because some imaginary super-secret assassin cut a brake line. You come back here after all these years and make accusations of my people when you have no basis for them. Your old man was worthless, and I see the apple ain't fallen too far from the tree. Get out of my office, or I'll have you arrested."

Swifty got to his feet, retrieved his small file folder and looked directly at the sheriff. "You just made a big mistake, Sheriff." With that said, he turned and stalked out of the sheriff's office. When Swifty got to the door, he paused, turned and looked back at the sheriff.

"I'll be back," said Swifty in a firm voice. Then he disappeared out the door.

CHAPTER SEVEN

Swifty was so angry he blew out through the waiting room of the sheriff's office without stopping to say anything to a surprised Melinda. He found himself sitting in the cab of his truck, waiting for his anger to pass. He thought about what had just taken place, he realized he should not have been surprised. Melinda had warned him. The sheriff was an asshole, just like his deputy. No one in authority in the sheriff's office gave a damn about how his father had died. They all disliked him and were no doubt pleased his old man was dead.

Swifty sat in the truck, going back through his conversation with the sheriff in his mind. Then he realized how absurd his anger was. His old man was an asshole. Always had been one. People didn't like him, and he didn't like anyone, except maybe Swifty's mother. If his old man had screwed up and gotten killed, Swifty would have felt very little remorse. The fact he was likely targeted and deliberately killed set off a different response in Swifty. Even if his father had been a jerk, nobody had the right to deprive him of his life. That's what really upset Swifty.

The real question in Swifty's mind was who killed his father and most importantly, why? He had no idea, and as he pulled out his file and reviewed his notes and the accident report once again, he came up with a big fat goose egg on motive.

All his father had was the ranch. he inherited it with no debt on it. With him dead, Swifty's mother now owned the ranch. She wasn't going to be able to run the ranch without help, which she really couldn't afford. At least if she sold the ranch for a fair price, she would have enough money to invest and live modestly on the income.

Swifty returned to the main question in his mind. Why would someone want to kill his old man? Dislike of someone is a long way from hate. Swifty had learned people kill for several reasons. One was hatred, usually born of some incident the person felt was unforgiveable. This was usually a revenge killing. Swifty knew of no one in the county or the state who disliked Eldon Olson enough to murder him.

Sudden anger was another motive but cutting a brake line to cause an accident would require time, planning and premeditation. All that planning and work seemed a long way from sudden anger.

Money was a strong motive, but his old man had no money. All he had was the ranch. The ranch was a nice piece of land with good water rights, but it held no minerals like oil or natural gas. The Hayfork Ranch was huge and had lots of water rights. The Hayfork folks might want his mom's ranch, but only at a cheap price. As far as Swifty knew, no one other than the guy from the Hayfork Ranch had ever approached his dad about buying the ranch.

Swifty closed his eyes and leaned back in the driver's seat of his truck. The only person who had shown an interest in the ranch was the foreman of the Hayfork Ranch. But he had told Swifty's mother he would wait until after the funeral to talk to her about it.

Swifty could see how the Hayfork Ranch might want their small ranch. It abutted their land and it had good water rights and access to the river. He knew his father would never sell the ranch to anyone for any price. All he had known was the ranch. If he had sold it, he would have been lost in a world he was totally unfamiliar with and unsuited for. It was common knowledge among the ranchers in the county his old man was a lousy rancher. But even he had done well enough to survive economically. Having no debt on the ranch was the foundation of his ability to make a living on the land.

Swifty started the engine and pulled his truck out into the local traffic. He was soon on the road to the ranch. He was deep in thought and mentally ignored the scenery he was driving by.

Maybe a talk with the Hayfork guy might give him some more clues. His mother had told him the guy would be at the funeral and would be available to talk to her about the ranch. Swifty could accompany his mother and see what the Hayfork Ranch guy was proposing. The funeral was in two days. Then Swifty had an idea.

He made his way out to the barn, and once inside he did a mental inventory of what he saw. Most of what he saw was old, worn, and in many cases, not worth keeping. The four horses were average stock at best. The best of the four was a grey gelding. He searched the tack room and came out with the best saddle blanket, saddle, and bridle he could find. Then he poured some oats into an old bucket and slipped inside the bay's stall. Swifty shook the bucket and the horse's eyes lit up at the sound and soon had his nose in the bucket, soaking up the oats. Swifty slipped a bridle on the grey and led him out of the stall. He tied off the reins to a post and proceeded to place the saddle blanket on the bay's back and then followed with the saddle. He tightened the cinch and tested it. Then he led the bay out of the barn and into the ranch yard. There, Swifty mounted the bay in one easy motion. He paused to pat the bay on the neck and leaned down to whisper in his ear.

"Let's go out and see what kind of hand we been dealt," whispered Swifty. With that he dug his heels in the bay's flanks, and they headed out of the ranch yard at a trot.

CHAPTER EIGHT

Swifty guided the bay down the entrance lane to the gate. Once there, he turned the bay, and they began a slow patrol of the boundary fence surrounding the small ranch. Swifty noted places in the fence that needed attention and made short notes in a small notebook he kept in his shirt pocket. He noted the places on the ranch that bordered or contained the river and its natural access to water for the livestock. He also noted small batches of cows and kept a separate count in his little notebook.

After almost half an hour, Swifty came to where the fence turned south. Across the fence was the edge of the huge Hayfork Ranch. Swifty followed the fence at a slow walk, looking at the ground and the area around the fence for any clues. He was over halfway down the fence line when he saw something in the dirt. He pulled back on the reins and the bay came to a stop. Swifty dismounted and holding the reins in his hand, he walked slowly in a circle and with each circuit, he widened the circle. By his fifth circuit of the area, he halted. In the ground in front of him on the other side of the fence, was the distinct mark of recent tire tracks. The tracks were smaller than a pickup truck, suggesting ATV. The tracks followed the fence.

Swifty mounted the bay and followed the tracks from his side of the fence. About seventy yards further south, he saw multiple tire tracks. The tracks were the same, so he determined they were made by the same vehicle, not several vehicles. Swifty dismounted and studied the ground across the fence. Then he saw a small flash of color. Looking closer, he saw several small stakes in the ground, with the top four inches of the stakes painted a bright red. He realized these were survey stakes used by a surveyor or a mineral prospector. He looked at the area where the stakes were located and then at the ground on his side of the fence. He could see nothing to indicate something of any importance. The ground did not appear to be disturbed and he could see no man-made holes in the ground. He took out his phone and took pictures of the area with the stakes and of the area on his side of the fence. He put his phone away and mounted the bay. He continued his patrol of the fence line, taking notes in his small notebook as he rode.

When Swifty had completed his circuit of the small ranch's boundaries, he had several pages of notes on fence repair, and a rough count of the cattle he had seen during his circuit ride. He had reached a point on the ranch road and his original starting point. He turned the bay's head and headed back to the ranch house and the barn. The bay sensed the change in direction and pulled against the bit in his mouth as he attempted to speed up their return to the barn. Swifty grinned, and let the bay have his head. Soon they were galloping down the ranch's dirt road.

Once they reached the barn, Swifty reined in the bay and dismounted. He led the horse into his stall and unsaddled him. Swifty put the saddle and saddle blanket on a nearby sawhorse and removed the bit and bridle. Then he went to the feed bunker and partially filled a small bucket with oats. He poured the oats into a feed bag and then slid the bag over the bays' head and positioned it over her muzzle. As the bay ate the oats, Swifty got out a long brush and proceeded to brush out the horse's coat. After about fifteen minutes, Swifty stepped back to observe his work. Satisfied, he put the brush away and removed the now empty feed bag. He made sure the water bucket in the stall was full and then closed the stall door and left the barn.

He pulled the small notebook out of the pocket of his denim shirt and checked his notes from today's ride. Satisfied, he put the notebook back and went to the tool shed. He removed the tools and materials he needed and dumped them in the bed of his pickup truck. Then he climbed into the cab and started the engine. He went through a mental checklist and after he was satisfied, he hadn't forgotten anything, he put the truck in gear and headed out for the first spot in the fence line he had noted in his little book.

He found the site on the fence line where he had first noticed a problem and brought the truck to a halt. Swifty stepped out of the truck and gathered his tools and material. Soon he had pulled out a few errant staples and then he was using the wire puller to straighten the fence. Once that was accomplished, he re-stapled the wire fence until it was straight and tight. Then he returned to the truck and moved on to the next spot he had noticed. Swifty continued working on repairing the fence line until he found himself back up where he noticed the painted stakes on the Hayfork Ranch. He got out of the truck and walked over to the fence line and sat down in the dirt, Indian style. He sat there and carefully looked at the colored stakes and the ground and ground cover they were arrayed in. His instincts told him the stakes were important, but try as he might, he could see nothing else out of place. He came up empty in his search for clues as to why the stakes were there in the first place.

Swifty got to his feet and returned to his truck. Once there he turned and again looked at the stake decorated spot on the Hayfork Ranch. Why would there be stakes and nothing else? Swifty then thought the stakes might be to mark something else, something temporary like a dead calf. But why bother? Finally, he returned to his truck, got in and drove off, still unsure of why someone would bother to pound painted stakes in the ground in plain open pasture. He pondered the thought all the way back to the ranch house. When he arrived, he still had no clue.

As he stepped up on the old porch, he could smell his mother's cooking. Swifty smiled. Some things never changed. He entered the ranch house to warm greetings from his mother, his sister, and the family dog. It felt like he had never left the ranch.

After supper was over, Swifty and his mother and sister had coffee and sat outside on the roughly roofed porch. The chairs were old and wooden and none of them matched. It felt fine to Swifty.

Swifty's mother asked what he had been up to and he told them about his unsuccessful trip to visit the sheriff and his tour of the ranch's fence line. He wasn't sure if he should bring up the painted stakes, he had seen over the fence on the Hayfork land, but finally he told them what he had seen

"Any idea why the Hayfork guys would be putting out painted stakes in the middle of nowhere?" asked Swifty.

"I know they've had some crews out there doing some surveying and testing," replied his mother. "But that was months ago, and I haven't seen them since. Your dad was not sure what they were lookin' for, but he thought it was a waste of money. There's been plenty of surveys done out there, and no one has ever found a trace of gas or oil," said his mother.

"So, those stakes have been out there for a while?" asked Swifty.

"I don't recall seeing any painted stakes," replied his mother. "But I could have missed them. I don't pay no mind to what's goin' on the other side of the fence. I got my hands full with what's goin' on over here."

Swifty thought about what his mother had said. The tire tracks he had seen were recent, not months old. Still, the tracks could have nothing to do with the painted stakes or when they were placed there.

They sat on the porch, sipping their coffee as the sun began to sink behind the mountains west of the ranch.

"What exactly are you trying to find out?" asked Swifty's mother.

"I don't think Dad's death was an accident," said Swifty. Then he went on to explain to his mother and sister what he had found at the site of the wreck and in the county impound lot. He went on to recount his conversations with the deputy and the sheriff.

"Let me get this straight," said his sister Melanie. "You think someone cut dad's brake line so he would run out of brake fluid and have a wreck?"

"That's what it looks like to me," replied Swifty.

"Why would anyone do that?" asked Melanie.

"I have no idea," said Swifty, "but I'm trying to find out. So far, I seem to be just spinnin' my wheels. Folks around here didn't like Dad, and they ain't shy about saying so."

"So, what are you going to do?" asked Melanie.

"I'm gonna keep on asking questions," replied Swifty. "Someone knows something, and I'm gonna keep asking folks until I find someone willing to talk about what they know."

"How long is that going to take?" asked Melanie. "You can only stay here so long. I know you have to get back to your job in Kemmerer."

"When I first got here, I was planning to head back right after the funeral," said Swifty. "Now, I plan to stay until I find out who killed our father."

"What will you do if you do find out?" asked Melanie. "You already said nobody here is interested in how or why dad died."

"That's true, little sister," said Swifty. "But I plan to find out who and come up with enough evidence to send the killer or killers, to jail."

"Isn't that the job of the police?" asked Melanie.

"It is," said Swifty. "But the cops around here seem like they'd like to just forget about the whole thing. Our old man was about as popular as pay toilets in a diarrhea ward in this county. And I admit I was not a fan of his, but he was our father, and nobody deserves to have their life cut short by some murdering asshole. Dad was an asshole, but he was still my dad. Nobody murders someone in my family and gets away with it."

"If you can't find out anything, will you bring your

partner Kit and his friends out to help you?" asked Swifty's mother.

"I don't plan to," replied Swifty. "This is a family thing and a personal thing to me. To my way of thinking, if someone attacks any member of my family, they are attacking me as well."

"You sound like something out of one of those old western movies you used to watch," said his sister.

"Maybe I am," replied Swifty. "Maybe I am."

CHAPTER NINE

Swifty was up early the next morning. He had coffee with his mother and then went out to check on the cattle. He drove his truck on the rude roads his father had create on the ranch and after almost an hour he was satisfied nothing was amiss. He returned to the ranch house and had breakfast with his mother and sister.

"So, what windmills are you going to try to hit with your lance today?" inquired his sister. Swifty ignored her sarcasm and took another sip of coffee. He put his coffee cup down on the table and looked directly at his mother and sister. "Frankly, I have no idea, but by the time I get to Cody I will have figured out some sort of plan. I don't intend to stop asking questions until I get someone to listen to me and give me some straight answers."

With that, Swifty rose from his chair, grabbed his cowboy hat off the wall rack and was out the door. Twenty minutes later he was driving through the outer edge of Cody. On the way into town he had made a mental list of people who might listen to him. First on his list was the county prosecutor. He drove to the courthouse and parked in the public lot. Once inside the courthouse, he asked a passing clerk for directions to the prosecutor's office. He had no idea who the current prosecutor was, but it was a good place to start. He found the right office and stepped inside. There he approached the first desk he saw and asked the older lady seated there if he could see the prosecutor.

"Do you have an appointment?" she asked Swifty.

"No, I don't," replied Swifty. "But I need to see the prosecutor on an urgent matter."

"If you want to see the prosecutor, you will have to make an appointment. The county prosecutor is a very busy man," she responded.

"All right," said Swifty. "When is his next available appointment?"

The lady opened a small leather-bound book and peered at it through her glasses. "The prosecutor's next available appointment is a week from tomorrow," she said.

Swifty knew the date was too far out to help him, but he had her make an appointment anyway. After taking a small card from her with the date and time of the appointment, he hurried out of the office and back to his truck.

Once in the cab of his truck, Swifty paused to decide his next step. An idea hit him, and he exited the truck and raced back into the courthouse. He went to the framed index of offices on the wall by the entrance and looked at the names of the five county commissioners. Not a single name rang a bell. He knew none of them, nor did he know anyone related to them. Still, it was worth a try. Twenty minutes later he had struck out. None of the commissioners were in or available, and any appointment was at least a week out.

He walked back to his truck and stood there by the driver's side door. Then he got an idea. He left the truck and walked a few blocks to the Irma Hotel. This was the hotel once owned by Buffalo Bill. The hotel had a sizeable restaurant and bar and if his memory served him correctly, this is where all the old ranchers hung out to drink coffee and tell lies every morning.

Swifty entered the restaurant. It was mid-morning and just two couples were having coffee at round tables with seating for four. Swifty looked to the bar. There sat seven old-timer ranchers having their morning coffee and bullshit session. They had been doing that every morning in the Irma since Swifty was a little kid. He thought he recognized at least two of the old ranchers, but he couldn't be sure. He had been gone for fourteen years, and likely some of the old timers has passed on to their reward in the sky during that time.

"Nothing ventured, nothing gained," thought Swifty. He walked up to the bar. His intrusion into the old-timer's private space drew instant stares. A couple looked annoyed, but most of them looked curious.

Swifty picked out an empty stool at the end of the line of old-timers and sat down. The bartender walked over with a puzzled look.

"Cup of coffee," said Swifty, acting like he had been stopping in for coffee every day for years.

The bartender brought him a cup of black coffee and Swifty took a sip, still ignoring his elderly bar stool neighbors.

"Sonny are you lost?" asked the nearest old guy.

"Nope," replied Swifty who took another swig of hot coffee.

"You ain't from around here, are you?" said the old guy.

"Actually, I am from around here," said Swifty. "I was born here."

"What the hell's your name?" asked the old timer.

"Swifty Olson," said Swifty. "Eldon Olson was my old man."

"Eldon's boy?" mused the old guy. "Didn't he have two sons?"

"Yep, he did," replied Swifty. "My older brother is Brad. He left here right after high school graduation and never came back."

"Where the hell have you been all this time?" asked the old guy.

"I went in the army the day after I graduated from high school," replied Swifty. "Seemed like the smart thing to do."

"What did you do in the army, son?" asked the old timer.

"I did a little of this and a little of that," said Swifty. "Mostly I did what they told me to do."

"Sounds familiar," said the old guy. "I went in the Marines when I was eighteen. Hated it, but it was damn good for me. I was a cocky kid and needed to have that crap knocked out of me. The Corps did that part in a hurry."

"I knew a few Marines," said Swifty. "Tough guys and good soldiers."

"My name is Martin Stevenson," responded the old guy. "My friends call me Shorty cause I ain't very tall."

Swifty extended his hand and the two shook hands. "Nice to meet you, Shorty," said Swifty.

"What brings you back to town?" asked Shorty.

"My old man got killed," replied Swifty. "I came back for the funeral."

"That's right," said Shorty. "I plum forgot about him gettin' killed."

"You know anything about his accident?" asked Swifty.

"To tell you the truth, I tend to ignore all the bad shit goin' on today," said Shorty. "Life's too damn short to fill it up with all the crap in the world people do to each other."

"Hard to argue with that line of thought," said Swifty. "So, you've not heard anything about his accident."

"I didn't say that, young feller," said Shorty. "I said I ignore bad shit." Shorty paused for a minute and then resumed speaking. "Your old man was about as popular as hoof and mouth disease in these parts. You couldn't find enough of his friends to hold a two-handed game of poker."

"I didn't care for him much, myself," said Swifty. "I couldn't wait to get away from him."

"Still, nobody deserves to die before his time," mused Shorty.

"Did he have any enemies in the county?" asked Swifty.

"He didn't have no friends, but I ain't so sure about enemies," replied Shorty. "Man can piss you off and you dislike him, but an enemy is someone who hates you. Lots of folks disliked your old man, but I can't rightly say I can think of anyone with a reason to hate him."

"So, no one was having a feud with him?" asked Swifty.

"I can't think of anyone who'd fit in them britches," said Shorty.

Swifty was silent, as though searching for something he could not find resting in his subconscious.

Shorty broke the silence. "Why all the questions about your old man's enemies?"

"Something just doesn't feel right about how he died," said Swifty.

"Something or someone?" asked Shorty.

Swifty paused, not sure how much he wanted to tell this old cattleman. Then he remembered how men like Shorty were often referred to as "brutally honest."

"Let me tell you what I've found," said Swifty. Then he went on to relate in step by step detail what he had discovered about his father's fatal accident. When he was finished, Swifty picked up his coffee cup and took a long drink from it.

Shorty paused before responding to Swifty's detailed story. He too, took a drink of coffee and then set his cup down on the scarred wooden bar top. "If your old man was killed, it was for a reason. Can you think of a reason?"

"I'm sitting here next to you because I am searching for a reason," replied Swifty. "I've been shut down or ignored by the sheriff, his deputies, the county prosecutor, and the county commissioners. I came here to the Irma hoping I could find someone who's been around the barn a few times who might know of a reason someone would want my old man dead."

"Well, I have been around the barn a few times, maybe too damn many times," said Shorty. "But I can't think of a good reason for someone to want to kill your dad. I honestly can't think of a soul who liked him, but that's a country mile from hating him enough to kill him."

Swifty thanked Shorty, laid down some cash to pay for his coffee and slid off his barstool.

Shorty put a hand on Swifty's shoulder. "I'll do some checking around and see if I can root out something. You make it a point to stop back in here and check with me. I didn't care for your old man, but I don't condone cold blooded killing," said Shorty.

The two men shook hands, and Swifty headed out of the Irma Hotel's dining room and bar.

CHAPTER TEN

Once he was outside the hotel, Swifty headed for his truck. Talking with Shorty had not opened any new doors, but it had confirmed his suspicions. Whoever killed his father did not do it out of anger or rage. It was a premeditated murder done for a reason, but the reason was as mysterious as ever.

Swifty sat in his truck. He was running out of ideas. Without a clear motive for murder and no clues leading to anyone, he was stumped. Then he remembered his Aunt Judy. She was his mother's sister. Judy had married a local boy, and it had ended in disaster. Then she met an army surveyor. He was in the area doing a job, and they began dating. They got married, and she followed him on his assignments around the country for the army. When he retired, they returned to Cody, and then bought a place in Meeteetse. She leased out the old drug store and ran an antique and gift shop for tourists there.

Swifty remembered her as a smart and thoughtful woman. She was also a good listener, and she had given him good advice when he was a boy. Unfortunately, he had ignored most of her advice and suffered the consequences.

Swifty put the truck in gear and headed south out of Cody. The drive was about twenty miles on a two-lane highway, and he encountered little traffic. When he reached Meeteetse, he drove around the corner of the block Judy's store was on and parked on the side street.

Meeteetse had a small business district about two blocks long and one block wide. It resembled an old western town with the false storefronts and wooden sidewalks.

He walked up to the front door of Judy's store and found the door locked and the lights out. Taped on one windowpane of the front door was a note.

"Gone to doctor. Be back tomorrow."

"Crap," thought Swifty. "A trip all this way for nothing."

Then his stomach rumbled, and he realized he had eaten nothing since breakfast with his mom. He continued north on the wooden sidewalk on the same side of the street and came to two side by side bars. The Elkhorn Bar and Grill and the Cowboy Bar and Outlaw Café.

Swifty had no idea which place was better or worse, so he flipped a coin in his head and walked through the front door of the Cowboy Bar and Outlaw Café. The place was narrow and dark. The bar was to his right along the wall and there were small tables with mismatched chairs around them on the left. At the back of the bar was a pool table and the restrooms. He was not sure where they had hidden the kitchen.

He picked out a table up against the side wall and took a chair, keeping his back to the wall and giving him a broad view of the entire bar. The waitress appeared at his table. She was an older lady, probably in her late fifties. She was short, a tad on the heavy side, and had short grey hair.

She put a glass of water, a paper napkin wrapped around silverware, and a plastic covered menu in front of Swifty and held a small pad in her left hand and a pen in her right. "What'll you have, Cowboy?" she asked.

Swifty glanced at the menu. He ordered a burger with everything on it with French fries and a beer. The waitress grunted and disappeared as quickly as she had appeared.

Swifty sat back and observed the occupants of the bar. It was late afternoon and there were about five older men at the bar, the bartender, and the now invisible waitress. Swifty could see nothing that appeared threatening, and he sat back in his chair and took a sip of water from his glass.

He looked the bar patrons and the bartender over carefully, but none of them looked familiar to him. Plus, it had been almost fifteen years since he had set foot in Park County, and people and things change in that much time.

Swifty took out his phone and checked for messages. He had some e-mails trying to sell him crap and no texts. He shut off his phone and stuck it back in his jeans pocket. About ten minutes later the waitress reappeared and served him his hamburger, fries, and cold beer. The sandwich was large and juicy, and the bun was fresh. Two things he appreciated, especially in a bar where the food tended to be a tad stale.

Swifty dug into his hamburger and fries and quickly polished them off. He was taking a long swig of his cold beer when the front door opened and three cowboys about his age stumbled into the bar. Swifty could tell by their gait and behavior that this bar had not been their first stop where alcohol was served.

As Swifty took a swig of beer, he noticed something familiar about two of the cowboys. They were loud and boisterous. The third cowboy was just clumsy with the muscle control of someone who had consumed too much alcohol for his body weight.

The three cowboys were all roaring drunk and thoroughly enjoying themselves. They stumbled up to the bar, grabbed stools, and knocked over the beer of one of the older men at the bar. Rather than confront the cowboys over the spilled beer, the old guy slapped a couple of bills on the bar and made a hasty exit from the bar. The three drunken cowboys watched him go and roared with laughter. Clearly, they saw themselves as kings of everything around them.

The largest of the drunken cowboys pounded the bar with his fist and yelled for the bartender to bring them a bottle of whiskey. That was enough for the other four old timers at the bar. They left money for their drinks and retreated to a table near Swifty with their remaining beers.

The bartender scowled at the three cowboys, but he reached under the counter and came up with a bottle of whisky. Swifty was pretty sure the bottle did not contain any fine Kentucky bourbon. More likely it was some hastily distilled rotgut whiskey from someplace in New Jersey. The bartender opened the bottle and provided each of the three cowboys with a shot glass and retreated to the safety of his cash register.

Swifty sipped on his beer and sat unmoving at his table. The cowboys began drinking shots and shouting and swearing at each other. Swifty watched as one by one, the four original old timers who had been at the bar when he came in, got up and slipped out the back door of the bar. Twice in the next fifteen minutes, people came in the front door and after a quick scan of the bar and taking in the three carousing cowboys, they beat a hasty retreat out the front door. The waitress had completely disappeared.

A normal person would have finished his beer, and slipped out the door, doing their best not to attract attention from the rowdy trio, just as the original five old timers in the bar had done. Better to get drunk where there was less chance of flying furniture, bottles, or bullets. That's what a normal person with any sense of self-respect and self-preservation would do.

Unfortunately, Swifty was not normal. At least not normal in relying on his sense of survival to avoid trouble spots. During his career in the army he had frequented many dive bars in foreign countries and the southern United States, which can sometimes be worse than foreign countries. He had been involved in more than his share of fights, some mild and some outright vicious. Later in his career, when he was in Delta Force, he and his pals often went looking for trouble and fights in the seediest bars they could find. To Swifty and them it was akin to blowing off steam. These occasions often rose close to the dangers of actual combat, which unfortunately made the experiences both exciting and memorable.

Swifty sat at his table, nursing his beer, waiting for the inevitable. As he studied the trio of drunken cowboys, he realized he recognized two of them. They had been classmates of his in high school in Cody. As he searched his memory, he realized they looked a tad different, but their voices and their crude language were the same as they had been over fourteen years ago.

Their names came slowly to him, but they came, just like the sun coming up in the morning. Nels Nelson was the biggest one. Teddy Post was the smaller one. He remembered them both from high school. They had been bullies since he first saw them in the seventh grade. They picked on the small and the weak. They stole lunch money and sometimes the home packed lunches themselves. They grew up on small ranches along the Shoshone River. They had tried picking on him in junior high, but Swifty had quickly taught both of them he was no one to mess with. He had given each of them a bloody nose one day after school when they were in the eighth grade.

They had left him alone after that memorable day. Getting your ass kicked does that to a person. Swifty went out for football as a freshman and quickly gained a reputation as someone who enjoyed contact and played the game with a fierce sense of controlled violence. Guys like Nelson and Post gave him a wide birth in high school. They never forgot the beating they took from him, and they were smart enough not to piss Swifty off. He had completely forgotten about them until just now.

Swifty finished his beer and sat at his table for a few moments. Then a grin came over his face and he pushed back his chair, got up, and walked up to the bar.

"Bartender, I'll have another beer," said Swifty as he leaned forward with his elbows on the old scarred bar top.

The bartender looked up from behind the cash register, which he seemed to have acquired as a safe haven. "Same as before?" asked the bartender.

"Yep, another Coors," replied Swifty.

"Right away," responded the bartender.

Swifty remained silent, awaiting his promised beer, leaning on the bar.

"Who the hell are you?" asked the third cowboy who Swifty did not recognize.

"A man ordering a beer," replied Swifty. "Are you deaf and dumb or just plain stupid?"

"What the hell did you just say to me?" demanded the drunken cowboy.

"You heard me unless your ears are full of cowshit," responded Swifty.

The bartender slid the opened Coors bottle in front of Swifty and hurried back to the safety of his position behind the large cash register.

"You can't talk to me like that!" snorted the cowboy.

"You must be deaf, because I just did," said Swifty evenly.

The drunken cowboy stepped closer, cocked his arm back as if to throw a round house punch at Swifty. He never got it off. Swifty hit the cowboy with a strong uppercut and the cowboy's head snapped back as he landed about two feet further back, flat on the floor and unconscious.

"What the hell?" snarled Nelson and he went to grab Swifty's arm. By the time his hands closed, Swifty's arm was gone.

Swifty stepped away from the bar and squared his shoulders, facing Nelson's surprised face. Then Swifty kicked Nelson in the balls, and Nelson bent forward in involuntary pain. Swifty put his hands together in a Delta grip and smashed Nelson on the side of the head. He went down like a sack of wet cement.

Swifty felt, rather than saw Post launch a round house punch at his head. He moved his head inches to the left and watched the punch fly past him, a good inch away from Swifty's head. Swifty grabbed Post's exposed arm and fist and used his momentum to pull him forward and then put his knee in Post's groin. Post went down like a polled steer and then rolled on the floor in absolute agony.

Swifty looked around the now empty room. The bartender was staring at him from behind the cash register. Swifty walked up to the bar and pulled out his wallet. He extracted a twenty-dollar bill and laid in on the bar.

"What's that for?" asked the bartender.

"Cover charge for the entertainment," said a smiling Swifty. "I haven't had this much fun in years."

Then Swifty looked down at the two still forms and the one writhing in pain on the floor. "If I were you, I'd call the sheriff," said Swifty. "These three are in no shape to drive themselves home today."

With that, Swifty retrieved his cowboy hat from the floor where it had fallen, placed it on his head and disappeared out the front door of the Cowboy Bar and Outlaw Cafe.

The bartender came out from behind the bar and the waitress magically appeared by his side. "Who the hell was that?" the waitress asked.

"I never saw him before," answered the bartender. "He's a complete stranger to me."

"I think you better call the cops," said the waitress.

"I'm on it," responded the bartender as he grabbed his phone from behind the bar.

He was in the middle of dialing the cops when he saw the waitress bending over one of the unconscious cowboys.

"What the hell are you doing?" he asked her.

"I'm getting us paid for the whiskey these cowpokes drank," she said.

"Make sure you get enough for a tip as well," he said. "I'll split it with you."

"You got a deal," said the waitress.

CHAPTER ELEVEN

Swifty stepped out of the bar onto the wooden sidewalk. It had gotten dark while Swifty had stopped for a late lunch or an early supper, and Meeteetse was a tad short on streetlights. Swifty turned left and walked south until he reached the corner where he turned and climbed into his truck.

He started the engine and put the truck in gear. He pulled up to the stop sign and turned on his turn signal. A lone semi flew past on its way to Cody and Swifty turned his truck north to follow it. He stayed comfortably behind the semi by about three car lengths. When they were about six miles out of Meeteetse, Swifty saw a county sheriff's car fly past with its lights flashing as it hurried toward the tiny town.

"Better late than never," thought Swifty. He knew the bartender would call the sheriff's office. The guy needed to get the three would-be troublemakers out of his bar as quickly as possible. Trouble follows trouble in the West, and the three busted up galoots were better off in the hand of the local deputy.

He drove through Cody and took the turnoff west of town that led to his family ranch. Swifty pulled up by the ranch house and got out of his truck. He decided to fail to mention what happened in the bar in Meeteetse to his mother or sister. He opened the door to the ranch house and was greeted by the sweet smell of fresh beef stew, along with the smell of freshly baked biscuits.

Ten minutes later, he had washed up and was seated at the kitchen table spooning a large helping of beef stew on his plate. He also snatched two of the fresh biscuits as well. In between bites of food, Swifty related his efforts during the day to get someone of authority to talk to him.

"The unfortunate truth is nobody cared much for your dad," said Swifty's mother. "He was a mean, ornery cuss, and never got along with anyone."

"Not even you, Mom?" asked Swifty.

"We got along," she replied. "But it was like living with a time bomb. You never knew when it was going to go off, and if it was going to affect you directly."

"Well, nobody is going out of their way to be of much help," said Swifty.

"They didn't like him, Son," said his mother. "I'm pretty sure most people who did know him are glad he's gone to his reward."

"Don't forget the funeral tomorrow at the church," said his sister Melanie.

"What time is the service?" asked Swifty.

"Service is at eleven in the morning," answered Melanie. "We're supposed to be there at ten thirty to go over things with the minister and approve any last-minute changes."

"What kind of changes can you possibly have at a funeral?" asked a puzzled Swifty.

"You'd be surprised," said his mother. "Things like songs

73

and hymns, and if folks want to stand up and say their piece. Things like that."

"Did you bring a suit?" asked Melanie.

"Yes, I brought a suit," responded Swifty. "I use the same suit for weddings and funerals, just like any good Wyoming cowboy."

Melanie made a face and got up and went to her room. Swifty looked over at his mother and saw she was smiling.

"What's so funny?" asked Swifty.

"You two may be older, but you haven't changed a bit," said his mother. "You rag on each other about everything and act like each of you is a big pain in the ass, but you both would be first in line to defend the other against anyone in the world."

"Only because she's my sister," said a protesting Swifty.

"You keep telling yourself that, Swifty," said his mother with a big grin on her face. "But I doubt the day will ever come when you'll actually believe it."

Swifty just shook his head and headed for his room. He was tired and tomorrow was a big day.

～

Swifty woke up before the sun was up. He dressed quickly and went outside to check the stock and do the morning chores. When he had finished, he returned to the ranch house and opened the side door. His senses were assaulted by the smells of bacon frying and coffee perking. He washed his hands and walked into the kitchen. There he was surprised to see his sister Melanie cooking breakfast and his mother was nowhere in sight.

"Where's Mom?" asked Swifty.

"She's on the phone with the minister," replied Melanie. "How do you want your eggs?"

"Scrambled," replied Swifty. He watched as Melanie broke eggs into a bowl and then whisked them, adding a few ingredients as she whisked. He grabbed a mug and poured himself a cup of hot black coffee and took a seat at the table. Five minutes later Melanie slid a plateful of scrambled eggs, bacon, and fried potatoes in front of him. Then she added a smaller plate of toast and a glass container of homemade cherry jam along with a small plate of butter.

"Thank you," said Swifty.

"You're welcome," replied his grinning sister.

"What's so funny?" asked Swifty.

"You act like you're surprised I can cook," said Melanie.

Swifty looked at his sister and started to speak, but then changed his mind and shut his mouth.

"What's the matter, big brother? Cat got your tongue?" asked Melanie.

Swifty looked down at the table and his plate full of hot food, and then back up at his sister. "One thing I learned in the army was to shut up when you think you're ahead of the game, even if you're not."

"And you're not?" she asked.

"Never argue with the cook who just put hot food in front of you," responded Swifty and he grabbed his fork and dug into his meal.

Melanie laughed and filled a plate with food and sat down across from her brother.

"So, what happened with the rodeo guy you married, little sister? Or is that a subject we should avoid?" asked Swifty.

"We can talk about him," she responded.

"What happened?" asked Swifty.

"He was a selfish asshole," replied Melanie as she took a bite of food. "Next question."

Swifty laughed and Melanie joined in.

CHAPTER TWELVE

Swifty's mom joined them in the kitchen.

"Everything all right?" asked Melanie.

"Yes, things are fine," said their mother. "The minister and I both seem to be on the same page. The service will be fairly short, depending on how many, if any, folks want to stand up and say something."

"How many people do you think will show up?" asked Melanie.

"I have no idea," said their mother. "Eldon was born here and lived his life here, but other than me, I don't think I can come up with a single person he treated as a friend."

"Have you heard anything from Brad?" asked Swifty.

"No, I haven't," replied his mother. "I'm not surprised. I haven't heard anything from him since he left home after high school graduation." She paused and lifted her napkin to wipe away a tear. "I get a birthday card and a Christmas card every year, always from strange places. Other than the cards I have heard nothing from your brother. I'm pretty sure he has no idea his father has passed."

Swifty nodded at his mother. He wasn't surprised. He had heard nothing from his brother since the day he left home. The cards to his mother meant at least he was still alive. Deep inside, Swifty wished his brother would suddenly walk through the outside door and into the kitchen where they had shared so many meals as children. Swifty excused himself and headed to his room to shave, shower, and get dressed.

Swifty reached into the closet and took out the white dress shirt and the black suit he had brought with him. He dressed and added a plain black tie. Then he pulled out his best pair of cowboy boots and buffed them with a rag. When he was finished, he put on the boots and stood and looked himself over in the small mirror in the bathroom. The face in the mirror stared back at him. He was older looking, his eyes more serious than the eyes of the young devil may care man he had been in the Delta Force. Back then he had sported a full beard because it was the cool thing for combat specialists to have. Since he got out of the army, Swifty shaved almost every day. He reached up in the closet shelf for the hatbox where he had placed it when he first arrived at the ranch. He opened the box and removed the white Stetson cowboy hat. He returned to the bathroom and carefully placed it on his head. The face in the mirror smiled back at Swifty. He walked out to the living room. There was no sign of his mother or sister. He took a seat in his father's easy chair and pulled out his phone.

He checked his messages and deleted most of them. He returned a couple of texts and then called his best friend Kit Andrews.

"Hello," said Kit.

"Hello yourself," responded Swifty.

"How are you holding up?" asked Kit.

"Pretty well," answered Swifty. "I'm dressed for the funeral and waiting on the womenfolk."

"Get used to it," said Kit. "It's the way of the world. Us waiting on women."

"Sad, but true," responded Swifty.

"When are you coming back to Kemmerer?" asked Kit.

"I'm not rightly sure," said Swifty.

"What the hell do you mean?" asked Kit. "You told me you were heading back here right after the funeral."

"I planned to, Kit, but I got a few loose ends I need to get tied up before I head back," said Swifty.

"How damn long is it gonna take you to get things tied up?" asked Kit.

"I ain't rightly sure," replied Swifty. "Probably no more than a couple of days."

"If you're sorry ass is not in my office in three days, I plan to come looking for you, and I won't be coming alone," said a bristling Kit.

"You know me," said Swifty. "I'll be there in three days, or I won't."

"That's what worries me," said Kit. "You sure there isn't something going on you're not telling me about?" he asked.

"Just loose ends, nothing more," responded Swifty.

"See you in three days or me and Big Dave will be coming with a posse," said Kit.

"See you then," replied Swifty and he hung of the phone.

Swifty glanced at his watch. It was almost ten o'clock. Time to get moving.

He had no sooner put his phone back in his jacket pocket, when his sister entered the room, followed shortly by his mother. Both women were wearing black dresses and shoes, typical western funeral attire.

Swifty opened the door to the ranch house and held it open as the two women in his life marched through the door and down the porch steps. He held the back door of his truck open so his mother could get in and then the front passenger door for his sister. As they were getting buckled in their seats, he slid into the driver's seat and started the engine.

"Everybody ready?" he asked. Both women nodded in the affirmative.

"Nobody forgot anything?" he asked. They responded in the negative.

Swifty put the truck in gear and they headed down the ranch road and out the front gate. It took him about twenty minutes to drive to the church in Cody. He parked the truck close to the church and opened the doors to let his mother and sister exit. Then he took each of them by the hand, and they walked together to the entrance to the church.

Swifty pushed open the big wooden front door to the church and held it for his mother and sister. They entered the church foyer and were immediately met by the minister. The minister was fairly young and was obviously nervous. He shook their hands and welcomed them. Then he led them to his small side office and offered them seats. There were only two seats other than his desk chair, so Swifty's mom and sister sat and he stood, leaning against the door jamb.

"I'm sorry I never had the pleasure of meeting the deceased," began the young minister. "I know that God treasures all of us, no matter what we are or who we have been. I have a few facts about your father I plan to share after talking with Mrs. Olson. I have made copies of my remarks and would like you to take a minute to read them. I want to make sure the remarks are accurate and are acceptable to each of you."

Swifty quickly read the paper he was handed by the minister. The paper contained items like Eldon's birth date, age, and the names of the family, along with mention of the ranch and how long it had been in the family. The minister had kept the details to the basics, and Swifty hoped he wouldn't suddenly be inspired during the service to come up with a long winded and platitude filled sermon. Keeping his words to the basics would be just fine with Swifty.

Swifty, his mother, and his sister agreed the notes were fine and after going over the songs Swifty's mother had chosen, the minister left them in his office as he hurried out to make sure the flowers were delivered and placed and the ushers had arrived.

Swifty looked at his watch. It was fifteen minutes until the service. He checked his phone and saw no new messages. He wasn't sure why, but he had this fleeting feeling that somehow his brother Brad had learned of Eldon's death and was about to appear at the church. The minutes ticked off and there was no sign of his brother.

Swifty found himself wondering where Brad was, what he was doing, and most importantly, how he was doing. He decided then and there if a miracle did not happen and Brad did not show up for the service, Swifty would use his now considerable resources to find him when he got back to Kemmerer.

The door to the small office opened and the young minister looked in. "Time to go," he said. Swifty stepped aside and followed his mother and sister through the door and into the church. An usher led them down the center aisle. There were a few people seated on both sides of the center aisle. Swifty glanced at them as they walked slowly to the front of the church. Most of them were old time ranchers with their wives. Swifty had no doubt the wives had made their husbands attend or suffer the inevitable domestic punishment, even if it was a cold silence. Husbands always get the final word, even if it is usually "Yes Dear."

Swifty and his mother and sister reached the front pew. The usher had stopped and stood just beyond the pew and turned to face his charges. Swifty stood aside as his mother and sister seated themselves and then he sat next to them at the aisle side of the pew.

Swifty had no sooner seated himself when he felt a tap on his right shoulder. He turned to see the smiling face of his Aunt Judy. She took his hand and squeezed it. Somehow, it made him feel better. He turned to face the front of the church as the minister strode up and took his place behind the lectern.

CHAPTER THIRTEEN

As the minister looked up from the lectern, the small crowd in the church fell silent. The minister welcomed the gathering and thanked them for attending. Then he gave them a page number for their hymnals and nodded to the organist. He turned his attention back to the congregation and asked them to stand and turn to the page containing the hymn *The Old Rugged Cross.*

The organist began playing and the combined voices of the small gathering sounded surprising loud and strong to Swifty. They sang well for a small group. He tried to think if he could remember his father ever going to church. His memory search came up short. His father was not a bit religious and Swifty could only remember attending church with his mother and his brother and sister. He did remember his old man berating his mother for giving money to the church, even if it was a few dollars in the collection plate.

The young minister gave his scripture reading and then led the congregation in prayer. They sang another hymn. When they finished and were seated in the pews, the minister cleared his throat and looked up and out at his small audience.

He began talking about Eldon, a man he had never

met or talked to. Swifty had to give the young minister credit. He had taken good notes when he talked to Swifty's mother and he related stories about Eldon that even Swifty had never heard. Swifty knew funerals were about the good things done on earth by the deceased, as though the bad things had somehow been whitewashed out of existence. When the minister had finished, he asked the congregation if anyone of them would like to share a story about Eldon. There were no takers. Swifty was not surprised. There was another hymn sung, and then the service was over. Swifty escorted his mother and Melanie from their seats and back up the aisle to the entrance of the church.

Once there, they formed a small line and greeted each of the attendees as they exited the church worship area. Then almost everyone headed down into the church basement for coffee, punch, and cookies. Swifty spent half an hour shaking hands and chatting with old ranchers he vaguely remembered from his childhood in Cody. He was surprised to see a few of his old classmates from high school. Most of them were women, but two of them were males who had been his classmates. Both were ranchers' sons who had stayed to work the family land. He talked with them about the weather, cattle prices, and the hay crop. They just about exhausted every topic still acceptable in a polite gathering like a funeral reception.

Swifty was about to disengage himself from his two classmates when he felt a hand on his shoulder. He looked to his side to see his sister Melinda.

"I found an old friend of yours," said his sister with a sly grin on her face.

Kit looked up and found himself face to face with

the girl he had dated for his last two years in high school. She was no longer the thin, boyish looking blonde he had known fourteen years ago. Ann Dexter had blossomed from a skinny teenager to a gorgeous young woman. She was tall, curvy, and had penetrating blue eyes that cut like lasers from her well-tanned face. Swifty searched for a clever thing to say, but his tongue remained frozen in place as his eyes took in a woman who was every inch a knockout.

"The great Swifty Olson is at a loss for words?" she asked. "I heard you were in the army. Did the enemy capture you and do the world a favor by cutting off your tongue?"

Melanie was still standing there enjoying her brother's discomfort, but she felt sorry for him and poked him in the ribs.

Swifty felt the poke and suddenly he found he could speak. "Ann, how great to see you again," said Swifty as he recovered from his temporary case of paralysis. "I thought you'd be long gone from Cody. When we were kids your plan was to escape to civilization as I recall."

"I did escape," said Ann. "I won a scholarship to the University of Wyoming and managed to get a degree in veterinary science."

"Veterinary science?" asked Swifty. "Isn't that like being a doctor for animals?"

"Glad to see you can still put pieces back together, Swifty," said Ann. "You were always good with puzzles."

"Is that an answer or another question?" asked Swifty.

"Still with the smart mouth," said Ann. "Even at your father's funeral."

Swifty realized he was being drawn into verbal combat

with a woman who was a lot smarter than he was. He tried to escape by changing directions.

"I'm glad you could take the time to come to my father's funeral," Swifty managed to get out.

"I knew your father and disliked him intensely," said Ann. "But I like your mother and your sister Melanie, and I came in support of them."

"You mentioned you escaped from Cody," said Swifty. "Are you back?"

Ann smiled at Swifty. "I heard you did some kind of investigative work, and now I can see why."

"What do you mean?" asked a puzzled Swifty.

"You ask good questions," replied Ann. "And you get right to the point."

"Why is that a bad thing?" asked Swifty.

"It's not a bad thing. I just gave you a compliment, you bonehead," she replied.

"So, it was a boneheaded compliment?" asked a now smiling Swifty.

Ann laughed. Her laugh was like a soft tinkling sound from a philharmonic orchestra.

"What's so funny?" asked Swifty.

"You are," said a smiling Ann. "You always were a smart ass with your mouth. Now you're still a smart ass, but a lot smarter one than the guy I knew in high school."

"You still haven't answered my question. Why did you come back to Cody?" asked Swifty.

Ann stopped smiling. A hard cast came over her bright blue eyes. She paused, as though trying to think through what she was going to say before she said it.

"I came back because I found out I wasn't so tough

and the world outside was a lot tougher," she said grimly. "I graduated near the top of my class at the University of Wyoming and went on to get my doctorate in animal science. I met a good-looking guy in vet school, and he swept me off my feet. We graduated, got married, and took jobs with the same vet group in Seattle. After about six months I came home from work early one day and found him and his female lab assistant in bed together."

Swifty wanted to interrupt and ask questions, but he wisely kept his mouth shut and listened.

Ann paused and looked away. When she turned her head back to face Swifty, he could see tears in her eyes. He wisely continued to keep his mouth shut.

"I kicked him out and we wound up in court. I had a good lawyer, but he had a great one. I took a licking in court and was embarrassed in public by him and his friends. I quit my job, holed up in a rented dump for three months, and then came home to Cody. I stayed with my folks until I got a place of my own. I went to work with one of the older vets in town and he retired two years ago. Then I bought his practice," said Ann.

"I've been working in Cody ever since. The practice has done well, and I've managed to pay off the loan I took out to buy the practice. I bought a nice home with some land and keep a couple of horses I like to ride," said Ann. "Things have worked out, and I like being near my family."

Swifty thought about what she had just told him. She had told him a lot more than he had anticipated, and he knew it was because the old bonds of trust between them from high school were still intact. She had needed to talk about what happened to her and he had provided the moment in a funeral reception in the basement of a church. The place and the timing weren't important but having the right person to talk to was.

Swifty found he had unconsciously put his arm around Ann, and she had melted into his chest. She was crying as quietly as she could. He could feel her tears on his cheek. He wasn't sure of the smart thing to do, so he continued to hold her and let her quietly sob. After a few minutes she stopped crying and then she started to pull away from him. Swifty let her pull away and saw she was red faced and her beautiful eyes were wet.

Ann pulled a handkerchief out of a small purse she was carrying, and she dabbed it at her wet eyes.

"I feel so stupid, crying in public like this," Ann said softly.

"You're at a funeral," said Swifty. "It's where most people cry. You look perfectly normal. Take a look around this room. I bet over half the women here cried during the service and they didn't like my father. If a woman doesn't cry at a funeral, people would think she was strange. You're just normal, for a woman."

At that remark, Ann fought back a grin, but was unsuccessful. As she smiled, it seemed to Swifty that a new sun had appeared in the church basement. Seeing her smile was influencing him. He could feel his defense mechanisms retreating into their long dark bunkers.

"Could I interest you in a cup of coffee and a cookie?" asked Swifty. "The price is right. They're free."

Ann laughed again, louder this time. She slipped her arm through his and said, "Lead on, Cowboy."

They walked up to the serving table and Swifty poured

her a cup of coffee and produced a chocolate chip cookie. He then supplied himself with the same combination, and they found two empty chairs at a small table by the far wall of the church basement.

Ann added cream and sugar to her coffee and after stirring it, she took a sip and set her cup down on the table. "So, I just spilled my guts to an old friend from high school," she said. "Now it's your turn. Where the hell have you been, and what have you been doing?"

Swifty took a sip of hot, black coffee and set his cup down. He thought about her question for a moment. Then he made a decision. She had told him the truth. She deserved the same from him.

"Since you are now divorced, do I call you Mrs., Miss, or Ms.," asked Swifty.

"My name is Ann. Always was and always will be," she responded.

"So, what last name do you go by now?" asked Swifty tentatively.

"I had it changed back to Dexter," said Ann. "He was Polish, and I had trouble pronouncing his last name, let alone spell it. That name is dead and buried."

"I escaped from Cody the day after graduation," said Swifty. "I hitched a ride to Casper and signed up with the army. I stayed with some friends I knew there from playing football and rodeoing, until I took a bus to boot camp. I got through infantry training and after about three years, I was approached by an instructor about applying for a special outfit. I decided to give it a shot. I qualified and they accepted me."

"What outfit was that?" asked Ann.

"It's called the Delta Force," replied Swifty. "Maybe you've heard of it?"

"I have," replied Ann. "I don't spend all my time looking up animal's butts. I manage to watch the news and do some reading as well."

"I trained with them and got assigned to a specific unit. I stayed in the unit until I left the army after about ten years," said Swifty.

"Why didn't you make a career out of it?" asked Ann. "If I remember correctly, you can retire after serving twenty years of active duty."

"Aren't you the military scholar," said Swifty with a mocking grin on his face. "You are correct. However, I was getting older and not every assignment I went out on was completely successful. I got wounded a couple of times. The last time was a pretty close call. I remember my nurse telling me that maybe I was running out of rabbit's feet. I thought about it and decided she was probably right. I got out and wound up back in Wyoming. I worked for a rancher down by Kemmerer and he referred me to a guy named Carson Andrews. He goes by Kit and he owns an investigative company called Rocky Mountain Searchers. I was hired to protect him from some bad guys who wanted him dead. We managed to get the upper hand and eliminated them."

"Eliminated them? You mean killed them?" said a shocked Ann.

"Some of them got killed, some went to prison," replied Swifty. "Either way they were out of our hair. After that, I went to work for Kit full-time and we have become close friends. I rent a place in Kemmerer and the work is mostly in the Rocky Mountain area, but I have gone to places like South Carolina, Illinois, Georgia, and Louisiana."

"What exactly does your company do?" asked Ann.

"We get to find missing people, things, documents, stuff like that," replied Swifty.

"So, you guys are bounty hunters?" asked Ann.

Swifty laughed. "No, not bounty hunters," he said. "Lost people are usually family members or relatives who have disappeared or gone missing. Sometimes it is a search for a family heirloom or valuable. Several times it has been a search for missing treasure, like gold or diamonds."

"Diamonds?" said Ann.

"Yep, one case was about lost diamonds," said Swifty. "We were hired to find a missing bi-plane owned by the U.S Post Office lost in 1929 that crashed in the Rocky Mountains with a bag of uncut diamonds."

"Did you find the diamonds?" asked Ann.

"We found the wreckage of the plane, the remains of the pilot and the diamonds," said Swifty.

"Your job sounds a lot more exciting than mine," said Ann.

"It is, if you don't mind getting shot at occasionally," replied Swifty.

"Shot at?" said Ann.

"Sometimes people didn't like what we were doing or were after the same things we were, and they took umbrage when we got involved. Occasionally they shot at us," said a smiling Swifty.

"I know I'm going to regret asking, but did you shoot back?" asked Ann.

"Hey, they were shooting at us," said Swifty. "Fair is fair."

"I can't make up my mind if you are confiding in me or dishing out a lot of bullshit," said Ann.

"You were straight with me about yourself," said Swifty. "Why would I lie to you. I still consider us best friends."

"I feel the same," replied Ann softly.

Swifty looked down at the table. Ann's hand had crept across the table and now rested on top of Swifty's hand. He did not attempt to remove his hand and the two old friends seemed lost staring into each other's eyes.

They were interrupted by Swifty's sister Melanie. "Sorry to break up this tender moment, but we're leaving to go to the cemetery. Are you coming with us, big brother?"

"Go ahead and take his truck," said Ann. "I'll give your big brother a lift to the cemetery. Give her your truck keys," she said to Swifty.

Swifty handed his keys to Melanie.

Melanie hid a smile, nodded, and left.

"Are you ready to go?" asked Ann.

"I was born ready," said Swifty.

"That always worried me in high school and still does," said Ann.

"Let's go," said Swifty. He rose from his chair and pulled out Ann's chair. She led him out to her pickup truck. On the way they talked about old times they had enjoyed together. When they reached the cemetery, Ann stood next to Swifty during the internment and then he walked her back to her truck. She gave him a hug and climbed into the driver's seat. Then she reached into her small purse and produced a small white card.

"This is my business card with my address, cell phone and office phone on it," said Ann. She grabbed a pen from her truck and quickly made a note on the card and handed it to Swifty. "I just added my personal phone and home address. In case of an emergency," she said with a grin.

"I ran into Melinda Swanson at the sheriff's office and she said there is usually a crowd at a place called the Calaboose tonight. Do you know the place?" asked Swifty.

"I know it," said Ann. "I'll see you there tonight."

"Where is the Calaboose located?" asked Swifty.

"Just find the place with the loudest music, most pickup trucks, and most empty beer bottles around the front door and you've found it," said Ann. "See you there."

With that, she fired up her engine and roared out of the cemetery.

CHAPTER FOURTEEN

Swifty stood there with a surprised look on his face. Then he felt a tap on his shoulder. It was his Aunt Judy. He turned just as she enveloped him in a hug.

"I'm so glad you came home," said Aunt Judy. "Your mother needs all the support she can get."

"I did it for her and for Melanie," said Swifty.

"I know you did," replied Aunt Judy. "Your father was a grade A asshole. Always has been and always will be. I bet he pissed St. Peter off at the pearly gates even before St. Peter had a chance to say a word."

Swifty smiled, even as he tried not to. His aunt was never one to mince words, and she always said what she meant.

"Walk me to my car," said Aunt Judy.

Swifty knew better than to disobey, and he escorted his aunt to her car.

"Your husband didn't come?" asked Swifty as he saw the empty car.

"He hated Eldon and never made any bones about it," said Aunt Judy. "He also hates funerals in general, so it didn't take much for him to back out of coming today."

"I can't say I blame him," responded Swifty. "I'm none

too fond of funerals myself, and my old man was never on my most popular list."

"I know he was hard on you as he was on your brother and sister," said Aunt Judy. "He was at least an equal opportunity asshole. He treated everyone he met like a piece of crap."

"If I had forgotten about his ill manners, I was reminded by almost everyone I've talked to since I got here," said Swifty.

"Your mother told me you got some concerns about how Eldon died," said Aunt Judy. "She said you're poking around trying to get some answers and not having much luck."

"I'd say that's a pretty accurate assessment," replied Swifty.

"I need to get back to the store," said Aunt Judy. "How about you stop by tomorrow morning at the store, and we can have coffee and chat?"

"Will you have any of those donuts you make at the store?" asked Swifty.

"I usually do," said Aunt Judy with a smile on her face.

"I'll be there with bells on," said Swifty.

He opened the car door for his aunt, and she slid into the driver's seat. "See you in the morning," said Aunt Judy, and she roared off out of the cemetery like a bat out of flying school.

Swifty walked over to where his sister had parked his truck. His mother and sister were already inside, waiting for him.

"How is your Aunt Judy?" inquired Swifty's mom.

"Feisty as always," replied Swifty. "She suggested I stop over at her store in the morning for some coffee and donuts."

"Before you get done with a cup of coffee and a couple of donuts, Aunt Judy will have squeezed every ounce of information out of you possible," said Melanie.

"As long as I get some of her donuts, she can squeeze all she wants," responded Swifty.

Swifty fired up the truck and drove out of the cemetery at a leisurely and respectful pace and then headed back to the ranch.

As they drove home, Swifty remembered something. "Did the foreman of the Hayfork Ranch talk to you at the church?" he asked his mother.

"He didn't show," said his mother. "One of his hands was there, and he told me the foreman had an emergency and couldn't make the funeral. He said the foreman would give me a call later today."

Swifty nodded at his mother and continued driving just under the speed limit all the way back to the ranch.

CHAPTER FIFTEEN

Once they arrived at the ranch, they all went into the ranch house. Swifty changed clothes and went into the kitchen for a cup of coffee. As he poured himself a cup, he saw a copy of the Cody Enterprise, the local newspaper, on the kitchen countertop. He grabbed the paper and scanned it as he drank his coffee. In the paper he found the brief obituary for his father. There were barely three small paragraphs summarizing Eldon's time on earth. Not much to say about his fifty some years on the planet. He folded up the newspaper and put it back on the counter. Swifty finished his coffee and washed out the cup in the sink.

He slipped out the door of the ranch house and headed to the barn. He checked on the horses and added some water to their trough. He peeked in at the chickens in the hen house and fenced in yard, saw nothing amiss and headed back to the ranch house. He saw a late model white Chevy pickup truck parked in the yard. As he passed the truck, he saw it had the brand of the Hayfork Ranch painted on the door.

Swifty entered the ranch house and as he came into the kitchen, he saw a middle-aged man seated at the kitchen table having coffee with his mother. The man was well short of six feet tall. His cowboy hat was on the table, resting on its top, and he could see the tan line on the man's face ending where the cowboy hat would have begun if he were wearing it.

The man pushed back his chair and stood with his hand outstretched. Swifty shook hands with the man and both sat down at the kitchen table.

"I'm Randy Smith, foreman of the Hayfork Ranch," said the man.

"I'm Gary Olson, but my friends call me Swifty."

"Good to meet you, Swifty," said Randy. "I just stopped by to see your mother and pay my respects. I'm sorry I got sidetracked and didn't make your dad's funeral."

"No apology needed," said Swifty. "Truth be told, my old man was not the most popular guy in Park County. The crowd at the funeral was small, but they sang pretty loud."

"I bet they did," responded Randy with a grin. Then Randy hesitated, as though he was trying to remember his lines in a school play. "I told your mother I'd stop and chat about the ranch."

"We're all ears, aren't we Mom," said Swifty.

"As you know, your ranch is contiguous to the Hayfork Ranch," said Randy. "We aren't currently trying to expand, but because of the location of your ranch and your water rights, adding your acreage to the Hayfork would be to our advantage."

Swifty smiled but said nothing in response.

Randy hesitated and then continued. "I assume with your dad gone, that running the ranch might be a problem for your family. If that is the case, then I have been authorized by the owner of the Hayfork Ranch to try to negotiate a sale price for your ranch. I know this is the day of the funeral, but like my old uncle Zeb used to say, 'There's no time like the present.'"

"Selling the ranch is entirely up to my mother," said Swifty. "With my father's death, she is the sole owner. Any questions of negotiating points need to be directed at her. I'm just her son."

Randy blushed slightly under his well-tanned face. "I meant no harm," he said.

"None taken," replied Swifty.

Randy turned to face Swifty's mother. "I guess I'm here to find out if you have any interest in selling the ranch, Mrs. Olson."

Swifty's mother was still dressed the in the black dress. She had sat in her chair quiet and motionless while the two men had talked.

"I would be interested in seeing an offer from your boss," she said.

"Do you have a price in mind, Mrs. Olson?" asked Randy.

"No, I do not," replied Mrs. Olson. "I'd like to see a formal offer so I can go over it with my son and daughter, and our attorney."

"I don't think that will be a problem," responded Randy. "I'll get back to my boss and have his folks draw up an offer and then bring it back so you can look it over, if that works for you."

"It works for me," replied Mrs. Olson.

"Well, thank you for your time, Mrs. Olson. I appreciate it. I'm sorry to intrude on your time of grief with something as mundane as business, but I'm just carrying out orders from my boss," said Randy.

"Thank you for coming, Randy," said Mrs. Olson.

Randy rose from his chair as did Swifty and his mother. The mother and son shook hands with Randy and walked him to the door. Swifty and his mother stood in the open doorway as Randy got in his truck. He waved to them and then drove out of the ranch yard. When all they could see was the rear of his truck through the dust, Swifty turned to his mother.

"What did you think?" asked Swifty.

"I got nothing to think about until I see a cash money offer," replied his mother as she shut the door to the ranch house after they had stepped inside.

Swifty followed his mother into the kitchen where she began to wash the coffee cups. Swifty got a pad of paper and a pencil out of the kitchen junk drawer and sat down at the table. He searched his memory and wrote down the word "ranch" with a figure of $340,000. Then he wrote down "water rights" and a figure of $160,000. The total of $500,000 was kind of impressive until he considered its investment value. Although the money would be tax free to his mother, $500,000 at 5% income was only $25,000 a year. Not bad, but not a fortune and skinny for retirement income for a woman in her fifties. When she hit sixty-five years of age, she would get about another $13,000 a year in social security. That would improve the total income to $38,000 a year, but still not a princely sum. Especially when she would have to rent a place to live.

Kit had stopped scribbling on the note pad, and his

mother looked over his shoulder to see what he'd been putting down on paper.

"You think we could get $500,000 for the ranch and the water rights?" asked his mother after she finished reading his scribbling.

"From what I've seen on the internet, that's an approximate total," replied Swifty.

"Is that before or after taxes?" asked his mother.

"There are no estate taxes on dad's estate," replied Swifty. "The total estate is too small."

"Well, we're getting worked up about nothing," said Mrs. Olson. "We have interest, but no specific offer yet. When we get one, then we'll have something to discuss." With that she left the kitchen and disappeared into her bedroom.

CHAPTER SIXTEEN

Swifty spent the next hour going through the tattered files containing the ranch financial and miscellaneous records. He took notes on his note pad and when he had gone through all the files, he put them away in the small office and tore the page off the pad. He put his written notes in the pocket of his shirt and went to his room. It was getting close to supper time, and he changed from his work clothes to some clean casual duds he would normally wear when going out on the town in Kemmerer.

Swifty emerged from his bedroom wearing a pair of clean Wrangler jeans, a white cowboy shirt with pearl snaps, and a wide leather belt with a Wyoming belt buckle. He was wearing his best cowboy boots and his grey Stetson hat.

As he walked through the living room, his mother and sister took notice of his attire.

"My, don't you look nice," said his mother.

"Don't get those nice duds all messed up tonight, Big Brother," said his sister with a grin on her face.

Swifty touched the brim of his cowboy hat at the ladies and slipped out the door of the ranch house. Soon he was behind the wheel of his truck, headed for Cody.

As he drove down the narrow highway, Swifty took out

his phone and looked up the Calaboose Bar in Cody. He glanced at the address and returned his phone to his shirt pocket. When he reached Cody's main drag, he turned east and headed toward downtown.

When he reached the cross street he was looking for, Swifty flipped on his turn signal and made a left turn when there was a break in oncoming traffic

He drove two and a half blocks north and passed what had been a blacksmith shop when he was a kid. Now it was a cowboy bar with a red neon sign announcing the location of The Calaboose.

Swifty slowed his speed and began looking for a parking place. He found one about a block past the bar and parked and locked his truck. He took a quick look in his side mirror, was satisfied with what he saw, and headed back down the street to the bar.

As Swifty approached the bar's front door, he saw two couples approaching from the other direction. Swifty got to the front door first, and held it open for the couples. They thanked him as they passed by and entered the bar. Swifty followed them into the poorly lit, loud, and smokey interior.

When he was inside the front door, Swifty stepped to the side and stopped, taking a minute to survey the surroundings. He identified the sign to the rest rooms, and he located a side exit across from the end of the bar. Then he began to scan the crowd. He attempted to locate some friendly faces. He saw no one familiar and stepped up to the bar to order a beer. The bartender quickly took his order and placed a large mug of beer in front of Swifty. He took his beer and found a small table back against the wall of the bar and pulled out a chair. He sat in the chair with his back to the wall where he could see everything in front of him and not worry about anything going on behind him.

Swifty sipped his beer and began to carefully scan the crowd. He had located the restrooms and a hallway likely leading to a back room and back door to the saloon. He broke each group of bar patrons into slices as he examined the crowd. He saw no familiar faces and he saw the men outnumbered the women by a ratio of three to one. It was a typical bar scene in Wyoming where the men outnumbered the women by at least two to one.

As he scanned the crowd, he kept on the alert for signs of possible trouble. He noted two separate groups of large bearded men who set off silent alarms in Swifty's mind. He had developed a nose for trouble in Iraq and Syria. He had learned to pay attention to his nose. Thus far it had never let him down and saved his ass more than once. Tonight, he was uncharacteristically wearing a leather vest over his shirt. He rarely wore a vest unless he was headed into a public place where a gun might come in handy. Swifty had a small Springfield .45 caliber automatic stuck in a small holster inside his pants in the small of his back. The vest did a good job of concealing the gun. The small Springfield only held five rounds. For Swifty, one or two rounds of a powerful .45 caliber hollow point bullet was all he had ever needed in the past, and that was in places where the other guys were heavily armed.

Twenty minutes passed, and he had finished his beer. He was about to get up from his chair and walk over to the bar for another when a waitress noticed him and slid over to his table.

"Need another beer, Cowboy?" she asked.

"Make it a Coors," said Swifty.

"Coors it is," she replied and grabbed his empty glass and headed for the crowded bar.

Five minutes later she was back with a cold Coors, and she set it on the table in front of him. Swifty paid her for the beer plus a good tip. She smiled and said, "Thanks, Cowboy. I'll keep an eye on your table, so I know when you need another."

Swifty thanked her, and she vanished into the swirling crowd of men and women letting off steam in a crowded bar on a Friday night.

A sudden movement from Kit's left caused him to stiffen in preparation for a quick move. His muscles relaxed as he saw Melinda's smiling face as she slid into an empty chair on his left.

"Welcome to The Calaboose, Cowboy," she said.

"Pretty noisy place," said Swifty.

"This noise?" asked Melinda. "This is just a mild roar. Wait for about an hour and things with get into high gear."

"Define high gear," said Swifty.

"A very loud Fourth of July celebration," said a grinning Melinda.

"I should have brought my earmuffs," said Swifty.

Melinda held up her half full bottle of beer. "That's what the beer is for," she said laughing.

"Where's your husband?" asked Swifty.

"He's in the far corner over there," said Melinda as she pointed to the corner of the room to Swifty's left. "They sent me to find you and drag your butt over to our table. Are you about done with that beer or are you bringing it with you?"

Swifty downed the beer in one long swallow. He

Robert Callis

slammed the empty bottle on the table. "Lead on, young lady," he said to Melinda.

Melinda laughed and got to her feet. Swifty rose from his chair and he followed her slowly and carefully through the tight packed throng on the floor of The Calaboose. It still took almost five minutes to navigate the crowd and make their way to the round table in the far corner of the bar.

There were five people at the table and two empty chairs. Melanie took one chair and Swifty took the other. Melanie introduced Swifty to Matt, her husband. Matt had gone to school with Swifty, but he had trouble placing him. The next couple was Shorty and Sandy. They were younger and unknown to Swifty. The last couple was different. The tall lanky cowboy grinned at Swifty, shook his outstretched hand and then pulled him tight in a man bear hug.

"My god, Lefty Phillips," said a surprised Swifty. Lefty had been one of his best friends in high school. He hadn't seen Lefty since they graduated. Lefty released Swifty and introduced him to his cute blonde wife Tammy. Swifty shook her hand and congratulated Lefty on his fine choice of a wife. Lefty grinned, knowing what Swifty said was the truth. Just like it had always been.

"Sit down you two big galoots, you're embarrassing the rest of us with all the man love," said Melinda. Still grinning, Swifty sat down in the empty chair in front of him along with the rest of the group who had been standing.

"So, what brings the great Swifty Olson back to tiny little Cody, Wyoming?" said Lefty.

"I'm here because of my father's funeral," said Swifty.

"Funeral? Your old man died?" said a surprised Lefty.

"I thought you had heard about it," said Swifty. "Seems

to me almost everyone else in Cody I've run into knew all about it."

"I've been working on an oil rig north of town, and this is the first I heard of it," said a still surprised Lefty. "Man, I'm sorry."

"Don't be," said Swifty. "My old man was an asshole to almost everyone he knew, including me, and he's the reason I joined the army the day after we graduated from high school."

"I heard you enlisted," said Lefty, "but that was a long time ago. What the hell have you been doing for the past fourteen years?"

"I spent about twelve years in the army and got to see some of the nastiest places on the earth," replied a grinning Swifty.

"Ouch," said Lefty. "That sounds bad, but you look good and appear to be still in one piece."

"More or less," said Swifty.

Lefty seemed to think for a few seconds and then he spoke. "Where the hell have you been for the past two years after you got out of the army?"

Swifty paused, to look around the small group at his table. They were all leaning forward as though they did not want to miss a word of this conversation.

"I hired on with a sheep rancher down in Kemmerer when I got back to the states. I worked for him a bit and then he had me do some bodyguard work for a friend of his. We hit it off and the friend started an investigation company called Rocky Mountain Searchers. Maybe you've heard of it?" said Swifty.

Lefty scratched his head and said, "Nope. Can't say I have. So, what do you do at this company?"

Swifty paused. He decided to give them the very short version of his story about the company. "We get hired to find things and people who are lost or missing."

"Things like what?" asked Lefty.

Swifty paused for effect, like he was searching for a suitable example for the group, all of whom were still silent and intent on hearing Swifty's story.

"Well, we were hired to find some missing diamonds," said Swifty.

"Missing diamonds?" said Lefty. "In Wyoming?"

"Yes," said Swifty. "In the late 1920's an airmail plane crashed in a snowstorm in the Mountains in western Wyoming and on board was a bag of diamonds. We were hired to find the plane wreck, the body of the pilot, and the diamonds."

"Did you find them?" asked Lefty.

"We did, but we ran into some trouble with some illegal treasure hunters who were looking for the same thing," said Swifty.

"Wow, what happened," asked Lefty.

"That's a story for another day," said a smiling Swifty. "I'd like to hear your stories about what all of you have done since I left Cody fourteen years ago."

"Well, hells bells, I ain't rightly sure where to start," said a grinning Lefty.

Everyone at the table broke out in laughter, some nervous, most of it natural.

CHAPTER SEVENTEEN

The small group at the table in The Calaboose were so engaged in their conversation, none of them noticed the five rough looking men who had entered the building and made their way forcefully to the bar. The five men pushed and roughly shoved both men and women who were in their path. Several of the men reacted angrily to the treatment until they got a good look at their assailants. Then they wisely melted away into the crowd, working to get as far away from the five as possible.

Even as he sat at the table with his friends, Swifty sensed a disturbance in the rhythm of the evening. The ebb and flow of loud music and loud talk and laughter seemed somehow interrupted. He surveyed the bar and quickly zeroed in on the five large men who had forced their way through the crowd like Roman Centurions who treated the crowd like so much driftwood they needed to kick out of their way.

Swifty studied the five men. They were all at least six feet tall. They had broad shoulders and hard lean bodies that came from hard work and a rough life. Their clothes were old and worn and looked like a generation away from any kind of washing machine. All of them had full beards, none of which were even slightly trimmed. Swifty knew trouble when he saw it, and he was looking at it in spades. He slipped his hand behind his back to make sure his pistol was still in his carry holster. Satisfied, he maintained his gaze on the five men who had made their way to the bar and ordered drinks in loud voices that had unsettled the already harried bartender.

Someone at the table had asked Swifty a question and it hung in the air as a now focused Swifty ignored it. The others at the table looked at Swifty in surprise until they followed his gaze and saw what he saw. The group fell silent. They were natives to Wyoming, and they knew trouble when they saw it. Lefty deliberately moved his chair away from the table to give him more room to move if he needed to. Swifty continued to silently stare at the five intruders.

The five men had gotten their drinks and downed them and demanded a refill which the bartender was quick to respond to. The five had turned with their backs to the bar and begun to survey the room. The music was still loud, the air thick with smoke, and the smell of sweat and beer was in the air, but something was different. Crowds are often oblivious to danger until it erupts. Crowds in a Wyoming bar are no strangers to sudden violence and the folks in The Calaboose were no different. People were drinking and talking and dancing, but they were also watching the five men, even if it was out of the corners of their eyes. Something was going to happen. They could feel it in the air. Everyone was watching and planning how they were going to exit from the bar as quickly as possible.

One of the men had finally spotted Swifty at the small table with his friends. The man had long blonde hair and a blonde goatee. He elbowed the man next to him and said something in his ear. Swifty was pretty sure the blonde guy had seen him and figured out who he was, and he was letting the other guy know. Within minutes word had been passed and all five men knew Swifty was in the bar.

Conversation at the table had died a quick death. Lefty whispered to Swifty. "Do you know those dudes?"

"Nope," whispered Swifty back. "Never seen them before."

"I recognize them," whispered Lefty. "They are all oil field roughnecks. I've bumped into them out in the oil patch a few times."

"Who are they?" whispered Swifty.

"I don't rightly remember their names," responded Lefty softly. "But they've been in a number of scrapes with the law here in Cody. At least three of them have done some time in the local hoosegow."

"Why would they be interested in me?" whispered Swifty.

"I've heard rumors they can be hired to scare or rough up people. They seem to like that kind of stuff," responded Lefty softly. "Did you have some kind of run-in with them?"

"This is the first time I ever laid eyes on any of them, let alone all five of them," whispered Swifty.

"Well, it looks like you're about to get acquainted," said Lefty. "They're headed this way."

Lefty was correct. The five men had finished their drinks and slammed their glasses on the bar top for effect. The blonde guy led the way from the bar. He was making his way through the crowd towards Swifty's table. He was taking his time, trying to make a statement. The other four followed closely behind him.

When the blonde one reached Swifty's table, he stopped about a yard from it. The other four men grouped behind him.

"Your name Swifty Olson?" asked the blond guy.

"Who wants to know?" responded Swifty.

"Me and my friends who plan on kicking your ass tonight," responded the smiling blonde man.

Swifty looked at the blonde guy and at each of the four guys behind him. He remained seated.

"If that's your plan, you look a tad bit outnumbered to me, Blondie," said Swifty softly.

"What the hell are you talking about?" asked Blondie, as he glanced around behind him. "They's five of us and only one of you!"

"What's your beef with me?" responded Swifty.

Blondie looked a bit confused. Swifty looked neither frightened nor concerned. He looked like his biggest problem was which brand of beer he was going to order next.

Blondie recovered from his momentary confusion. "You beat up three of our friends in a bar in Meeteetse when they was dead drunk and couldn't defend themselves."

"I did beat the crap out of three buttholes I used to know in high school who were acting like they belonged to the Wild Bunch. They had it coming," said Swifty.

"You ain't gonna sweet talk yourself out of this one," snarled Blondie.

"I'm not planning on doing any talking other than this," said Swifty. "I'll give you boys five minutes to clear out of this bar and never come back. If you're still here after five minutes, then we'll go out in the parking lot and I'll teach all five of you how it feels to get stomped so bad you regret the day you were born."

Blondie looked stunned. This was not what he had expected. He looked back at his four friends. They were as surprised as he was. Then he looked at the crowd surrounding them. A lot of the men and some of the women were smiling. They were enjoying this unscheduled entertainment.

Swifty sat in his chair and waited. When five minutes had passed, he rose from his chair and confronted the five thugs.

"All right boys, you had your chance," said Swifty. "Let's go outside and settle this where damage to the premises will be limited."

With that Swifty pushed his way through the five men before they could react and headed for the front door of the bar. As Swifty walked, the crowd parted in front of him like the Red Sea for Moses. He exited the bar first, slipping a roll of quarters from his vest pocket and sliding it into his right hand.

Swifty strode to the side of the bar where the parking lot was located. The lot was filled with pickup trucks and cars, but there was some space between the building and the lot. When he reached the first line of parked vehicles, he turned to face his attackers.

The five men had followed him out of the bar and into the lot. Right behind them was a mass of bar patrons wanting to see something more than a bloodless confrontation.

As the five thugs stood in a line facing Swifty, the crowd flowed around behind them, scrambling for positions with a good view of the mayhem to come.

Lefty emerged from the crowd and stepped up next to Swifty.

"Stand back," said Swifty. "This isn't your fight."

"Well, from what I heard in the bar, this ain't your fight either," said Lefty. "Them boys ain't got no friends I know of. It's likely they got paid by them three yahoos you pounded over in Meeteetse."

"Maybe so, but it is what it is, and I don't want you getting involved," said Swifty.

"You're gonna take on all five of them?" asked Lefty.

"Hopefully there's only five of them," said Swifty.

Lefty cracked a smile. "You ain't changed a lick since we was in high school." With that said, Lefty moved about five yards away from Swifty, staying slightly left and behind him.

Swifty studied the five thugs in front of him. They were all bigger than normal, but none of them had moved very gracefully when he had watched them in the bar. He guessed they were strong, but not very agile. The five were about four yards from where Swifty was standing. The thugs momentary surprise from his actions in the bar had faded. Now out in the parking lot, the five of them saw only Swifty and they reeked with overconfidence because of their superiority in numbers. Swifty's training told him to attack before they expected it.

Without warning, Swifty moved quickly forward and nailed Blondie on the jaw with his right fist wrapped around the roll of quarters. There was a loud snapping sound and Blondie went out like a light and flopped to the ground like a sack of wet cement. Swifty then kicked the next thug in the balls. As he fell forward, Swifty hit him with his right fist wrapped around the roll of quarters, and he went down hard.

One of the thugs threw a punch and it slid off Swifty's upper left arm as he slid away from the telegraphed punch. Swifty stepped inside the missed punch and hit the side of the man's face with a two-handed fist smash. He dropped to his knees, dazed from the blow.

Swifty managed to duck a punch from a fourth thug that still bounced off the top of Swifty's skull. He felt that one, and it dazed him and made his eyes water. Swifty danced away from the thug and warily looked for the location of the other thug. He couldn't see him between his watering eyes and his constant movement. He knew he needed to dispatch the thug in front of him quickly before he got too tired or outmaneuvered.

Swifty slipped inside a round house punch launched by the guy. He could feel the wind from the punch it was thrown so hard. Then Swifty grabbed the front of the guy's shirt and pulled him into Swifty's chest as Swifty head butted him. The guy went down hard and Swifty pivoted to check behind him, searching for the fifth thug. He couldn't see him. Then he saw Lefty pointing to the ground to his right.

The fifth thug lay on his back on the parking lot. His legs and arms were out at angles to his body. Swifty slipped the roll of quarters back in his vest pocket and turned to scan the lot with a puzzled look on his face.

"Did you do that" Swifty asked Lefty, pointing to the prone body of the fifth thug.

"Nope," said Lefty, "I stayed out of it just like you told me to."

"So, what happened to this guy?" asked Swifty, pointing to the prone body in front of him.

Lefty walked over, went to one knee, and reached to the thug's chest.

"I think this happened," said Lefty as he held out a tranquilizer dart he had removed from the thug's chest.

Swifty walked over to Lefty and took the dart from him. He held it up to take a good look at it.

"Never seen a tranquilizer dart before?" came a female voice from the crowd.

Swifty looked toward the source of the voice. There, stepping towards him was Ann Decker, a long-barreled tranquilizer gun in one hand. The gun looked out of place held by a lovely blonde woman, dressed in a pretty red dress and wearing red cowgirl boots.

"You shot him?" asked an incredulous Swifty.

"Part of my job is to tranquilize crazed animals," said a smiling Ann. "This seemed like a good occasion to get in a little practice."

Lefty stepped in front of the gathered crowd. "Show's over, folks. Time to go back inside and party," he said.

The crowd began sifting back into the front door of The Calaboose and was soon dissipated like smoke from a fire on a windy day.

Lefty followed them toward the front door. He stopped by the one remaining conscious thug who was on his hands and knees trying to shake the cobwebs out of his head.

Lefty leaned down near the thug's head. "Are you all right?" asked Lefty.

The thug mumbled something, and he extended his hand as if he expected Lefty to help him to his feet. Instead,

Lefty stood and kicked the thug in the head with his cowboy boot as hard as he could. The thug hit the parking lot and lay there moaning.

Lefty stood next to the moaning thug and looked around the now empty parking lot. He cupped his hands and called out, "Is there a doctor in the house?" Then he laughed and headed back into the bar.

Almost as fast as the fight had started, it was over. Swifty and Ann soon found themselves alone in the parking lot, along with the five unconscious thugs.

"I think you need some medical attention," said Ann as she examined Swifty's head. "Let's head over to my office and take a closer look at your head."

Swifty touched his finger to his head and it came away dripping with blood. "Maybe you're right," said Swifty.

"Maybe, my ass," retorted Ann. She strode to her truck, slipped into the cab and started the engine. Swifty came around to the passenger side and slid in. Ann drove them at the speed limit back towards her office. About two blocks from the bar they met two Cody police cars with their lights flashing as they hurried toward The Calaboose.

"Looks like a busy night at The Calaboose," said Ann.

Swifty looked at her in surprise.

"Of course, I wouldn't know, because I was never inside of the place tonight," she continued.

Swifty smiled and leaned back in the passenger seat. He touched his head again. His hand came away with blood on it.

Ann noticed his motion. "Leave it alone until I can get a good look at it. Head wounds always bleed like a stuck pig, so it's not likely as bad as it might look," she said.

She soon drove behind her office and parked in the back. She got out of the truck and Swifty followed her. He had noticed there were parking spaces in front, but he suspected she was not interested in having anyone know she was inside the office.

She unlocked the back door and held it open for Swifty to enter. He did and she followed, locking the door behind her. She turned on a few lights and led him to an interior examining room. Swifty noticed the room had no windows, so no interior light escaped to the outside world. Ann pointed to a chair and motioned for him to take a seat.

Swifty sat in the chair and she put on a white tunic over her dress. Then she put on rubber gloves and pulled down a movable light so she could get a good look at his injured scalp. She probed the wounded area and then went to a cabinet and removed some medical materials. She swabbed the wound with an antiseptic and cleaned it with cotton swabs. Then she examined the wound again. Satisfied with what she saw, she threw away the used materials and sat down opposite Swifty on a movable stool.

"Did you get hit anywhere besides your noggin?" she asked.

Swifty thought for a moment and then said, "I don't think so, but I can't be sure."

"Spoken just like a man," said a smiling Ann. "Take off your shirt and let's have a look."

"Did you bring me in here on false pretenses?" asked Swifty.

"False pretenses? What the hell are you babbling about?" asked Ann.

"I think you got me in here just to see if you could get me to take my shirt off," said a too innocent looking Swifty.

"My god," said Ann. "Fourteen years and you're still a sex maniac."

"Can't blame a guy for trying," said Swifty.

"That's the same line you used back in high school," said Ann.

"Yeah. As I remember it didn't work too well back then either," said a grinning Swifty.

"Get the shirt off, Cowboy," said Ann.

Swifty removed the shirt. There were no cuts, but he had the beginnings of a couple of pretty good bruises on his shoulder and chest. Ann checked his chest out with her stethoscope and then went back to the cabinet and took out a couple of small packets.

"I advise you to take these pills," said Ann. "You're liable to have a pretty good headache in a bit and these will help you sleep. Take two pills now and two more every four hours until you run out of pills."

Swifty held up one of the packets to the light to read it.

Ann smiled at him. "These are pain killers. They're samples I get from pill peddlers. I often give them to patients who are short on money."

Swifty seemed to relax.

"Of course, those patients are animals who can't talk, so I assume there are no after affects," grinned Ann.

"Very funny," retorted Swifty.

"Put your shirt on and follow me," said Ann.

Swifty donned his shirt and asked, "Where are we going?"

"My office, where I have a good bottle of bourbon," replied Ann.

"Works for me," said Swifty and he followed her out of the exam room, down a short hall and into what appeared to be her private office.

Ann switched on a side lamp and gestured towards two easy chairs in front of a low coffee table. "Have a seat, Cowboy."

Swifty took the nearest chair while Ann went to a cupboard behind her desk and returned with a bottle of good bourbon and two glasses.

"If you want ice, you're out of luck," said Ann. "I don't waste good bourbon by watering it down."

She opened the bottle and poured a good two fingers into each glass. She sat down in the other chair. They raised the glasses and clinked them together and each of them took a strong swallow of the rich bourbon.

CHAPTER EIGHTEEN

Swifty felt the rich bourbon slide down his suddenly parched throat. He felt as if the bourbon was spreading to the rest of his body. As if his tensed muscle system was finally relaxing from the adrenaline driven high of hand to hand combat.

He looked up to see Ann staring at him with an intensity he found a bit unnerving.

"Thank you," said Swifty. "And I don't mean just for patching me up. Thank you for nailing that fifth bozo before he got to me. I hate to admit this, but I was starting to run out of steam. I must be getting old."

Ann laughed. She had a rich melodious laugh that was very female and yet felt like more.

"You're welcome on both counts," she said. "I watched the fight unfold and then realized no one was going to step in to help you, so I grabbed my dart gun, loaded it and plunked that fifth guy in the chest. It was a pretty big target and hard to miss."

"I find it interesting you were the only one to come to my defense," said Swifty. "Did you shoot that galoot because it was the right thing to do or because you felt some compassion for poor old Swifty?"

"It was a fight and someone I know and like was

outnumbered," said Ann. "I was just trying to even out the odds."

"Damn," said Ann. "I forgot to retrieve the dart."

"You mean this dart," said Swifty, as he pulled the now empty dart out of his shirt pocket.

"You retrieved it?" asked Ann.

"Actually no. Lefty pulled it out and gave it to me," said Swifty. "I just stuck it in my shirt pocket and forgot about it until just now."

Swifty reached over and handed the dart to Ann. She took the dart and laid it on top of a side table.

"So, you felt no compassion for poor old Swifty?" he asked.

"Like I said, I didn't want a friend of mine to get the crap kicked out of him," replied Ann.

"So, I'm just an old friend?" asked Swifty.

Ann looked at him with an exasperated expression on her face. "You disappeared from my life the day after high school graduation. I never heard from you again until you spoke to me at the funeral today. As far as I knew you were dead and buried on some piece of crap desert in the middle east," she said.

"How did you know I was in the desert in the middle east?" asked Swifty.

"I didn't, but I knew you were in the army and knowing you, if there was a fight going on somewhere in the world, you were bound to be in the middle of it," Ann responded.

Neither of them spoke. Swifty took another sip of the excellent bourbon and Ann did the same.

Ann broke the silence after a few minutes. "I was really hurt when you left to join the army the day after we graduated. You didn't say goodbye. You didn't write. You didn't call. You just left. You left like I meant nothing to you. It was the worst time of my life," she said.

Another silence enveloped the two of them.

Finally, Swifty broke the silence. "I'm sorry, Ann. I know I was young and pissed at my dad, but you're right. I took it out on you as well as him. I'm truly sorry."

Swifty paused and took another sip of bourbon. Then he continued. "Thinking about you was the one thing that kept me going in the early days of my army career. Knowing how you believed in me and encouraged me in high school kept coming back to me in my mind when I faced obstacles, I was not sure I could overcome. I was immature and selfish back then," said Swifty.

"I knew you'd be fine," he said. "You were smart and pretty and kind. I knew you would do well in college and become someone who was both good and successful at whatever you chose to do. I was a different case entirely. I had to learn most of my lessons the hard way. Later, I got a little smarter, but I have more than a few scars from my early mistakes."

Swifty paused. "For me that's one hell of a long speech. Talking is not my game. Am I embarrassing myself like I feel I am?" he asked.

"No, you're not," replied Ann softly.

"I knew you'd find someone else," continued Swifty. "You were too smart and too cool not to. You were way out of my league when we were in high school and I knew it. I just used to thank God you didn't realize it and thought of me as a friend you wanted to hang out with. I knew it wouldn't last when you went to college. I wasn't good enough for you and I knew you'd figure it out pretty quickly. I'm sorry the guy who did was an asshole. You deserved much better."

"I got what I deserved," said Ann. "When you're young, you are being propelled by your hormones and sometimes you make really bad choices. I did, I paid for it, and then things got better. I like who I am now, and I like my life."

"You should," said Swifty. "You've done really well here in Cody. You should be proud of yourself."

Ann didn't answer him. She took another sip of bourbon and stared at Swifty. Her eyes were intense, and they seemed to be boring into Swifty's mind where he hid all his personal secrets.

"What's wrong?" asked a now nervous Swifty.

"I'm studying you, Swifty Olson. I just discovered I have the ability to make you very nervous and I'm enjoying it," said a smiling Ann.

Swifty did not respond. He found his throat was dry, his mind confused, and his instincts were sending him mixed messages that didn't seem to make any sense. He wanted to say something, something hip and funny, but no words came to him. She was right. She had made him as nervous as a ten-year old sent to the principal's office. It was cool in Ann's building, but he was sweating profusely.

He took another drink of bourbon. This time he took a swig, not just a sip. The rich bourbon burned on its way down his throat. He looked up at Ann. She was still staring at him. He could see the light reflecting in her blue eyes, their intensity was startling.

Neither of them broke the silence by speaking. They just sat there with glasses of bourbon in their hands, staring at each other like they were seeing each other for the first time. To Swifty it was both unnerving and irresistible. He could not make himself tear his eyes away from her. She was sitting there in her chair, dressed in a white medical smock, a glass of bourbon in her hand, a smile bordering on a smirk on her lovely face.

Ann broke the silence. "Tell me," she said.

Swifty looked confused. "Tell you what?" he asked.

"Tell me about your twelve years in the army," said Ann. "I want to know what happened to you. I want to know how you felt. And I want to know why you never called or wrote me in those twelve years. I want to know how someone who made such an impression on me could just leave and forget all about me."

Swifty looked at Ann. He was not sure how to answer her. He was afraid he would say the wrong thing. He didn't want this connection he felt toward her to end. He didn't want to say something like he had said to many women over the years. He wanted her to know how hard it had been to not contact her. He took another swig of bourbon and sat the glass down. He looked Ann in the eyes. He wanted to drown in the deep blue of her eyes. He wanted to hold her. He wanted to taste her lips. But he felt like his tongue had been cut out. He couldn't seem to form the words he wanted to say. This was totally unlike any experience he had ever had with a woman.

Finally, he forced his tongue and his mouth to function. "Are you sure you want to hear about it?" he asked. "Most of it was pretty boring."

"Do you have a better topic to talk about?" replied Ann.

Swifty knew she had him cornered. He took a deep

breath and began to tell her about some of his experiences in Delta Force. He chose some stories he felt were safe to talk about. But, as he talked, he felt himself beginning to loosen up and soon he was talking about experiences that were both violent and emotionally draining. Finally, Swifty told her about his darkest moments. Moments when he thought he would die. Moments when he thought he would never see the sun again.

Ann said nothing. She listened intently as Swifty released memories and feelings he had kept purposely repressed for years. Things he had never told anyone, including his best friend, Kit Andrews. Finally, Swifty stopped talking. His lips were dry. His body hurt. His breathing was shallow and swift. He was shocked to find his eyes were wet.

Then the unexpected happened. Ann got out of her chair, set her glass on a side table and walked over to where Swifty was seated. She slid into his lap and put her arms around his neck. She used her fingers to wipe away his tears. She took the fingers into her mouth to lick them. Then she kissed him. He returned the kiss and soon they were embracing each other like two lovers who have been separated by vast amounts of time and distance.

Ann held Swifty and he suddenly felt like huge weights had been lifted and constricting chains had suddenly slipped away.

They sat like that, holding each other tightly, for a long time.

CHAPTER NINETEEN

Swifty wasn't sure what time he left Ann's office. All he knew was he felt better than he could ever remember. It was like his best birthday, his best Christmas morning, and his greatest days of triumph and success in the army all rolled into one morning.

When he started his truck's engine, it was very dark out. He turned on the headlights and headed out of Cody and back to the ranch. When he reached the ranch, only a small light in the kitchen was on. Swifty smiled. It was the same small lamp his mother used to leave on when he was in high school and had been out carousing. He quietly made his way to his room, stripped off his clothes and slipped into bed. As he made himself comfortable, he felt the sharp pang of pain from several bruised parts of his body, including the top of his head. He no sooner found a comfortable position and began to recount the events of the strange evening before he was fast asleep.

Swifty awoke to the smells of fresh coffee and bacon cooking on the stove. He showered and dressed and headed out to the kitchen. There he found his mother and Melanie cooking breakfast and drinking coffee. He greeted them and filled a mug with hot, black coffee.

"I'm surprised you survived the night," smirked his sister.

"What are you talking about?" asked Swifty as he sipped his coffee.

"From what I heard you created quite the ruckus at the Calaboose bar last night."

"Define ruckus," said Swifty.

"I heard you got into a brawl with five roughnecks from the oil patch," said Melanie.

Swifty scowled at his sister. "Where the hell did you hear that?" asked Swifty.

"They have this new thing called the internet and social media," said his smirking sister. "You may have heard of it, but maybe it hasn't made its way to Kemmerer yet."

"The internet?" said Swifty.

"Yes, you know, that wireless thingabob," said Melanie.

"I know it," said Swifty.

"It was all over Twitter last night and this morning about the big fight at the Calaboose last night. There were even pictures," said Melanie.

"Pictures?" said Swifty with surprise in his voce.

"Yeah, you know about how they developed photographs and even moving pictures in the last century," said a smirking Melanie.

"I know," said Swifty, sullenly.

"According to eyewitnesses, some cowboy beat the crap out of five big roughnecks in the bar's parking lot. Most of the accounts I read did not know who the roughnecks were or who the cowboy was, but from the descriptions I read, it wasn't hard to figure out," said Melanie.

"So, my name wasn't mentioned?" asked Swifty.

"Nope," replied his sister. "Just some cowboy type dressed just like you were when you went out last night. I checked your clothes in the laundry hamper this morning while you were still asleep, and they looked to be in a lot worse shape than they were when I last saw them on you."

"I have no idea what the hell you're talking about," said Swifty.

"Would you like to see this short film someone took on their cell phone?" asked Melanie.

"Those things are probably doctored and produced in Russia," retorted Swifty.

Swifty thought for a second and then came up with an idea to shut up his nosy sister. "I have no memory of last night," he said, and took a sip of his coffee.

"This from the man who remembers what he had for breakfast last Christmas," snorted Melanie.

"I have no idea what you're talking about," said a calm Swifty.

"Then maybe you can explain the phone call we got about an hour ago," said a grinning Melanie.

"What phone call?" asked Swifty.

"The one from your old high school pal, Lefty Phillips," retorted Melanie.

"Lefty called here?" asked Swifty.

"He certainly did. He wanted to know if you were all right after beating up those five yahoos from the Calaboose bar last night. I told him you hadn't made it home till late last night and you were sound asleep. He laughed and said you must have had a pretty good night and asked me to have you call him," said a grinning Melanie. "Here's his phone number," she said as she handed Swifty a piece of paper.

Swifty took the paper and stuck it in his shirt pocket without looking at it. He ignored his sister and drank his coffee.

Melanie grimaced and returned to the stove. Minutes later, she was back with a plate of eggs and bacon along with some buttered toast. She shoved the plate in front of her brother and disappeared out the door of the kitchen.

Swifty ate his breakfast and thought about the events of last night. He was crystal clear about what had happened with the five roughnecks, but not so sure about his involvement with Ann. He finished his breakfast and took his dishes to the sink where he washed and dried them and put them away. Then he remembered his appointment with his Aunt Judy.

He showered and shaved and put on clean clothes. He noticed either his mother or sister had laundered, dried, and folded his dirty clothes and stacked them on an old wooden chair by the closet in his bedroom.

He headed out of the bedroom and found his mother in the kitchen drinking coffee. He kissed his mother good morning and gave her a hug.

"I promised Aunt Judy I would stop by and chat, so I'm headed over to Meeteetse," said Swifty.

"Say hello to her for me," said his mother. "And be careful."

Swifty was out the door, wondering if she had also heard about the fight at the Calaboose bar last night. As far as he knew, ranch women gossip was probably still faster than the internet.

CHAPTER TWENTY

Twenty minutes later he was pulling into the outskirts of Cody. He stopped to fill up the truck with gas and then headed south to Meeteetse. The day was sunny with some wind, and Swifty drove with the driver's side window down.

He pulled into the outskirts of Meeteetse about twenty minutes later and drove down the main drag of the tiny town until he reached the intersection where the gas station was on the southwest corner and turned to the left and parked up against the side of the commercial building on the end of the block. Swifty exited his truck and strode up onto the wooden boardwalk until he reached the front door of his Aunt Judy's shop. As he opened the front door, the tiny bells attached to the top of the door tinkled, announcing his arrival.

Aunt Judy swooped out from behind the long glass cased counter and gave Swifty a big hug. Then she released him and looked him up and down.

"Looks to me like you could use a cup of coffee, young man," she said with a grin.

"I can't say no to a cup of your coffee, Aunt Judy," replied Swifty.

Aunt Judy retreated behind the counter and returned

with two cups of fresh coffee. She gestured for Swifty to sit down at a small round metal table. He pulled out a chair for her and then sat down next to her.

Swifty sipped the hot coffee and set his cup down on the small table. Aunt Judy took a tiny sip of her coffee and held her cup in her right hand.

"So, tell me just where the heck you have been for the past fourteen years, young man," asked Aunt Judy.

Swifty thought for a minute, then grinned and began talking. He had always had a special bond with his Aunt Judy. He had confessed things to her when he was growing up, he could never bring himself to tell his father or mother. He trusted her. She had never let him down. Swifty spent the next twenty minutes regaling his aunt with stories about his experiences in the army and the Delta Force and many of them made her laugh. He carefully sanitized many of the stories and related only the things he felt she would find interesting or funny. His Aunt Judy had a great sense of humor, and it was one of the things he appreciated about her the most.

"So, you came back to Wyoming, and you're working for this Kit guy and living in Kemmerer," said Aunt Judy. "Who called you to let you know about Eldon's death?"

"My sister, Melanie called me, and I packed up some stuff and drove to the ranch the next day," replied Swifty. "She said she got my number from you. I remember I sent it to you some time ago."

"She called me, and I told her I could give her a number to reach you," said Aunt Judy.

"I figured as much," said Swifty. "You are the only one I've given it to."

"I get the distinct feeling something is wrong," said Aunt Judy.

"What do you mean, wrong?" asked Swifty.

"I've known you since the day you were born, Swifty Olson. You never were very good at lying. It was unnatural for you. Something is bothering you, and I'm pretty sure it's not the fact that your father is dead. You and he were like oil and water. Never got along. But something is eating at you. I can see it in your face and hear it in your voice," said Aunt Judy.

Swifty paused and took another sip of coffee to give him a chance to collect his thoughts. He had always trusted his Aunt Judy, and she had never let him down. He put down his cup and looked directly at her.

"I've done some digging into what happened to my dad," said Swifty. "I discovered some things that make me pretty sure his death was no accident."

"What things?" asked Aunt Judy, her facial expression now very serious.

"I discovered the brake lines on his old truck had been cut," said Swifty.

"Are you sure they didn't just snap off from old age?" asked Aunt Judy.

"I examined the wreck of the old truck in the county impound lot, and they had been cut with a sharp object," said a grim faced Swifty.

"Cut?" exclaimed Aunt Judy.

"Yes, cut," responded Swifty. "I also examined the site and quite simply, Dad tried to brake for the curve, and nothing happened. When he tried to turn the steering wheel, it was too late, and he went off the edge of the cliff by the river. A neighbor heard the crash and came out to investigate. He called the sheriff's office and the deputy who showed up didn't even bother to go down to the crash site to check on Dad's body."

"Good lord," said Aunt Judy, a shocked expression on her face reflecting her surprise.

"I went to the sheriff's office and talked to the Deputy who turned out to be one of those worthless twits who likes to wear a uniform and play cop. He's both lazy and not very bright. He hadn't even investigated the wreck," said Swifty.

"Really," said Aunt Judy.

"So, I went to talk to the sheriff, and he got all upset because I trespassed on county property by going on the impound lot and searching the wreck of Dad's old truck. We got into a shouting match, and he basically tossed me out of his office," said Swifty.

"Good lord," said Aunt Judy.

"Then I went to see the county attorney and was told he was out. So, I tried to see any of the county commissioners, but none of them were available. Any appointment I could make to see any of them was at least a week out," said Swifty.

"That sounds like our public servants at work," snorted Aunt Judy. She'd always had little use for politicians.

"Public servants, my ass," said Swifty.

"So, it sounds like you investigated the wreck, found evidence and tried to report what you found to the authorities and then got stonewalled," said Aunt Judy.

"That's a pretty good summary of the last few days," replied Swifty.

"So, nobody you've talked to has the slightest interest

in helping you find out who cut the brake lines on Eldon's truck?" asked Aunt Judy.

"Not one single person," replied Swifty.

"Do you have any old friends from high school who could help you?" she asked.

"I have a couple of old friends, but they've got jobs, families, and responsibilities and I can't see trying to get them to help me," said Swifty. "Especially in something that isn't really their fight."

"Sounds like your fresh out of options," said Aunt Judy.

"I hate to admit it, but that sums the situation up pretty well," said Swifty.

"How about your partner and your friends back in Kemmerer?" asked Aunt Judy.

"If I called them, they'd be here in a few hours," said Swifty. "But this isn't their problem and I don't see myself asking for their help. I'm not sure what I can do next, or even how to do it."

"When you're at the bottom of the barrel, it's time to get a new barrel," said Aunt Judy with a faint smile on her face.

"What the hell are you talking about?" asked Swifty.

"You need a new barrel," said Aunt Judy. "One you didn't even know you had."

"I'm sorry, Aunt Judy. I have no idea what the hell you're talking about," said Swifty.

"You do have another option," said Aunt Judy. "One you never knew you had."

"What option are you talking about?" asked a puzzled Swifty.

Aunt Judy got up from her chair and walked over to the coffee maker behind the glass counter, refilled her cup and then returned to her seat at the small table. She took a sip of her coffee. Then she set the cup down on the table. Then she leaned forward as if she was about to share a secret with her nephew.

"You do have another option," said Aunt Judy. "One no one has ever told you about, not even your mother."

Swifty looked at his aunt as if she had just grown another head. His face reflected utter confusion.

"What option is that?" he asked.

"Tell me what you know about your grandfather Olson," she said.

Swifty thought for a moment and then he answered his aunt's question. "My grandfather Olson bought the ranch and then went into the army during the Vietnam War. He was a Green Beret and served two tours in southeast Asia. He got killed during his second tour," said Swifty.

"Have you ever been to the cemetery where he was buried?" asked Aunt Judy.

Swifty thought for a bit and then answered his aunt. "I don't remember ever going to his grave or know where it is," he said.

"Why do you think your mother or father or even your grandmother never took you to visit your grandfather's grave?" asked Aunt Judy.

"I have no idea," replied Swifty. "I guess I never thought about it before."

"That's because your grandfather Olson was not killed in Vietnam," said Aunt Judy.

"He wasn't?" said Swifty. "Then why did everyone tell me he was dead?"

Aunt Judy took another sip of coffee and then set her

cup the table. She sighed and then began speaking to Swifty. "I promised I would never tell you this, but I think it's time I told you the truth. After what's happened to your father, you are entitled to know what happened back before you were born," she said.

"When your grandfather came home from the war, he was a different person than the man I had known before he shipped out for Vietnam," said Aunt Judy. "He was angry and frightened and had trouble sleeping or even talking to people. It got so bad he finally went to a lawyer, divorced your grandmother, left her the ranch, and then disappeared, leaving her with your father as a small child."

"He disappeared?" asked Swifty. "To where?"

"No one knew where he went," said Aunt Judy. "He never called, came back for a visit, or even wrote a single word to your grandmother. The family treated him like he died in Vietnam and has ever since."

"Where the hell is he?" asked Swifty.

"What makes you think I know where he is?" asked Aunt Judy.

"You wouldn't be telling me this story if you didn't," said Swifty. "You were the only one who knew where I was and I suspect you managed to find out where my grandfather is as well," said Swifty.

"You were always too damn smart for your own good," said Aunt Judy with a faint smile on her lips.

CHAPTER TWENTY-ONE

Aunt Judy got up from her chair and walked to the front door of the store. She closed it tight, locked it, and hung the closed sign from the hook on the glass in the door. Then she refilled her coffee cup and Swifty's and returned to the table.

She sat down and handed Swifty his cup. Then she took a long swig from her cup and set it on top of the small table.

"Your grandfather was not a nice man," she said. "He was cantankerous, ill-tempered, and prone to violence with the slightest provocation. And that was when he was in a good mood. When he came home from the war, he was angry. He couldn't sleep and when he did, he often woke up in the middle of the night from nightmares and he would be soaking wet from sweat. Your grandmother told me she was terrified of him and what he might do over something that was literally nothing."

"She told me he was collecting guns and ammunition and all kinds of survival gear. He would go to gun shows and swap meets and come home with loads of stuff in his truck. He would take it all into the barn where he stored stuff in an old tack room he kept locked with a big padlock. He had the only key. He'd go into town and get into fights at ridiculous places like the post office or the grocery store. It was like he went everywhere just looking to start a fight."

"Didn't he get arrested?" asked Swifty.

Aunt Judy smiled and took a sip of coffee. "I believe he actually did get arrested once, but just once. He beat up four deputies and almost destroyed the jail. The sheriff gave up and just let him go. No one ever tried to arrest him again. They were all scared to death of him. Frankly, so was I," she said.

"Was he a drunk or a druggie?" asked Swifty.

"I don't believe he ever had anything to do with drugs," replied Aunt Judy. "He might have smoked an occasional marijuana cigarette, but I can't say for sure. He wasn't a drunk, but he did occasionally have a drink."

"What did he drink?" asked Swifty.

"He drank some brand of Rum," answered Aunt Judy. "I'm not sure of the brand, but I think it was named after some mountain."

"Mount Gay?" asked Swifty.

"That's the one," said Aunt Judy. "He mixed it with coke or Pepsi."

"So, what happened to him?" asked Swifty.

"One day he came home with an army surplus Jeep and a two wheeled trailer. He loaded all his stuff in the Jeep and the trailer and covered it with a tarp and tied it down tight. Then he handed his wife, your grandmother, an envelope. In the envelope was a deed to the ranch where he signed it over to her. A cashier's check for most of the money they had in the bank, and a letter," said Aunt Judy.

"What was in the letter?" asked Swifty.

"Basically, the letter just told her he was tired of people

and civilization and he was leaving her and the baby and he never wanted to hear from her, the baby, or anyone else for the rest of his life," she said.

"Did he say where he was going or where she could contact him in the future?" asked Swifty.

"He did not. He made it clear he was done with her, the boy, the ranch, and the town of Cody plus the rest of the country. He said nothing about where he was going or why, or what he planned on doing," said Aunt Judy. "That reminds me," she said. Aunt Judy rose from the table and went over to the bar. She got behind it and then bent over until she disappeared behind the bar. When she reappeared, she had an old white faded envelope in her hand. She returned to the table and laid the envelope down in front of Swifty.

"What's this?" asked Swifty.

"This is a copy of the letter I had made. I snitched the letter from your grandmother's desk and had it copied and then I returned the original to her desk," said Aunt Judy.

"Why did you do that?" asked Swifty.

"I wanted a copy of the letter in case the original got destroyed or someone like you wanted to know what really happened to their grandfather, "said Aunt Judy.

"Can I read the letter?" asked Swifty.

"That's why I made a copy and kept it hidden in my safe all these years," said Aunt Judy. "Open the envelope and have at it."

Swifty carefully opened the envelope. It was not sealed. He took out the one page of faded white paper. Then he unfolded the letter and began to read it. After about five minutes he had read it and re-read it and he stared at the signature at the bottom of the letter.

"My grandfather's name was B. R. Olson?" asked Swifty.

"Those are his initials, not his first name," replied a smiling Aunt Judy.

"What's B. R. stand for?" asked Swifty.

"Bushrod," said Aunt Judy. "Bushrod Olson is your grandfather."

"What the hell kind of name is Bushrod?" asked a puzzled Swifty.

"I have no idea," said Aunt Judy. "All I know was he hated his first name and never used it and always went by B. R. Olson."

"I don't think I've ever heard of anyone named Bushrod," said Swifty. "What the hell does Bushrod mean?"

"I have no idea," said Aunt Judy.

"Let's take a look," said Swifty as he pulled out his cell phone and typed in Bushrod on Google. A few seconds later he had his answer.

"I'll be damned," said Swifty. He found several Bushrods in Google. There was a Bushrod Johnson, a teacher, University Chancellor and confederate general in the civil war. A Bushrod Washington, a U.S Supreme Court Justice and nephew of George Washington.

"Looks like Bushrod was used as a first name during the Revolutionary War, but not much since," said Swifty.

"Well, your grandfather hated the name, no matter where it came from," said Aunt Judy. "And I can tell you, I never heard anyone brave enough to address him in public as Bushrod."

"While I'm in Google, let's see if maybe there is a hint of where he might be now," said Swifty. He typed in the name and waited. A few seconds later he had a few possibilities.

He began to search each one of the items which popped up on his tiny screen and was down to the last one when he hit paydirt.

He found a reference to a B.R. Olson owning a plot of land near Clark, Wyoming. Swifty looked up Clark on his phone. It was a tiny unincorporated town of about three hundred people on about fifty thousand acres of wilderness and mountains.

"This might be our man," said Swifty. "Tiny place of about three hundred people surrounded by about fifty thousand acres of wilderness."

"Actually, he doesn't live in Clark," said Aunt Judy. "That just where he picks up his mail, if he ever gets any."

"How do you know that?" asked Swifty with a puzzled look on his face.

"I hired a private detective about ten years ago," said Aunt Judy. "He was able to trace him to a piece of land by Beartooth Pass."

"Where the heck is that?" asked Swifty.

"The pass is on the map," said Aunt Judy. "He has some sort of cabin up about ten thousand feet?"

"How high is the pass?" asked Swifty.

"The pass is about eleven thousand feet," said Aunt Judy. "It's just south of the Montana state line."

"Do you happen to have a map of Wyoming," said Swifty.

"Sure do," said Aunt Judy. "I've got lots of them. The state of Wyoming provides them to stores like mine to give out to tourists." She got up out of her chair and went over to the bar. She returned with a brand-new road map of Wyoming in her hand. She gave it to Swifty and sat down.

Swifty opened the map and spread it out on the small table. He studied the map for a few minutes and then looked up at his aunt. "Highway 212 goes through the pass into Montana, but it says here the road is closed during most of the winter."

"They get a lot of snow up at that altitude," said Aunt Judy.

"Shouldn't be any snow up there now," said Swifty. He continued to study the map. "Looks like Clark is about fifty miles from Cody, but his cabin site is more like a hundred miles away. There is no straight shot from Clark to where his land is located."

"I doubt he has had any visitors in the past forty years or so," said Aunt Judy with a smirk. "Nor do I think he wants any now."

"Considering what's going on in our country and the world right now, I'm not sure I can totally disagree with him," said Swifty. Then he looked up at his aunt. "Do you think he'd see me and talk to me?"

"I have no idea," said Aunt Judy. "I rather doubt being isolated from the world for over forty years has added anything to his interest in other people, but you are his grandson."

"I think I need to find him and talk to him," said Swifty.

"Why?" asked Aunt Judy.

"There's a reason my Dad got killed. I think it has something to do with the ranch. B.R. Olson bought the ranch and worked it before he left for the war. If there is something on the ranch that is worth killing for, he just might know what it is," said Swifty. "Plus, if the folks who own the Hayfork Ranch are behind the death of my father,

I'm gonna need some help and I have a feeling the kind of help I'm gonna need is the real nasty kind. And nasty seems to be grandpa's middle name."

Swifty rose from the table. He handed back the envelope containing the copy of the letter to his aunt, but he hung on to the map of Wyoming. He gave her a long hug. When he released his aunt, he said, "Thank you for sharing your family secrets with me. You have no idea how much I appreciate this."

"I only hope I've done more to help you than harm you," said Aunt Judy. "That crazy old coot is liable to shoot you for trespassing and not give a crap about the fact you're his grandson. Promise me you'll be careful."

"I'm always careful, Aunt Judy," said a grinning Swifty. With that he strode to the front door, unlocked it, flipped the closed sign to the open sign and disappeared out the door.

CHAPTER TWENTY-TWO

When he got to his truck, Swifty climbed into the cab, started the engine, and pulled out his cell phone. He punched in a familiar number and waited for the phone to ring at the other end.

"Let me guess," said the familiar voice on the other end of the line. "You got drunk and the hogs ate you."

"That'll be the day," said a now grinning Swifty.

"What's up?" asked Kit. "Time's money and you're wasting mine."

"I need a favor," said Swifty.

He heard a loud groan from the other end. "I can only imagine that hopefully this is just a dream," said Kit in a pained voice.

"Got a pen and paper?" asked Swifty.

A minute passed as he heard some shuffling of papers over the phone. "O.K., I'm ready," said Kit. "Let's hear your grocery list for the day."

Swifty read from a list he had written down before he had talked to his Aunt Judy, but he added some items as a result of that talk. When he was finished there was a pause before Kit spoke.

"Did we declare war on Canada, and I missed it?" asked Kit.

"Nope. This is a private matter between me and some people who have managed to really piss me off," replied Swifty.

"When do you need this stuff?" asked Kit.

"Yesterday," answered Swifty.

"Send it to your mom's ranch address?" asked Kit.

"That'll work," responded Swifty.

"There are a couple of items I don't have on hand," said Kit. "Not to mention possession of them is more than likely illegal."

"I know," replied Swifty. "You remember your dad's old friend in Buffalo?"

"Bill Eckberg?" responded Kit.

"That's the one. He'll have them. Do you have his number?" asked Swifty.

"Sure do," replied Kit. "I'll call him as soon as we're done."

"We're done," said Swifty.

"Are you sure you couldn't use some help,?" asked Kit. "This stuff is enough to start your own small war."

"If I do, it'll be my own private war," replied Swifty. "But, thanks for the offer. This is something I need to do for myself. I don't want you or any of my other friends involved. If this goes sideways, I can always disappear. You, not so much."

"It's your call," said Kit. "I hope you know what you're doing."

"As usual, I probably don't," said Swifty. With that, he broke the connection with his best friend.

Swifty put the phone in his shirt pocket and pulled out of Meeteetse, headed north for Cody and his mother's ranch.

CHAPTER TWENTY-THREE

When he arrived back at the ranch, Swifty went to his room and retrieved his laptop computer. He took it out to the kitchen table and plugged it into an outlet. As soon as the laptop was ready, he fired it up and began a methodical search for his grandfather's property. He utilized simple things like real estate tax records he knew his grandfather could not stay hidden from. Then he used Goggle Search to get aerial view of property plots including his grandfather's and the surrounding land parcels. He saved each pertinent item and soon he had a good idea of the property and those surrounding it.

It appeared his grandfather's property was one of the few with any dwellings on it. Even then, he found it very difficult to find much that resembled a habitable structure. He found aerial views of a small broken-down cabin and a nearby barn with the roof caved in. He could see no signs of roads or even well-worn areas in the land to indicate regular vehicle traffic. The old cabin and barn were surrounded by waist high weeds and looked uninhabited.

Swifty stared at the pictures on the small screen and pondered them. Maybe the old man had died. Even his Aunt Judy had not seen him in many years. Having a post office box didn't tell him much. He could have paid the rent on the box for years ahead.

He took another look at the satellite pictures. Then he used a hand-held magnifying glass to study the images. He could see no sign of recent habitation. One item stood out. The taxes were current. Someone had paid them. He checked the tax record. The taxes were minimal, but they had been paid six months ago. Someone had paid them, and he was pretty sure it was his grandfather. There was only one way to find out. He needed to get near the property. Then leave his truck and hike up into the property and have a look for himself.

Swifty closed his laptop and sat back in his chair. It would probably be at least two days before he received the supplies he had requested, and he might have to drive to Buffalo to pick up the items from Bill Eckberg. In the meantime, he had seen several things on the ranch that needed attention and repair so he could make himself useful.

He put the laptop back in his room and headed out the door to the barn. He had noticed two stall doors needed repair and there was no time like the present. He went into the tack room, found the tools he needed, and then proceeded to take off the stall doors and repair them. It took him a couple of hours to complete the repairs, but when he was finished, the doors were rehung and worked perfectly. He put away the tools and headed for his truck. He drove the truck out of the ranch yard and drove slowly along the fence line. After about half an hour he had identified about three places where the fence needed repair. He made a mental note and then headed back to the ranch house.

He parked the truck and headed into the kitchen where

his mother was making supper. He offered to help, and she waved him away. He went to the living room and turned on the television. He watched a news program and all it did was remind him how fortunate he was to live in Wyoming instead of a place like New York City, Los Angeles, San Francisco, or Portland.

Dinner that evening was pot roast with roasted potatoes. He had missed lunch and he was famished. He forced himself to stop after two helpings of pot roast and potatoes. His mother didn't seem to mind his appetite one bit. His sister just made little piggy faces at him. It reminded him of when they were little kids. Some things never changed.

Swifty woke early and quickly dressed and headed out to feed the horses and check on the cattle. He returned to the ranch house about an hour and a half later and was greeted by the smell of bacon frying. After breakfast he shooed his mother and sister out of the kitchen, and he did the dishes and cleaned the kitchen. Then he went to his room and checked his phone. He had a text from Bill Eckberg.

"Your package is ready. It's been prepaid," read Bill's text.

Swifty smiled. Kit didn't let any grass grow under his boots. He texted Bill back that he would be there by noon to pick up the package. Then he said goodbye to his mother and sister and drove the truck back through Cody. It took him over three hours to get to Bill's place just outside Buffalo. He drove the old road slowly to make sure he didn't miss the almost hidden cutoff and soon he was parking in front of Bill's cabin.

When he stepped outside the truck and onto the gravel covered parking area, Swifty paused and checked his surroundings. He could hear the wind in the pines and a couple of songbirds. He could see the open area with their pine boundary fences enclosing it. He could smell the fresh air and the scent of both pine and sagebrush. Other than the wind and birds, he could sense nothing else moving. He knew from previous experience Bill was probably not in the house. He had surely heard his truck engine making its way up the rough road to the cabin. Bill was likely located up above the cabin, hidden in the pine trees. He was also likely to be looking at Swifty through the scope of a high-powered rifle.

Swifty turned so he was facing the cabin and he spread his arms out at his sides with his hands open to assure Bill he came with no ill intent and not armed. He kept his position for a couple of minutes until Bill suddenly appeared from behind a large pine tree just uphill from the cabin.

Bill looked as Swifty remembered him. He wore old army camo pants and shirt with a boonie hat in the old forest camo long abandoned by the army in favor of new digitized clothing. Slung over his shoulder was a .300 Win Mag rifle with a powerful scope.

The two men shook hands. "You're looking downright healthy," said Bill. "I can't imagine how you stay in such good health with so many trying to put a hole in you."

Swifty laughed. "Hey, I'm not the one living up in the wilderness and greeting his guests with a high-powered rifle from concealment."

Bill laughed. "I still believe in one basic rule. Trust nobody."

Swifty looked around the cleared compound and cabin. "Looks like it's worked pretty well so far."

"That it has," said Bill with a grin. "I got fresh coffee in the cabin." Swifty followed him up on the front porch of the cabin and followed Bill inside.

The inside of the cabin was much nicer than the outside and showed both the touches of an experienced mountain man with a previous military background. Stuffed animal heads and skins adorned the walls. Hanging on pegs on one wall were all kinds of outdoor tools from snowshoes to animal traps.

Bill motioned Swifty to a small round kitchen table with three chairs. Swifty took one chair and Bill produced two mugs and a pot of coffee. He poured each of them a cup and then took a seat.

"I got the request from Kit, but I admit I was a little surprised to find out it was for you," said Bill.

"Why is that?" asked Swifty.

"I guess it was a surprise you needed something this powerful for an ambush. You never struck me as an ambush kind of guy," replied Bill.

"When the odds are stacked against you, it's a good idea to cover all the bases," said Swifty.

"Well, these boys should do the job for you," said Bill. He rose from his chair and walked over to where he had three cardboard boxes stacked on top of each other. He opened the top box and extracted a curved metal object about eighteen inches high and about two feet long. He returned to the table and handed the object to Swifty.

Swifty held the object in his hands out in front of him and turned it until he could read the message inscribed on one side of the object. "Front toward enemy," was the message.

Swifty read the message out loud and then set the Claymore mine down on the table. "Sounds like good advice to me," he said.

"You use Claymores before?" asked Bill.

"More times than I care to remember," replied Swifty.

"The clackers and wiring are in the box," said Bill.

"The best thing about the army is they assume all of us are stupid," said a grinning Swifty. "And a lot of times they were right."

Bill laughed and the two men clinked their coffee mugs together in agreement with Swifty's sentiment.

"How many Claymores in the boxes?" asked Swifty.

"A dozen total," replied Bill. "That's what Kit requested when he contacted me. Will it be enough for you?"

"If it isn't, I'll be too dead to complain," replied Swifty.

Bill took a sip of his coffee and shot Swifty a serious look. "Do you need some help?" he asked.

"Nope. This is a personal matter, and I need to handle it myself. I don't want any of my friends involved," replied Swifty. "If things go to hell in a handbasket, I can just disappear. Most of my friends can't do that."

"The offer still stands if things get dicey," said Bill. "I'm a hell of a lot closer than Kit or anyone else in Kemmerer," said Bill.

"I appreciate the offer, and I will keep it in mind," said Swifty.

The two men sat in silence and finished their coffee. When Swifty rose to his feet, Bill did as well and each of them picked up a box of Claymores and carried them out to the truck. When they had finished loading the truck, Swifty turned to Bill. "What do I owe you?" he asked.

"Bill's been taken care of by your partner," answered Bill. The two men shook hands. "Don't do anything stupid out there," said Bill.

"Doing stupid things is part of my way of life," replied a grinning Swifty.

He climbed in his truck and started the engine. As he turned the truck around, he waved goodbye to Bill and drove out through the ring of pine trees back to the dirt road.

CHAPTER TWENTY-FOUR

Swifty stopped in Buffalo at the Busy Bee Café and grabbed a quick lunch. It was almost a three-hour drive back to Cody. Along the way, Swifty thought about his next move. He had made an inventory of items he had requested from Kit and Bill, plus items he already had on hand. He took the list out of his shirt pocket and read it, ticking off each item as he determined he had, in fact, possession of all the equipment listed.

He began to think about how he could best approach his newly discovered grandfather without getting shot or killed. None of the ideas he came up with came across as sound, so he decided the best strategy was to get all the aerial reconnaissance he could and then map out the best approach to his grandfather's cabin. He would park his truck about three miles from the cabin. Then make his way on foot to a point where he could have a good view of the entire area. Then he could decide on the best route and the best method to approach his grandfather.

Before long, his thoughts were interrupted by traffic coming out of Cody to the east. Within half an hour he was in downtown Cody. He stopped to fill up the truck's tank with gas and then drove through Cody, turning left onto Wyoming Highway 291. He pulled up next to the ranch house and parked the truck. He decided to leave the Claymores under a tarp in the bed of the pickup. He would wait until the shipment from Kit arrived and then take everything down to the shop in the barn and repack it for his trip to his grandfather's place. He walked down to the barn and pushed open the big sliding barn door aside so he could enter. He flipped on the overhead lights and made his way to the tack room. He spent about twenty minutes rearranging things so he would have space to store the Claymores and the rest of his gear. When he was finished, he stood back to examine his work. Satisfied with what he saw, he headed for the barn door. Before he got there, he heard the sound of an engine just outside the barn.

Swifty paused. Stepping outside the barn door to see who was there would be natural for most people. Swifty was not most people. He did not like surprises. He stepped back until he was up against the wall of the barn. Then he walked silently into a nearby stall where he slipped inside and went to one knee where he had a good view of the entrance to the barn. The barn door slid open and light from the outside world flowed into the interior darkness of the barn. A figure was silhouetted against the sunlight, but Swifty could only see it as a dark figure. Then the figure spoke.

"Swifty? Where the hell are you?" said a calm female voice, he knew to be Ann's.

"Over here," said Swifty as he rose to his feet and stepped out of the stall and into the open part of the barn.

"Were you cleaning out that stall or just being sneaky?" said Ann with a grin.

"I was being sneaky," said Swifty. "Just like always."

Ann walked forward and stopped barely a foot from Swifty. Her eyes darted over him as though she was taking some sort of inventory. "You look like you've been sweating. Since I suspect you are averse to manual labor, what have you been doing that would work up a sweat?" she asked.

Swifty tried to keep a straight face, but he failed miserably. His grin started small and then spread across his entire face.

"I just spent some time cleaning up the tack room," replied Swifty with an attempt at presenting a face of innocence.

"I highly doubt that," replied Ann. "On your best day, you were always a trouble-making scamp."

"Me?" exclaimed Swifty with a phony sense of innocence.

"You couldn't fake innocence if your life depended on it," retorted Ann. "On your best day you were still up to something bound to get you in trouble."

"I admit I always leaned toward having a good time, no matter what I was doing," said a grinning Swifty.

"That may be the first truthful words I've ever heard come out of your mouth," said Ann.

"I'll prove to you I was actually working," said an innocent looking Swifty.

"Show me," said Ann with doubt in her eyes.

Swifty led her to the tack room and once inside, he showed her the rearranged room with the clean space he had cleared out on one wall.

"I am finding it hard to believe you may have actually told me the truth about something," said a still doubting Ann.

"I'm a changed man," said Swifty with a look of false innocence.

"That'll be the day," said Ann. "You are who you are, and I doubt it will ever change. Unfortunately, that's what draws me to you. You may be impulsive and crazy and often reckless, but those are the things that attracted me to you in the first place and nothing has changed. I'm still attracted to you, but lord knows why."

Swifty put his hands up, palms out, in mock surrender. "I'm just a cowboy trying to find his place in the world," he said.

"What a crock that is," said Ann. "You may be a cowboy, but you are, and always were, a guy trying to remake the world to fit what he thinks it should be for his personal enjoyment."

"I'd like to argue against that, but I can't fight the truth when it gets tossed in my face," said Swifty.

"You know what I really hate?" asked Ann.

"What?" replied Swifty with a puzzled look on his face.

"I hate the fact I am still as drawn to you as I was in the tenth grade," said Ann. She stepped forward and slipped her arms around Swifty and hugged him tightly to her.

Swifty responded with a hug of his own. When he released his hold on her, Ann leaned forward and kissed him on the mouth. Not a peck, or a swipe of lips, but a full-bore mouth on mouth kiss with a tongue inserted like an exclamation point.

"Wow, where did that come from?" asked Swifty as Ann pulled slightly back from him.

"You know damn good and well were it came from," said a slightly irritated Ann.

"You're right," responded Swifty. "I do." Then he pulled

Ann tightly against him and kissed her hard on the mouth, adding an exclamation point with his own tongue.

Without warning Ann suddenly pulled back from Swifty's embrace.

"Is something wrong?" asked a puzzled Swifty.

"Nothing's wrong, I'm just a lot smarter than I used to be," said a smiling Ann.

"What the hell does that mean?" asked Swifty.

"It means I've taught myself to go a lot slower when dealing with a man," said Ann. "Rushing into something was not smart, and it was a hard lesson to learn."

"I'm confused" said a frowning Swifty.

"It's pretty simple," responded Ann. "I like an occasional jolt of excitement to make sure I'm on the right track, but then I need to hit the brakes and make sure this path leads to something good and not falling into a swamp."

"Is there a translation for guys or is this just a learn as we go kind of deal?" asked Swifty.

Ann grinned at Swifty. "You catch on pretty quickly for a guy who skipped college," she said. "All it means is I've learned to take important things slowly and to make sure of my footing as I go."

"So, where are we?" asked Swifty.

"We're getting to know each other all over again," said Ann. "I think I know you pretty well, but I'm sure lots of things have changed."

"And?" asked Swifty.

"And I have a lot I need to learn about you, Swifty Olson. I'm pretty sure you are not the same boy I knew in high school," replied Ann.

Swifty thought about what Ann had said and then he

looked at her and smiled. "You're right. There's a lot about me you know nothing about," he said.

Ann turned and walked out of the tack room and headed for the barn door.

"Where are you going?" asked a surprised Swifty.

"Don't get your underwear in a bunch," said a smiling Ann. "I'm going out to my truck to get the surprise I brought for you."

"A surprise? For me?" said Swifty. "I'm not sure if I should be happy or looking for a weapon to defend myself with."

"You'll be happy. You can count on that," said Ann and she disappeared out the barn door.

"I hate surprises," muttered Swifty under his breath.

Ann soon returned to the barn carrying an old-fashioned picnic basket. She set it on the work bench after clearing some tools off it. She pulled up two mismatched work stools next to the work bench. She opened the basket and took out an honest to god red and white checked small tablecloth and spread it out on the work bench. She emptied the contents of the basket out and set them on the tablecloth covered bench surface. She brought out a bottle of champagne, two glasses, and two plastic place settings. Then she brought out two large sourdough meatloaf sandwiches laced with horseradish mustard, two large dill pickles, two small bags of potato chips, and a plastic bag containing six large home-made chocolate chip cookies. When she was finished, she sat down on one of the work stools and smiled at Swifty.

For one of the first times in his life, Swifty was speechless. He just looked at Ann and the picnic lunch spread before him in amazement.

Finally, Swifty found his voice. "How in the world did you remember all these things I liked when we were back in high school?" he asked.

"I have a long and excellent memory," said a smug Ann. "Besides, I like all of these things as well."

Swifty sat on the other stool and waited as Ann opened the bottle of champagne. The cork popped and shot somewhere over Swifty's head.

"Damn, missed," said a grinning Ann.

"Not by much," said a surprised Swifty.

Ann poured champagne into each of their glasses and set the bottle on the workbench. She held up her glass as if to make a toast. Swifty lifted his glass.

"To us," said Ann. "May the best of friends we'll always be."

"I'll drink to that," said Swifty.

Both drained their glasses, and then Ann placed portions of food on their paper plates and passed one to Swifty.

"Before I dig into this lovely meal, what is the real reason for this surprise feast?" said Swifty. "The Ann I recall never did anything without having a purpose."

"You are correct, Mr. Cowboy," replied Ann. "There is a purpose to this meal."

Swifty said nothing and he sat on his stool, waiting patiently. He had learned long ago Ann was a very smart woman, but she could not help herself when she wanted to know something. All he had to do was outwait her curiosity, which usually was not for long.

Ann sat there with a straight face for about three minutes. Then she broke into a grin and reached over and punched Swifty in the shoulder. "You know me too well, Swifty Olson," she said.

Ann took a swig of champagne and looked Swifty directly in the eyes. "I want to know everything that has happened to you since the last time I saw you at high school graduation."

"Everything?" said a surprised Swifty. "Even the boring stuff?"

"Everything," said Ann.

"Some of it is pretty violent and nasty," said Swifty. "I've done and seen things I've never shared with anyone who wasn't there with me at the time it happened."

"Everything," repeated Ann.

"You seemed a bit squeamish when I mentioned a few things the other night," said Swifty.

"Everything," said a determined Ann.

Swifty took a bite of his tasty sandwich and washed it down with champagne. Then he looked up at Ann and began to talk.

His talk took longer than he had expected. He found himself elaborating and going into detail he had never done before for anyone, including Kit. Ann never blinked or gasped or got red in the face. In fact, she peppered his story with questions which required more detailed explanations.

When Swifty was finished with his story, he and Ann had eaten all the food from her basket and the champagne bottle was empty. Ann's face was calm, but her eyes betrayed her concerns.

When Ann was sure Swifty was finished with his story, she got up and put the tablecloth, the food, and utensils back in the picnic basket. Then she picked up the basket and slipped out of the tack room and out of the barn. Swifty sat on his stool, unsure of what to do next.

Then Ann reappeared and stood in front of him. She took Swifty's face in her hands and leaned down and kissed him hard on the mouth. Then she helped him to his feet. She hugged him and kissed him. He responded. Ann broke the kiss and headed out to her truck with Swifty following behind her like a puppy. When she got to her truck, she turned and looked Swifty in the eye.

"This was a good start, Cowboy," said Ann. Then she got in her truck and drove down the dirt road. Swifty watched her until the dust from the road engulfed the truck and swept Ann and her truck from view.

CHAPTER TWENTY-FIVE

As he made his way back to the ranch house, Swifty found himself a bit confused about what had just happened. Swifty was knowledgeable about a lot of things in the world, but a woman's motivation was not on his list. He tried to rerun the previous events in his mind like you would rewind a vide. When he had finished, he was as clueless as ever.

He made his way back to the porch of the ranch house and paused there. He looked back at the ranch road. It was empty. Not even a tiny cloud of dust remained to mark Ann's passing. It was like she had never been there. Swifty shook his head, shrugged his shoulders, and continued into the front door.

His mother and sister were putting dishes away in the kitchen. Melanie looked at him with a smirk on her face. "Glad you could finally make it home, Swifty," she said. His mother said nothing, but she too was smiling. "We decided not to wait dinner on you, but you don't look too hungry to me. You look a bit confused, but not at all hungry." Then both she and her mother broke out laughing.

Swifty turned on his heel and quickly made his way to his room where he shut the door to reduce the sound of female laughter. He made his way to his old desk. There he pulled out his laptop and plugged it into a wall outlet. Once he had a connection, he used his fingers to move to a section he had reserved for his trip to try to find his grandfather. When the screen came up, he found himself staring at a list he had made of items he had determined he might need soon. He went over the list. He had everything in his truck or the barn except the items Kit was shipping. Swifty looked at the date on the laptop screen. The shipment was due the next day. Since it was coming FedEx, he was unsure of what time of day the delivery guy would arrive at the ranch. He assumed he would spend the next day itemizing things and then packing what he felt he would need for his trip up to the Montana border.

Satisfied with his list, Swifty turned off the laptop and shut it. Then he looked around his room and found what he was looking for. All alone in a small drawer of his desk was a beret. Not just any beret. This one was green, and it was the only thing Swifty had ever seen of his grandfather's. He had found it when he had snuck up into the dusty attic as a young boy. He had been searching for treasure in old cardboard boxes when he found the beret. In the hat band he found a name inscribed. The name was "B. Olson." He had known then it had belonged to his grandfather. He had taken it and stored it in his small desk drawer where he knew no one would ever look for it. Occasionally, when he was growing up, he would take the beret out of the drawer and place it on his bed and stare at it.

Swifty smiled as he took the beret out of the drawer and slipped it into his backpack.

He was unsure of exactly how he might use the old

beret, but he had decided it might help him when he finally confronted his long-lost grandfather.

Swifty emerged from his room and found the ranch house strangely empty. He finally found his mother and sister sitting outside on the front porch. He found another old chair and dragged it next to where the ladies were sitting. He plopped into the chair and looked directly at his mother and sister. "So, what have I missed so far?" he asked with a wide grin on his face.

"Your sister has some news," said his mother with a sly smile on her face.

"What's your news, Melanie?" he asked.

"I have a new job," said his grinning sister.

"Doing what?" asked a surprised Swifty.

"I'm an assistant in training for Dr. Dexter," replied Melanie with a note of pride in her voice.

"You're working for Ann?" said a surprised Swifty.

"Yes, I am," retorted Melanie. "I start out doing filing and secretarial stuff and taking phone calls, answering mail, and ordering supplies for her clinic. She is also paying my way to Northwest Community College. I attend classes here in Cody at night and after the first year, I can attend classes on-line until I get my associates degree," said Melanie with a note of pride in her voice.

"You didn't happen to get this job because you're my sister, did you?" asked Swifty.

"No, it's more like I got the job in spite of my being your sister," retorted Melanie.

"Seems a tad suspicious to me," said Swifty.

"Don't flatter yourself, big brother," said Melanie. "In case you haven't noticed, Ann is still a very hot looking woman. She's been beating guys off with a stick ever since she came back to Cody. She can do a whole lot better than you and so far, she has said no to every guy who has asked her out."

"She came to see me today," responded Swifty. "What do you call that?"

"She feels sorry for you, just like she would for an injured little puppy," snapped back Melanie. "She only got involved with you because you got hurt in that fight at the Calaboose."

"So, I'm just another injured puppy to Ann," said Swifty.

"I doubt she could see the difference," retorted Melanie.

His sister's words stung Swifty, but he did his best not to let it show. He rose to his feet, said a curt good night to his mother and sister and headed on into the ranch house. He went to his room, undressed, and slipped into his old bed. It was some time before he finally fell asleep.

Swifty woke early. It was still dark outside. He dressed and headed out to the kitchen. He found it dark and empty. He went out the door and walked toward the barn. The morning air was crisp with just a slight breeze blowing. He tugged his jacket closed and was soon in the barn. He turned on the light switch and went into the tack room. There he turned on another light switch and looked at the space he had made. He pulled out his list and went over it mentally. When he was satisfied, he had not forgotten anything, he went out to the barn and began cleaning out the four horse stalls. He used a pitchfork to muck out the stalls and then he spread fresh straw in them. The old mucked out straw he pitched into an old wheelbarrow and moved it out to the side of the barn where he added to the existing pile of old straw. He knew his mother would use it for compost. Then he went back outside the barn and fed the horses hay with a bit of grain. He left the chicken coop and the small hog house to his mother and sister. He also ignored the two milk cows after feeding them. Some things a cowboy didn't do unless he absolutely had to.

When he was finished with his chores, the sun was coming up. He headed to the ranch house. When he got to the front porch, he could smell coffee brewing and bacon frying. Swifty smiled. Few things smelled better to him first thing in the morning. He made his way inside the ranch house and found his mother and sister making breakfast. He was tempted to tease his sister about her new job as an animal doctor's helper. Then he thought better of it. He was secretly glad his sister had found something and was even happier she was working for Ann. His mother would need all the help she could get running the ranch and while he was happy to help his mother, running their small ranch was not high on his list. Swifty went out to the small alcove off the front porch and washed his hands and face, drying them off with an old worn hand towel.

His sister plopped a big mug of black coffee in front of Swifty. He accepted the coffee without a word, grateful for hot coffee without a lecture. After a breakfast of bacon and scrambled eggs and toast, he finished his coffee and headed out the door. He went to the barn, saddled up the bay, and set out to check on the cows. The sun was up, and he felt its warming rays on his shoulders and back. He felt good in the saddle. He had the first time he ever rode a horse, and nothing had changed over the years. Swifty had always felt he was born to be a cowboy. He took his time moving out to the main pasture and let the bay have its head and only used the bridle when the bay began veering off course to some other part of the ranch. He checked the cattle herd and saw nothing amiss. Then he rode the fence line, taking his time. He had learned long ago you could see things from the back of a horse you could never see from the cab of a pickup truck.

Nothing had changed since his last fence inspection and when he reached the spot where he had seen the survey stakes on the other side of the property fence, he was surprised to find the stakes were missing. When he looked carefully, he could see a couple of small holes where some of the stakes had been. Swifty thought it puzzling someone would come out and remove the stakes, but maybe they realized they had forgotten them and someone else had reported them. It was hard to say with an outfit as big as the Hayfork Ranch.

Once he had completed his circuit of the ranch, he headed for the barn. He saw dust from the ranch road and then saw the FedEx truck headed back to Cody. Swifty grinned. Kit had been correct, as usual. The shipment from Kemmerer had arrived. He spurred the bay and they galloped back to the barn. When he arrived, he led the bay into the barn and his stall. There he unsaddled the horse and removed the bridle and saddle blanket. He brushed the bay with a curry comb and used an old blanket to wipe the horse down. Satisfied with his work, Swifty gave the bay a little grain and headed for the ranch house.

When he reached the front porch, he found three large boxes stacked by the front door. Swifty checked the labels and they were all addressed to him. He picked up the boxes one at a time and took them back to the tack room in the barn. Once he had all three boxes secured, he closed the door to the tack room and locked it so he wouldn't be interrupted. Then he opened each box, emptied them of their contents and cataloged each item he had received. Once he was done, he compared the list of items with the list he had originally written. Everything he had asked for was there. Included were a couple of items he had not asked for. One was a small box of smoke grenades and the second was a state-of-the-art satellite phone with a charger.

Swifty grinned. His partner was always thinking ahead and when he thought about it, he should have included the items in the first place. He was doing this caper on his own, and if he got in trouble, he had no backup. The phone and smoke grenades would help Kit find him if he was injured and unable to move around.

He placed all the items on the old work bench and then covered them with a small tarp. It was not a lot of concealment, but he didn't think he'd have a lot of surprise visitors to the tack room. When he was finished, he exited the tack room and closed the door. Then he pulled out a new padlock from the shipment he had just received and locked the tack room door. He added the padlock key to the small ring of keys he kept in his jeans pocket. Then he made his way to the house.

When he reached the house, both his mother and sister were gone. He moved through the silent old ranch house to his room. There, he opened his laptop and began to do some research of Google Earth and other sites to learn as much as he could about the area where he believed his long-lost grandfather was located. When he was finished, he went out to his truck and retrieved a small portable printer with a package of letter sized copy paper. He returned to his room and began printing out the pages he had earmarked. When he was finished, he returned the printer to the truck and went back to his room. There he began studying the pages he had printed out and making notes on the margins of the printed pages.

CHAPTER TWENTY-SIX

It was still dark outside when Swifty was out of bed and taking a shower. He dressed quickly and made his way out to the kitchen. The ranch house was dark and quiet. For one of the first times in his life on the ranch, Swifty had gotten up before his mother. He made a pot of coffee and three pieces of toast. He buttered the toast and added some jam. Then he drank black coffee and ate his breakfast.

When he was finished, he washed his dishes in the sink and put them on the drying board. Then he made his way out to the barn and unlocked the padlock on the tack room door. Once inside, he locked the door and then began putting items in piles on the workbench. When he was finished, he unlocked the door and made his way out to his truck. There he retrieved several zip-up bags and two packs. He took them back to the barn and soon had each bag filled and placed in the packs along with a few individual items. He also slid a long, wicked looking black rifle into a padded rifle case.

Satisfied with his work, he took two trips to the truck transporting his packed items. When he was finished, he locked the padlock to the tack room and walked back to the ranch house. His mother and sister were still not up. Swifty found a pad of paper and a pen and wrote a brief note to his mother letting her know he was going up by the Montana border on a scouting trip and might not be back until the next day. He added his cell phone number, knowing it was unlikely he would get any cell service where he was headed. Then he left the note on the kitchen table and left the ranch house. Five minutes later he was driving out the entrance to the ranch and headed toward Cody.

Swifty stopped in Cody and gassed up his truck. Then he stopped at the grocery store and bought some food items. When he returned to the truck, he distributed the food items into his two packs. When he was finished, he got in the cab of his truck and pulled out his road map of Wyoming.

He found Cody on the map and traced his finger on route 120 north of town until he got to the intersection with route 296, about seventeen miles. Then he ran his finger on 296 for forty miles to the intersection with US highway 212. At the intersection he moved his finger east on 212 to the Montana border up on Beartooth Pass. The map showed the summit of the pass at 10,947 feet above sea level. He was pretty sure his grandfather's property was at an elevation of almost ten thousand feet. He checked his notes and sure enough, the property was at nine thousand nine hundred and twenty feet. He exited the truck and pulled out one of the packs from the truck bed. He dug through it until he found his altimeter and stuck it in his shirt pocket. He replaced the pack and returned to the cab of his truck. He pulled out the altimeter and put it in one of the truck's cup holders. He slipped on his sunglasses and started the truck's engine.

"Well, here goes a really smart move or a really dumb

one," thought Swifty, as he put the truck in gear and headed north out of Cody and closer to a grandfather he had never met.

As he drove, Swifty kept an eye on his odometer. He knew there was no direct route from Cody to Beartooth Pass. He had to take a roundabout path to get there and there was no short cut. He estimated the trip would take almost two hours and he wasn't far off. Again, he checked his odometer. Finally, the road curved to the north and began a steep climb as he rapidly gained altitude.

Swifty checked his pocket altimeter in the cup holder. He was at eight thousand, four hundred feet and quickly gaining altitude. He slowed the truck and began to look for possible crude side roads on his right. He knew from his research his grandfather's land was east of highway 212. Just after he passed nine thousand, one hundred feet, he saw a crude road on his right. He noted it, but felt it was too low to be an access road to his grandfather's land. He kept driving but slowed even more down to thirty miles an hour. He thought the access road might be hidden and he didn't want to miss it.

As he made his way slowly up the steep incline, he noticed what looked like an old, abandoned logging road to his right. The weeds were high, but the cleared trees made the road look like an alleyway through the forest. Swifty stopped the truck on the side of the road and got out. He walked over to what he thought was a logging road and sure enough, it was rough, but wide enough for a big truck. Weeds and small saplings about two feet high dotted the old logging road. Swifty guessed it hadn't been used in several years. He returned to his truck and once in the cab, he pulled out his printed copies of the Google maps he had previously selected. He quickly found a satellite photo showing the traces of the old logging road. He set the copy on the passenger seat of the truck and checked the altimeter. He was at nine thousand four hundred and eighty feet. He noted the information on the margin of the map and pulled back out onto the highway.

Swifty noted no vehicle had passed him since he started up the pass nor had he met any vehicles coming from the Montana side. He knew the road was closed during much of the winter and apparently it didn't get much use in the summer months either.

He kept the truck's speed down to twenty miles an hour and soon he saw faint traces of an access road on his right. He glanced at his odometer and saw he was at ten thousand-and eighty-feet above sea level. This had to be the access road to his grandfather's place.

As he passed the access road, Swifty accelerated the truck's engine and pushed it up to a respectable forty-five miles per hour. He kept a sharp eye on the right side of the road but saw no other signs of a road or a path, or a trail. Soon he hit the top of Beartooth pass. His altimeter showed he was slightly over ten thousand nine hundred feet above sea level. He continued on highway 212 and half an hour later he was entering the outskirts of Red Lodge, Montana.

Red Lodge was an old coal mining town that peaked just before the great depression. Today it is an aging town of about two thousand people. It originally was on the Crow Indian reservation, but when coal and then gold were discovered, the government either bargained or cheated the Crow people out of the land, depending on who you talk to.

Swifty drove down the small town's main drag and pulled into an ancient gas station that had seen better days. He gassed up his truck and then pulled it out of the station. He drove less than a block and then parked the truck in front of a café with a weathered wooden sign proclaiming it to be the best food in Red Lodge. Swifty was unsure if that was positive or negative, but he often found excellent food in out of the way cafés in small towns. He had also experienced some food so bad it was hard to remember it was supposed to be eatable by humans.

The restaurant was called The Wild Table, and Swifty was pleasantly surprised at the menu. It featured numerous wild game dishes, and he quickly selected a buffalo burger with fries and a cup of coffee. While he waited for his meal, Swifty went over his maps and notes. There were only about eight other people in the café, and he had chosen a table in the far corner of the building. His table was next to a window, so he had excellent light. He also had a good view of anyone entering or exiting the café.

Swifty was only about halfway through his photos and notes when the waitress brought his meal. The aroma from the freshly cooked buffalo meat was delicious. After his first bite of the burger, he knew the aroma was spot on to the taste in his mouth. He had not realized how hungry he was, and he devoured his meal in an embarrassingly short time. He was about to signal the waitress when she appeared at his table like she had been reading his mind.

"Dessert?" she asked with a nice smile.

Swifty took one glance at the menu and ordered one of his favorite desserts he seldom saw on a menu.

"I'll have a slice of the rhubarb pie and a refill of coffee," said a smiling Swifty.

"Coming right up," said the smiling young waitress and she headed to the kitchen.

Swifty had barely begun checking his notes again when she appeared at his table and slid a large slice of fresh rhubarb pie in front of him. Then she refilled his coffee cup from the decanter she had in her other hand, and left a bill, face down, on the table. Swifty thanked her and took his time eating the pie. He savored each bite. It was delicious. When he finished the pie and his coffee, he left enough cash to cover the bill plus a generous tip. He would remember the Wild Table in case he returned to Red Lodge.

Swifty stepped out of the café and onto the sidewalk. He felt the warmth of the sun on his hands and his face. He took a deep breath. The mountain air was fresh and clean. It was moments like this that made Swifty glad he did not live in a big city.

He returned to his parked truck. Once inside the cab, he rolled down the windows and sat back in the driver's seat and re-checked his notes and photos. He put the notes and photos aside and leaned back in his seat and closed his eyes.

In his mind, Swifty tried to envision what his grandfather's property would be like. He had studied the satellite photos and was amazed at how detailed they were. He had studied the photos of the old cabin and while the detail was very good, something bothered him, and he was trying to understand why.

Then it came to him. While his grandfather was old, probably in his mid to late seventies, he was not helpless. He had lived up in the mountains for over forty years.

Anyone who had survived up at almost ten thousand feet for that long was both tough and knowledgeable about the mountains and the weather. Add that experience to his training and experience as a Green Beret in Vietnam and the result was a very capable survivor. The old man was comfortable living off the land, on his own, without the help or the need for help from anyone in the more civilized part of the world. People who lived in Wyoming and Montana were normally made of pretty tough material and were folks who knew how to survive in the mountains. Add all his grandfather's experience and training as a Green Beret and you came up with one tough customer.

Swifty decided to get a room for the night and then return to Bearfoot Pass and do some reconnaissance on foot. He wanted to have a good understanding of the land making up his grandfather's property and the area around it before he walked in and announced himself. Based on what he knew about his grandfather, being innocent was like being stupid. Nothing good could come of just wandering onto his grandfather's land and saying, "Here I am."

Swifty started the truck and drove down the main drag of Red Lodge. He pulled into the parking lot of the Lupine Inn. It was modest and inexpensive according to his notes. He got a ground floor room for a cheap price. He preferred ground floor because he could park his truck directly outside his door and if something bad happened, he wasn't trapped on a second floor with limited escape routes.

He moved his two bags into the room. Then he stepped outside onto the sidewalk in front of his room. He scanned his surroundings. When he was confident that he was not being watched, he grabbed his rifle case and took it quickly inside his room as well. Once inside, he locked the door and got undressed. He placed his Kimber .45 semi-auto pistol under his pillow and was soon fast asleep.

Swifty woke from his nap about six o'clock that evening. He dressed and then walked the three blocks to The Wild Table and had a quick supper. Then he walked back to his room and re-inventoried all the contents of his two bags. When he was satisfied, he had missed nothing, he pulled out his notes and photos and did another thorough search of all the photos of his grandfather's land. By now, Swifty was pretty sure his grandfather no longer lived in the old cabin he saw in the photos. Partly because he felt the cabin had too many signs of neglect and needs for repairs, and partly because he had a feeling about his grandfather. After all his training and experience and all the years he had spent isolated up in these mountains, Swifty was pretty sure his grandfather had developed animal like survival instincts and it was likely the old cabin was a decoy and his grandfather's real living quarters were somewhere near, but well hidden.

Swifty took all the satellite photos of his grandfather's land he had and spread them out on the bed. he placed them in their proper location and order, so he had the equivalent of a bird's eye view of the land. Then he took a little magnifying glass out of one case and slowly began to study each photo. He started by trying to follow the faint outlines of a road or trail from the highway to the old cabin. Then he first took the north side of the trail and studied it as he moved from the highway to the cabin. After he was done, he began again on the south side of the road and again followed it all the way to the old cabin. He found nothing suspicious on either search. Then he broke the area around the cabin into four-inch quadrants. He carefully studied each quadrant with the small magnifying glass, looking for anything that did not belong. He located a decaying old outhouse due east of the cabin, but the trail to it was almost invisible and the outhouse was in bad shape. He knew then he was right about the cabin no longer serving as his grandfather's residence.

He searched two more quadrants without any success. Then he set the magnifying glass on the bed and sat back in the wooden chair and rubbed his eyes. He was frustrated with his lack of success. Then he remembered Big Dave's words of advice. "Look for what don't belong."

Swifty closed his eyes and tried to envision the property from his memory of the satellite photos laid out on the bed. When he opened his eyes, he again searched the photos and saw nothing amiss. Then a thought struck him. If he were creating a home and hiding place where would he put it. He knew he would place it somewhere with a commanding view of all its surroundings. That meant the highest point on the property. He studied the photos and determined a spot he felt had the most commanding view of the surrounding land. Then he looked away from that point towards each point of the compass.

Then Swifty saw what he had missed before. As his eyes moved away from the high point on the land to the borders of his grandfather's property, he could see how the trees had been thinned and even trimmed to provide good avenues of sight and more important, good fields of fire to each boundary. Swifty's eyes got wide. He was right. Somewhere around the high point of the land was his grandfather's new home.

Swifty rose to his feet, rubbed his eyes, and walked to the door. He unlocked the door and walked down the old sidewalk to the side of the office. There he found a vending machine and he bought a cold can of Coke with change from his pocket. He took the Coke and returned to his room, locking the door behind him.

He sat in his chair, opened the can of Coke, and took a long swig. Then he set the can on the floor and took the magnifying glass and began to slowly and carefully study the photo of the high point on his grandfather's land.

CHAPTER TWENTY-SEVEN

After over two hours of studying the maps and the satellite photos Swifty got out of his chair and rubbed his eyes. He was tired and his butt was sore from sitting in the uncomfortable motel chair for so long. He took off his boots and unbuckled his belt. He was so tired he didn't bother to undress. He just crawled up on the bed and was fast asleep in a matter of minutes.

When Swifty awoke, the sun was barely up. He got up, undressed and proceeded to shower and shave. Then he made a cup of coffee from the tiny coffee pot in his room. He sat down to compile a list to pack for the day long reconnaissance he had planned for his grandfather's land. After a few minutes of writing, he reached for his coffee cup and took a long swig. It was awful. He got to his feet and fled to the bathroom where he spit out what he had left in his mouth and then took a drink of tap water to try to wash the taste out of his mouth.

When he was finished, he left his room and walked about a block and a half to a little bakery. There he bought a large cup of black coffee and two doughnuts. He returned to his room and consumed his hasty breakfast. He almost inhaled the doughnuts, but the coffee was good, and he took his time drinking and enjoying it.

While he drank his coffee, Swifty finished his check list. Then he rechecked it and pulled the listed items out of the two canvas bags. He took out a small backpack and filled it with his list of selected items. Then he zipped the canvas bags shut and locked them. He slid them under the bed and then grabbed the small backpack and exited his room. He slipped into his truck and tossed the backpack on the passenger seat.

Minutes later, Swifty was headed south out of town and headed for Beartooth Pass. In a little over half an hour he was at the top of the pass. He slowed his speed down to about thirty-five miles an hour and carefully studied the east side of the highway. When he spotted the barely obvious entrance to his grandfather's place, he slowed down even more. Then he spotted the old logging road on his left and turned off the highway onto it.

As he moved slowly down the road, the weeds and small pine trees rubbed against the undercarriage of his truck. He kept going until the old road made a turn to the north. As soon as he was sure the truck was completely out of sight from anyone driving down the highway, he stopped the truck and shut off the engine.

Swifty sat in the truck and carefully surveyed his surroundings. The old road was fairly wide. He assumed it was that way to allow large logging trucks to get through without hitting mature pine trees that bordered it. Because of the pine trees, he could see little or nothing past the screen they created. He knew the screen worked for him as well. Nobody could see him or his truck unless they were right on top of it.

Swifty grabbed his backpack and exited the truck. He stepped away from the truck and looked up. The wall of pine trees on both sides of the old road screened all but the middle of the road from the sky. Only someone or something with a camera directly above the truck would have a clear view of it. Swifty pulled out his compass and Topo map from his pocket and studied them. He oriented the compass to true north and then set out on foot.

As he moved, Swifty worked hard to maintain as much silent movement as possible. He paused every few minutes to listen for sounds, smell the air, and study his surroundings. The more he walked, the better he got at keeping any noise to a minimum. Because of the pine trees and heavy undergrowth, he had to keep adjusting his path, but he used his compass to keep him on a course to reach the edge of his grandfather's property.

After about forty-five minutes, Swifty halted and took a swig of water from the canteen on his belt. He checked his map and compass and then leaned up against a pine tree trunk and remained motionless. He listened. He sniffed the breeze, and he studied the area around his position. Satisfied he could not detect any threat; he continued his journey.

After almost one and a half hours, he stopped to again check his position. He was almost positive he was on the edge of his grandfather's land. He looked at the map and his compass. Then he checked his watch. At his current pace, Swifty estimated he would reach the observation point he had chosen in another hour.

He reminded himself he was now on his grandfather's land. He could not afford to underestimate the former Green Beret and Vietnam War combat veteran. Being careless now could easily result in getting shot or worse.

Swifty moved forward slowly and cautiously. He had moved this way for about twenty minutes when he thought he saw a flash of light. He froze in place. Then using only his eyes, he scanned the area where he thought he saw the light. It was difficult as the pine trees overhead blocked out much of the sunlight, creating a darkened forest with slivers of light slipping through openings created by growth or the slight movement of branches due to the occasional breeze.

He was careful to not move any part of his body other than his eyes. On his second pass of the area he saw what caused the flash of light. About five feet up the tree trunk of a healthy pine tree was a small box-like object. After satisfying himself his location was not in the object's path, Swifty lowered his body to his knees. He slipped his hand slowly into his backpack and came out with a small pair of powerful binoculars. He lifted them to his eyes and slowly scanned the object. Then he smiled and lowered the binoculars and slipped them into his shirt pocket, leaving their strap around his neck. The object was a trail camera. It was painted in forest camo and would have blended in with the pine tree. But it was strapped to the trunk of the tree where there were no limbs full of pine needles. The flash was a random ray of sunshine striking the lens of the camera.

Swifty didn't know how sophisticated the camera was, but he had to assume it wasn't a wireless device because the terrain there didn't seem to allow for any line of sight connections to a data source. After a quick study of the terrain and his surroundings, he was satisfied he was looking at the only camera in the immediate area. He slipped backwards and crawled through the underbrush at an angle away from the range of the camera. When he had crawled for about fifty yards, Swifty rose slowly to his feet and carefully surveyed his new surroundings. He could see no other cameras and after checking his handheld GPS map and compass, he set a new heading to allow him to bypass the area around the camera, he carefully set out on his new heading.

Swifty moved very slowly and deliberately. He studied the ground in front of him before he took each step. After a few steps, he would pause and freeze in place. Then he would use his eyes to scan the terrain in front of him, being careful not to move his head or upper body. As he followed the natural slope of the terrain and picked his way through the sometimes-dense undergrowth, he found himself moving away from his intended target of the highest point of his grandfather's land.

He started to pick a short-term landmark and work toward it. Then he realized he was safer if he approached his target obliquely rather than head on. An hour and a half later he reached a point where there was a clearing in front of him. He stopped and went to his knees next to a tall pine tree next to the clearing. He extracted his small binoculars from his shirt pocket. Swifty pulled the binoculars up to his eyes and began a scan of the land in front of him. He was in a position slightly above the clearing, so he had a fairly clear view of the land to his west.

He realized his view of the high point he had targeted was still mostly hidden by trees. He slipped the binoculars back in his pocket. Then he slipped his small backpack off and leaned it against the tree. Swifty got to his feet and using a rock next to the pine tree, he began to climb up the trunk of the tree. He was able to reach a good-sized branch and then pull himself up. Once he had his foot on the branch, he searched and found other handholds and climbed higher up the tree. As he climbed higher, he paused at each opportunity and tried to see through the thick pine branches, but there were few good openings. When he was about two thirds up the tree, he found an open space where the branches had thinned. He maneuvered around the tree until he found a decent perch. Once he settled onto the perch, he pulled out his binoculars and scanned the land in front of him. He had a clear view of the top of the high point of his grandfather's land. He pulled out a strong canvas strap out of one of the pockets on his utility pants and secured one end to a strong branch next to him and the other end to a D-ring on his vest. It was a trick he had learned in Delta. Even the best soldiers couldn't avoid getting tired and falling asleep. He had no idea how long he would be up in the tree and the last thing he wanted was to fall asleep and find himself in a free fall from about twenty feet in the air.

He scanned the area around him every few minutes and made as little noise as possible. He also kept any movement to an absolute minimum. After what he thought was about an hour, he checked his watch. It was almost noon. He had seen no movement and even though he had a higher view of the ground at the high point of the land, he was unable to see anything unnatural. As Big Dave had taught him. "Look for what don't belong."

He was thirsty and drank from his belt canteen. The

water was warm, but it felt good going down his now dry throat. As he was slipping the canteen back in the holder on his belt, he sensed movement. He pulled the binoculars to his eyes and scanned the hill. He saw nothing. Then he sensed movement again. He looked below the hill to a clump of bushes about four feet high. Then he saw the movement again. A four- point buck stepped out from the bushes into the open. The buck sniffed the air and nervously turned his head as he scanned the area for any possible danger. Sensing none, the buck bent his head down and began munching on some high prairie grass.

As Swifty watched, the buck suddenly jerked his head up. Before the deer could move Swifty saw a sudden blur in the air and the buck, now stricken, took about ten steps and fell to the ground. Swifty kept his binoculars glued to the deer. He didn't have long to wait. A couple of minutes later a tall, gaunt figure dressed head to toe in camouflage emerged from a stand of pine trees. The man moved cautiously toward the fallen buck. He wore a boonie hat and dark sunglasses on a band that went around his neck. As the man moved closer to the fallen deer, Swifty could see his weapon. In his left hand he carried a black crossbow. When he got next to the deer, the man used his crossbow to touch the deer's eye with the end of the crossbow.

"He's making sure the buck is dead," thought Swifty.

Satisfied the buck was a kill, the man laid the crossbow on the ground and pulled a knife out of a scabbard on his belt. The man grabbed the deer by the hind legs and pulled it into a position where the head of the deer was downhill from the rest of the body. Then the man used his knife to slit the deer's throat.

"He's using gravity as a drain for the blood. He's done this before," thought Swifty.

The man removed a vest and put it over the crossbow. Then he used his knife to cut off the deer's head. He rolled the decapitated head and antlers to the side. Then he carefully used the knife to cut open the buck's belly from top to bottom. When he was finished, he rolled up his sleeves and found and then cut off the gland sacks on the legs. He then reached into the deer's open body cavity and slowly and carefully he pulled out the buck's intestines and organs in one large package. He had to pause occasionally and use his knife to remove an obstacle to his operation. It was obvious the man was experienced and skilled. He had done this many times before. Finally, he pulled out the buck's gut pile and dumped the entire mess on the ground about five yards from the buck's remains. Then the man used his knife to cut the deer's legs at the knee joint. Then he put the knife in its sheath and bent the legs against the joint until they cracked. At that point, he simply bent the legs against their natural joint and broke them off. He tossed the broken legs on top of the gut pile and proceed to drag the carcass to the nearest tall pine tree. He reached into a side pocket in his camo pants and produced a long rope. The rope was thin, and while it retained a few patches of its original white color, most of the rope was stained dark with the dried blood of other deer.

The man cut slits in the upper portions of the hind legs and ran the rope through them and tied them together. Then he stood and coiled the remainder of the top and threw it over a lower branch of the pine tree. He tugged on the rope until he was satisfied the branch was strong enough. Then he pulled on the rope until he had hoisted the deer carcass about four feet above the ground. He then tied the loose end of the rope to the lower trunk of the pine tree, so the deer carcass was suspended above the ground.

The man then pulled a canteen off his belt and poured water on his bloody hands to wash them off. He wiped his wet hands on a nearby clump of grass and replaced the canteen. He walked over to the hanging deer carcass and inspected it. Apparently satisfied with what he saw, he walked over and retrieved his crossbow and vest. He donned the vest and after a quick look around, the man strode back into the clump of trees and disappeared from Swifty's sight.

Swifty lowered his glasses and slipped the binoculars back into his shirt pocket. He had just seen an expert hunter use a crossbow to take down a good-sized buck deer and then field dress him like an expert. Swifty had no doubt he had just seen his mysterious grandfather displaying many of the skills of the mountain man the old Green Beret had become.

Swifty was impressed by the old man's skill and professional hunting ability. There had been no wasted motion, no mistakes in cutting, and an almost scary efficiency with a knife. Swifty sat back in his perch in the tree and let out the breath he found he had been storing in his gut. He remained in the tree for almost another hour. He knew from his training a man like his grandfather had likely circled around the kill site and waited to see if the now hanging deer carcass had any visitors.

When he was satisfied that he was alone, Swifty carefully and as quietly as possible descended from his perch in the pine tree. When he reached the ground, Swifty went to his knees and waited for another ten minutes. He smelled the air, listened to the breeze in the top of the pine tree and watched the area around him carefully.

After taking those precautions, he gathered up his backpack and slipped it on. Then he moved slowly and as quietly as possible back the way he had come. Once he was a good distance from his perch on the pine tree, he increased his pace, but was careful to follow his old path, including avoiding the trail camera he had seen earlier.

It was over two hours before he found himself standing next to his truck on the old logging road. He tossed his backpack onto the passenger seat and climbed into the cab. He started the engine and after several movements forward and backward he had turned the truck around and was carefully making his way back to the highway.

Swifty drove the speed limit all the way back to Red Lodge. He pulled into the parking lot of his motel and grabbed his backpack and duffel bag and went straight to his room. Once inside, he locked the door and removed his clothes. He took a hot shower for almost ten minutes which was a rare luxury for him. His muscles were sore and cramped from his long stay in his perch in the pine tree. The hot water relaxed his tired muscles. When he was finished, he toweled off vigorously and changed into clean clothes.

He was about to open his computer when his stomach reminded him, he had eaten nothing but a few swallows of water since breakfast and it was almost six o'clock. He slid the laptop back on the bed and headed out the door. A few minutes later he was sitting at a table in the back of The Wild Table restaurant. The same waitress came to his table. He ordered a buffalo steak dinner and a large rum and coke from the bar. She brought the drink promptly as if she sensed he needed it more than the steak. Swifty thanked her profusely and sipped on his drink as he waited for his steak and ran the events of the day through his mind like it was a tape recording.

CHAPTER TWENTY-EIGHT

Swifty was interrupted in his thoughts by the waitress bringing him another rum and coke.

"You went through that first one so fast I thought you might need a back-up," she said.

Swifty thanked her and after taking a drink from her offering, he knew she was right. He needed it. This time he set the drink on the table and reminded himself to slow down. The waitress returned with his steak dinner and he proceeded to pace himself. He cut each piece of meat to a reasonable size and then ate it, chewing it slowly and savoring the taste and flavor. When he had finished his steak, he still had a small amount of rum and coke in his glass. He swallowed the last of the drink and when he caught the waitress's eye, she promptly brought him his check. He left enough cash for his meal along with an even more generous tip than his previous one. He didn't often receive excellent service, but when he did, he liked to reward it.

He left the restaurant and took his time on the short walk back to his motel. On his walk he stopped at a small bar and went inside. He bought a bottle of rum and paid for it. Then he resumed his walk back to the motel. There were a few people out and about and Swifty made a point of saying hello to perfect strangers and tipping his hat to the one lady he encountered on his walk.

Back at the motel, he placed his laptop on the rickety old desk and sat down in the equally old chair. After opening his laptop and allowing it to warm up, he sat back in his chair and thought about what he had learned on his expedition to his grandfather's property. He'd learned his grandfather had some level of security. He'd avoided the trail camera, but he was pretty sure there were more cameras. If one had caught him on the property, he had neither seen nor heard any evidence of an alert to his presence.

His grandfather was likely pretty self-sufficient. He had been hunting deer out of season and Swifty doubted his grandfather had bought a hunting license in years, if ever. The old man had a lot of experience in field dressing wild game. Swifty had been impressed by his methods and his efficiency with a knife.

Despite all of that, Swifty had not been able to pinpoint where old Bushrod had built his dwelling. He had seen a lot of the old man in the open, but after hanging up the field dressed deer, he just seemed to disappear into the grove of trees. The other thing that struck Swifty was the lack of noise. During the entire episode he had watched from the tree, he had heard literally nothing out of the ordinary. Even the deer had died quietly.

The real question in Swifty's mind was simple. What should he do now? If he tried more reconnaissance forays, he was more likely to be discovered by the old Green Beret. And that might not end well for Swifty. After mulling over several ideas and plans, he decided the best method might just be to try the direct approach. Then he focused on just how direct his approach should be.

He finally decided he would drive his truck into his grandfather's hidden drive and see how far he could get before he was stopped by a physical barrier or one that was armed. His real purpose was to find and talk to his grandfather. He didn't want anything from the old man except some information. After his chat with his aunt, he knew he really needed more than information. He needed the old man's help. Old Bushrod might know why someone would kill his less than popular son. He might know if there was something on the small ranch worth killing his father over. But, to get any answers to those questions, he needed to find, meet, and talk to the old man.

Swifty thought about the direct approach. Then he thought about what he should bring with him. He mentally went over several options and then settled on a very basic plan. He would equip himself for a hike into the mountains as if he was not sure where to start his search. The plan limited the options for equipment but was one he could most easily defend if confronted by his grandfather.

He made a list of things to take with him on the next day's hike, and then gathered them up from his duffel bags and placed them in the small backpack. Satisfied, he turned out the lights and went to bed.

CHAPTER TWENTY-NINE

Swifty was up at dawn. He showered and dressed quickly and was standing outside his motel room when the first rays of sunshine were hitting the side of the motel. He walked down the main drag to a small place on a corner he had noticed before. In two and a half blocks he had reached the Café Regis. He had checked his computer and the cafe was the number one spot in Red Lodge for breakfast.

Once inside he took an empty booth and had soon ordered a full breakfast along with strong, black coffee. After ordering, Swifty looked around the restaurant as he waited for his breakfast. The place was about half full and almost all the customers looked to be working men. He was pretty sure six A.M. was a tad early for tourists and travelers, but just the beginning of the day for the average guy.

After breakfast, Swifty walked back to his motel room. He checked his pack and again went over his list. He could think of nothing else he might need, and he didn't want anything on his person or in his pack that might alarm his grandfather. He needed to look just like what he was, a young man on a hike looking for something.

Swifty zipped the pack closed and exited his room. He slipped into the cab of his truck and put the pack on the passenger seat. Then he started the engine and pulled out of the motel parking lot, heading south.

There was very little traffic on the highway and Swifty reached the old logging road turnoff in under thirty minutes. When he reached the old logging road, there was no traffic, so he turned off on the road and drove to the same place he had stopped the previous day. He exited the truck, pulling his small backpack out with him. After closing the truck door, he checked himself out in the driver's side mirror. He wore old hiking boots, jeans, and a denim shirt with a canvas vest. All the clothing items were older and worn. Then, he put on a slightly soiled white Wyoming Cowboys cap and slipped on his sunglasses.

After one last look in the mirror, he was ready. He hiked back out on the logging road to the highway. Then he worked north to the entry road to his grandfather's land. Swifty paused at the entrance for a brief moment. Then he took a deep breath and began hiking into the interior of his grandfather's property.

Swifty took his time. He walked slowly and carefully. He was on high alert and kept his head on a swivel. As he walked, he carefully scanned his surroundings and stopped periodically to smell the air and just listen. He walked for about twenty minutes when the road came to a thick stand of pines. Where the road ran through the pines, a stout steel gate had been erected. Swifty walked up to the gate and read the weathered metal sign attached to the gate.

"Private Property. No trespassing. Survivors will be arrested."

Swifty grinned to himself. He had seen a similar sign on a ranch north of Kemmerer. The rancher had a good trout stream on his property and people were constantly trespassing on his land to fish. He put up the signs, but they were ignored. Finally, he shot a trespasser in the leg and got sued. He had to pay a fine, but after that incident, nobody every trespassed on his land again.

Somehow Swifty had a feeling if his grandfather shot someone trespassing the person was more than likely to just disappear forever. He had the strong impression if his grandfather said something, he meant it.

Swifty slipped around the end of the gate and continued down the barely visible road. He walked for about five minutes and then stopped and stood perfectly still. He looked all around him. He listened carefully for any sounds. He sniffed the air for any scents. Finding nothing amiss, he continued walking slowly for another five minutes and repeated the same sequence. After walking and stopping for a total of about twenty-five minutes, he reached a clearing. He stopped at the edge of the clearing and looked around the mountain meadow of tall native grasses, disturbed by only the occasional small pine tree. In the middle of the meadow he saw the old log cabin. The front door was missing. The roof had holes in it. And the roof was sagging in the middle like an old, swayback horse.

He approached the cabin slowly, keeping alert with his head on a swivel. Once he reached the front of the old cabin, he stopped. The old porch was falling in. He could see through the front door without a door and the place was mostly empty and forlorn looking. Sunlight streaming through a window on the east side of the cabin provided the only illumination inside.

As he stood silently outside the front of the old log

cabin, Swifty had a sensation of being watched. The longer he stood there the stronger the feeling became. He was sure his grandfather was watching him but staying hidden from sight.

He was trying to decide what to do next. He didn't want to anger or provoke his grandfather, but he needed to find a way to confront him without provoking him to violence. Swifty slowly turned around. As he did, he carefully scanned his surroundings. He was looking for evidence of some other buildings or shelters, but if there were any, he could not see them. As he was finishing his turn, he saw something next to a tree trunk that did not seem to belong. He paused, focused his eyes on the location and soon found the outline of a tall, gaunt looking man dressed entirely in cammo as he had been the day before when Swifty watched him kill and field dress the buck deer.

Swifty continued to stare at the man. Then he had an idea. He lifted both hands and arms straight up in the air in a gesture of surrender. He held his hands open, facing his grandfather to show he had no weapons. Then he stood there and waited.

CHAPTER THIRTY

After five long agonizing minutes, the cammo clad figure began to move. He moved slowly toward Swifty. As he moved closer, Swifty saw he was armed with a pump shotgun. It looked like a Remington 870.

As the figure continued to advance toward Swifty, he brought up the barrel of the shotgun, so it was pointing directly at Swifty. Swifty forced himself to remain motionless. He slowed his breathing and did his best to relax his tense and agitated muscles. When the cammo clad figure was ten yards away he halted.

"Who the fuck are you?" thundered out a deep base voice. "And what the hell are you doin' trespassing on my private property. Don't bother telling me you didn't see the sign on the gate unless you are deaf, dumb, and blind, which I sincerely doubt."

As his grandfather spoke, Swifty was busy both listening to the old man and studying him. His grandfather was tall, slightly over six feet. He was broad shouldered, but trim, almost thin. His hair was grey and looked to be in some type of buzz cut. His eyebrows were bushy, but he was clean shaven. He had piercing blue eyes and a strong jaw. His skin was dark and tanned from living outdoors and constant exposure to the sun, which shown in Wyoming almost all the three hundred and sixty-five days every year. A glance at the shotgun told Swifty his grandfather had large hands.

Bushrod took two steps closer to Swifty and pointed the shotgun directly at his chest.

"Cat got your tongue, mister?" asked Bushrod. "Are you an idiot or can you speak English?"

"I speak English," said Swifty, not taking his eyes off the shotgun in Bushrod's hands.

"What are you doin' tresspassin' on my land?" asked Bushrod.

"I came to find you, if your name is Bushrod Olson," responded Swifty.

"Well, this is your lucky day, stranger," said Bushrod. "Cause I'm Bushrod Olson and I ain't blown your head off, yet."

"Would you mind lowering that shotgun?" asked Swifty.

"Yes, I mind. I'm keepin' this scattergun aimed at your guts until I decide otherwise," said Bushrod. "Who the hell are you to be up on private land looking for the likes of me?"

Swifty hesitated before responding. He needed to choose his words carefully or this situation could get ugly very fast.

"My name is Gary Olson, but my friends call me Swifty," he finally uttered.

"Never heard of you," said Bushrod. "Why are you trespassing on my land?"

"I came to see you," said Swifty.

"I said I don't know you, and I never heard of you," said Bushrod. "Why the hell are you here to see me?"

"My Aunt Judy told me about you," said Swifty.

At the mention of Aunt Judy, Bushrod's eyes narrowed and he tightened his grip on his shotgun.

"What's your Aunt Judy's last name?" asked Bushrod belligerently.

"Her last name is Vannoy, her married name," responded Swifty.

Bushrod's eyebrows lowered, as if he had just heard a name from a long dead past.

"Vannoy? Judy Vannoy?" he queried.

"She's my aunt. My mother's sister," replied Swifty.

"What's your mother's name?" asked Bushrod tersely.

"Her name is Janet Olson," said Swifty.

"I don't recollect ever hearin' of either of them ladies," said Bushrod. "How'd this Judy Vannoy even know my name?" he asked with a puzzled look on his face.

"Her sister Janet married your son, Eldon Olson," replied Swifty.

"Eldon got married?" asked Bushrod.

"He married Janet, my mother," said Swifty.

"Your mother?" asked a now incredulous Bushrod.

"Yes, my mother. She and Eldon had three kids. My brother Bradley, me, and my kid sister Melanie," said Swifty.

"So, my son got married and had three kids?" asked Bushrod. "And your one of them? You're my grandson?" he stated with a bewildered look in his eyes.

Swifty wanted to lower his hands, but he could feel there was still doubt and tension in the air. Then he noticed a possible good sign. Bushrod had slightly lowered the muzzle of his shot gun. Now if it went off, it would only blow off Swifty's lower legs.

"You got any proof of all this crap you bin spoutin?"

asked Bushrod. "Today any fool can look all this junk up on the internet and claim to be someone or something he ain't."

"I do," said Swifty. "Can I lower my hands?"

Bushrod gestured downward with the muzzle of his shotgun, which was not very reassuring to Swifty, but he took a chance and slowly lowered his arms.

"Check my wallet in my vest inside pocket on my left side," said Swifty.

Keeping the shot gun in the lowered position, Bushrod stepped closer to Swifty. Then he took his left hand off the weapon and slipped it inside Swifty's vest and extracted his wallet. Then Bushrod stepped back three paces and told Swifty to sit on the ground. Swifty complied with his command.

Bushrod cradled the shot gun in the crook of his right elbow and then used his hands to open Swifty's wallet. He extracted a Wyoming driver's license and Swifty's military ID card.

"You're ex-army?" Bushrod asked.

"Yep," said Swifty.

"What branch?" asked Bushrod.

"Three years in infantry, the rest in Delta Force," replied Swifty in an even voice.

"What do you do now?" asked Bushrod.

"I work for an investigative firm out of Kemmerer," replied Swifty. "My business card is in the wallet."

Bushrod fished the business card out of the wallet, examined it, and returned it to the wallet.

"All this crap says your name is Gary Olson, you got a Wyoming driver's license, and you work for an outfit in

Kemmerer," said Bushrod. "All of this could be fake. Today they can fake any kind of ID. What else you got?"

"I got this from your old footlocker stored in the attic of your old ranch in Cody," said Swifty. "I found it when I was a kid, and I hid it away and kept it in my room." Swifty slowly reached inside his vest and pulled out the old Green Beret. He held it out in front of him like an offering to some old Nordic god.

Bushrod's face drained of color. His eyes got wide. He stepped forward and grabbed the proffered beret. He looked the beret over carefully and turned it over and over in his hand. Then he saw the name on the hat band. When he looked up at Swifty, he had tears in his eyes.

"You found this in my footlocker?" he asked.

"Yes, sir," responded Swifty.

"My god," said Bushrod as he touched the beret to his cheek. "I never thought I'd see this again."

"I also got this," said a now more confident Swifty.

"What?" asked Bushrod.

Swifty slowly reached back into his vest and drew out a small metal flask and offered it to Bushrod.

Bushrod stepped forward and took the flask. Then he opened the flash and smelled the contents. He looked down at Swifty.

"Rum?" he asked.

"Mount Gay Rum," said Swifty. "Aunt Judy said it was your favorite."

"It was," said a now-smiling Bushrod. "I ain't had a drop of this in twenty years," he said.

"Help yourself," said Swifty. "I brought it for you."

Bushrod put the open flask to his lips and took a swig.

He closed his eyes and savored the taste and let it slide slowly down his throat. Then he replaced the cap on the flask, slipped it in a pocket on his cargo pants, and turned his attention back to Swifty.

"Git on your feet, son," said Bushrod. "You're too damn old to be groveling in the dirt like some damn lost puppy."

Swifty slowly and carefully got to his feet and then stood there, unsure about what was yet to come.

CHAPTER THIRTY-ONE

"Follow me," said Bushrod and he turned and headed back into the clump of trees he had originated from. Swifty followed him at a respectful and safe distance.

They walked for a few minutes under the canopy of fir trees and then things changed. The trees thinned out and then Swifty saw some wooden poles scattered about, but all upright although some were at odd angles. Sunlight filtered through to the ground, but it was not filtering through pine tree limbs, it was coming through camouflage netting. The netting was about ten feet above their heads.

Swifty noted his grandfather walked at an easy lope and he never looked back to see what the trespasser might be up to. Swifty had a feeling the old man could sense what he was doing, even if he couldn't see his grandson.

A few more minutes walking and they came to a clearing. There were no trees, but there were plenty of wooden poles supporting the artificial canopy. Bushrod walked past several smaller sheds and headed directly for a large door in what appeared to be a solid log wall. Swifty followed.

Once Bushrod reached the door he opened it and stepped aside, motioning for Swifty to enter the doorway. Swifty did as instructed and stepped into a large room. As he looked around, he realized he was half in and half out of a large cave or a cut into what looked like solid stone. At the back of the cave/room was a large bed and several military looking foot lockers. The walls were lined with rough wooden shelves. The shelves were stocked with everything from food, to clothing, to ammunition. The lone exception to shelves on the walls was a huge metal safe, which Swifty assumed contained his grandfather's personal arsenal.

In one corner near the front of the room was a wood-burning stove with a metal flue that disappeared into the roof. The roof in the front of the room was log, but the roof of the rear of the room was stone. On two sides of the stove was a crude counter with a stone countertop. In the middle of the room was an old couch and a ratty looking easy chair. There was a small round wooden table with two mismatched chairs on the right side of the room.

Swifty was surprised to feel a hand on his shoulder. He turned suddenly as if to defend against an attack. He turned to face an old man with a grin on his face.

"Pretty touchy, ain't you boy," said Bushrod.

"I was just surprised," said Swifty.

"You reacted pretty damn well," said Bushrod. "Them Delta boys taught you pretty well."

Swifty did not respond. He just stared at his grandfather with a combination of amazement and curiosity.

"How long have you lived here?" asked Swifty.

"I bin here a damn long time," replied Bushrod. "Have a seat, and I'll make us some coffee. Then we'll jaw a bit."

Swifty took a seat on one of the chairs at the small round table. He turned his chair so he could keep an eye on his grandfather.

Bushrod went to the stove and started a fire. When he had a small blaze going, he grabbed a battered old metal coffee pot from a shelf under the counter and sat it on the stone top. Then he produced a large plastic jug and poured water into the coffee pot and sat the coffee pot on top of the stove. He produced two slightly chipped ceramic cups and placed them on the countertop. He pulled out an old metal can and measured out coffee into one of the cups. He pulled out a plastic container of some white chipped pieces which Swifty recognized as eggshells.

When Bushrod was satisfied the stove was hot enough, he tossed the eggshells and the coffee into the water filled coffee pot and placed it on top of the old stove. All during this domestic exercise, he never spoke a word. Swifty took the time to continue to examine the contents of his grandfather's unique homestead.

The room was silent, except for the sound of the coffee percolating on the old stove. When he was satisfied the coffee was ready, Bushrod took the old coffee pot off the stove and placed it on the stone countertop. He opened the coffee pot lid and poured in a bit of cold water from the water jug. Then he poured the coffee into the two mugs. He picked up the mugs and walked over to the table, handing one of them to Swifty.

"You need a cow?" he asked.

"Nope. I take mine black," said Swifty.

"It must run in the family," said Bushrod and he smiled as he said it. It was the first time Swifty had seen his grandfather smile since he had first seen him.

Both men took sips of their coffee and each of them

made a sign of satisfaction, then took solid drinks of the strong hot beverage.

Bushrod broke the silence. "I ain't rightly sure how this should go, but I think I'll tell you a bit about me, let you ask all the questions you want and then it'll be my turn. That all right with you?"

"Works for me," said a relieved Swifty. He wasn't sure how to start and now his grandfather had laid out the ground rules.

"Well, for starters, I guess I should kinda set the stage for this yarn," said Bushrod. "I ain't gonna tell you nothin' about my time in the Nam. If you got the stomach for it, I'll tell you about things good folks can't possibly imagine. But that'll come later. I got out of the army and I'd had my fill of killin', jungles, crappy food, heat, bugs and snakes. When I got home, I was pissed to find out all those draft dodgers protesting a war I never wanted to fight in the first place. I remember getting off that freedom jet in California. I was dressed in my army fatigues and was delighted to be back in the good old U.S.A. That didn't last long. As me and my buddies walked through the terminal, we got assaulted by dirty looking hippies dressed in rags and smelling worse than the shit the Vietnamese used to fertilize their fields. They literally threw shit at us. We just marched right through those assholes. We knew if we stopped and cold cocked any of those assholes, we'd wind up in the guardhouse. I wanted out of the army, not staying in as a prisoner in some army jail. As soon as I got out of that airport, I got a ride to a bus terminal. There I went into the men's room and changed out of my uniform and into some old civies I had bought in Saigon.

Bushrod paused and took a long drink of coffee. "Sorry for the interruption, but I ain't had no guests for some time and I ain't used to talking this much."

"No problem," said Swifty. "You're doing fine."

"I bought a ticket to Salt Lake. From there I bought a bus ticket to Casper. My wife drove down and picked me up and took me back to Cody and the ranch," said Bushrod.

Then the old man paused. He sat there for a few seconds, just looking out at the wall of his cabin as if he could see something Swifty couldn't.

"When I got home, things had changed. I discovered I didn't like change. I got pissed at just about everything I saw. I got pissed at all the chicken shits I knew who didn't serve who badmouthed those who did. I got pissed at the cops who busted poor bastards like me for jaywalking and let big money stiffs go scot free for stealing from their neighbors and friends and their country," said Bushrod.

"I got drunk. I got into fights. Hell, I looked forward to gettin' into fights. I beat guys up and occasionally I got beat up. I was pissed at the government. I was pissed at the ranch. I got so bad I was pissed at my poor wife. She was a hell of a woman. My biggest disappointment was my son. When he was born, I was thrilled to have a son. I was dumb enough to believe he would grow up to be another me. I was wrong. He was a worthless pussy. He had no guts, no backbone, and no real ambition."

Bushrod paused to take a long swig of coffee. Then he set his mug down and looked directly at Swifty. "So, you found my old beret?"

Swifty paused to take a swig of coffee. Then he set his mug down and spoke. "When I was a kid, I got to poking around in the attic at the ranch. I found your old footlocker and when I opened it, I found your beret. I didn't know what it was or who it belonged to, but I knew it was something special. I hid it inside my shirt and snuck it down and into my room. It's been there ever since until I took it out this week."

"I wasn't sure who the hell you were, and I ain't normally very nice to strangers, let alone trespassers, but there was something about you that I could sense, but didn't know what it was," said Bushrod. "When you pulled out that beret, I knew you weren't lying to me."

"Was that when you left the ranch?" asked Swifty.

"Yep, once I figured out I was toxic to the place and everyone there, I knew I had to get out and go someplace else where there were no damn people to deal with. I gave my good wife the deed to the ranch and half the cash I had stashed and took my old truck and left," said Bushrod.

He paused for a moment and then took another swig of coffee. He looked over at Swifty and said, "I ain't never been back."

"I know," said Swifty.

"I wandered about a bit and found this property. It was for sale and it was dirt cheap. It wasn't good for much then and it hasn't changed. It was good for me because it gave me what I wanted. Privacy. I wanted to be left alone. I wanted no part of people, civilization, laws, governments, and all that crap. So far, it's held up its part of the bargain," said Bushrod with a wry smile on his face.

"What did you use for money?" asked Swifty.

"I bought the place for cash. I trapped and hunted and

fished. I traded hides for cash. Then an old army buddy looked me up and hired me for a job in Africa," said Bushrod.

"Africa? What kind of job in a place like Africa?" asked a surprised Swifty.

"Nasty work," said Bushrod. "I hired on as a mercenary in one of their many brushfire wars and revolutions. I was lucky to get out of there alive, but I did. I was lucky and got paid a chunk of cash for that caper. And I got out uninjured and alive. I got other offers to do similar work, but I'd had enough, and that job reminded me how much I hated getting shot at."

"What'd you do with the money?" asked Swifty.

Bushrod smiled. "My buddy got out at the same time. He became a stockbroker. Said his clients got pissed occasionally, but they didn't shoot at him. He invested my money for me. I get a statement every month and I can draw on my account. That's when I had to get a post office box in Clark. I hike over there once a month," he said.

"Even in the winter?" asked Swifty. "I thought the road up here was closed in the winter."

"It is," replied Bushrod. "I use snowshoes and cross-country skis to get there and back. I pull a small sled and use it to bring back supplies."

"But there's no bank in Clark," said Swifty.

"There ain't, but I don't use no bank. The brokerage firm is my bank. I got checks I can use to draw on my money and I use the mail to order stuff. UPS delivers up here, except in the winter when the road is closed," said Bushrod.

"How do they get in your property?" asked Swifty, remembering the gate and sign.

"They don't," said Bushrod. "They deliver to the gate

and I pick it up there. I put an old wooden crate hidden in the trees to the left of the gate. They leave my stuff in there."

"I didn't see the crate," said Swifty.

"You weren't supposed to," replied a smiling Bushrod.

"So, you have no electricity up here?" asked Swifty.

"I didn't say that," said Bushrod. "I got a bank of solar panels just outside the cammo top and I got a large converter and storage batteries just inside the top. They supply power to one of my sheds where I keep my ham radio and a small freezer."

"Ham radio?" asked Swifty.

"It's damn handy and I use it for lots of stuff," said Bushrod.

"Where does your water come from?" asked Swifty.

"There are two springs on the property. One of them is above this cave, and I have pipe run from a small pool above the cave. When I want water, I turn on the valve in the pipe and I have cold water here in the main cabin," said Bushrod.

"How do you take a bath?" asked Swifty.

"You noticed I don't stink much?" asked a smiling Bushrod. "I have a pipe bypass that runs water into a big tub I have outside. Water runs from the tub into an outdoor shower. The sun heats the tub in the summer months. In the winter I had an inflatable tub I set up in here and I heat water on the stove. When I'm done, I toss the water outside and deflate the tub. Same goes for how I wash clothes."

"I'm impressed," said Swifty.

"You should be," said Bushrod. "People today have no notion of how to survive in the wilderness. Some crazy person ever figures out to destroy our power plants is the day millions of clueless people start to die."

"Nature don't give a shit about who your parents are, or where you went to college, or how smart you think you are. Nature can kill you or help you survive, but you gotta be smart enough to figure out how."

Bushrod paused, and then drank the remains of his coffee. He looked over at Swifty. "Want more coffee?" he asked.

Swifty nodded and handed Bushrod his empty mug. Bushrod rose and walked over to the stove. He refilled both mugs and brought them back to the small table.

"You got any more questions, son?" asked Bushrod.

"I think I'm done for now, but can I ask more if they come to me later?" he asked.

"Fine by me," said Bushrod.

"Well, I guess it's my turn to try to answer your questions," said Swifty.

"Let's start with this one," said Bushrod. "Did my wife ever remarry?"

"No, she didn't," replied Swifty.

"Is she still alive?" asked Bushrod.

"No," said Swifty. "She died of cancer about ten years ago."

Bushrod took the news hard. Swifty could see it in his eyes. He could see hurt in the blue eyes that had revealed very little up until this moment.

"Did she suffer long?" Bushrod asked.

"I have no idea," answered Swifty truthfully.

"How is my son?" asked Bushrod.

"He was killed in an auto accident about a week ago," said Swifty.

"Killed?" said Bushrod.

"Died in the crash," said Swifty.

Bushrod was silent. He had just learned his wife was dead and so was his son. His only previous links to his past were gone.

"How did my son, your father, turn out?" asked Bushrod.

"He was an asshole," said Swifty, surprising himself with being so candid about his father to his grandfather.

"Not surprised," said Bushrod. "Something was not right with that boy. I knew it the day he was born. I felt bad about leaving his mother to deal with him, but I wanted out and I got out."

Swifty chose not to respond to his grandfather's statement about his son, Swifty's dad.

"Who did my son marry?" asked Bushrod.

"He married Janet McMain," said Swifty. "She was a high school classmate, one year younger than he was."

"I remember the McMains," said Bushrod. They were good people."

"They still are," said Swifty.

"My son had three children?" asked Bushrod.

"Yes," replied Swifty. "Like I said before, there was me, my older brother Bradley, and my younger sister Melanie."

"Are they alive?" asked Bushrod.

"Brad left home the day after he graduated and never came back. I have no idea if he is alive or dead and if he's alive, I don't know where he is," said Swifty. "Melanie married a local loser and got divorced. She is living at the ranch with our mother."

"So, I may have three grandchildren depending on whether this Bradley is still alive?" asked Bushrod.

"That's correct," said Swifty.

"The ranch is still in the family?" asked Bushrod.

"It is, but with Dad gone, I'm not sure how Mom is going to be able to keep it going," said Swifty.

Bushrod did not respond. He sat in his chair and drank coffee. Then he rose to his feet and walked to the door of the cabin. He opened it and peered outside. "I'm going to the outhouse. It's getting dark. I suggest you stay for supper and for the night. That all right with you?" he asked.

"Fine with me," responded Swifty. He was enthralled with what he was learning. It was like opening the pages of a long-lost history book about his family.

Bushrod disappeared out the front door. When he returned, he was carrying an armload of firewood for the stove. He set the wood next to the stove and then turned to face Swifty.

"The outhouse is the first shed on the left. I suggest you use it to drain all that coffee you bin drinking," he said.

Swifty nodded and headed out the front door to do his nature business. When he returned, his grandfather was preparing a supper of venison stew with freeze dried potatoes and sourdough bread.

He was startled to realize the cabin had no windows but had ample light. The light came from fixtures in the ceiling that were supplied with power from the solar panels his grandfather had mentioned before.

Swifty sat on the couch and watched his grandfather skillfully prepare dinner. He was amazed at how agile and skillful the old man was in a kitchen, especially as rustic a kitchen as this one was.

"How about you set the table while I finish up?" said

Bushrod. "Plates and flatware are in that cubbyhole under the counter."

Swifty found the plates and flatware and set the table. Then he searched and found real cloth napkins and folded them and placed them next to the plates.

His grandfather served them deer stew with potatoes and thick slices of sourdough bread and coffee. The stew was delicious as were the potatoes. Both men used the bread to sop up the gravy left from the stew with the chunks of sourdough bread. When they were finished, Bushrod heated water on the stove and washed the few dishes and utensils. Swifty dried them and put them away.

Bushrod went to one of the wall shelves and produced an old rolled up sleeping bag and a pillow. He placed them on the old sofa and turned to face Swifty. "This don't look like much, but it's damn comfortable. I'll see you at breakfast." Swifty took off his shirt, pants, and socks and slid into the unzipped bag. He hadn't been there more than three minutes when the lights went out. Ten minutes later, Swifty was sound asleep.

CHAPTER THIRTY-TWO

Morning came early. Swifty woke, took a few seconds to get oriented, and then the front door opened and Bushrod entered the cabin. The open door let in a few rays of the early morning sunlight.

"Mornin' kid. How'd you sleep?" asked Bushrod.

"I slept like the dead," said Swifty.

"Ain't heard that phrase since I was in the army," said Bushrod.

"Must have been where I picked it up," said Swifty as he rolled out of the sleeping bag onto the floor of the cabin.

"I'll have breakfast in a jiffy," said Bushrod. "Fried Spam and eggs and hot biscuits all right with you?"

"Eggs?" asked Swifty.

"I got a chicken coop and some layin' hens and one lazy rooster," said Bushrod.

"Sounds great," replied Swifty. "What can I do to help?"

"Go on out to the outhouse, do your business, and wash up," replied Bushrod.

Swifty dressed and took care of his personal business. After he washed up, he filled his mug with hot coffee and took a seat at the small table. He watched his grandfather work in the kitchen. He moved swiftly and efficiently. No wasted motion. He knew what he was doing.

Five minutes later Bushrod announced breakfast was ready. "Grab a plate and help yourself," he said. "I'm a cook, not a waitress."

Swifty grabbed a plate and filled it from the stove. Then he sat at the table where he was joined by his grandfather.

"I cook, you clean up," said Bushrod.

"Works for me," replied Swifty.

When they were finished, the two men pushed their plates aside and Bushrod got up, retrieved the coffee pot and refilled their mugs. He returned the pot to the stove and then sat down at the small table.

"I got to thinking about our talk," said Bushrod.

"Yes sir," said Swifty.

"I think I got a few more questions. That all right with you?" he said.

"Fire away," said Swifty. "Questions are fine, bullets not so much."

Bushrod actually laughed out loud and it startled Swifty.

"Kinda jumpy this morning, ain'tcha boy," said Bushrod.

"I think I was born jumpy," said Swifty.

Bushrod laughed again. "Any doubts about you bein' my kin are fadin' fast," he said.

Then the old man sat back in his chair and stared at the ceiling. Swifty felt the weight of the silence but did not speak. Finally, his grandfather looked at him and asked a question.

"Tell me about the ranch," he asked.

"I'm not sure what you want to know," said Swifty.

"Everything and anything," responded Bushrod.

"Well, it needs a lot of work," replied Swifty. "My dad apparently wasn't up to the task of maintaining it well. He had about two hundred head of cattle, and they were in pretty good shape. I didn't see any bull, so I figure he must have used artificial insemination or hired out for a stud bull. The machinery I saw was old, but most of it looked workable. The fencing is decent but needs some maintenance."

Swifty paused, not sure of what other information his grandfather was looking for.

His grandfather broke the silence. "Can your mom keep the ranch goin'?" he asked.

"You want an honest answer?" asked Swifty.

"Son, the only answer I ever want is the truth," said the old man.

"No, she won't be able to keep the ranch. Even if she hires help, the ranch is too small to support itself and her," replied Swifty.

Bushrod was silent again, and he looked up at the ceiling as if he were looking for something. Finally, he looked straight at Swifty and spoke.

"If she sells the ranch, what kind of money could she get for it?" asked Bushrod.

"Not enough for her to live on," said Swifty. "I worked on some numbers and checked on the local market for land and possible buyers and no matter how I looked at it, the numbers don't work for my mom."

Bushrod rose and took his coffee cup and Swifty's and walked over to the stove. He refilled the cups from the old coffee pot and returned to the table. He slid Swifty's cup over to him and then took a sip of the hot brew. He placed the cup on the table and then spoke.

"Any would-be buyers hanging around?" he asked.

"Just one," replied Swifty. "The foreman of the Hayfork Ranch has inquired about buying the ranch."

"The Hayfork Ranch. I never trusted any of those assholes when I was running my ranch. Bunch of thieves and scoundrels if you ask me. I remember when they was running some kind of land tests on their property next to mine. They asked if they could test on my land and I told them to pound sand," said Bushrod.

"They were doing test on the ground?" asked Swifty.

"Yep," replied Bushrod.

"When was this?" asked Swifty.

"Let me think," said Bushrod. He scratched his head and seemed lost in thought. Then he looked at Swifty and said, "It was in the spring, about ten months after I got back from the Nam."

"Did they do any digging?" asked Swifty.

"Digging?" asked Bushrod.

"Digging test holes, boring in the ground for samples," said Swifty.

"They might have," said the old man. "But I didn't give a shit what they did on their land as long as they stayed on their side of the fence."

"Would they be looking for oil or natural gas?" asked Swifty.

"They might have been, but I had my land tested before I went to the Nam and there was no trace of oil or gas," said Bushrod.

Swifty did not respond, and Bushrod could see the wheels in his grandson's mind were spinning at high speed.

"What?" asked Bushrod.

"I'm not sure," said Swifty.

"Not sure of what?" asked Bushrod.

"I'm not sure why the Hayfork boys would be digging new test holes on their land just on the other side of ours," he said.

"They were digging test holes?" asked Bushrod. "When was this?"

"I'm not sure, but I don't think it was very long ago. I saw the test holes and flags when I was riding the fence this past week," said Swifty. "When I went back a couple days later, the holes were filled in and the flags were gone."

"If it ain't oil or gas, what the hell could they be lookin' for?" asked Bushrod.

"I honestly have no idea," said Swifty.

"I never trusted those bastards," said Bushrod. "You give them snakes an inch and they'll likely take a mile."

Swifty did not respond to his grandfather. As he sat at the crude table in the old cabin, he suddenly got a flash from a long dormant part of his brain.

"I've been trying to figure out what happened to my dad and why, and I think I just came up with a possible motive," said Swifty.

"Motive. Motive for what?" said Bushrod.

"I think my dad was murdered," said Swifty.

"Murdered? By whom, and why?" asked Bushrod.

"I know someone tampered with the brake lines on his old truck," said Swifty. He took out his phone, thumbed up photos he took of the brake line and showed them to Bushrod.

"Holy shit," said Bushrod. "Them brakes lines have been cut!"

"That's exactly what I think," said Swifty. "The question is who cut them and why. I've been struggling to come up with a motive let alone a connection to who might have done it."

"I don't see where this is leading to," said Bushrod.

"I'm not sure, but I think my dad was killed because he refused to sell the ranch to someone," said Swifty.

"Who tried to buy the ranch?" asked Bushrod.

"According to my mother, the foreman at the Hayfork Ranch had tried to buy it and my old man turned him down cold," said Swifty.

Both men were silent for a while. Then Bushrod broke the silence.

"Why would the Hayfork boys want the ranch?" asked Bushrod. "It does have good water, and it does adjoin their land, but I don't see why they would need it. They got plenty of land and water as it is. The original ranch at its peak in the 1880's was about 250,000 acres. Over the years and three owners, they sold off about a hundred thousand acres. They kept the best land along with most of the water. It don't make sense."

"Exactly," said Swifty. "Something doesn't add up. Why would anyone kill my dad to get a chance to buy the ranch when they don't appear to need it for anything?"

Again, both men were silent as they sat sipping their now cold coffee, and deep in thought.

"What if there was something else on the ranch they wanted?" offered Bushrod.

"Like what?" asked Swifty.

"Gold, Silver, Diamonds," said Bushrod. "Something worth a passel of money."

"I didn't read about there being a trace of any of those things anywhere near the ranch," said Swifty.

"Maybe it's something else," said Bushrod. "Something we don't know nothin' about."

"You could be right," responded Swifty. "Whatever it is, it has to be worth enough that they had no problem killing Dad to get him out of the way."

"From what you said, your father Eldon was an asshole by any man's standard," said Bushrod. "But he was my son and your father. He deserves some justice."

"What kind of justice are you talking about?" asked Swifty. "I got nowhere when I tried to get the sheriff interested in the evidence I had collected. Had no luck with the county commissioners or the district attorney either for that matter."

Bushrod's eyes took on a hard metal like cast. He stared at his grandson and showed a steel resolve in his face.

"If my son was murdered, then I aim to get justice done for him," said a grim toned Bushrod.

Swifty started to react, but then he realized he needed to keep his mouth shut and let his grandfather talk.

Both men sat at the table and said nothing for several minutes. Finally, Bushrod broke the silence.

"I saw a lot of things in the Nam no man should ever see. I thought I could forget them when I mustered out of the army. I was wrong. They kept coming to me in dreams in my sleep. When I woke up, I was covered in sweat and felt like I'd been in a fistfight all night long," said Bushrod.

"PTSD?" asked Swifty.

"I went to the VA hospital and that's what they called it. I tried therapy, medicine, and all that crap. Nothing worked.

I knew I had to get the hell away from people, even my wife and son, or I would seriously hurt someone," said Bushrod.

"I left and then bought this place. I've done my best to clean up my life and my mind. I steered clear of people of any kind and kept to myself. I just wanted to be left alone. After about a year, the dreams stopped. I got no idea why. I just know they stopped, and I was no longer afraid to fall asleep. It was a terrible thing, not wanting to fall asleep because I knew what was waiting for me. I've spent years avoiding people to make sure nothing triggers those dreams again," said Bushrod.

Swifty wisely kept his silence and continued to listen.

"I've talked to a few people in the past five years," said Bushrod. "I took an adult education class in town on basic computer skills. I got the hang of it and then I used the computers at the library to try them out and practice. I learned about e-mail. I used Google to find old army buddies and used e-mail to connect with them."

"How did that go?" asked Swifty.

"It was hit and miss," replied Bushrod. "Many of them were dead. I found their obituaries. Some were in VA hospitals. Some were certified nuts. And some were like me. Holed up somewhere private and keeping a low profile."

"That's kind of sad," said Swifty.

"Damn right it's sad," said Bushrod. "Men like me served their country in a shitty war and came home to protests from chicken shit people who didn't know what we went through and couldn't care less. Piss on the lot of them."

Once again, Bushrod paused and stared at the ceiling. After a couple of minutes, he spoke again.

"But not all of us are out of the fight," he said.

"What do you mean?" asked Swifty.

"Some of us are making a life for ourselves. We try to keep connected to help ourselves feel we're a part of something," said Bushrod.

He paused and looked directly at Swifty. "You served. You fought. You know what I'm talking about. Men like me faced combat every minute we were in the field. You learned who you could trust and avoided those you couldn't. We who survived combat became tight, like brothers. We're still tight and we're still brothers," said Bushrod. "We are all fiercely loyal to our country, our flag, and each other. If one of us ever needed help, the others would respond."

"What do you mean by respond?" asked Swifty.

"Just what I said," replied Bushrod. "If one of us asked for help the rest would respond if they were at all able."

"I get that, but what does that have to do with my dad's murder?" asked Swifty.

"Well, grandson, to my old-time way of thinkin', you and me need to find out who killed my son and why. After hearin' everything you've told me about his death, I have a hard time coming up with any other motive than ownership of the ranch. It was all Eldon had," said Bushrod. "The only folks who have expressed an interest in the ranch before Eldon died was them assholes at the Hayfork Ranch. To my simple-minded way of thinking, them boys at the Hayfork wanted the ranch and Eldon was in the way. Why they wanted it don't matter to me except for one thing."

"What's that?" asked Swifty.

"If there's something on that ranch of value, it belongs to my daughter-in-law and I aim to see she gets it. I also aim to make those Hayfork bastards pay for what they did.

I don't give a shit about the Sheriff, the cops, the state police or the Wyoming National Guard. I want justice and I intend to get it the old-fashioned way," said a grim voiced Bushrod.

"I agree with you we need to find out who did it and why, but I don't see taking the law into our own hands," said Swifty. "What good is it if we wind up in jail for the rest of our lives?"

Bushrod turned his hard eyes on his grandson. "I know you fought those Arabs in the desert. I know they tried to kill you, but you killed them. I know how that feels. I know you had friends killed and watched them die. I know you did your best to kill those responsible and you were good at it. In the jungle it was the same for me. Only we were on foot in the jungle. No trucks, no tanks, no armored vehicles. We were a small unit of six or seven and we were out in the bush for weeks at a time. We lived off the land. We worked with the local Yards and trained them to fight the Cong and the North Vietnamese. We sweated, fought, bled, and suffered together. Few units were ever tighter no matter how far back in military history you go."

Bushrod paused and stared directly into Swifty's eyes.

"If you want me to help you find out who killed Eldon and why, I'm in, but only on my terms," said Bushrod grimly.

"What terms?" asked Swifty.

"I make the rules," said Bushrod. "I lead, you follow. I give orders, you obey."

"I'm all right with that," replied Swifty.

"I intent to kill the mother fuckers who killed my son. Then destroy their remains and leave no evidence how they died, or who killed them, or what happened to their remains," said Bushrod. "Those are my terms. Take them or leave them."

Swifty paused for a whole three seconds. "I'll take them," he said. "I understand what you just said. I understand because I've been in combat and sometimes, I had to do things that were not by the book. Some of the things I did aren't even in any book."

Bushrod nodded his approval. "Any more questions?" he asked.

"Just one," said Swifty. "What do we do first?"

CHAPTER THIRTY-THREE

Bushrod smiled at his grandson. He got up from the table and returned with a bottle of Kentucky Bourbon whiskey and two small shot glasses. He opened the bottle and filled both shot glasses, sliding one glass in front of Swifty. Both men took their glasses and got to their feet.

"Here's to our mission's success and the complete death and destruction of our enemies," said Bushrod. The two men clinked glasses and drank the contents in one swallow. Then both men sat down at the old table.

"Okay," said Bushrod. "Just how much help can we get from this outfit you work for and your friend who runs it?"

"You name it, and I'm pretty sure I can get it," replied Swifty.

"Good," said Bushrod. He got up from the table and returned with a pad of paper and a pencil. "We need to make a list of things we need and then work to complete the list."

"I get you need me to get all the material things, but we're likely to need some more bodies on our side," said Swifty.

"You leave that part to me," said Bushrod with a grim look on his face.

They spent the next two hours compiling a list. The

list had two columns. One column contained a list of information they needed. The other contained a list of items they thought they would need. When they were done, Bushrod pushed his lists aside and got up from the table.

He went to his small kitchen and soon came back with sandwiches made with thick homemade bread. He also emptied the coffee cups and refilled them with fresh coffee.

Swifty looked at his sandwich suspiciously. "What's in the sandwich?" he asked.

"Try it and find out," said Bushrod as he bit into his sandwich with obvious relish.

Swifty decided caution over valor and lifted off the top of his sandwich to inspect it. "What the hell is this?" he asked.

"Peanut butter and sliced sweet gherkin pickles," replied Bushrod.

"You've got to be kidding me," said Swifty.

"What the hell are you babbling about?" asked Bushrod.

"I never heard of this in a sandwich," said Swifty.

"Try it before you run your mouth, young man," retorted Bushrod.

Swifty lifted the sandwich in one hand and inspected it carefully as though he expected ants or spiders to come crawling out. When they didn't, he bit into the thick bread and started to chew.

"Well?" asked an observant Bushrod.

"Not bad," said Swifty. "In fact, it's pretty damn good. Where did you come up with this concoction?" he asked.

"The Nam," said Bushrod. "When you got almost nothing but C-rats, not much will survive time in the jungle, so you learn to improvise. I learned to make do with what I could scrounge. And, I grew to like them."

Between mouthfuls, Swifty thought about what Bushrod said. "Are you sure you're not bulllshitting me?"

Bushrod looked at his grandson and smiled. "Of course, I'm bullshitting you. In what universe could you find bread in a jungle?"

"So, when did you start eating these sandwiches?" asked Swifty.

Now Bushrod was positively beaming. "When I was in junior high, the school lunches were awful and in pitiful sizes. They had a surplus food table with bread, butter, peanut butter, and dill pickle slices. I learned to improvise, and I grew fond of peanut butter and pickle sandwiches. As I got older, I switched to sweet gherkin pickles. I make the bread from sourdough starter and the peanut butter and pickles last forever without any refrigeration."

Swifty just shook his head and kept eating.

When they finished eating, they both cleaned up and went back to their lists.

"We should make additional lists for each of us as we divide up who is supposed to get what and do what," said Bushrod.

"Good idea," said Swifty. They spent the next hour dividing up the original list into a list for each of them, broken down by tasks needed doing and supplies and equipment and information needed.

When they were finished, Bushrod looked at the lists and said, "We need to make a copy for each of us, and he pulled out his tablet of paper.

"No need for that?" said Swifty.

"What do you mean?" asked Bushrod.

"Watch this," said Swifty. He pulled out his cell phone and carefully took pictures of each of their handwritten lists. When he was finished, he tapped his phone and showed the photos of the lists to a puzzled Bushrod.

"Amazing," he said. "I never would have thought of that."

"You don't own a cell phone or a smart phone, and you never have. How could you know?" said Swifty.

Swifty gathered up his belongings and stuffed them into his backpack. He walked out the door of the hidden shelter. When he was out in the open, he turned and looked at Bushrod. The two men's eyes met, and they shook hands.

"Good-bye, Grandpa," said Swifty. "Thanks for everything."

"Travel safe, Swifty," said Bushrod, "And my friends call me Bushrod. You're not just my grandson, you're now my friend."

Swifty walked away from the old man. He fought the urge to look back. He knew Bushrod would consider it a sign of weakness. As he walked under the afternoon sun, he felt somehow taller, stronger, and smarter. He was no longer just Swifty Olson, ex-soldier; he was the grandson of Bushrod Olson, a Green Beret veteran of the Vietnam War.

CHAPTER THIRTY-FOUR

Swifty was soon driving north in his truck. In about half an hour, he entered the outskirts of Red Lodge. He entered his room. There he showered, shaved, and changed to fresh clothes. Then he checked out of the motel and drove to the library. There he called up his photos on his phone, transferred them and had them printed out. He took the printed sheets to the front desk and paid for them. Then he slipped them into his pack and headed back to his parked truck.

After stopping to fill up the truck with gas, he headed south and back to Cody and the family ranch. As he drove, Swifty reran the events of the past twenty-four hours in his mind like it was a movie on a CD. He had started this trip looking to find his long-lost grandfather and seek his help and advice. He had done well on both counts. Now he needed to get started on his lists. When he drove into the outskirts of Cody, he pulled over to the side of the highway and stopped. He pulled out his cell phone and called a stored number.

"Tell me what jail you're in, and I'll come and bail you out," was the response when his call was connected.

"Well, hello to you too, Mr. Andrews," retorted Swifty into the cellphone.

"How much cash do I need to bring?" asked Kit.

"I don't need no cash, but I do need some stuff I'm pretty sure you can get your hands on," said Swifty.

"I already sent you stuff," said Kit. "What the hell did you do with all that?"

"I'll need the stuff you sent, but I will also need more," replied Swifty.

"What the hell have you got yourself into?" asked Kit.

"Kind of a family war," said Swifty.

"Those are the worst kind," said Kit. "Your family?"

"Yep," replied Swifty.

"Are you gonna need my help?" asked Kit. "I can be there in no time with some very experienced help."

"I don't think so," said Swifty. "If things do get dicey, you'll be the first one I call."

"I appreciate that," replied Kit.

"I assume you have a list," said Kit. "As I remember, you always do."

"You're right again, as usual," said Swifty. "You got something to write with?"

"I was born with something to write with," retorted Kit. "Start the list but read slowly and stop if I say so."

"Here it comes," said Swifty.

Then he began to read slowly, each item on his equipment list. The list was long, and it took several minutes to relay it to Kit.

"Anything else?" asked Kit.

"Of course," said Swifty.

"I should have known," groaned Kit.

"I need information," said Swifty.

"What kind of information?" asked Kit.

"I need to know everything you can find about the Hayfork Ranch from the day it was founded right up till today," said Swifty.

"I can do that," replied Kit.

"I also need to know its ownership history and all you can find on the current owners," added Swifty.

"Got that," said Kit.

"I also want to know if there are any studies showing any kind of valuable minerals known to be located on or near the Hayfork Ranch, and including my family ranch," said Swifty. "I also want to know about any permits requested by the ranch owners for the property including minerals and artifacts."

"That should be pretty easy," said Kit. "Anything else?"

"Nope, at least for now," said Swifty.

"When do you want this stuff?" asked Kit.

"As soon as you can get it together," replied Swifty. "I'd appreciate a rush on the information on the ranch owners and the mineral studies."

"I'll do the best I can," said Kit. "Anything else?"

"I'm probably gonna need a shit pot full of luck," said Swifty.

"Sorry, I'm fresh out of that," retorted Kit. "You're sure you don't need me out there?"

"I'd like nothing better, but this is a personal, family thing and I don't want you involved. It could go sideways on me without much effort," said Swifty. "If I get deep in the shit over this, I'm gonna need your help then and you're gonna be needing that thing you're always talking about."

"Plausible deniability?" said Kit.

"Yep, that's the one," said Swifty. "Thanks for your help."

"I'm here if you need me," said Kit.

"I know it, Kit," said Swifty.

Swifty disconnected the call and put his list away. Then he pulled back on the highway and headed for the ranch.

CHAPTER THIRTY-FIVE

By the time he reached the ranch, Swifty had started to formulate a plan. Before he exited his truck, he pulled out his phone and called Kit back.

Kit answered on the first ring. "Now what?" said Kit, with exaggerated impatience.

"I got another request," said Swifty.

"Why am I not surprised," said Kit.

"If I send you the legal description of my mom's ranch, can you check the public records and see if any outfit has pulled permits to do testing on the land?" asked Swifty.

"Fire them over, and I'll find out," replied Kit.

"Thanks," said Swifty. He was grinning as he terminated the call. He knew Kit would move heaven and hell to find out if anyone had pulled permits in the past five years. Wyoming as a state had the smallest population of any state in the country. People knew each other. If Kit ran into a roadblock, he would turn to Big Dave for help. Big Dave knew everybody in Wyoming who was anybody, and he had done lots of favors for folks over the years. He couldn't remember anyone ever saying no to Big Dave. Or at least they didn't say no twice.

Satisfied he had done all he could do at the moment,

Swifty slipped his phone in his pocket and got out of his truck. As he walked to the ranch house, he sniffed the air. He could smell something good cooking inside. His mouth was already watering as he pushed open the door to the kitchen.

Swifty was up early the next morning. He took hay out to the cattle, fed the horses and cleaned out the stalls, and then he made his way back up to the ranch house. His sister was gone, but his mother was in the kitchen making breakfast.

Swifty sat at the table with a cup of fresh coffee. He took no more than a couple of sips when his mother plopped a plate full of eggs, bacon, and fried potatoes down in front of him. He thanked her profusely. She sat down on the seat opposite him with a cup of coffee.

"What's going on?" she asked. In between bites of breakfast, Swifty told her about his trip to Red Lodge and his search for his grandfather. She was surprised about where his grandfather was living, but she did not interrupt him once. She knew if she kept quiet, Swifty would tell her everything she wanted to know and some things she'd just as soon not know.

After about twenty minutes of eating and talking, Swifty finished his story and took a long drink of coffee.

"I can't believe old Bushrod is still alive," she finally said. "And living that close to us all of these years. Why in the world didn't he ever get in touch with us?" she asked.

"He wanted nothing to do with people, even his own

people," said Swifty. "He felt he was toxic to the human race, and they were just as toxic to him."

"What a waste," she finally said. Swifty could see tears forming in her eyes.

He put down his coffee cup and looked softly at his mother. "All that is now in the past, Mom," he said. "Grandpa wants to help us, and he and I are formulating a plan that could help us get justice for Dad and maybe provide a windfall for you so you can keep the ranch."

"I think that would take the hand of God," replied his mother.

"Bushrod isn't God, by any stretch of the imagination," said Swifty. "But he has promised to help, and I am reaching out to my friend, Kit for some assistance and he agreed as well."

"What kind of help?" asked Swifty's mother.

"It's better if I don't tell you," said Swifty. "The less you know about what we are planning to do the better. My friend Kit calls it plausible deniability. I'm not sure what that exactly means, but he's a lot smarter than I am."

"All right," said his mother. She rose from her chair and started to gather up the breakfast dishes. Swifty got up and helped her clear the table. She washed the dishes, and Swifty dried them and put them away on the shelves and in the cabinets in the old kitchen.

After they were done, Swifty grabbed his laptop and headed for the door. As he passed his puzzled mother, he said, "I'm going into town to do some work at the library," and then he was gone.

As his mother heard his truck engine start, she was even more puzzled. In all the time Swifty had grown up on the ranch, she had never heard him even mention the word library, let along say he was going there. She just shook her head.

Kit drove into Cody, but before he headed to the library, he stopped at the local United States Department of Agriculture office. There he got copies of several maps. He had to wait as the young lady who waited on him had to call up the parcels of land and then have the system print them out.

She checked each map against her list and then rolled them up and put them in a cardboard tube. She set the tube on the counter and then added up the items on her register.

"That's a lot of maps, Mr. Olson," she said. "The total will be two hundred and ninety- eight dollars and thirty-two cents."

Swifty handed her his credit card and when she handed him his receipt to sign, he took her proffered pen, signed it, and slid it back to her. She handed him the receipt, and he thanked her for her help. She beamed.

Swifty checked to make sure the plastic plugs on each end of the tube were secured and then headed out to his truck. Then he drove to the library and took the tube with him as he entered the old brick building.

The library was old, but in good condition with high ceilings and contained rows and rows of bookshelves filled with all kinds of books. He went to the main desk and filled out a form to rent a computer terminal. He gave the clerk a credit card to pay for the rental and she slipped it through a reader and then handed him back his card along with the receipt.

Swifty pocketed the receipt, and she directed him to

the section where the computers were located. He found his designated computer and put his cardboard tube on the small stand and sat down. He turned on the computer, waited a few seconds for it to come on, and then entered the code he had been given by the clerk. In a few seconds he was online.

Swifty took out a list he had made and then began to do a Google Earth search of certain land parcels based on the list he had made. As he found what he was looking for, he studied the maps and photos, and then pushed a button to print them out.

The process took him almost three hours. He also made notes in his notebook during his search and referenced them to the appropriate map. When he was finished, he gathered up his tube and returned to the main desk. He told the clerk he had copies to pay for from his terminal. She noted the terminal number and then disappeared into a back room. Fifteen minutes later she was back with a small stack of printed papers. She counted out the pages manually, and then entered data into a calculator.

"My goodness," she said.

"Something wrong?" asked Swifty, who was a little irritated the printing of the pages had taken so long.

"No, nothing's wrong," said the clerk. "It's just the total pages are the most I've ever had requested."

"How many pages?" asked Swifty.

"One hundred and thirty-seven," said the clerk, who was now a little embarrassed and red faced because of her outburst.

"Sounds right to me," said Swifty.

He handed her his credit card and soon he had a receipt

and was out the door of the library with his tube of maps and his pile of printed pages. He opened the passenger door of his truck and deposited the tube and the pages on the passenger seat. Then he slipped around the truck and piled into the driver's seat.

As soon as Swifty was out of sight, the clerk excused herself from the main desk and went to the ladies' room. She slipped into a stall and took her cell phone out of her pocket. She dialed a number from memory. When someone answered, she identified herself and gave the man a short message. Then she hung up, returned the phone to her pocket and left the stall. She stopped at the sink to wash and dry her hands and returned to the main desk.

On the way out of Cody, Swifty noticed he was getting low on gas. He pulled into a gas station and got out to fill his tank. While he was pumping gas, he was running a checklist through his mind to make sure he had not forgotten anything on his trip to town. His thought process was interrupted by a sharp smack on his left shoulder.

Irritated, he turned to find himself face to face with a not smiling Ann.

"I haven't heard a peep out of you since I went out of my way to bring you a picnic lunch," she said without a trace of humor in her voice.

"I'm sorry," said Swifty. "I've been kind of busy."

"That's the kind of crap I used to heard from you when we were in high school," came her sharp retort.

Swifty started to explain what he had been doing, but he quickly realized he was already way downhill with a long uphill fight in front of him.

"How about I buy you lunch?" said a somewhat hopeful Swifty.

Ann's face did not change, but she did have a quizzical look in her eyes. She was silent for almost a minute. Then she spoke.

"You got a deal," she said. "Be at my office in fifteen minutes. And don't be even a second late."

"Yes, ma'am," said a sheepish Swifty.

CHAPTER THIRTY-SIX

Five minutes later, Swifty was parked behind Ann's office in her small parking lot. He could see his sister's truck in the lot, but no sign of Ann. He drove there as soon as he finished gassing up his truck. He knew he was on thin ice, and he was taking no chances.

The next ten minutes dragged by. Swifty began to think of excuses he might use if his sister suddenly appeared in the parking lot and wondered why he was sitting there. He gave up on several ideas and settled on telling her the truth. When you told the truth, you didn't have to worry about what you had said later.

At exactly fourteen minutes after she told him to be at her office in fifteen minutes, Ann roared into her parking lot in her veterinary pickup truck. She pulled up next to him and lowered the window on her passenger side.

"Get in," she commanded.

Swifty obeyed without saying a word. As soon as he was seated and before he could buckle his seat belt, Ann roared out of the parking lot. When she hit the street, she floored the big V-8 engine, and the truck shot down the street like it had been launched by a catapult.

She drove like a madwoman until she pulled into the

driveway of her home in Cody. She stopped the truck, shut off the engine, and grabbed a McDonalds bag from behind her seat.

"Get out!" she commanded.

Swifty obeyed.

Ann got out of the truck with her bag, slammed the door shut, and marched toward the front door of her house. She opened the door and marched inside, leaving the door open, but not looking back to see if Swifty was following her.

He was.

She went through the kitchen, dropped the bag on the counter and marched through the living room and down the hall. Swifty followed at a safe distance.

She entered a door and Swifty followed. He found himself in the middle of her master bedroom. She stopped, turned and faced him with a look that was anything but friendly.

"Get your clothes off and be quick about it," she commanded.

Swifty obeyed. By the time he was finished, she was wearing only some rather sexy red underwear and sitting on the edge of the huge king-sized bed.

She looked up at Swifty with a slightly less ferocious face. "Do you like what you see?" she said.

A light went on in Swifty's brain. He finished undressing and took a step toward the bed.

"Hold it," said Ann. "That's far enough."

Swifty looked confused and stopped in his tracks.

"I just wanted you to get a good look at what you were missing," said Ann.

"What?" sputtered Swifty.

"You heard me," said Ann. "Now get out of my house and take your damn clothes with you."

Swifty was in a state of shock. Then luckily his brain took over his body. As he pulled on his clothes, he came up with an answer.

"Would you like to hear what happened or would you rather just gloat over your Pyrrhic victory," said Swifty evenly.

"What the hell are you talking about," replied Ann.

"Just what I told you," said Swifty, as he finished dressing. "I'm going out to your kitchen. If you're interested in what has happened that was more important to me than getting back to you, I'll be happy to explain. I'll be there for ten minutes. If you're interested, join me. If not, stay in here until I leave."

For the first time that day, Ann was speechless. Swifty left the room and closed the bedroom door behind him.

Five minutes later, Ann appeared in the kitchen fully dressed.

Swifty had made coffee and sat at her kitchen table with a cup of coffee in his hand and the paper sack from McDonalds next to him.

"Please have a seat, Doctor," said Swifty.

Ann sat down in a chair without saying a word. She looked confused.

Swifty got up and put the contents of the paper sack in the microwave and set it to reheat, closed the door, and hit the button. Then he filled a cup with coffee and set it and a bowl of artificial sweetener and a small carton of half and half in front of her.

When the microwave dinged, he got up and took out

the contents. He split them up and put half in front of Ann and kept the other half. He got a bottle of ketchup out of the refrigerator and set in on the small table, right in front of Ann.

Ann sipped her coffee and looked directly at Swifty. "Care to explain why you failed to follow up your words of endearment to me with any semblance of a physical presence," she said grimly.

Swifty was not a college graduate, but he was not stupid. He knew anytime a woman asked you a question like this one, he was in deep trouble unless he came up with the right answer.

Swifty did what he always did in situations like this. He picked up his coffee cup and took a long sip to give him as much time as possible to come up with a satisfactory response to her question. Once again, he decided on the honest truth.

"I met with my aunt and found out my grandfather was still alive and living on land he owned near the Montana border, up near the top of Beartooth Pass," said Swifty slowly and distinctly. "I did a recon of his property and then returned to confront him."

"Why?" asked a puzzled looking Ann.

"My aunt thought he might be the only one who could and would be able to help me with the mystery of who killed my dad and why," replied Swifty

"So, what happened?" asked a curious Ann.

"I walked into his property and he surprised me. Then I talked my way into getting him to hear me out about why I was there," said Swifty.

Ann stayed silent, waiting for him to continue his story.

Swifty spent the next fifteen minutes telling Ann about his grandfather, his grandfather's place, and what they discussed. When he was finished, he looked directly at Ann. Her face was devoid of any emotion.

"Are you finished with your story?" asked Ann.

"Yep," replied Swifty.

Then Ann responded, angrily, as she rose out of her chair. "You are the most disturbing man I have ever met," she said. "You ignore me after I make you a special picnic lunch. Then just when I am ready to come down on you like a ton of bricks, you go out and come up with the almost unbelievable story about your suddenly reincarnated grandfather and his mysterious place up on Bear Tooth Pass."

"But I'm telling you the truth," protested Swifty.

"I know you are," responded Ann. "That's what pisses me off. I want to beat the crap out of you for ignoring me, and then you go and tell me this true story I thought only existed in books and movies."

"So, you're not mad at me?" asked a puzzled Swifty.

"Of course, I'm mad as hell at you," Ann practically shouted back at him. "But I'm also damn proud of you and feel bad because I misjudged your ability to deal with a really bad situation. But......"

"But what?" asked Swifty.

"But I feel bad you didn't ask me to help you," said a now much calmer Ann.

A light went on in Swifty's brain. With all his planning and work to assemble assets to help him, he had overlooked one of the most important.

"I do need your help, Ann," said Swifty.

CHAPTER THIRTY-SEVEN

Swifty spent the next hour drinking coffee and explaining his plan to Ann. She interrupted him several times with questions, mostly to make sure she understood what he was referring to, and then he was finally finished.

"You think this will work?" asked a still dubious Ann.

"I do," he said. "Most of it is Bushrod's idea. It depends on getting my hands on the right equipment and having enough of his old Green Beret pals showing up to help us. He seems to think that won't be a problem."

"So, where do I come in?" asked Ann. "I want to help, but I can't do anything illegal."

Swifty grinned at her. "Your part in this will be strictly legal and above board. I promise you."

"Explain to me in words I can understand what it is you need me to do?" asked Ann.

"You may want to take notes," said Swifty.

Ann got up from the table and returned with a pad of paper and a pen.

"Fire away, Cowboy," said Ann.

Swifty noticed her smile had returned, along with the usually bright glint in her eyes when she was doing something she really liked.

"Remember when you came to my aid during the fight outside the bar?" asked Swifty.

"Yes, I remember," replied a somewhat puzzled Ann.

"You used a tranquilizer dart on that guy to put him down, right?" he said.

"Yes, I did," said a still puzzled Ann.

"What kind of animal was that tranquilizer made for?" asked Swifty.

"A mature pig," said Ann. "A load for a horse or cow would have been too much. One for a dog or a cat would have been too little."

"How many tranquilizer darts with that load of drug do you have in stock?" asked Swifty.

"It doesn't work that way, Swifty," replied Ann. "I load the dart with the proper load of tranquilizer for the type of animal I need to use it on. I only have three sizes of darts and I load a dart with the proper type and amount of tranquilizer."

"If you used a dart on a human, like you did that night at the bar, how many darts that size do you have?" asked Swifty.

"I have about a dozen I think," said Ann, "but I'd have to check my supply to be sure."

"If you wanted to use a dozen darts on mature pigs, do you have enough tranquilizer on hand?" asked Swifty.

"Sure," said Ann. "I've got more than enough for three dozen if I needed them."

"If you needed to order more darts, how long would it take before they were delivered to you?" asked Swifty.

"A week, maybe less," replied Ann.

"Excellent," said Swifty.

"Why are you asking me about my supplies of darts and tranquilizers?" asked Ann.

"I plan on using non-lethal weapons in this operation and your darts would be perfect," said Swifty. "Do you happen to know how much the darts cost and while you're at it, how much for a tranquilizer gun and how long would it take to get a gun if you ordered it today," asked Swifty.

"I don't remember the cost, but I can look it up," replied Ann. "I think the last time I ordered one it came in less than a week."

Swifty thought for a minute and then said, "I'm gonna' need about five of them and about thirty doses of tranquilizer appropriate for a large pig."

"We can go back to the office, and I can look up the price," offered Ann.

"Actually, I really need to get home," said Swifty. "My mom hasn't heard from me for a couple of days, which is my fault, and I need to make sure everything is still all right at the ranch."

"I'll go down to the office and look up the price and then text it to you," said Ann. "You can text me and let me know how many guns you need, and I can order them."

Swifty looked a bit perplexed as if he were trying to select the right words to respond to her offer.

"If you're worried about me paying for the guns and tranquilizers, don't," said Ann. "I'm charging you retail so there's still a little profit in it for all my trouble."

Swifty started to protest, and then realized Ann was having a little fun with him.

"Whatever works for you is fine with me," Swifty carefully responded.

Ann tried to keep a straight face, but then she burst out laughing.

Swifty joined in, and then he rose from the table. Ann stood and Swifty took her in his arms. They kissed a long, slow, and passionate kiss. Then Swifty patted her on her butt and headed out the door.

Two minutes later he was back in her kitchen.

"I seem to have misplaced my truck," said an embarrassed Swifty.

"I think I know where you left it," responded a smiling Ann. She led him out to her truck and soon she was dropping him off at his truck.

Swifty exited her truck and climbed into the cab of his pickup. He looked back at Ann and said, "Later."

"Better make it sooner, if you know what's good for you," she retorted.

Swifty grinned, and drove away, heading back to the ranch.

CHAPTER THIRTY-EIGHT

Twenty minutes later, Swifty was pulling his truck up next to the ranch house. After getting out of his truck, he headed to the barn to make sure the chores had been taken care of. A quick check of the horses found them still munching the last bits of hay and oats from their stalls. Satisfied the chores were done, he headed to the house.

He entered the ranch house and walked into the kitchen. The kitchen was empty, but a pot of coffee was still hot. Swifty grabbed a cup from the shelf and filled it with coffee. The coffee was jet black and probably stronger from brewing longer. He took a sip. It was very strong.

Swifty walked into the living room and found his mother in her favorite chair. She was fast asleep with a book lying open in her lap. Swifty carefully removed the book, put a piece of paper in it to mark the page she had been reading, and set the book on the small table next to her chair.

Then he took the coffee to his room. On his desk, he found some mail and a note from his mother. The note said some packages had arrived and were stored in the barn. "Good old reliable Kit," thought Swifty. He opened his mail and then opened his laptop. He found several messages with attachments from Kit. As he opened each attachment, he studied the contents carefully. One attachment was a history of the Hayfork Ranch and its ownership. The current owners were two guys from New York City. They were partners in a large venture capital business and appeared to have bought the Hayfork Ranch as an investment. The two men were in their late forties and had been partners for almost twenty years.

According to some attached newspaper articles, the two men were gay and lived together as life partners. "Gay Ranchers?" thought Swifty with a slight grin on his face.

The two men had been involved in several run-ins with the Securities and Exchange Commission for dubious trading practices, but never convicted of any crime. The articles alluded to the high-priced tony New York City law firm they used to defend themselves as a probable reason why there were no convictions.

After reading the other attached articles, Swifty learned more about the gay partners. They were smooth, they were connected, and they were wealthy. They were also very aggressive in their business dealings and based on the numerous suits over breach of contract issues, not very good at keeping their word to anyone.

Kit had also obtained recent photos of the two partners. One was named Barney Kimbell. He was white, forty-eight years old and a graduate of Harvard Business School. The other was Theodore Lincoln, a black forty-six-year-old man who was a graduate of the University of Alabama where he earned both bachelors and master's degrees in finance. The two men lived in the same penthouse in New York City.

From other articles, it appeared the two men spent most

of their time in New York but traveled to Wyoming at least three times a year. One of those three times was the annual Hayfork Ranch Day, celebrated by the people of nearby Meeteetse, Wyoming. The two men hosted a one-day tour of the ranch. The two men provided buses for transportation and then a barbeque on the ranch. They limited the guest list to three hundred people and more than a thousand signed up, so they did a drawing to choose the lucky folks who could enjoy the visit and barbeque.

Kit had written a note and attached it below the article. He noted his opinion was the owners did this to satisfy curiosity and cut down on possible trespassing by locals to satisfy their curiosity about what went on at the historic ranch.

Swifty reread the article about the annual outing at the Hayfork Ranch. The outing was usually in late May or early June. He could find no specific date for this year's celebration. He would check for the information later. He wrote himself a short note to that effect and went back to the articles. When he was finished, he sat back in his old wooden chair and closed his eyes. The ranch owners were older, gay, wealthy, and ruthless in business dealings.

He searched his memory and remembered something Big Dave had once told him. He had said, "Take what you need, leave what you don't." It had been his advice to Swifty on what to take on a re-supply trip to a sheep herder's camp up in the mountains in late summer.

As he continued to think about what to do, he remembered a second story he had heard from Big Dave one night when they were sitting round a campfire on a sheep drive. Big Dave was telling a story about an old gold prospector up in Alaska. In 1895, the prospector sent a letter to Sears and Roebuck. In the letter he requested a case of toilet paper and enclosed about twenty dollars in cash to cover the cost of the toilet paper and shipping.

The prospector got a letter from Sears and Roebuck clerk. In the letter the Sears employee informed the prospector he needed to use their catalog to order his toilet paper.

Disgusted, the prospector wrote the Sears employee a return letter. In the letter he said, "If I had your catalog, I wouldn't need your damn toilet paper."

Swifty smiled to himself. Sometimes you needed to assess what you had, not what you needed and rework your plan to deal with a problem.

The more he thought about how he might lure the two ranch owners to Wyoming, the more frustrated he got. He even considered organizing a team to go to New York City and confront the two men on their own turf. The more he thought about it, the more ridiculous it seemed. He needed to come up with a way to get Kimball and Lincoln to make an unscheduled trip to Wyoming. He sat up in his chair and grabbed a piece of paper and a pen and began to write down various scenarios to entice the two men to come to their ranch for an unscheduled visit.

He was still looking over his list when his mother poked her head into his room and told him supper was almost ready. Swifty closed his laptop and followed her into the kitchen.

CHAPTER THIRTY-NINE

Dinner was roast beef, mashed potatoes, gravy, and green beans. Swifty suddenly felt famished and had two large helpings. He and his mother talked about the ranch, and his sister sat quietly, listening carefully, but looking at her brother like she was inspecting an insect impaled on a pin.

Swifty had helped his mother and sister with clearing off the table and he and his sister did the dishes. When everything was put away, Swifty went to pour a fresh cup of coffee into his mug when his cell phone rang. He looked at the phone and saw the call was from Kit. He promptly answered the phone while pouring coffee into his mug.

"What's up?" asked Swifty.

"Am I disturbing anything?" asked Kit.

"No, we just finished cleaning up after supper," replied Swifty.

"Well, I found something I felt would be better to tell you about over the phone instead of a text," said Kit.

"What?" asked Swifty.

"You remember you asked me to look into any geological or mineral searches done recently on the Hayfork Ranch," said Kit.

"I remember," said Swifty.

"I found the smoking gun," said Kit.

"Smoking gun? What smoking gun?" asked Swifty.

"I believe we now know why your father was killed, and who wants your mom's ranch and why," said Kit.

"Let me get to my room, so I can jot all this down," said Swifty

"I'll wait patiently on my phone," said Kit in a quiet voice.

Swifty almost dashed to his room. He shut the door and sat at the old desk.

"O.K., what did you find?" Swifty asked.

"There have been several tests for minerals on the Hayfork in the past three years. The last tests were done less than a year ago and they were all on Hayfork Ranch land adjacent to your mother's ranch," said Kit.

"And?" asked Swifty.

"Are you sitting down?" asked Kit.

"Of course," replied a now impatient Swifty.

"Ever heard of rare earth deposits?" asked Kit.

"Rare earth what?" asked Swifty.

"Rare earth deposits," replied Kit.

"Can't say I have," answered Swifty.

"I'll read you the summary," said Kit.

"Go ahead, I'm listening," said Swifty.

"Rare earths are a combination of 17 elements on the periodic table. These deposits and how much they're worth vary by the amount and quality of each type. Among the 17, a handful are considered to be critical rare earths, which means they are both rare and valuable," said Kit.

"Wyoming has 10 of the rare earths in quantity and quality worth mining," said Kit. "Apparently the Hayfork

Ranch has large traces of six of the most valuable rare earths. The traces increased the closer they tested to your ranch."

Swifty was silent for a minute, as he processed what Kit had just told him.

"You mean Mom's ranch could have large deposits of these rare earth minerals?" asked Swifty.

"Bingo," said Kit. "You win first price for logic."

"What are these rare earth minerals?" asked Swifty.

"Glad you asked," replied Kit. "I just happen to have the report in front of me. Neodymium is what makes your phone vibrate and are used to produce tiny magnets used in cell phones, ABS brake systems, lasers, and cruise control."

"Yttrium is used in lasers, LEFs, metal alloys, and superconductors. Praseodymium is the most valuable of the rare earth elements and is used primarily in florescent lamps, anti-counterfeiting devices and glass making. Dysprosium is used in hybrid vehicles, wind turbines, and cruise missiles. Last, but not least is Terbium which when mixed with neodymium produces super magnets used in electric vehicle motors and used in fuel cells and lighting," said Kit. "Did you get all of that?"

"Hell, I got lost after hearing the first one," said Swifty

"Well, to make it short and sweet, your mom's ranch is sitting on a virtual gold mine of rare earth minerals," said Kit. "My guess is the owners tested for the rare earth stuff and had some, but the strongest traces led straight to your mom's ranch."

"So the ranch owners had their people try to buy the ranch from my dad, but he wouldn't sell, and because he was probably an asshole about it and shut them down, they decided to eliminate him and buy out my mom," said a shocked Swifty.

"I kept telling Big Dave you were smarter than you looked," said Kit.

"Screw you and the horse you rode in on," said Swifty.

"Now, that's something I'd actually pay to see," retorted Kit.

"You couldn't afford it," Swifty shot back. "You got any more?"

"Thought that would be enough for one day," said Kit. "I'll e-mail you the reports as attachments."

"How'd you get your hands on the actual reports?" asked Swifty. "I thought they were the property of the people who ordered them along with the state of Wyoming."

"They are until they aren't," said Kit. "Gotta go. I'll see you later."

"Not if I see you first," responded Swifty, but he was talking to a dial tone. Kit was long gone.

CHAPTER FORTY

Swifty was up early the next morning. When he left the ranch house everything was dark and quiet. Not even his mother was up and about. He walked to the barn, fed the horses and checked their water. Then he got in his truck and drove out to the pasture area of the ranch to check on the cattle. He did a head count and accounted for all the cattle. They looked to be in good shape to him. He returned to the ranch and parked his truck.

As he made his way into the ranch house, he could smell breakfast in the kitchen. He arrived in time to snag a piece of bacon before his mother smacked him on the hand and told him to wash up first. He grinned and went to the wash area to wash his hands and face.

When he returned to the kitchen, he filled a mug with coffee and sat at the table. His sister immediately slid a plate full of eggs, bacon and potatoes in front of him. He thanked her and she just looked at him like he was an escapee from a lunatic farm. He grinned and dived into his breakfast.

After breakfast he helped his mother clean up while his sister left to go to work. When Swifty was sure she was gone, he poured his mother a fresh cup of coffee and motioned for her to join him at the kitchen table.

"What's up?" she asked. "Have you learned some news about your dad?"

"I've got some news for you, Mom. I'm pretty sure I now know why dad was killed and by whom," replied Swifty in as even a voice as he could manage.

His mother sat there, her coffee untouched, as she waited for him to explain.

"I had asked Kit to do some investigating for me," said Swifty. "He can do things and get into places I can't."

"He's a good friend," said Swifty's mom.

"Yes, he is," replied Swifty. "I asked him to see if he could find out if anyone at the Hayfork Ranch had been ordering mineral testing on their ground. It turns out they had been doing testing over the past three years. The most recent testing showed traces of rare earth minerals on the Hayfork Ranch."

"What's that got to do with us and your father?" asked his mother.

"The tests revealed that the closer the tests got to your ranch, the stronger the traces got," said Swifty.

"What does that mean?" asked his mother.

"It means that it is more than likely large deposits of these rare earth minerals are located on your ranch," said Swifty.

"I still don't understand what that means," said his mother. "Is this stuff dangerous?"

Swifty smiled. "No, Mom, it's not dangerous. But it is valuable. In fact, rare earth minerals are quite valuable, and the ranch appears to have some that are among the rarest and most valuable," he said.

"I'm confused. Why are these rare earth minerals so valuable?" asked his mother.

"To simplify it, let's just say these minerals are used in lots of high-tech stuff. One example is their use in cell phones," said Swifty.

"Cell phones?" asked his mother.

"Yes," replied Swifty. "Cell phones and lots of other high-tech stuff. According to Kit, Wyoming is one place where lots of these rare earth minerals are found, but not usually in a sufficient quantity to commercially extract them from the land."

"And our land has that much?" asked his mother.

"Apparently so, but we would have to test to be absolutely sure," replied Swifty.

"What does this have to do with getting your father killed?" she asked.

"I think the folks who own the Hayfork Ranch tested their land and in doing so discovered the closer they got to our land, the larger the deposits of these rare earth minerals got. They tried to get dad to sell and when he refused, they had him killed," said Swifty.

"Why would they kill your father?" his mother almost shouted the words.

"Because they were sure you couldn't make a go of the ranch by yourself and would have to sell, and they'd be right there to take it off your hands," said a grim Swifty.

"Oh my god," said his mother. "They murdered Eldon!"

"They killed him so they could get their hands on your ranch," said Swifty.

"What are you going to do?" asked his mother with a fearful look in her eye.

"I'm going to get even for what they did," said Swifty in a soft, but firm voice. He hugged his mother to him and held her as she began to cry. Swifty held her close until she stopped weeping. Then he grabbed his unused napkin and handed it to his mother so she could wipe the tears from her face. As she wiped away her tears, Swifty gently released her from his arms.

When she was composed, his mother looked at Swifty and put her hands on his arms.

"This is a job for the authorities. You need to go tell the sheriff and let him do his job," she implored Swifty.

"That fat old politician couldn't find his ass with both hands tied behind his back," said Swifty sarcastically.

"If not him, then go to the state police," said his mother.

"I promise I will go to the authorities," Swifty told his mother. "But only when I have enough proof to send those two fat cat bastards to prison for the rest of their lives."

"How will you do that?" asked his mother.

"I'm getting help from Kit and from my grandfather Bushrod," replied Swifty.

"Bushrod?" exclaimed his mother. "That man is too old to do much more than manage to stay alive."

"Bushrod is more of a man than most who are thirty years younger. He wants justice for Elon and for you, and I intend to use his help and Kit's help to see that justice is done," said Swifty.

"Promise me you won't do anything illegal," pleaded his mother.

"I promise I will do everything I can to see that justice is done for Eldon," said Swifty. "I promise."

CHAPTER FORTY-ONE

Swifty returned to his room, showered, shaved, and put on clean clothes. Then he turned on his laptop and sat down at his small old desk. He changed the setting to email and then sent a message to Kit. Satisfied, he closed his laptop and unplugged it. He took the laptop and cord and slipped into a carry bag.

Swifty stood up and walked to the door, carrying the bag. At the door he stopped and turned and looked back at his boyhood bedroom. He nodded as if in a salute, and then turned on his heel and walked out to the kitchen.

In the kitchen he stopped to speak to his mother.

"Mom, I'm going to be gone for a few days. It's better if I don't tell you where I am going," said Swifty. "You can't tell anyone what you don't know."

"Who would ask?" his mother said.

"I have no idea, but it's pretty likely someone will," said Swifty. "I'll see you in a couple of days."

Swifty grabbed his carry-on bag of clean clothes and his laptop and headed out the door of the ranch house. Once outside, he tossed the bags into the back of the cab of his pickup truck. Then he got in the truck and drove it over to the barn. He backed the truck up to the large barn door and then shut off the engine.

He got out of the truck and entered the barn, leaving the barn door wide open. He went to the tack room and unlocked it. He began picking up the various boxes and crates he had stored there and began carrying them outside the barn where he packed them in the bed of the truck. After about twenty minutes he was finished. He did a head count of the items in the truck bed and went back to the tack room to make sure he had not missed anything. The tack room was empty of his boxes.

Satisfied, he got in his truck and drove into Cody. When he was just outside of town, he called Ann on his cell phone and told her to meet him at a local coffee shop. When he arrived in downtown Cody, he drove to the coffee shop and parked about half a block away. He exited the truck and walked to the shop. When he got there, Ann had already arrived and was sitting at a small table outside on a small patio. She had two containers of coffee on the table in front of her.

"Hello, Cowboy," she said with a smile.

"Hello, Ann," replied Swifty. "Thanks for meeting me with such short notice."

"What's up?" she inquired.

"I'm loaded up and headed to my grandfather's place," replied Swifty.

"I assume you want to know if I've got your order ready," said Ann with a sly smile on her face.

"Once again, you are way ahead of me, just like always," said a grinning Swifty. "How did you get them so soon? I thought it would take a week?"

"Ever heard of an overnight order?" asked Ann.

"To Cody, Wyoming?" said a surprised Swifty.

"Cody has an airport, Swifty," said Ann

"I didn't think of that," said Swifty.

"What have you learned?" asked Ann.

"I got a call from Kit, and now I know why my Dad was killed," said Swifty.

Ann's smile disappeared, and her eyes became intense. She chose not to speak and waited for Swifty to tell her what had happened.

Swifty told her what he had learned from Kit and gave her a brief overview of his plans.

Ann was silent for a bit. Then she reached out and put her hand over his. "I understand why you are doing this, but I still want you to be careful. This is likely to be risky and dangerous."

"I'll be fine," said Swifty. "I'll do my best to keep you informed, but there's no phone or data service up at Bushrod's place."

"Just don't forget me," said a very serious Ann.

"I won't. I promise," said Swifty.

Ann laughed. "That's what worries me," she said.

Swifty put down his empty coffee cup and looked Ann in the eyes.

"Ready?" he asked.

"Born ready," was Ann's response.

Swifty laughed. Ann was using his lines.

Both of them rose and went to their respective vehicles. Ann led the way back to her office and when she parked her truck, Swifty pulled in next to her and parked his. They entered the veterinarian's office from the rear. Then Ann showed him where she had stacked the supplies, she had promised him. Swifty began picking up boxes and loading his truck. When he was finished, he turned to face Ann.

But Ann was not alone. Swifty's sister Melanie was standing beside Ann.

"Be careful, big brother," said Melanie as she gave him a hug.

"Don't get yourself killed, or I'll dig you up and kill you myself," said a half-smiling Ann.

Swifty gave Ann a strong hug, and then paused to kiss her on the lips.

Swifty walked to his truck and turned to face the two women before he climbed into the cab.

"I'll be back," he said.

"You damn well better be back, or I'll hunt you down and shoot you," said a half-serious Ann.

Swifty got in his truck and started the engine. As he pulled out of the little parking lot, he turned and waved to Ann and Melanie.

Ann made her fingers into the shape of a pistol and pointed it at Swifty. Swifty laughed and touched the brim of his cowboy hat. Then he put the truck in gear and drove out of the lot. He turned the corner and then he was gone.

CHAPTER FORTY-TWO

It was only a few minutes before Swifty was driving out of town and headed toward Beartooth Pass and his grandfather's place. The day was sunny with only a little wind. As he drove, Swifty went over the list of items in his mind to make sure he had not forgotten anything. He couldn't think of anything he had missed or forgotten.

It seemed to take longer than before, but soon Swifty was driving up toward the crest of Beartooth Pass. He scanned the side of the road and slowed down as he saw some familiar sights. Then he saw the almost hidden entrance to Bushrod's place. He turned into the narrow drive and drove slowly until he came to the closed steel gate.

Swifty brought his truck to a stop and started to get out of the truck cab to open the gate. He made it as far as the front of the truck when a loud voice said, "That's far enough, Pilgrim."

Swifty stopped in his tracks and put his arms straight out at his sides with his hands open to display he was not hiding any kind of weapon.

"On your knees, Pilgrim, and lace your fingers behind your head," ordered the loud voice.

Swifty went to his knees and laced his fingers behind his head.

"State your business here," commanded the loud voice.

"I'm Swifty Olson, grandson of Bushrod Olson, bringing him supplies as we had agreed on," said Swifty.

"I'm coming out to take a look at your truck," said the voice. "Don't move a muscle or I'll blow your head off."

Swifty's ears strained to hear footsteps or movement. He heard nothing. Then he heard the canvas tarp he had tied down over the load in the bed of the truck being loosened. He heard the flap of the tarp being pulled away, then he heard nothing.

"All Right, Pilgrim, get to your feet," the voice commanded.

Swifty got to his feet and stood there with his hands down at his sides.

Without making any noise, a man in cammo appeared at his left side. The man was old, with a white gunfighter mustache. He wore a boonie hat, and he carried an M-16 rifle at port arms.

"You're Bushrod's grandson?" he asked.

"Yes," replied Swifty.

"Duke Wayne, weapons specialist," said the man and he held out his right hand. Swifty shook his hand. Duke had a very strong grip. "I'll open the gate and close it behind you," said Duke.

Swifty nodded he understood, and he got back in his truck and started the engine. Duke opened the gate with one hand, the M-16 cradled in the other arm. Swifty drove through the gate. He looked in his side rear mirror and saw Duke talking into a small handheld device.

"He's radioing ahead to let them know I'm coming," thought Swifty.

Swifty drove slowly down the narrow road until he came to the clearing. As he drove slowly toward the old shack, he could see Bushrod and two other men standing in front of it, obviously waiting for him.

Swifty pulled the truck up near Bushrod and brought it to a stop and stepped out of the truck.

"Them all the supplies?" asked Bushrod.

"Yep," replied Swifty.

"Let's move your truck over to the supply depot we've set up," said Bushrod. "Doc here will show you where to pull up to."

As Swifty slid into the driver's seat of his truck, one of the men next to Bushrod started walking toward the area with the cammo canopy overhead. Swifty started the truck and slowly followed the man. He was short and stocky. He had white hair and a white beard. He directed Swifty to a spot and Swifty parked the truck.

Swifty exited the truck and stuck out his hand. The short man grabbed it in a powerful grip. "Swifty Olson, Sergeant, United States Army retired," said Swifty.

"Sergeant Bobby Manning, Medic, Green Berets, United States Army retired," said the grinning shorter man. "Good to meet you, Sergeant. Heard a lot of good things about you from your grandpa."

The two men were soon joined by Bushrod and the other man. Both were dressed in cammo. Bushrod introduced Swifty. "This here is Sammy Four feathers, former Green Beret engineer. We call him Chief. He's a full blooded

Commanche, or at least he claims he is," said Bushrod. "He's our intelligence guy."

Sammy was about five foot six inches high and built like a scarecrow. He was thin and wiry. He had no beard and his hair was long and white and had one large braid running down his back.

Swifty looked at the three men in front of him. "I met Duke at the gate," said Swifty. "Are we expecting more men?" he asked Bushrod.

"Nope, what you see is what we got," replied Bushrod.

"I thought a Green Beret unit was twelve men," said Swifty.

"You would be correct," replied Bushrod. "Five of my old unit are dead and three others ain't in good enough shape for a trip like we're plannin'."

"So, it's four men in the unit?" asked Swifty.

"Five, counting you, grandson," replied Bushrod. "We figure even a young buck like you with ten years in special forces can keep up with four old codger Green Berets."

Bushrod, Sammy, and Doc all laughed loudly.

Swifty grinned at the old warriors. "I'll do my best," he said.

"Well then," said Bushrod. "Let's get this truck unloaded and stacked inside the supply tent. Doc, you man the tote board and make sure you note everything we unload."

"Will do, Bush," replied Doc. He grabbed and clipboard with a pencil attached by a string. He noticed Swifty staring at the apparatus and grinned. "Only the most modern equipment for this outfit," he said.

The three men began unloading the bed of the truck. As each man grabbed a box or crate, he read off the contents

271

to Doc who noted it on his clipboard. Then the men toted their loads into a large wall tent located at the back of the area covered by the cammo netting.

In less than an hour they had unloaded the truck and opened the boxes and crates to make sure the contents were correct. When they were finished, Bushrod led the way to his hidden cabin. The four men sat down on old chairs on the wooden front porch of the cabin.

"I forgot something in the truck," said Swifty.

He ran to the truck and returned with a cooler full of ice and beer he had stored in the back seat. His return with the cold beer was greeted by cheers from the other three men.

"What the hell is all the ruckus about?" said a loud voice. Elwood "Duke" Wayne strode into view from his guard spot out by the property gate. When he saw the cooler of ice and beer a broad smile filled his face. He joined the other men on the porch and grabbed a can of beer.

Soon the only sound was the sound of beer cans popping open and the sighs of content by the beer drinkers.

Swifty paused midway through his beer and looked at Bushrod. "Do we not have a guard at the gate?" he asked.

"We do," said Bushrod. "We have a sensor out there powered by a solar collector." He reached into his pocket and pulled out a small device. "Here, I'll give you a sample." He pushed a button on the device and suddenly the quiet of the area was destroyed by the sudden blaring of a trumpet sounding the notes of a cavalry charge.

"Does that work for you, Swifty?" asked a grinning Bushrod.

"Works for me," said Swifty. "I could use another beer."

"One beer coming up," said Doc, as he tossed a cold can of beer to Swifty.

Swifty caught it in midair like an outfielder snagging a fly ball.

"Looks like you've done this before," said Doc.

"More than a few times," replied a smiling Swifty.

CHAPTER FORTY-THREE

After about an hour of socializing and beer drinking, the men headed inside the cabin for supper. As they all crowded into the small cabin, Duke bellowed out, "What's for supper?"

Bushrod gave him a disapproving look, and then said, "We have a limited menu tonight. I've got fresh deer meat and potatoes on hand."

"I've got a better idea," said Chief Four feathers.

"Oh, god, not more rattlesnake stew," moaned Doc.

"Nope," said Chief, "I've got a much better item than that."

"What?" challenged Duke.

"Well, on my way over here, I came across a local crisis in a small town," said Chief. "I was slowly drivin' through this small settlement and saw all these townsfolks bunched up alongside the road. It seems there was this runaway wild sow causing havoc in the town. The sow was rootin' up all the ladies' gardens and chasing off the dogs they tried to use to drive her off. They had called for the Sheriff, but he was over two hours away. I sized up the situation and offered my services to the ladies," said Chief with a dead pan face.

"What happened?" asked Bushrod.

"I pulled out my rifle and shot that insolent sow. Then I dragged the damn thing over to my truck by her hind legs. I had to use a hand winch and some boards to get the brute into the bed of my truck," said Chief. "Then I tipped my hat to the ladies and drove off. When I came to a pull off spot on the road next to a small stream. I pulled over and parked the truck. Then I climbed in the bed and gutted the sow. I got a collapsible bucket and went to the stream and filled it. Then I washed down the carcass until it was clean. Then I sharpened my knife and proceeded to butcher it. I put the best pieces in my empty ice chest and drove to the next town. When I got to the outskirts, I heaved all the guts over the side. Then I pulled into town, bought some butcher paper and wrapped up the meat and got a couple of cheap ice chests and some ice and filled them up. When I was done, I drove to the self-serve car wash and washed out the bed of my truck."

"So, where's the meat?" asked Bushrod.

"Sittin' in three ice chests by the side of the front porch," said the expressionless chief.

"Why the hell didn't you tell us sooner?" asked Doc.

"Didn't see no need till now," said the stone faced Chief.

"Let's go," said Duke and he led the way out to the porch where the men retrieved the three heavy ice chests and brought them into the cabin.

Bushrod opened his small refrigerator and a small freezer running on propane and filled them, leaving a large portion of pork roast out on the table.

Doc patted the paper wrapped pork. "Looks like dinner to me," he said.

"So, what was your excuse to the ladies for shooting the pig?" asked Duke.

Chief looked at Duke like he was a moron. "Obviously the damn pig was a menace to society. I told the ladies, it was the pig or me, so I shot the pig to protect them and their fine town."

The other four men looked at each other and then laughed and gave Chief a round of applause.

Bushrod interrupted their fun and gave directions and chores to every one of them. He and Doc stayed inside the cabin to fix supper. The others scattered outside to complete their respective assignments.

About two hours later, Duke, Chief, and Swifty had finished their assignments and met back at the cabin. Dinner of pork roast and roasted potatoes and gravy was ready, and the men sat at the table on chairs, turned over pails, and a nail keg. The food was hot and delicious, and everyone had at least two helpings.

When the meal was over, everyone helped to clean up and wash dishes. When they were done, they all gathered around the small kitchen table. Swifty had created an inventory on his laptop. He had entered the items he had inspected before dinner and added the items Chief and Duke had covered. When they were done, and everyone was aware of all the gear and equipment they had on hand, Bushrod held up his hand for silence.

"I have been thinking about how to plan this operation," he said. "Swifty has told you about the rare earth minerals on the ranch and how when the owners of the Hayfork Ranch couldn't get my son to sell it, they killed him and tried to buy it from his widow. The objective of this mission is to get justice for my son. I plan to get it from these two greedy assholes from New York City who own the Hayfork Ranch, and this is how we aim to do it."

Bushrod was silent, and he turned to face Swifty. He gave Swifty a nod.

Swifty cleared his throat and began talking. "These two men rarely come to their ranch in Wyoming. They come three times a year. They come once for the annual open house they throw for the folks in Meeteetse and two other times during the summer months," he said.

"When are those times?" asked Duke.

"Other than the open house date, we have no idea," said Swifty.

"So how can we plan for something without a specific date?" asked Doc.

"There's an old saying," said Swifty. "When Mohammed won't go to the mountain, we get the mountain to go to Mohammed."

"Bad enough I spent part of my life wasting gooks," said Duke. "Now we're talking camel jockeys?"

"A figure of speech, Duke," said a smiling Swifty.

"Oh," said Duke.

"We need a plan to lure those two peacocks to the ranch at a time we want," said Swifty.

"How do we do that?" asked Chief.

"We give them an urgent reason to come as fast as they can," said Swifty.

"I'm startin' to warm up to your grandson," said a grinning Doc.

The four old Green Berets sat silently in their seats, waiting for Swifty to explain how that was going to happen.

"I have the outline of a plan," said Swifty. "I want all of you to hear me out, and then you can shoot holes in it until we come up with the best plan possible."

"Fire away," said Bushrod.

"My plan is we pick a time when things are slow," said Swifty. "Based on what I know, the middle of the week, like a Wednesday, is when all the hands and workers are at the ranch. We wait until dusk, then we quietly move in on the ranch in two-man teams, leaving one of us as a lookout and guard. We advance at dark, using night vision goggles and moving on foot."

"What about weapons?" asked Duke.

"We leave rifles and pistols at the place we hide our transportation," said Swifty. "We carry knives and dart rifles."

"Dart rifles?" asked a scowling Duke.

"Yep," said Swifty. "We use the rifles veterinarians use to put down animals with drugs. Our rifles will have darts with loads of drugs large enough to knock out humans, but not hurt or kill anyone."

The other four men nodded their understanding, but Duke still had the look of serious doubt on his face.

"We use the dart guns to subdue everyone on the ranch while they're sleeping," said Swifty. "Then we secure their hands and ankles with plastic zip ties. When we have them all secured, we borrow a long horse trailer from the ranch and load all of them into it. We hitch it to one of our trucks and we haul all of them up here. We leave one of us hidden at the ranch with a good long-range radio to watch the ranch and report what happens after we leave."

"What happens when we get the hands back to Bushrod's place?" asked Doc.

"We build a small stockade with a canvas roof and we keep them in it with hoods over their heads, so they are unable to see anything," said Swifty.

"So that way they can't see who snatched them or where they are?" asked Doc.

"That's the plan," said Swifty.

"Then what?" asked Bushrod.

"I'm sure someone at the ranch reports to a boss at the end of each day or submits some kind of report," said Swifty. "When no one calls or makes a report, someone will head out to the ranch to see what's wrong. They show up, find everyone gone, and panic and call the two owners in New York."

"How can we be sure the owners will run to the ranch?" asked Bushrod.

"We can't be sure," said Swifty. "But if you were an owner and found out your multi-million-dollar ranch was unattended and the staff unaccounted for, even if you called the sheriff, you'd fly out to Wyoming to see for yourself."

"I'd bet those two assholes would charter a private jet to Cody and have someone pick them up and run them out to the ranch," said Duke.

"Me too," said Doc.

"What happens next?" asked the Chief.

"Glad you asked," said Swifty with a big grin on his face.

CHAPTER FORTY-FOUR

While Swifty was explaining his plan, Bushrod rose from his chair and went to a cupboard. He extracted a good bottle of bourbon and five glasses of various sizes, shapes and condition. He returned to the table and poured two fingers of bourbon in each glass and handed a glass to each man at the table.

After every man had a drink in his hand, Bushrod stood and held up his glass. The other four men followed suit. When all were standing, Bushrod said, "To victory." The other men repeated it, and all took a drink from their glasses. Then they took their seats and Swifty turned on his computer and used his fingers to click on keys until he found what he was looking for.

The vision on the laptop computer screen was an aerial view of the entire Hayfork Ranch. Then Swifty brought up an aerial view of the homestead area where the ranch house and all the outbuildings were located. The homestead took up about seven acres.

"This is our target area," said Swifty. He pointed to several buildings and explained what they were. He zeroed in on the bunkhouse and the foremen's quarters. "These two buildings are our main targets. The plan is to launch our attack at two thirty A.M. when everyone should be asleep. I have a thermal scanner we will use first to make sure we have everyone on the ranch located before we attack."

"How do we stage the attack?" asked Doc.

"Good question, Doc," replied Swifty. "We leave one man, probably Chief, to oversee the entire operation and act as our security backup in case things go south. We divide up into two-man teams and one team takes the bunkhouse and the other team takes the foremen's quarters. I doubt the doors are locked. The two-man teams enter the buildings and shoot each occupant with a tranquilizer dart. When they are finished subduing the targets, I will call Chief. Her will drive his truck drive onto the ranch, go to this barn, hook up to this four-horse trailer and pull it to the bunkhouse. Then we will drag the targets out of the bunkhouse and over to the trailer. We will drag them inside the trailer. We use zip ties to tie their hands behind them and then tie their ankles together. Then we will slip black hoods with nose and mouth holes cut in them over their heads and secure them."

"Do we have enough hoods?" asked Bushrod.

"I estimate the total number of targets at the ranch at about twenty. I have thirty hoods in case we encounter more targets," replied Swifty.

"Good," responded Bushrod.

"Then we move the truck and horse trailer to the foremen's quarters, and we repeat the process," said Swifty.

"Are twenty or more guys gonna fit in that horse trailer?" asked Duke.

"It might be a bit tight, but the passengers aren't gonna notice and they'll be in no condition to complain," replied Swifty.

That brought a chuckle from the old Green Berets.

"Then we haul the horse trailer back here to Bushrod's place and dump them in the compound we've been building. It's walled and gated with a wire roof," said Swifty.

"What about their hoods? Do we remove them?" asked Bushrod.

"Nope. We leave them on. When they can't see anything, it adds to the disorientation we want," said Swifty.

"How about feeding them and letting them take a leak or a crap," asked Doc.

"One of us will guard them, and we'll feed them army field rations. We'll have a lister bag of water with a plastic cup attached by a small chain," replied Swifty. "We have an old toilet seat over a hole in the ground and once they're in the compound, we'll retie their legs so their ankles have a two-foot spacing so they can shuffle walk. The guard will give them oral instructions on how to reach the privy and find their toilet paper. Any other questions?"

"What kind of army rations are we giving them?" asked Doc.

"Probably a mixture of what we have," replied Swifty.

"I vote for lots of ham and lima beans," said Duke.

"Why ham and lima beans?" asked Doc.

"I hate ham and lima beans," replied Duke.

All five of the men laughed. Almost no one in the army liked the ham and lima beans ration.

"How long do we hold these dudes?" asked Chief.

"Until the deal is done," replied Swifty grimly. "Once the mission is accomplished, we'll tranquilize them and haul them to a spot outside Cody and leave them by the highway after we remove the bindings on their hands and ankles and remove the hoods."

"Sounds like no harm, no foul to me," said Doc.

"I like it," said Bushrod.

"What happens then?' asked Duke.

Swifty smiled as he recalled how he obtained the information he was about to share. His Aunt Judy had been on three of the annual ranch open house visits and she told Swifty the two owners traveled with two bodyguards. They flew into Cody, rented the biggest car available, and drove to the ranch. The biggest rental car in Cody was an older black Lincoln Continental. Swifty knew, because he had called the rental car company in Cody and asked about the biggest car they had available to rent.

"We hope the two owners will fly into Cody with two bodyguards. I'm pretty sure they will rent the older black Lincoln and drive to the ranch to meet with the sheriff," said Swifty.

"If they do, where do we snatch them?" asked Duke.

"I've ruled out the airport," said Swifty. "Too many people and eyes around there. The ranch is likely to have lots of law enforcement around, so that's out."

"So, where then?" asked Duke.

"We have a lookout near the ranch with a radio," said Swifty. "When the two owners leave the ranch, our guy radios us and we set up a fake army roadblock with two of you in uniform and fake beards and a black sedan with phony license plates and fake lettering. They stop the Lincoln, shoot the guards with tranquilizer darts and then do the same to the two owners. We pull the Lincoln off on a side road and leave it with the guards in it. Then we take the two owners to a secret place to interrogate them."

"I like the plan," said Bushrod. "Who plays the army guys?"

"I think that falls to Doc and Duke," said Swifty.

"Aren't they gonna be suspicious of army guys wearing beards?" asked Chief.

"The car will be lettered as part of the Wyoming National Guard," replied Swifty. "Part-time soldiers often have beards."

"That's true," said Doc.

"Where is this secret place?" asked Duke.

"Glad you asked," said a grinning Swifty. "Part of the plan is to scare the shit out of these two rich New Yorkers."

Swifty hit some keys on the laptop and a picture of a riverbank with a high stone hillside next to it came into focus.

"What the hell is that?" asked Bushrod.

"That is a place called Legend Rock," replied Swifty. "It's a little-known state park located about thirty-one miles south of Meeteetse. You leave highway 120 on a paved road on the west side and follow it five and a half miles until you come to a fork in the road. You take the right fork and follow a gravel road for three miles. After you cross the second cattle guard you take the road to your left heading south. In about one hundred yards the road takes you to a green steel gate. On the other side of the gate is a parking area. From there you walk on a path southwest of the parking area to an area with a large cliff that faces Cottonwood Creek. On the cliff are hundreds of petroglyphs. This is a historic site and a sacred site for Indians."

"What the hell are petroglyphs?" asked Duke.

"Petroglyphs are images that have been pecked or incised into a rock surface. The pecking is done with an object harder than the rock surface. Sometimes they are pecked as an outline of animals or birds or objects. Often eyes, clothing, or other details can be pecked inside the feature. Some are fully pecked where the pecking has totally filled in the outline and it is more like a shadow with no internal features. Most of the petroglyphs are hundreds of years old and some are older," said Swifty.

"Who the hell made them?" asked Bushrod.

"Many Indians from many places over a long period of time," said Swifty. "Nobody really knows. Most Indians consider this a sacred place."

Chief asked no questions and made no comments. He just stared intently at the pictures of the site.

"Why this place?" asked Doc.

"It's scary as hell in the daytime and we'll be there at night. It's isolated and there are no lights. No one visits the place at night," said Swifty.

"How do you know that?" asked Duke.

"I talked to an employee at the sheriff's office I went to school with, and she told me even the deputies don't like to go near there," replied Swifty.

"Sounds ideal for our purposes," said Bushrod.

"Who does the interrogating?" asked Duke.

"That's something we have to decide now," said Swifty. "Who has experience in questioning prisoners?"

There was about a minute of silence. The four old Green Berets looked at each other and then three sets of eyes setting on one of their number.

"Why's everybody lookin' at me" said Bushrod.

"Cause you could get the truth out of a granite statue," said Doc. "Bushrod's the man for the job. I've seen him get tough NVA officers to spill their guts in less than ten minutes."

"You may remember I used some tactics not exactly sanctioned by the Geneva Convention," said a grim faced Bushrod.

"Last time I checked, the Geneva Convention deals in war crimes," said Duke. "This here ain't no war crime. It's frontier justice. Anybody here disagree?"

"Not me," said Doc.

"Nor me," said Bushrod.

Chief just grunted his approval. Then all four sets of eyes swiveled until they focused on Swifty.

"Well, Swifty," said Bushrod. "What's your vote?"

"This is about family justice, not the legal system," said Swifty. "Count me in."

CHAPTER FORTY-FIVE

After breakfast the next morning, the five men went out to the supply tent. Swifty had pulled out a bale of hay and stood it up on one end. Then he attached a paper plate to the hay bale near the top with some long nails. When he was done, he stepped back to face the small group of old Green Berets.

Swifty walked back about fifteen yards to another bale of hay where he had placed a tray full of dart guns and old empty darts. He picked up a gun and an empty dart. Then he demonstrated how the dart gun worked and how to load it and shoot it. He repeated the process to make sure its operation was clear to the four men.

Then, Swifty had each of the four old Green Berets pick up a dart gun and an empty dart and demonstrate how to load it. He had each of them do this five times until it became almost automatic.

Then Swifty had each of the four men come up to him, one at a time, and pick up a dart gun and an empty dart. On Swifty's command, they loaded the dart into the dart gun and cocked the gun. Then each man pulled the dart gun to their shoulders, aimed it, and fired it at the paper plate. Swifty had each man fire six darts at the target. By the third dart, the old Green Berets were hitting the paper plate dead center.

Satisfied with their accuracy, Swifty gave them a short lecture about handling the dart gun with a loaded dart. "A loaded dart gun is just like any loaded gun and I'm not worried about you guys screwing it up," said Swifty. "But the part where you have to be careful is when handling the dart and then loading it into the gun. You must be careful not to jab yourself with the sharp end of the dart. Remember, this is going to be at night. It will be dark. There will be no light. You will be relying on night vision optics. All of you have used these optics when on night-time operations. Your advantage is you can see, and they can't. If for any reason somebody pops on the lights, quickly remove the optics and use your eyes to make your shots. Any questions?"

There were none and they spent the next two hours simulating moving to the target points, entering them, and then moving in the bunk areas to insure they shot each target as swiftly and quietly as possible. When they finished the drills, they broke for lunch.

Lunch was powdered lemonade and ham and cheese sandwiches, and the five hungry men made short work of the thick sandwiches.

Bushrod appeared with a pitcher of the lemonade and a small flask of whiskey. He refilled each man's glass and added a shot of the bourbon.

While the men sipped on their home-made cocktails, Swifty went over the plan again and in slow, meticulous detail. Then he asked each man questions about their role in the operation. Finally, he asked for their responses to things going wrong and possible changes to the plan. When he was finished, he was satisfied they all understood not only their roles, but the roles of everyone else in the team.

Swifty raised his glass and took a swig of his bourbon laced lemonade. He set his glass on the table and looked around the table at each of the men.

"Any questions?" asked Swifty.

Duke raised his hand.

"You have a question, Duke?" asked Swifty.

"I sure do. What the hell does a man have to do to get a decent drink in this godforsaken place?"

Everyone laughed, and Bushrod pushed the pitcher of lemonade and the flask of whisky over to Duke.

"We have some duties to perform and some items to procure in the next two days," said Swifty. "Is everyone clear on what they need to do?"

As Swifty looked around the table, everyone nodded their assent. They were all on board and ready to finish their raid preparation tasks.

Swifty stayed in the cabin to help Bushrod with the dishes and cleanup while the other three old Green Berets slipped outside and disappeared from sight as they headed out on their assignments.

When he and Bushrod finished with the dishes, Swifty hung his dishtowel on a hook to dry and he and Bushrod went out to the front porch. As they got to the porch steps leading down to the ground, Bushrod put his hand on Swifty's shoulder.

"Remember Swifty, once we start this thing, there ain't no turnin' back," said Bushrod.

"I've known that from the day I came up here looking to find a grandfather I thought was dead," replied Swifty.

CHAPTER FORTY-SIX

Swifty was up at five the next morning. He rolled out of his sleeping bag and smelled the scent of freshly brewed coffee. By the time Swifty had crawled out of his sleeping bag and gotten dressed, he was surrounded by sleepy men looking for hot coffee and food.

Breakfast was eaten quickly and in almost complete silence. Every man had jobs to accomplish and a limited time to get them completed.

Swifty helped wash up the breakfast dishes and headed for the front door of the small cabin.

"Where are you headed?" asked Bushrod.

"I'm headed to Meeteetse to see my aunt. I have some questions concerning our mission and she's a very reliable source of information when it comes to the Hayfork Ranch," replied Swifty.

"When can I expect you back here?" asked Bushrod.

"Tonight, or tomorrow morning at the latest," responded Swifty.

"See you then," said Bushrod. "Be careful out there."

"Always," responded Swifty and he left the cabin. Ten minutes later he was pulling onto the highway and headed toward Cody. When he arrived in Cody, he pulled into the parking lot of an office supply store. When he exited the store, he was carrying a new small portable printer with printing and paper supplies. He put his purchases on the back seat and climbed into his truck. He pulled out of the lot and headed for Meeteetse.

Half an hour later he was parking just off the main drag in Meeteetse and locking his truck. He walked down the old wooden sidewalk to his aunt's store. When he pushed open the store's front door, a tiny bell chimed.

Swifty stopped after entering the store and turned around and looked up. Sure enough. Up above the door was a tiny photo-electric cell device that hadn't been there before. He turned around and had barely gotten to the middle of the store when his Aunt Judy appeared from a back room. There was no door to the room, only a curtain.

His Aunt Judy gave him a hug and then led him over to the old drug store counter where there were stools on one side. Swifty took a stool, while his aunt went behind the counter and quickly poured two large mugs of hot, fresh coffee. She slid one mug across the countertop to Swifty and took a sip out of her mug. Swifty followed suit. To a Swede, drinking coffee was like breathing air. It was a necessity and Swifty did it automatically without giving it a thought.

"What brings you to Meeteetse?" asked his aunt.

"I'm doing a little research and I needed to see an expert on the subject," replied Swifty.

"Who's the expert?" asked his aunt.

"You are," replied Swifty.

"What's the subject?" she asked with a surprised look on her face.

"The Hayfork Ranch," said Swifty.

"What about the ranch?" she asked.

"If you have a place I can plug in a portable printer, I can tell you and show you," replied Swifty.

"There's an electrical outlet on my side of the counter," said Aunt Judy.

"I'll go get the printer," said Swifty. He rose from his stool and left the store.

A few minutes later, he returned with a bag and a box. He set them on the counter and produced his laptop computer from a bag. Then he pulled the small printer from the box and set it up. He plugged the printer into the outlet on the side of the counter.

After he turned on the laptop and made a few keystrokes, the small printer whirred into life. Swifty produced paper and loaded the printer and tested it. Then he took out a pad of paper, a pen, and a yellow highlighter and laid them on the bar.

He did a quick search on his laptop and clicked on the laptop keyboard until he pulled up an aerial photo of the buildings grouped together on the Hayfork Ranch. He turned the laptop so his Aunt Judy could clearly see the screen.

"Is that the Hayfork Ranch?" she asked after studying the screen.

"The one and only," replied Swifty. "Do you recognize the buildings?"

Aunt Judy studied the screen and then responded to his question. "I do. Every year the ranch invites the folks in Meeteetse out for a day visit with a barbeque lunch. I've been to the last three of them and have taken the walking tour each time," said Aunt Judy.

Swifty hit a key and the little printer spit out a copy of the image on the laptop screen. Swifty took the image and slid it in front of his aunt. He took the pen and pointed to one of the buildings. "What's this building?" he asked his aunt.

"That's the main ranch house," replied his aunt. Swifty wrote on the printout labeling the building.

"Which of the buildings is the bunkhouse?" asked Swifty.

His aunt pointed to a long narrow building, and Swifty labeled it with his pen.

"Which building is the residence for the ranch foremen?" asked Swifty.

His aunt pointed out a building, and Swifty used his pen to label it.

One by one, Swifty went through all the buildings in the printout and labeled them after his aunt identified them.

When he had gone through all the buildings, Swifty asked, "Are there any sleeping quarters other than the bunkhouse, the foremen's house, and the main house?"

His aunt studied the printout and shook her head no.

"Do you know who sleeps in the main house?" asked Swifty.

"I'm pretty sure the main house is only used when the owners stay there," replied Aunt Judy. "They only come a few times a year. They only come in the summer or fall, never in the winter. When they come, they bring some help with them while they are on the ranch."

"What kind of help?" asked Swifty.

"I think they bring a cook and a maid," said Aunt Judy.

"They also bring a couple of big tough looking guys who they call assistants, but they look like bodyguards to me."

"So, no other buildings on the ranch are used for sleeping quarters?" asked Swifty.

"No, I'm sure of it," said Aunt Judy.

"Why are you so sure?" asked Swifty.

"The previous owner had a few cabins he rented out to city folks. People who were dudes and wanted to have a dude ranch experience. The state shut him down for all kinds of safety violations and that was the end of that," said Aunt Judy. "I think the cabins were these four little things here," she said as she pointed to four small shed-like structures setting in a row on the edge of the ranch building area.

"Are there any other structures on other parts of the ranch?" asked Swifty.

"Not that I'm aware of," replied Aunt Judy. "There might be some old line shacks on isolated parts of the ranch, but I doubt any have been used in years and they'd be in bad shape. Winters here are tough on old uninsulated wooden shacks. I've seen one or two hay storage places, but they are just a roof over a concrete floor with no sides or anything else."

Swifty studied the picture carefully until he was satisfied his aunt had helped him identify the use of each and every building structure on the ranch grounds. Then he turned and smiled at his aunt.

"You've been very helpful, and I really appreciate you taking the time to go over this with me," said Swifty.

"I'm always glad to help my favorite nephew," said a smiling Aunt Judy.

"One out of two ain't bad," responded Swifty with a grin.

"Have you heard from your brother?" asked Aunt Judy.

"Not since the day he packed his stuff and left, one day after he graduated from Cody High School," replied Swifty.

"I'm kind of surprised he never came home for your dad's funeral," said Aunt Judy.

"So was I," replied Swifty. "But I figured he probably never got the news Dad had passed."

"You're probably right," said Aunt Judy. "Still, it's a shame. I know it made it a little harder on your mother."

"I'm sure it did, but that's water over the dam now," said Swifty.

"Is there anything else I can help you with?" asked Aunt Judy. "We'd love to have you come over for supper soon," she hinted.

"Maybe later," responded Swifty. "I've got kind of a full plate right now."

"Doing what?" asked his ever-inquisitive aunt.

Swifty looked over at his aunt. He'd never been good at fooling her. She was too smart and too perceptive.

"I'd tell you, but then I'd have to shoot you," he said with a poker face.

"That's pure baloney and you know it, Swifty," said Aunt Judy.

"Let's just say you're better off not knowing anything about what I'm up to," said Swifty with a serious note in his voice.

His aunt studied Swifty's face. Then she said, "Maybe so, but when whatever you got planned is over, I expect a full accounting from my favorite nephew."

Swifty got to his feet. "I promise," he said. Then he gathered up his equipment and took it out to his truck. His aunt followed him. He gave her a big hug and a kiss on the cheek.

"You be careful out there?" said his Aunt Judy with a warning tone in her voice.

"I'm always careful except for the times I forget," said a smiling Swifty.

He started the engine of his truck and soon was heading down the highway back to Cody.

CHAPTER FORTY-SEVEN

Swifty stopped in Cody to gas up his truck. He then stopped at the grocery store and did a bit of shopping. Then he placed his purchases in the bed of the truck and headed back to his grandfather's place.

About five miles north of Cody, Swifty's cell phone rang. He glanced at the screen to see who was calling. Then he slowed the truck, pulled off on the side of the highway, and stopped the truck. He hit the answer button on his phone.

"Ain't you got nothing better to do than bother honest people in the middle of the day," said Swifty.

"I know lots of honest people, and you ain't one of them," retorted Kit.

"So why are you botherin' me when there's so many other folks in the world who are honest?" asked Swifty.

"Because I need your permission to do something," replied Kit.

"What in the hell do you need my permission to do. As I recall, you ain't never asked for my permission to do anything before?" asked Swifty.

"I need your permission to hire a professional team to

do an extensive mineral search on your mother's ranch," responded Kit.

"To do what?" said a surprised Swifty.

"You heard me, you dumbass. I need your permission to hire a team to do a search of your mom's ranch for those rare earth minerals we talked about," said Kit.

Swifty thought for a minute and then he replied. "It's fine with me if it's fine with my mom. You need to talk to her."

"I was planning to, but I wanted to make sure you were all right with the idea before I made the call to her," replied Kit.

"I got no problem with it," said Swifty. "I'm just kicking myself for not thinking of it myself."

"Well, this ain't the first time and it won't be the last," replied Kit. "Are you making any progress on finding your dad's killer?" he asked.

"None I can tell you about if you plan on staying out of jail," replied Swifty.

"The only jail I've been in is the old territorial prison museum in Laramie and I have no desire to improve on that experience," said Kit.

"I hear breaking out of jail is a lot of fun," said Swifty.

"You need your hearing checked, along with most of your worthless hide," said Kit.

"Same to you. Talk to you later," said Swifty as he disconnected the call. He put his phone away and drove back onto the highway.

Swifty checked his phone for a number and when he found it, he pressed the button to call.

He could hear the phone ring and then a female voice answered.

"Sheriff's office, Melinda speaking," she said.

"Melinda, it's Swifty Olson," he said.

"How the hell are you, cowboy?" asked Melinda. "Since that big fight at the bar you seem to have disappeared."

"I've been busy," said Swifty, "but I'm still around and still trying to find out who killed my old man and why."

"I've heard nothing," volunteered Melinda.

"I'm not surprised," said Swifty. "Look, I need a favor."

"Oh boy, that can only mean trouble with a capital T," sighed Melinda. "O.K., what the hell is the favor?"

"I heard a rumor that something strange is going on out at the Hayfork Ranch," said Swifty.

"Strange like what?" asked Melinda.

"I can't say because I'm not totally sure," responded Swifty.

"What's that got to do with me?" asked a puzzled Melinda.

"I think those two dudes from New York who own the Haystack Ranch might be flying into Cody real soon," said Swifty.

"I've heard of those two rich assholes," said Melinda. "The sheriff usually has his nose up their butts."

"It'd be worth a hundred bucks if I was to get a text when they arrive in Cody," said Swifty.

"Why would you want to know that?" asked Melinda.

Swifty said nothing, knowing how Melinda would interpret his silence.

"I see," said Melinda. "Well, I sure could use a hundred bucks. Give me your cell phone number."

Swifty rattled off his number, then he repeated it to make sure Melinda had it down correctly.

"Got it," said Melinda.

"I owe you," said Swifty.

"You probably owe me more than a hundred bucks, but I'll settle for that," said Melinda slyly.

"Thanks," said Swifty and he broke the connection. A few minutes later he was driving north out of Cody. On the way, he called his mother and told her to expect a call from Kit, and why.

After Swifty was finished, he paused. "Do you have any questions, Mom?" he asked.

"No, I don't. I trust you and know you're working hard to help me out now that Eldon is gone," she said. "Is your friend Kit coming, too. I hope so. I so look forward to meeting him after hearing so much about him from you," she said.

"I'm not sure, Mom," replied Swifty. "I know the exploration team is coming, but they'll call and let you know when to expect them."

"Please take care of yourself and come home as soon as you can," she said.

"I will, Mom, I promise," said Swifty and then he disconnected the call.

Swifty brushed the edges of his eyes with his fingers. They came away wet. Talking to his mother had been more emotional than Swifty realized. He shook his head as if to clear his brain and accelerated the truck to about five miles per hour over the legal speed limit in Wyoming.

By the time Swifty returned to his grandfather's place, it was late in the afternoon. As he drove along the narrow road, he came to a clearing on one side where Bushrod had built a makeshift firing range. As he eased past the range on the bumpy dirt road, he saw Chief, Doc, and Duke taking turns firing at targets. He waved to them, and they waved back. When he reached the old ranch house, he parked the truck and walked over to the camouflage covered compound.

When Swifty entered Bushrod's cabin, the old man was sharpening a large combat knife at the small dining table.

Bushrod looked up from his work and smiled at his grandson. "So, you managed to hang on to your scalp for another day," he said with a twinkle in his eyes.

Swifty ran his fingers through his thick hair as if testing to see if Bushrod was correct. "Yep, it's still all there," he said.

Swifty took a rickety chair at the table and placed his laptop computer case on the scarred tabletop.

"How is your Aunt Judy?" asked Bushrod.

"Feisty and as nosey as ever," said Swifty. "She was very helpful. She knows a lot about the ranch layout, but she kept digging at me to find out what we are up to and why I needed this information about the Hayfork Ranch."

"What did you tell her?" asked Bushrod.

"I told her I could tell her but then I'd have to kill her," said Swifty.

"I bet that didn't slow her down one iota," said Bushrod.

"You'd be right as you usually are," responded Swifty.

"So, what did you learn?" asked Bushrod as he sat at the table and pointed at the still closed laptop.

Swifty opened the bag and took out the photos and printouts he had made and spread them out on the tabletop.

"Appears to be the layout of the Hayfork Ranch," said Bushrod.

"It most certainly is," said Swifty. Then he began briefing Bushrod on everything he had learned from his Aunt Judy and one by one he pointed to each building and explained its use on the ranch.

Bushrod studied the photos and listened to Swifty as he stroked his chin. "It appears to me there are only three sleeping quarters on the ranch," he said.

"That's correct," responded Swifty. "The main bunkhouse is here, the foreman's quarters are here, and the main house is here." Swifty moved his index finger to point to each building as he described it.

"Are they all currently being used?" asked Bushrod.

"It seems only the owners and their guests use the main ranch house when they visit. Any other time only the bunkhouse and the foreman's quarters are used," said Swifty.

"If we pull off the raid and kidnap all the hands, how will we know if the owners are coming and when?" asked Bushrod.

"I've got an old friend at the sheriff's office and she'll call me if the owners are coming in. She told me the owners always call the sheriff just before a visit to make sure they get special treatment at the airport and at the ranch," said Swifty.

"That was smart of you," said Bushrod. "I was wondering how we were gonna know if them rich boys were gonna take the bait and fly out here."

"Did we get a car to set up as a Wyoming National Guard vehicle," asked Swifty.

"We did better than that," said Bushrod. "Chief found an old sedan the guard just traded in at the Ford dealer in Cody. It still has the army paint job and army markings on it."

"How did he get his hands on it?" asked Swifty.

Bushrod looked at his grandson and slowly shook his head side to side. "He stole it. I told you he was a damn Commanche."

"If it's old and beat up, will it pass as an official National Guard car?" asked Swifty.

"Chief went to some detail shop run by a Ute he knows and had him clean it up. The old Junker looks almost damn respectable," said Bushrod.

"Anything else?" asked Swifty.

"I could use some help with dinner if you're done with your executive duties," said Bushrod.

"What do you need me to do?" asked Swifty.

CHAPTER FORTY-EIGHT

Bushrod and Swifty had just about finished preparing a supper of pork chops, potatoes and gravy when the other three old Green Berets came filing in through the cabin door.

"What's for supper?" bellowed Duke.

"More of Chief's damn wild hog," replied Bushrod in an even louder voice.

The five men sat down to supper and attacked the food placed in front of them. Unlike most of their meals, this one was eaten mostly in silence. There were a few comments, a few friendly insults, but conversation was kept to a minimum.

When supper was over, everyone, even Duke, pitched in and the table was cleared, the dishes were washed and put away, and then the men returned to the table.

Swifty brought his printouts and outlines to the table. He placed a small box at the far end of the table and placed his largest satellite photo of the Hayfork Ranch on it. Everyone at the table had a good view of the photo.

"This is our objective," said Swifty. "We'll approach the ranch from two directions. Chief will drive my pickup truck south to Meeteetse and then west to a point one mile from the entrance to the ranch." He used a pen like a pointer to highlight the location where Chief was to wait parked in the truck.

"The rest of us will drive to a spot in a clump of woods located on the north side of the county road that intersects with the paved road just east of the ranch. We park two vehicles there, out of sight," said Swifty. "Once there, we will advance on foot through the trees to the ranch. We cross the fence and continue on foot to the ranch headquarters. This will be a hike of about three miles. I estimate the travel time to be slightly more than one hour. We will be hiking at night, with no lights. If we encounter anyone during the hike, we will neutralize them and bring them with us to the ranch. Any questions so far?"

Duke raised his hand. "When you say neutralize them, do you mean like what we did in Vietnam or what you did in the Middle East?"

Swifty grinned. "My mistake," he said. "The object of this mission is to render everyone we encounter unconscious and under the influence of a tranquilizer dart. Our object is not to harm or kill anyone on this mission. Is that perfectly clear?"

The four old Green Berets looked at each other and all nodded their agreement with Swifty's point.

"When we reach the outskirts of the ranch buildings, Bushrod will make radio contact with Chief and let him know we are in position. Chief will then start the engine on his truck and wait for our call," said Swifty. "It that clear to everyone?"

Again, the four old veterans nodded agreement.

"We determine our location on the ranch photo and

then divide into two teams. Bushrod and I move quietly to the bunkhouse, while Duke and Doc move to the foreman's quarters. When we are ready, Bushrod and I will enter the bunkhouse and shoot each occupant with a tranquilizer dart. When we are finished, we will flick the interior lights on and off twice. That will be the signal for Doc and Duke to enter the foreman's quarters and tranquilize them," said Swifty.

"When everyone in both buildings has been tranquilized, each team will check to make sure everyone in their target area is unconscious and no one is hiding in the restroom or some other area of the building. When each building has been swept and each target has been checked, we'll meet outside the bunkhouse. Is this clear so far?" asked Swifty.

Again, the four old warriors nodded yes.

"Then Bushrod will call Chief on his cell and Chief will drive the truck onto the ranch and up to this equipment area," said Swifty, using his pen to point to the equipment area on the photo. "Chief will hitch up a four-horse trailer and then drive to the bunkhouse. Once there, we will drag the unconscious targets out of the bunkhouse and place plastic ties on their hands and feet. Then we will load them into the trailer. Once done, we move the trailer to the foreman's quarters and do the same to the unconscious targets there. Are there any questions?"

"What if we have a runner?" asked Doc.

Swifty frowned. It was a good question. On a raid like the one planned, someone was always where they shouldn't be and created a problem. They could be in the bathroom or sitting outside sneaking a smoke. Whatever the reason, it happened, and it happened often.

"When we finish tranquilizing both buildings, we do a sweep of the buildings," said Swifty. "If there is a runner, we track them down, tranquilize and restrain them and toss them in the horse trailer."

Swifty looked at the four grim and serious faces sitting around the small table. "Anything else?" he asked.

He was greeted with silence this time.

"When all the targets are accounted for and loaded into the horse trailer, Chief will drive the truck and trailer out the front gate of the ranch. Then on to Meeteetse and then north to Cody and up to Bushrod's place," said Swifty.

"You are to maintain radio silence all the way back to Bushrod's place. Chief is that clear?" asked Swifty.

"Yup," said the Chief.

"The rest of us will police the area and make sure we've left nothing behind," said Swifty. "Then we will hike back to our hidden trucks and use them to return to Bushrod's place. Any questions, gentlemen?"

"What's the time-line for this caper?" asked Doc.

"The assault is set for 0300," said Swifty. "We leave wooded area about 0200. Chief drives to his spot outside the ranch by 0230."

"When are we planning to hold this party?" asked Duke.

"In my experience, the best day for an attack like this is a Wednesday. The best time is 0300," said Swifty. "Any disagreement with the day or the times?"

"Nope, the times and the day sound good to me," said Bushrod.

"The next Wednesday is two days away," said Doc. "Do we go this Wednesday?"

"I think we're ready so this Wednesday works for me," replied Swifty.

"I agree with that," said Bushrod.

"So do I," said Duke.

The Chief just sat in his chair and his face broke into a rare grin. "Good time to hunt," he said.

"Wednesday it is," said Swifty.

"Tomorrow we should do a dry run and an equipment check," said Bushrod.

"How about right after breakfast?" asked Swifty.

"Works for me," said Duke.

"Same here," said Doc.

"Let's get some sack time," said Bushrod. "We got a full day tomorrow and a lot to get done."

The five men rose from the table and wandered off to their respective sleeping pallets. Ten minutes later the lights were out, and some disorganized snoring broke out.

CHAPTER FORTY-NINE

After breakfast, everyone helped clean up and then they assembled in front of the cabin.

Bushrod had taken several empty cardboard boxes and arranged them on the ground in front of the old cabin. He had placed them the approximate distance apart that the men's target buildings would be on the ranch.

"Let's see how we will carry out this mission," he said. Then he, Doc, Swifty, and Duke moved to the end of the improvised compound of the ranch. Using only hand signals, Bushrod and Swifty advanced quickly, but silently, until they reached the box designating the bunkhouse. Duke and Doc moved silently to the box designating the foreman's quarters. At a hand signal from Bushrod, the two teams entered the grassy area behind the cardboard boxes and proceeded to go through the motions of firing their dart guns and reloading, moving and shooting again, until they had subdued all of the estimated imaginary inhabitants.

They repeated this exercise several times, each exercise ending with Chief pulling up to the area in Swifty's pickup truck. Finally, it was time to break for lunch. At the lunch table while eating a grilled Spam sandwich, Swifty had an idea.

He put down his sandwich and tapped his metal coffee cup on the table until the other men looked up at him.

"I've got an idea," said Swifty. "Can you, Doc, and Duke all ride a bicycle?" he asked Bushrod.

"Of course," replied Bushrod after looking at Duke and Doc, who were nodding their heads in assent.

"From the fence by grove of trees where we will be leaving our truck to the target area is almost five miles," said Swifty. To illustrate his point, he took out his topo map and spread it out on the table. He used his finger to point out where the team would be starting from and then traced it along the road from that pasture to the headquarters area of the Hayfork Ranch. "If we used bikes, we could make the trip in less than an hour, maybe in forty-five minutes," he said.

Bushrod looked at the map. "Remember we are moving at night and not using any lights. Seems to me it'd be really easy to have a simple wreck on the way, and that would screw up our plan. Our only backup is Chief, and his job is to serve on overwatch duty," said Bushrod.

"We could wear our new NVDs," said Swifty. "Using bikes is much faster, and it makes it easier on us with packs and a weapon."

"Where the hell are we gonna get bikes one day before the mission?" asked Duke.

"I'll run into Cody," said Swifty. "There are several places renting bikes to tourists there. Renting four bikes would seem normal and not unusual, so we'd raise no suspicion."

"Sounds like a plan to me," said Doc.

"Me, too," said Duke

"Go get the bikes but get back here as fast as you can," said Bushrod.

"I'm on my way," said Swifty, as he tossed the remains of his Spam sandwich on the table and headed out the door.

Ten minutes later Swifty was driving onto the highway and headed for Cody at the speed limit. As soon as he had cell service, he called Ann.

"Is something wrong?" Ann said when she answered his call.

"Nope, nothing's wrong," said Swifty. "I just had an idea, and I need your help."

"Let's hear it," said Ann.

"I need you to rent me four mountain bikes for two days and pick them up for me, so they're at your office when I get there," said Swifty.

"Mountain bikes?" asked a surprised Ann.

"Yes. Mountain bikes," said Swifty.

"For men or women?" said Ann sweetly.

"Very funny," said Swifty. "Men's mountain bikes."

"They'll be here when you get here," said Ann and she hung up.

Swifty replaced his phone in his pocket and pushed the accelerator down, pushing five miles an hour over the posted speed limit.

When Swifty pulled into the small parking lot behind Ann's office, he saw her truck parked, but there were no bikes in the bed it. Then he got out of his truck and saw the four bikes leaning against the side of the back wall of her office building.

Before he got to the bikes, Ann stepped out of the back door of her office.

"Thanks for getting the bikes for me," said Swifty.

"I did a little better than you asked," said Ann.

"What do you mean?" asked Swifty.

"I got electric bikes," she said with a grin on her face.

"Electric bikes?" asked a surprised Swifty.

"Yep, electric bikes," said Ann. "They have a small battery, and they charge when you peddle them, but they can self-propel themselves for quite a while. I figured you old timers could use all the help you could get."

Swifty looked at her in amazement. He had never thought of electric powered bikes. Not only would they save the team's energy, they would be silent.

"Thank you, Ann. This is really a big help," said Swifty.

"You'll be getting a bill, Cowboy," said Ann with a smirk on her face. "Try to return them in one piece or your bill is going to be really high."

"I promise," said Swifty.

He and Ann loaded the bikes into the bed of his truck. Then Ann gave him an instruction book and a quick tutorial on using the electric bikes. When they were finished, she stood to the side to give him room to get to the cab of his truck. He put his hands on her shoulders and pulled her into him and gave her a long, lingering kiss. Then he released her and stepped up into his truck.

Swifty waved to her as he left her small parking lot and roared down the street, heading north out of Cody.

CHAPTER FIFTY

A little over an hour later, Swifty was pulling up in front of the old cabin on Bushrod's place. He shut off the engine, got out and proceeded to unload the four electric bicycles. He leaned the bikes up against the old porch. Then he pulled out the instruction manual and sat down on the steps of the rickety old porch. He began reading and was so intent, he didn't hear the footsteps approaching him. When he did, he looked up and saw the four old Green Berets approaching.

He returned to his reading until he was finished. Then he looked up at the faces of four very puzzled old men.

"What in the blue blazes are these funny lookin' bikes for?" asked Duke.

Swifty stood up and faced the four old men. "These are four of the latest electric bicycles in the world," he said. "In the next hour, Bushrod, you, Doc, and I are going to learn how to be silent cavalry."

"Silent cavalry? What the hell do electric bicycles have to do with silent cavalry?" asked Bushrod.

"It's a little over three miles to the ranch headquarters from the fence line just past that grove of trees," said Swifty. "That's more than a long stroll, for four old men at night, carrying plenty of gear. These bikes can carry us and our loads easily. They run on batteries when you're not peddling, and we can mount portable GPS units on the handlebars."

Doc strode over to the bikes and picked it up, testing the weight. Then he examined the handlebars and fenders. "You want us to ride these contraptions in the dark? Hell, we'll all be casualties in the first couple of miles."

"We use these," said Swifty, as he held up one of the NVDs. When you turn your head, the lighted view turns with it."

"This idea is so stupid it might actually work," said Bushrod.

"Where'd you get these contraptions?" asked Duke. "I never heard of electric bikes."

"Ann, my veterinarian friend, rented them for us. Try not to bust them up, or we'll be buying them, not renting them," said Swifty.

"I ain't been on a bike since I was about fifteen," said Bushrod.

"Me neither," said Doc.

"No time like the present to get reacquainted," said Swifty.

"What the hell," said Duke, "It's a pony with wheels. Let me have one of those damn things."

Swifty and the other three men each took a bike. Then Swifty pulled out the manual and prepared to give a fast lesson on how to use and ride the bicycles.

Chief sat down on the old porch with his back to a post and stared at the spectacle in front of him.

Swifty noticed the Chief's puzzled look. "What do you think, Chief?" he asked.

"I think white men are plumb crazy," said the Chief without cracking a smile.

"No time like the present to find out," said Swifty.

He had the other three Green Berets line up with their respective bikes. Then he went through the manual making sure the old men knew where the brakes, steering, gears, and battery transfer switches were. Then Swifty conducted a drill for each of them.

He had each Green Beret stand in front with his bike. When Swifty yelled out a part, each of the old Green Berets were forced to point to the part. He made them do it three times until he was satisfied they understood all the components of the bike and where they were located.

Next Swifty had them mount their bikes, one at a time and demonstrate how to ride and shift them and change to battery power and back to manual peddling. The four men rode the bikes back and forth over the flat ground and then ventured over some small hills where they were forced to use the gears for the uphill segments.

After forty minutes, Swifty called a halt to the exercise. The four men dismounted from their bikes and leaned them up against the porch of the old cabin.

Swifty looked up at Chief who hadn't budged from his spot. "What do you think, Chief. Will the bikes do the job?" he asked.

Chief nodded his head. Then he spoke. "I think I can cobble together some crude saddlebags so there is less weight in the packs and the bikes will be more balanced," said Chief.

"How soon can you get it done?" asked Swifty.

Chief looked up at the sun and shaded his eyes. "I can have them ready by suppertime," he said.

"That sounds good to me," said Swifty. "We need to use tomorrow to check all our gear and get loaded up for the trip to our rendezvous site tomorrow night. Having these bikes means we can leave the rendezvous site on the bikes about 0200. That allows an hour for travel to the ranch headquarters."

"Let's make it 0145, just to be safe," said Bushrod.

"0145 it is," said Swifty. "I'd tell you guys to hit the hay early, but you're old and will probably take a nap tomorrow anyway," he said.

This announcement was met with catcalls and boos and various pieces of spare equipment cascaded in Swifty's general direction.

Swifty ran around the corner of the old cabin with four old Green Berets in hot pursuit.

CHAPTER FIFTY-ONE

Supper that night was light and quick. After the dishes were washed and put away, the five men walked over to a small sand table Bushrod had erected. On the sand table was a small mockup of the Hayfork Ranch headquarters area. Each building was represented by a small block of wood. One by one, each man stood and identified each of the buildings including the bunkhouse and the foreman's quarters. They also identified the location of the four-horse trailer they would be using.

They did this mock-up study five times. Then they each stood to identify their rallying point and the exit route they would be taking. Each of the five men led a study and peppered the others with questions. One of the questions was alternative exit routes, and they had developed three. Two hours later, they were finished.

By ten o'clock that night, every man had slid into his sleeping bag, and it was lights out.

By sunrise the next morning, every man was up and within an hour, they had been fed, cleaned up the area, and were each checking and re-checking their personal gear and testing anything with a battery. Each of them carried extra batteries in case of a power failure.

About noon, Swifty left the camp and drove about ten miles south until he got a decent signal for his cell phone. He called his aunt and got a weather report and an estimated head count of Hayfork Ranch hands likely to be staying at the ranch that night. She promised to stay at the store that night and watch the road to get an estimate of hands who left the ranch. Swifty would call her about midnight, and then she would head for home.

The day seemed to crawl by for Swifty. The four old Green Berets each managed to snag a nap in a cool, dark spot in Bushrod's place. Swifty admired their cool and their ability to take advantage of down time. They were veterans of war and wasted no energy unnecessarily.

Chief finished his modified bike saddlebags and after a few adjustments they fit snugly behind the bicycle seats.

At midnight, Chief left the camp in Swifty's pickup truck. Swifty saw him toss in a light rucksack, an M-16, and a crossbow. He wore a combat vest stuffed with magazines of .223 ammo. His outfit included a worn canvas shirt, jeans, and old combat boots. On his head, he wore a battered straw cowboy hat.

Ten minutes later, Swifty and the other three Green Berets piled into Doc's truck, the four electric bikes riding obediently in the bed of the truck. They were dressed casually like Chief. They also wore combat boots like Chief.

At 0100 they were at the rendezvous site. Swifty had picked a place he knew well. On the state highway to the Hayford Ranch was a junction with a county road. The road was gravel and veered to the southwest toward other smaller ranches. There was a large stand of pine trees about three miles down the gravel road. The north edge of the grove butted up against the fence line separating the land from the Hayfork Ranch. The night was cool, the sky partly cloudy. There was less than a quarter moon. Swifty drove the truck well into the grove of pine trees and parked it. After they arrived, the four men quickly changed clothes to all black. On their heads they wore black hockey helmets with the red lights attached. They all checked their gear and triple counted everything. When they were satisfied, they leaned back against the truck and waited. Swifty called his aunt, and she reported that two pickup trucks she recognized as belonging to hands at the Hayfork Ranch had driven in from the ranch about eight o'clock and headed toward Cody. Swifty thanked her and told her to go home and get a good night's sleep. She laughed and hung up. "Two less hands to deal with was fine with him," thought Swifty.

At 0145, they eased the bikes over the fence and then climbed over it. With Swifty in the lead, they mounted their bikes and soon were peddling in single file, each man following the bike in front of him. Swifty glanced at his GPS and soon he found the fairly visible ranch dirt road. He checked the GPS every five minutes and was pleased to see they were right on target heading for the headquarters area of the Hayfork Ranch.

It took the team exactly forty-one minutes to reach their rallying point at the edge of the ranch building complex. There had been no incidents and no noise on the entire ride in from the fence line. They had startled the hell out of a small group of cows, but other than that there were no incidents. They neither saw nor heard anyone during their ride.

The four men dismounted their bikes. They walked their bikes and hid them in a small grove of trees. After retrieving their small packs from the home-made bike saddlebags, each man did an equipment check. When they had finished, each man shouldered a pack, extracted his dart gun, and loaded it with a full needle cartridge.

Using only hand signals, Bushrod led the other men forward. They moved single file, as they silently flowed over the terrain, their small head lights replaced by night vision goggles. When they reached the ranch foreman's quarters, Bushrod signaled to Doc and Duke and they both went to one knee to wait. Bushrod silently led Swifty to the larger bunkhouse. The two men crept up to the door, each standing on either side of the bunkhouse entrance. They were both checking their weapons prior to entering the bunkhouse. The bunkhouse door suddenly swung open. A very sleepy cowboy with an urge for a tobacco fix he could not ignore stepped out of the bunkhouse. He was in the process of pulling a cigarette out of a pack when Bushrod shot a dart into the cowboy's upper back, just below his neck. The cowboy took a somewhat puzzled step forward and started to raise his hand when he pitched forward off the small front porch of the bunkhouse and was out like a light.

Swifty knelt by the fallen cowboy and checked his pulse while Bushrod reloaded his dart gun. When the gun was reloaded Bushrod nodded at Swifty. Swifty quietly opened the door to the bunkhouse and the two black-clad figures entered in single file.

Once inside, Swifty went to the right and Bushrod went

to the left. Simultaneously they approached the first bunk on their side, found a suitable target and fired a tranquilizer dart at their target. Then each man reloaded and moved to the next bunk. They found eleven bunks occupied. When every occupant in the bunkhouse was accounted for, the two men slipped out the front door as quietly as they had entered.

Once outside the bunkhouse and at the foot of the small porch, Bushrod stood upright and gave a hand signal to Doc and Duke. Doc returned the hand signal, and he and Duke silently made their way up to the door of the foreman's quarters. Once there, each man stood on either side of the door with their backs to the wall of the building.

When Swifty and Bushrod reached the front of the foreman's quarters, they took up protective positions and Bushrod gave Doc a hand signal. Doc and Duke then slipped inside and less than five minutes later they were back outside and joined Swifty and Bushrod.

"Everything go all right?" asked Bushrod.

"Slicker than snot on a brass doorknob," replied Doc.

"How many?" asked Bushrod.

Doc held up two fingers.

"The bunkhouse?" asked Doc.

Bushrod held up one finger on one hand and two fingers on the other.

"Less than we thought," said Doc.

"Any problems?" asked Duke.

"We got surprised by one cowboy coming out for a late-night smoke, but he is now conveniently asleep at the foot of the porch stairs," said Bushrod.

"One less we have to carry out of the bunkhouse," said a grinning Duke.

Swifty pulled out his phone and texted Chief. He waited and got a quick response.

"He's on his way in," said Swifty as he pocketed his phone.

"Let's get these two galoots out of this place and then head down to the bunkhouse and tend to them boys," said Bushrod.

It took only a few minutes to drag the two limp bodies out of the foreman's quarters and out in front of the building. Duke used snap ties to tie the unconscious cowboys' hands behind them and tie their feet together.

While he was doing that, Bushrod, Swifty and Doc returned to the bunkhouse and were soon dragging the limp bodies of the drugged cowboys out of the building and onto the ground outside. When they were done, Duke joined them, and they used snap ties as Duke had done until all the sleeping cowboys were trussed up.

Less than five minutes passed before they heard the sound of a truck engine heading toward them. Swifty's pickup truck appeared at the edge of the row of buildings and turned and drove slowly toward them. Chief pulled the trailer up to the bunkhouse and they proceeded to drag the unconscious cowboys into the four-horse trailer, dropping them unceremoniously on the trailer floor.

When they were finished with the bunkhouse, Chief drove to the foreman's quarters where they collected the last two victims of the nighttime raid. As soon as they had finished loading the trailer, Duke shut the tailgate and used a hunk of rope from his pack to tie the locking bar in place where a padlock would normally have been used. When he was done, he slapped the side of the trailer and Chief pulled away until his truck and the trailer disappeared into the darkness.

"Back to the bikes," said Bushrod and the four men trotted back to the small grove of trees. Once there, they placed their spare items in the saddlebags. Bushrod stepped into a small clump of pine trees with his knife. When he emerged, he had several broad branches in his hand. He tied them together at the ends where he had cut them with some strong cord he produced from his vest. Then he tied the branches to the rear fender of his bike. "I'll be tail-end Charlie," he said. Swifty nodded he understood, and the four men mounted their bikes. Swifty switched on the GPS. When everyone was ready, Swifty led them back the way they had come.

This time they took their time and reached the fence line separating the two ranches in slightly over an hour. Once there, Doc and Duke climbed the fence and Bushrod and Swifty lifted the bikes over the fence to them. When that task was accomplished, they climbed the fence and helped load the bikes into the bed of the truck. Swifty cut the pine branches from Bushrod's bike and tossed them in the bed of the truck.

Doc grabbed an old duffle bag from the truck and the men stripped off their black clothing and stuffed it into the bag. When they were done, Doc tossed the bag in the truck bed and all four men slipped into the truck.

Ten minutes later they were driving out the edge of the grove of pine trees and headed to Meeteetse. Swifty glanced at his watch. It was almost 0500. He looked to the east and could see light along the edge of the eastern horizon. The sun was making its slow rise into the sky.

CHAPTER FIFTY-TWO

Swifty drove slowly through Cody, being careful to stay under the speed limit and making complete stops at stop signs. He had no intention of having some bored cop pull them over on a whim. The other three old Green Berets were fast asleep in their seats. He drove into the small parking lot behind Ann's office and quickly unloaded the bikes, leaning them against the side of her office building. Then he returned to the truck. His passengers were still dead to the world.

Swifty grinned to himself. He still had adrenaline pumping through his veins. Every time he had been in combat, the emotional rush of it had taken time to dissipate. Usually the process took several hours. He marveled at these old war veterans who simply shut off the strains of emotions. When he reached the entrance to Bushrod's land, he turned off and drove slowly until he came to the gate. There was no sign of Chief, so he stopped the truck, got out and opened the gate and then climbed back in and drove through it. He stopped the truck, jumped out and shut the gate.

On the drive to the old log cabin, the road was pretty rough. Even at slow speeds there was a lot of bouncing and soon he had three grumpy old men bitching at him for being such a lousy driver. They found themselves rudely awakened inside the truck.

Swifty pulled into the clearing and he could see his truck and the horse trailer parked by the camouflage netting. He parked the truck, and he and his passengers disembarked. Chief emerged from under the netting and the five men all high-fived each other. After various jibes and insults were exchanged, Chief drove the truck and trailer to the back area of the netting and stopped. There the men had built a small containment yard of barbed wire topped with razor wire. The yard was covered by the netting and contained a port-a-potty Doc had stolen from somewhere, along with a lister bag and a tin cup attached by a cord. On a small piece of canvass were twenty old army blankets Doc had picked up at an Army-Navy surplus store in Bozeman.

The trailer door was lowered, and the five men worked to drag the still unconscious cowboys into the small compound. Once they had the cowboys inside, they removed the ties on the men's hands but left the ties on their feet. When they finished the task, they exited the compound and padlocked the sturdy entrance. Chief drove the truck back out and unhooked and parked the horse trailer.

The sun was now up, and its warming rays felt good on the tired muscles, especially the four old geezers. All five made their way to the cabin porch where they fell or collapsed into the old chairs and overturned buckets. Bushrod disappeared and then reappeared with a large cooler filled with ice and beer. He sat it on the porch and lifted the lid. Then he proceeded to toss cold cans of beer to each of the ranch raiders.

Duke snapped open his can and drained it in one long

and determined swallow. "Another," he managed to blurt out. Bushrod complied and tossed him a second beer.

"Breakfast of champions," said a grinning Doc, as he held his beer up for a toast.

"Green Berets all the way," shouted Doc, and the other men joined him in drinking to his toast.

When Swifty woke up, he was lying on the floor of the small cabin. His sleeping bag was nowhere in sight. When he sat up, he felt light-headed and his tongue felt like it was three inches thick. He recognized the symptoms. He had gotten slightly drunk. He slowly made his way upright and standing on his unsteady feet. Duke and Doc were still asleep on the floor and Duke was snoring loudly.

When he was able to somewhat focus his eyes, he could see Bushrod at the stove and he could smell bacon cooking. Normally the smell of bacon was enticing to him. This morning his body's response was his stomach started to gurgle. He staggered over to the small counter and poured himself a cup of steaming black coffee into a mug. Then he groped his way along the counter until he could grab a rickety old chair. He managed to get himself seated without falling or spilling the coffee. Once safely seated, he sipped on his coffee. After about five minutes he began to feel like he might actually live. He finished his coffee and got up and refilled his mug.

"Ready to join the ranks of the living?" said Bushrod from his position at the stove.

"I think so," said Swifty.

"I got flapjacks and bacon when you're up to it," said a bemused Bushrod.

"One more cup of coffee, and I think I'll be up to it," responded Swifty.

After Swifty had finished his second cup of coffee, he began to take in his surroundings. Doc and Duke were still out on the floor, but he noticed Chief was missing.

"Where's Chief?" asked Swifty.

"He's monitoring the prisoners," replied Bushrod.

"Where they can see him?" asked a surprised Swifty. Part of his plan was none of them was ever to be visible to the cowboys.

"He's about one hundred feet away in a little lean-to," said Bushrod. "We used solar panels to set up a camera with voice communication so we can see and hear the cowboys, but they can see or hear nothing. We'll trade off watch duties and wear all black with hoods when on duty."

"Who's up next?" asked Swifty.

"Doc is up next. Each of us gets a three-hour shift," said Bushrod.

Swifty rose from his seat and got a plate of flapjacks and bacon and refilled his mug with coffee. He returned to the table and began eating, knowing the best thing he could do was fill his stomach with food.

"Any word from the ranch?" asked Swifty.

"Not a peep so far, but it's early," replied Bushrod.

"How long before the owners get wind the ranch is deserted?" asked Swifty.

"My guess is around noon," said Bushrod. "Someone will call and get no answer and then come out to see what's wrong with the phones and find the place deserted and report it."

"I'll drive down the pass around noon and call my aunt for a sitrep," said Swifty.

"That won't be necessary," said Bushrod.

"Why not?' asked a puzzled Swifty.

"Doc brought one of them fancy satellite phones with him. I ain't got no idea of how to use it, but I'm pretty sure you do. You can call her from here," said Bushrod.

"Great!" said Swifty. "Can I have a look at it?"

"It's over on the shelf under the window over there," said Bushrod, pointing to the far side of the cabin.

Swifty got up and strode over to the window and retrieved the satellite phone. It was an older model, but after a couple of minutes he was sure he had it figured out. He replaced the phone and after refilling his mug with coffee, he went outside and sat on the porch. The sun was up, and he could feel the warm rays on his legs. He was feeling better.

When he finished his coffee, he went back inside and grabbed another mug and filled both of them. With a mug in each hand he walked out to where the lean-to was located. There he found Chief, sitting in a canvas chair, watching the small screen filled with the image of the detention cage. He handed the mug to Chief who accepted it without a word, and Swifty grabbed a nearby bucket and turned it upside down and sat on it.

"Any activity?" he asked Chief.

"None so far," replied Chief. "Them cowboys been very quiet and obedient."

"That'll change when they wake up," said Swifty.

"Yep," replied Chief. "Likely to get damn loud and disorderly over there when that happens."

Swifty nodded his agreement. He wondered how long it would be before the two wealthy owners of the Hayfork Ranch got the word and finally showed up at the airport in Cody.

CHAPTER FIFTY-THREE

Two days passed. The cowboys had awakened from their drug induced sleep and they were none too happy. Their leg ties were sufficiently long enough for them to get up and awkwardly walk, which was useful in making it to the portable outhouse. They were fed three meals a day, each time by a team member dressed all in black with a hood over his head, while a second team member similarly dressed held an M-16 rifle on them.

The team members remained silent. They listened when the cowboys had a question or a problem, but they said nothing in return. Duke got the bright idea of giving them two packs of playing cards and that seemed to help a bit with their boredom and anger.

Swifty had driven down the pass to a spot where he had previously gotten good cell reception. He texted Melinda at the sheriff's office with the number for the satellite phone Doc had provided. She had responded with a text letting him know she had received the number. He also texted his aunt and provided her with the number as well.

Shortly after breakfast on the third day, Swifty got a call on the satellite phone from Melinda. He answered it after the third ring.

"Hello. Is this Swifty?" asked Melinda.

"It's me, Swifty," he replied.

"We just got a call," she said. "The sheriff is supposed to be at the Cody airport at two this afternoon. Them two rich dudes from New York are arriving on a private jet at about that time. Got that?"

"I got it, Melinda. Thanks. I owe you," said Swifty.

"You bet your ass you do. I expect that hundred bucks pronto," she said. "And by the way, the sheriff will be giving them a personal escort to the ranch."

"How are they getting to the ranch?" asked Swifty.

"I heard they rented that Lincoln from the Hertz guy," replied Melinda.

"I'll send you two hundred, Melinda," said Swifty.

"Ohh, you are my favorite cowboy," she squealed. "Gotta go." And she hung up.

Swifty put the phone away and ran out on the porch of the cabin. There he found Doc, Chief, and Bushrod drinking coffee.

"I just got the call," said Swifty. "The two owners are arriving at the airport in Cody at about two this afternoon. The Sheriff is meeting them and will escort them out to the ranch. Apparently, they rented the Lincoln from Hertz and will be driving out in it."

Bushrod thought for a bit and then he said, "It's likely they'll bring the two guys as muscle, so there might be four in the Lincoln. Any way you can verify that?"

"I can call Melinda a little after two," said Swifty. "She'll likely know and if not, I can call my aunt. They have to drive right past her store. She can watch for them and then call us."

"Give her a call," said Bushrod. "The more we know, the better we can prepare."

Swifty called his aunt and gave her the details, including the estimated time of arrival of the private plane in Cody. She promised to be on watch and give him a call. Swifty thanked her and hung up.

Within half an hour the men were dressed appropriately and were gathered around the kitchen table in the small cabin. Bushrod had a map spread out on the table and they were discussing exactly how they wanted things to go down. The plan was for Duke and Doc to dress in army fatigues and use the old car they had snagged to head out to Meeteetse right away. They would drive to Meeteetse and then take the highway out to the Hayfork Ranch. About two miles before the highway reached the ranch, there was a gravel county road which split off from the highway and headed south west. They would take the county road and drive until they were out of sight of the highway and wait for a call from Swifty.

Bushrod was about to ask a question when the satellite phone rang again. Swifty picked it up. It was his aunt. Swifty listened intently and then said, "Hell yes we can use it. Have him park it by the south wall of your building in Meeteetse?" Then he hung up.

"What the hell was that all about?" asked an exasperated Bushrod.

"That was my aunt. My uncle has a World War II Willy's Jeep completely restored with army paint and insignia. She wanted to know if we wanted to use it. I told her yes. It'll be parked on the north wall of her building in an hour with the keys under the mat," said an excited Swifty.

"Great!" said Bushrod. He turned to Doc and Duke. "Take your truck to Meeteetse and park it on the north side of his aunt's building. Move your stuff to the Jeep and get out to the hiding spot as fast as you can. We'll call you when the targets are exiting the ranch. Is that clear?" he asked.

"Clear!" said both Doc and Duke almost in unison.

They gathered their gear and dashed out to Doc's truck. Within minutes, they were roaring out of the small clearing.

Bushrod pointed to Swifty. "You are probably in the best shape of all of us. And you know the country better. Head for your mom's ranch, saddle a horse and get in position to observe the ranch. When those jaspers leave the ranch, call Doc and let him know. Is that clear?" he asked.

"Crystal clear," replied Swifty.

"Well why the hell are you still standing here? Get your ass moving," said Bushrod.

Swifty bolted out the door of the small cabin, unable to keep a smile off his face as he ran. Within minutes he was out on the highway, headed for Cody at a tad over the legal speed limit.

He reached the ranch in record time, although he did slow down to ten miles an hour over the speed limit outside of Cody and carefully drove the speed limit in town. When he reached the road to the ranch, he hit the gas again. Soon he was roaring into the yard in front of his Mom's ranch house. He slid out of the truck, stopped to grab his small rucksack and checked to make sure his binoculars were in the pack. Then he threw the rucksack over his shoulder and ran to the barn. There he saddled the bay. He paused just long enough to pull out the satellite phone and stick it in the rucksack and then he swung his right leg over the saddle.

He rode out the door of the barn without stopping to close the door.

Once out in the pasture, he pushed the bay to a gallop and was soon at the fence line separating his mother's ranch from the Haystack. Swifty slid out of the saddle and pulled a pair of wire cutters out of the rucksack. He quickly cut the fence and pulled the wires to the side. Then he remounted the bay and rode through the new opening. He checked his watch and saw he had over an hour and a half before the owners were likely to arrive at the ranch. He pushed the bay to a trot and headed for the Haystack Ranch. He passed several head of cattle, but never even glanced at them. Swifty's face had a grim and determined look. He couldn't afford a mistake on this mission, and he knew it.

CHAPTER FIFTY-FOUR

It took Swifty almost forty-five minutes to reach the outskirts of the headquarters of the Hayfork Ranch. He slowed the bay to a walk and headed to a point south of the ranch buildings. He knew there was a butte running north and south for a few hundred yards. He would have a good vantage point up on the butte, and he headed to the west end of it.

The sun was out and only a few sparse clouds interrupted the rays of sunlight streaming down on the ranch. Since he entered the Hayfork Ranch, he had not seen any living thing other than cattle. He had slowly circled the bottom of the west end of the butte, looking for a path to the summit. He soon found a well-worn trail and urged the bay up it.

It took him almost fifteen minutes to get to the top of the butte. The top was narrow and rocky, and he let the bay slowly pick her way along the ridgeline. When he was directly even with the cluster of ranch buildings, he continued on until he could see much of the road approaching the ranch entrance.

He found a good place further back on the ridgeline and tied the bay to a slice of rock jutting out of the ground. He made his way to a spot on the ridgeline where he had a good view of the ranch buildings and the road leading up to it. Swifty found a spot between some rocks and made himself as comfortable as possible. He sat in the rocks where he was almost invisible to anyone on the ranch or the road.

He pulled out his field glasses and his phone and checked his cell signal strength. He had two bars, which was good enough. He leaned back against a rock and kept his eyes on the road. After about twenty minutes, he saw the Jeep with Doc and Duke heading toward the ranch. When the Jeep reached the junction, it took the left fork and disappeared behind a grove of trees.

Swifty grinned to himself. Doc and Duke were in place. He shifted his view back to the road and waited. Fifteen minutes later his cell phone buzzed. He pulled out the phone and looked at the screen. He had a text from Melinda. "Sheriff and guests leaving airport for ranch."

Swifty clicked off the phone and returned it to his shirt pocket. Depending on their speed, he estimated the sheriff and his guests were about fifty minutes from the ranch. He shifted his position so he could observe the ranch. He pulled his binoculars up and studied the ranch grounds. He could see two men on a John Deere Gator heading out from a barn. They were heading to the west. He studied the cargo area and saw what he thought were mineral or salt blocks for the cattle. He watched them until they were out of sight. When he scanned the main ranch house, he saw a sheriff's SUV parked in front of the building. He could make out a deputy in uniform leaning against the SUV. The man appeared to be talking to someone in the vehicle. There were likely two deputies on duty watching the ranch. Then

Swifty returned to his position where he had a good view of the incoming road.

He made himself as comfortable as possible, but he knew he needed to stay awake. The sun was warm and the temptation to close his eyes and enjoy the day was strong, but he resisted it.

Forty minutes passed. Then fifty, and still no traffic on the road. He swiveled his view back to the ranch house. Now, both deputies were out and leaning against their SUV. He could see no other activity at the ranch.

An hour and ten minutes after he received Melinda's text, he got a second text from his aunt. "Sheriff car and a Lincoln just passed through town on way to ranch."

Swifty smiled. He had tried to keep things from his aunt, but she was one smart lady and she'd figured things out for herself. He focused his attention on the road to the ranch.

In fifteen minutes, he was rewarded with the sight of the sheriff's car and the black Lincoln heading toward the ranch. He watched as they passed the junction to the wooded area where the Jeep lay hidden. The two vehicles continued on toward the ranch, passing the intersection without any hint of a pause.

Swifty shifted his position so he could concentrate on the ranch house. He watched as the two vehicles parked in front of the building and the sheriff and a deputy emerged from their car. They walked up to the deputies on duty and the four men engaged in an exchange for about two minutes. Then the sheriff gave a hand signal to the Lincoln and the doors opened. Two large men emerged from the front seat of the Lincoln, followed by the smaller and much more slender men from the back seat.

Swifty felt a chill as he had his first real look at the two men who had ordered his father's murder. Anger threatened to consume him, but he repressed his emotions and feelings and calmed himself down.

Down on the lawn of the ranch house, the two owners and the sheriff were engaged in a lengthy discussion with the sheriff doing a lot of pointing and gesturing. Then the three of them got in the sheriff's car, leaving the three deputies and the two bodyguards standing on the ranch house lawn. The sheriff's car drove around the buildings and pulled up in front of the bunkhouse. The three men got out and walked into the bunkhouse, the sheriff leading the way. They were in the bunkhouse for about ten minutes. Then they reappeared next to the sheriff's car. The sheriff was pointing in the direction of the foreman's quarters and gesturing. The two owners shook their heads at whatever the sheriff had said, and the three of them got back in the sheriff's car and returned to the ranch house.

Back at the ranch house, the three men emerged from the sheriff's car, and engaged in a fairly heated exchange. In the middle of their conversation, the John Deer Gator appeared and drove up to the ranch house. The two ranch hands got out of the Gator and shook hands with the sheriff and the owners. The two hands were obviously being questioned about things they had zero knowledge of. The conversation was short, and the two hands climbed back into the Gator and drove off.

The heated conversation with the sheriff continued. Finally, the owners shook hands with the sheriff and he and the deputy got into his car and drove off, heading back towards Meeteetse. The two owners and their bodyguards entered the ranch house, while the remaining two deputies stayed leaning against their SUV.

Swifty had no idea what was going on in the ranch house. All he could do was wait and hope he was right about the two owners. They were rich men. This was their ranch, but all of their employees, including a cook, were gone. Swifty had bet they wouldn't stay at the ranch house. He had assumed they would either return to Cody and stay at a motel, or they would drive directly to the airport in Cody and fly back to New York. Either way, they would have to drive past the phony National Guard roadblock, manned by Doc and Duke.

Swifty shifted his position so he could observe the road junction. He watched as the sheriff's car drove past the junction and headed toward Meeteetse. He texted Doc, "Move to roadblock position."

Almost immediately, the Jeep appeared on the county road and drove up to the intersection where they pulled the Jeep across the road and got out to stand next to it. They wore army uniforms with helmets, and they carried M-16 rifles. They also wore dark sunglasses. "Nice touch, Doc," thought Swifty.

The helmets covered up the two old Green Berets' grey hair. The sunglasses covered up the wrinkles around their eyes.

Swifty shifted his position so he could observe the ranch house. He studied the area with his binoculars, and he waited. He remembered the age-old army complaint,

"Hurry up and wait." It had been true in 1940, and it was just as true today.

After almost twenty minutes, the owners and their bodyguards emerged from the ranch house. They headed straight for the Lincoln. The bodyguards opened the back doors for the owners and then climbed into the front seat of the Lincoln. Swifty noticed they completely ignored the two deputies fifteen feet away. He considered that a good sign. Arrogant assholes.

The Lincoln backed up and turned and then roared out of the ranch house yard. Swifty grabbed his phone and texted Doc. "Target on the way."

Swifty replaced the phone and shifted his position, so he could see the roadblock clearly in his binoculars.

A few minutes later he saw the Lincoln approaching the roadblock. Duke was out between the Jeep and the road from the ranch, while Doc stood behind the Jeep, his M-16 at port arms. Duke had his M-16 across his chest. As the Lincoln slowed and came to a stop about ten yards from the Jeep, Duke approached the driver's side window with his hand out in the traditional military halt signal.

As Swifty watched, the driver lowered his window and leaned forward to hear what Duke had to say. Meanwhile, Doc approached the passenger side front door and when he was next to it, he ripped the door open and produced a dart gun which he used to shoot the bodyguard. At the same time, Duke brought up his M-16 and pointed the muzzle at the driver's head. The driver put his hands up. Doc reloaded and shot the driver in the neck. Soon both bodyguards were slumped down in the Lincoln's rich leather-bound front seat.

Duke then pointed his rifle at the two owners who

were cowering in the back seat of the Lincoln. He shouted something and both men carefully got out of the Lincoln with their hands up. Doc quickly tied both men's ankles and wrists together with snap ties and the two men were shuffled to the waiting Jeep. When they reached the back of the Jeep, the two prisoners were forced to their knees. Doc then shot each of them in the back of the neck with the dart gun. Duke dumped the two smaller men in the back of the old Jeep and covered them with a tarp, which he snugged down to tie-downs on the Jeep.

Then Duke and Doc got in the Jeep and turned it around and headed back toward Meeteetse. As they drove out of sight, Swifty got to his feet and made his way back to his bay. He untied the bay and swung up onto the saddle. Then he headed back to the trail and down the ridge. In less than an hour, he was back at the fence. Once on his mother's ranch, he dismounted the bay and tied it off to a fence post.

Then Swifty removed some tools from the bay's saddlebags and began the work to reconnect the break in the fence he had created earlier in the day. When he was done, he replaced the tools in the saddle bags, untied the bay, and mounted her. Soon he was back at the ranch. He led the bay unto the barn, unsaddled her, and wiped her down. They he gave her an extra ration of oats and returned to his truck. Soon he was driving slowly and carefully through Cody. When he passed the city limits, he pressed the gas pedal, anxious to get back to Bushrod's place and see his father's killers face to face.

CHAPTER FIFTY-FIVE

When Swifty reached Bushrod's drive, he approached the gate ready to jump out. He was surprised when Chief was at the gate. Chief opened the gate and Swifty drove through and then stopped. Chief closed the gate and he jumped into the passenger seat. Swifty looked at Chief and the old Commanche just pointed toward the old abandoned cabin on Bushrod's property. Swifty drove as fast as the bumpy road would allow, and they pulled into the clearing in front of the old cabin.

Bushrod was standing on the cabin's porch. As soon as Swifty had the truck stopped, he and Chief got out and were met by Bushrod. He shook hands with each man, and they walked into the hidden compound to Bushrod's log cabin. The three men climbed up on the porch and each took a seat on the old chairs. Bushrod opened a cooler and tossed a cold beer to Chief and Swifty, finally taking one for himself.

"How'd it go?" asked Bushrod, as casually as if he were inquiring about riding fence.

"It went just like I hoped," said Swifty. "The two owners and their two bodyguards drove to the ranch, talked to the sheriff and looked at the bunkhouse. Then they argued with the sheriff and he left, leaving two deputies to guard the place. The two dudes and their bodyguards went into the ranch house. They were in there for over half an hour."

Swifty paused, to take a swig of beer. Then he continued. "I watched the sheriff's car until it passed the road junction and headed for Meeteetse. Then I called Doc, and he moved the Jeep out onto the road setting up the roadblock. I watched the ranch house and when the four of them got into the Lincoln, I called Doc to alert him," said Swifty.

"What happened at the roadblock?" asked Bushrod.

"Duke stopped the Lincoln. While he talked to the driver, Doc slipped up on the other side of the Lincoln, pulled open the door and shot the guard in the passenger seat with a dart. Duke pulled up his M-16 on the driver, and then Doc shot the driver with a dart," said Swifty.

"Did they resist?" asked Bushrod.

"Nope," said Swifty. "They sort of folded down on their seats. Then Doc and Duke ordered the two owners out of the car. They shackled them with zip ties and made them duck walk over to the Jeep. Doc tranquilized them. He and Duke folded them into the back of the Jeep and covered them with a tarp. Then they drove off toward Meeteetse like they were heading to a church service."

"I'm surprised it went that easy," said Bushrod.

"Surprise is a great weapon," said Swifty. "Those boys had no idea what was coming. The whole thing took less than five minutes. Doc and Duke did a great job."

Swifty took another swig of his beer. "Have you heard from them?" he asked.

"They called after they got to Meeteetse and changed clothes and vehicles and moved the two owners into the truck bed. They were driving slowly up the highway to Cody," said Bushrod.

He looked at his watch. "If they maintained the same pace, they should be here in about twenty minutes," he said.

"How are the cowboys doin'?" asked Swifty.

"They were pretty rowdy this morning and I got tired of it, so I fired a blast from my twelve gauge over their heads and things have been pretty damn quiet since," replied Bushrod.

"So, when do we take the ranch owners to Legend Rock?" asked Swifty.

Bushrod cast a glance over at Chief and Swifty sensed something unspoken between them. Then Bushrod took a sip of beer before answering Swifty's question.

"I think we'll wait till Doc and Duke and their guests get here before we make that decision," said Bushrod.

"I think we should do it as soon as possible," said Swifty.

Bushrod frowned. "I told you in the beginning I was in charge of what we do and don't do," he said. "You can think all you want, but I have the final say on what happens to those two jaspers."

Swifty wisely decided to keep his mouth shut. He drank some more beer, and Bushrod changed the subject.

CHAPTER FIFTY-SIX

It was almost forty minutes before Duke and Doc pulled into the clearing by the abandoned log cabin. They drove the truck over by the cammo netting and parked it. They got out of the truck and Doc went to the bed and took off the tarp covering the truck's cargo. Then he and Duke, with the help of Chief and Swifty unloaded the two unconscious men out of the bed of the truck and onto the ground.

Bushrod walked over and stood directly over the two unconscious bodies. "We'll see how tough these two assholes are tonight."

With that said, he directed the others to put the unconscious duo into sitting positions with their backs to separate trees. Then each of them was tied to their respective tree with strong rope.

"Let's have a beer and decide just how we're gonna' proceed," said Bushrod.

The four men made their way to the cabin porch and took seats on whatever was available, Swifty ending up with an overturned metal bucket. Bushrod handed out cold beers and then he gave everyone a briefing of how the snatch and grab went down. When he was finished, he looked at the other four men.

"Any questions?" Bushrod asked.

There were no questions. There was no noise except for the occasional loud swallow of beer. Swifty had forced himself to keep quiet, but finally he decided to speak up.

"I think we should take the owners to Legend Rock tonight," he said. "The longer we wait, the more chance for something to go wrong with the cowboys or the two owners, or something else we haven't even thought of."

His outburst was met with silence. Finally, Doc spoke. "I think Swifty's right. In Vietnam we got in, and we got out. No dilly dallying and no wasted time. Nothing good can come of waiting for what we got planned."

Bushrod cleared his throat. Then he spoke in a soft, even, but stern voice. "I think Doc is right. The sooner we get this over with, the sooner you boys can get the hell out of here and go home." He looked at the four other men, his gaze lingering on Swifty for a moment or two. "Shall we vote?"

The four other men nodded their agreement. Bushrod put his beer down on the porch floor. "Do we deal with the two New York dudes tonight at Legend Rock?"

Bushrod looked at the four men. "Duke?" he asked.

"Tonight," said Duke

"Doc?" Bushrod asked.

"Tonight," replied Doc.

"Chief?"

"Tonight," grunted Chief.

"Swifty?"

"Tonight," responded Swifty.

"Tonight, it is," said Bushrod. He finished his beer and tossed the empty can on the porch floor.

"Now, gentlemen, this is how it's gonna go down," said Bushrod. He outlined his plan for the evening and gave each of the four other men their assignments and responsibilities. When he was finished, he looked at each of the four men directly. "Any questions?" asked Bushrod.

There were none.

"All right," said Bushrod. Each of you has your assignments. Let's get everything we need together and load it on Doc's truck. We'll plan on leaving here for Legend Rock at midnight. Let's move out."

All five men rose and left the porch to finish their assignments. They gathered at Bushrod's place for a quick supper of brats and beans. When Duke brought in a beer, Bushrod grabbed it from him.

"No booze," said Bushrod. "We have a mission tonight."

Duke nodded his head and didn't complain.

Supper was unusually quiet. When it was over, Doc went out to feed the cowboys and Duke took food out to the now conscious owners of the Hayfork Ranch.

Swifty ate very little. He wasn't sure why, but he had little appetite. Something was bothering him, but he couldn't put his finger on it. He felt he should feel elated, but for some reason all he felt was a sense of foreboding.

CHAPTER FIFTY-SEVEN

By eleven that evening, everything had been packed in the bed of Doc's truck. Each man carried a rucksack with black clothing, including a black ski mask. Every man had checked his weapons several times, and Doc and Swifty had checked and rechecked the tranquilizer darts and guns.

When everything was loaded in the bed of the truck, Bushrod and Chief appeared with Mr. Kimball and Mr. Lincoln. Both men had their hands and ankles zip tied and wore black hoods over their heads. Both had their mouths taped shut. Their once clean, well pressed and pristine designer clothes were now torn and dirty.

"Here are our guests," said Bushrod, "although they seem a bit worse for wear and tear."

Bushrod nodded his approval and then he looked at the three old Green Berets and Swifty.

"Put them in the backseat of the truck and engage the child locks so there is no way they can open the rear doors," said Bushrod. "I'll keep a gun on them in case they suddenly get a sense of gentlemen's outrage at our backwards Wyoming customs."

The two were loaded roughly into the back seat of Swifty's truck, and the child locks engaged. Once the prisoners were secured in the truck, Bushrod turned to Doc. "How are the cowboys?" he asked.

"We gave each of them a shot of tranquilizer," said Doc. "They'll be asleep for about twelve hours."

Bushrod nodded his approval and gave a hand signal for the team to load up.

Then Swifty got behind the wheel, and Bushrod took the front passenger's seat. He produced a large .45 caliber semi-automatic pistol and half turned in his seat, so he could watch the rear seat passengers and hold the gun on them.

Chief, Duke, and Doc got in Doc's truck with Doc driving, Duke in the shotgun position, and Chief taking up the rear seat. Bushrod looked at his watch. It was two minutes until midnight. He rolled down his window and yelled over to Doc, "Let's roll."

Swifty's truck led the way out of Bushrod's property, and he pulled out on the highway headed south, followed by Doc's truck. They drove right at the speed limit with a respectable distance between the two pickup trucks. Swifty kept his eyes on the road. It would be almost a two-hour drive, and he wanted nothing to go wrong on the drive to Legend Rock.

On the drive south from Cody, the highway was almost deserted. Swifty thought he might have seen three vehicles on the entire drive from Bushrod's place. He slowed to drive through little downtown Meeteetse. The two bars were still open. Swifty glanced at the clock on the dash of his truck. It read 1:15 A.M. He passed his aunt's place on his left. It was dark and quiet. The black windows seemed to convey a sense of foreboding. Swifty felt an involuntary shiver run down his back.

An hour and fifty minutes after leaving Bushrod's place, Swifty was pulling into the small, gravel parking lot for visitors to Legend Rock. He parked his truck, and Doc pulled in and parked next to him. Bushrod handed his pistol to Swifty and said, "If they try to escape, shoot them in the head." The two hooded and bound men in the back seat visibly flinched at his words. Swifty allowed himself a small grin at their discomfort. He felt it fitting the two rich, arrogant assholes were probably so frightened they were shitting their pants.

The other three old Green Berets were busy unloading Doc's truck and carrying the contents down the path and out of sight. Swifty rolled down the window on the driver's side of the truck to let the night air in. The air was cool but felt welcome to Swifty's warm and clammy skin.

After almost twenty minutes, Doc appeared in the small parking lot. He motioned for Swifty to get out of his truck and join him about thirty feet away from the truck. Swifty rolled up the window and got out of the truck. Then he walked over to where Doc was standing.

"We're ready at the site," whispered Doc. "How are they doing?" he asked.

"No change, but that's not surprising considering they can't talk or walk, or see anything," replied Swifty.

"Let's get them out of the truck and walk them slowly down the path to the site," said Doc.

"Let's do it," said Swifty.

The two men approached the truck. Swifty opened the rear door on the passenger side while Doc held his sidearm in his hand, giving Swifty protective cover. Swifty reached in and slid his hands under the trussed-up man's armpits and pulled him out of the back seat. Then he stood him up against the side of the truck bed. When he was sure the prisoner wouldn't fall to the ground, Swifty went to the other side of the truck and removed the second prisoner. He forced him to perp walk to the other side of the truck and propped him up against the truck bed, next to his partner. Then he stepped back and turned to Doc.

Doc smiled. He produced two headband lamps from his rucksack and tossed one to Swifty. Both men put the headband lamps on their heads and turned them on. The light created was both bright and powerful.

Doc motioned for Swifty to follow him.

"Works for me," thought Swifty.

Doc walked to the truck and grabbed Kimball and turned him toward the path. Then he grabbed his arm and ordered him to walk. Swifty grabbed Lincoln by the arm and propelled him forward. The zip tie restraints forced both prisoners to take small steps. They ended up walking like the geisha girls Swifty had seen in Japan. He had to force down a smile.

Because of the slow pace, it took a while to reach the creek. Once there, the ground between the creek and the rock cliff was quite level and easier to walk on. As they rounded a large rock against the base of the cliff, they could suddenly see the pit fire Duke had built. It was large and impressive. The flames leaping high into the star-studded night sky.

As Swifty's eyes adjusted to the brightness of the fire, he began to make out the scene in front of him. Behind the fire stood Bushrod and Duke. Chief was nowhere to be seen. That puzzled Swifty. Seeing Chief in the light of a fire would scare the crap out of most men. Especially guilty men who were bound and helpless to resist.

Ten yards from the fire, between it and the cliff were two metal fence posts in the rocky ground. The posts were about four and a half feet high and about six feet apart. Doc led his prisoner over to the farthest fence post and slipped his bound arms over the post and then pushed the man down on the ground until he was sitting on his butt on the rocky surface.

Then Doc came to Swifty and relieved him of his prisoner. He took the other bound man to the other fence post and repeated the procedure he had used on the first prisoner. Once he was finished. He motioned Swifty to join Bushrod and Duke on the other side of the fire.

As Swifty moved to comply with Doc's unspoken directions, Doc moved toward the creek and quickly set up a camera on a tripod. After he adjusted the tripod, he switched on the camera which caused a small red light on the camera to begin pulsing. Satisfied, Doc joined the line of the other three raiders.

Once Doc was in position, Bushrod removed his ski mask and motioned for the others to do the same. This puzzled Swifty, because now their faces would be known to Kimball and Lincoln. Suddenly he began to have a bad feeling about what was to come.

Then Bushrod motioned to Doc who came forward and removed the hoods and the gags on the two prisoners. Both men's eyes were blinking, and their heads turned as they adjusted to the light of the fire and the scene before them.

Kimball was the first to speak. "What the hell is going on here? I demand you release us immediately or I'll bring down the power of every court in the land and put all you assholes in the gas chamber."

"I order the prisoner to be silent, unless he is asked a question," said Bushrod in a loud and stern voice.

"Kiss my ass, you reprobate hillbilly," said Lincoln who was as confused and angry as Kimball.

"You open your mouth one more time without permission of the court, and I'll cut your tongue off," said a grim Bushrod as he pulled a very large knife from its scabbard on his belt. "And believe me, I'll enjoy doing it. Nod your heads if you understand what I've just told you," he commanded.

Both bound men suddenly realized they were in a situation unlike any they had ever encountered except in watching a movie or reading a book. Both of them nodded their heads that they understood Bushrod's command.

"You two are in the presence of the court of true justice," said Bushrod. "Tonight, you will be tried for the crime of murder in the first degree for the intentional death of Eldon Olson. If you are found guilty, the penalty is death."

Shock spread across the faces of the two accused men. The reality of what might happen seemed to overwhelm their normal senses. Fear and shock seemed to overtake their bodies and minds. Neither of them uttered a word. Their voices were literally frozen with fear.

"The jury for this court consists of the four men in front of you. All four of them have fought against the foreign enemies of the United States of America. All of them have served their country heroically and are prepared to stand in judgement of greedy cowards who killed an innocent man to steal his land from him for their ill-gotten gain," said Bushrod.

Bushrod paused, and then turned toward Doc.

"Please read the charges, Bailiff," Bushrod said to Doc.

Doc took a slip of paper out of his shirt pocket and began to read. "Earlier this year, Theodore Lincoln and Barry Kimball ordered and paid others to sabotage the vehicle of Eldon Olson, causing a wreck and Mr. Olson's untimely death. The charge is murder. The punishment is death," said Doc with finality and then he replaced the paper in his pocket and stepped back in line with Duke and Swifty.

"You have heard the charges against you, Mr. Lincoln and Mr. Kimball," said Bushrod. "How do you plead?"

Kimball weakly raised his hand as if asking for permission to speak.

"You have a question, Mr. Kimball?" asked Bushrod.

"Yes sir," said Kimball nervously and haltingly. "Are we allowed the services of an attorney?" he asked.

"You are not," replied Bushrod sternly.

Kimball's head fell forward as if in defeat, and Lincoln still looked dazed as if he was witnessing a bad dream.

"How do you plead, Mr. Kimball?" asked Bushrod.

Kimball started to speak and then caught himself and tried to assert some pride in his response. Then he straightened his posture as best he could. "I plead not guilty," he said.

Bushrod turned to face Lincoln. "How do you plead, Mr. Lincoln?" he asked.

Lincoln still looked confused, and he did not respond.

He looked as though he was trying to swim out of a bad dream.

"I repeat, how do you plead to the charges, Mr. Lincoln," asked Bushrod.

Lincoln finally seemed to assert himself and stared straight at Bushrod. "I plead not guilty to this nonsense," he snarled at Bushrod.

Bushrod turned to Swifty. "Enlighten the defendants, Mr. Prosecutor," he said nodding at Swifty.

Swifty was slightly surprised. He recovered from it and stepped forward toward the defendants and when he was about ten yards from them, he stopped.

Swifty looked at the two bound men. He saw hatred and contempt in their eyes. Contempt not only for him, Bushrod and the others, but for their way of life and the laws of the United States of America. A country he, Bushrod, and the others had sworn to defend against all enemies, foreign and domestic.

"When I returned for Mr. Olson's funeral, I obtained a copy of the police report of his fatal accident. I examined the accident site and then his damaged vehicle in the sheriff's impound lot. I found the brake lines cut," said Swifty. Then he powered up his phone and displayed the photo he took of the sliced brake line.

"I next obtained copies of mineral searches done on the Hayfork Ranch, ordered by Mr. Lincoln and Mr. Kimball. The report showed traces of rare earth minerals. The closer the search got to Mr. Olson's ranch, the stronger the amount of minerals. Based on that search, I suspected the bulk of the valuable rare earth minerals were located on Mr. Olson's ranch. I had this verified by a separate mineral search done a week ago. The foreman of the Hayfork Ranch tried to buy Mr. Olson's ranch. When Mr. Olson refused, he was killed on orders from Mr. Kimball and Mr. Lincoln so they could buy the ranch from Mrs. Olson for a fraction of its true value," said Swifty.

When he finished, Swifty turned and walked back to stand in line with Duke and Doc.

"After hearing the evidence, would either of the defendant like to change their plea?" asked Bushrod.

"Fuck you," said Kimball and Lincoln attempted to spit at Bushrod. Both his range and aim were inadequate.

Bushrod had a grim smile on his face. "Both of the defendants have a serious lack of respect for the laws of the United States of America and for the jurisdiction of this court. This is not New York, gentlemen. This is Wyoming. The evidence is overwhelmingly against both of you. I will give you one more chance to change your plea, before we resort to western justice. How do you plead?" asked Bushrod.

Both men exploded in an avalanche of curses aimed at Bushrod and the rest of their captors.

Bushrod waited until they ran out of breath. Then he spoke with an evil smile on his face. "You gentlemen leave me no choice. The East you inhabit may seem a rough, but sophisticated place to you. The West, and in particular Wyoming, has a savage form of justice. Whenever proper justice fails to take hold, western justice intervenes and asserts itself."

With that he motioned towards the darkness at the edge of the creek. From the shadows appeared the defendants' worst nightmare.

CHAPTER FIFTY-EIGHT

From the edge of the night's darkness and onto the edge of the flickering light produced by the fire, a figure emerged. Swifty blinked to make sure he was seeing what he thought he was seeing.

Chief emerged into the circle of light created by the fire. Only he didn't look like the Chief Swifty knew. He wore his hair in two braids. A beaded headband surrounded his head. He was naked except for a loin cloth. His body was painted with streaks of crude colors and his body gleamed like it had been covered in oil. The light from the fire reflected on his body.

In his hands, Chief held a tomahawk in one hand and a long ugly knife in the other. The fire reflected off the burnished steel of the knife blade. Chief slowly walked until he was between the fire and the two captives.

Swifty glanced at the two bound men. They were shocked at the sight of the warlike painted body of Chief. The horror in their faces gave evidence they began to understand what was in store for them.

"You can't do this," screamed Kimball. "This is barbaric. It's inhumane."

Bushrod stood by the fire with his arms folded. He said nothing, but his grim face said volumes.

Chief stopped and stared intently at the two captives. Then he swung the tomahawk and then the knife toward the two bound men. As he swung each arm, the weapons he held made a swishing sound that penetrated the night like a siren.

"You people are perverts," screamed out Lincoln, as he thrashed about and tried to get to his feet.

After several minutes of silence and no movement from Chief, during which the two men screamed and pleaded for mercy, Chief moved slowly toward the two bound men, expertly swinging the tomahawk and knife in the night air as he did.

He reached Kimball first and knelt on one knee next to him. After a few seconds of staring into Kimball's terrified face, Chief laid the tomahawk on the ground next to him. Then he took his now freed hand and grabbed Kimball's hair with it and jerked his head forward.

Without any warning he brought the sharp knife up and pressed the point into the flesh on the man's head began cut Kimball's skin on his head to the skull. Kimball screamed and then he fainted. Chief paid no attention to Kimball's condition, and he continued to use his knife to begin the ritual scalping by cutting the skin to the bone in a circle around the top of the skull.

Lincoln began shouting, "I'll talk, I'll talk, please stop!"

Then Chief stood, holding the bloody knife in one hand. Kimball's head was covered with blood as the knife inflicted head wound bled freely. Then Lincoln fainted.

Chief stepped back a few paces and stood there in front of the fire, holding his bloody knife.

Duke stepped forward and carried a collapsible pail of water which he proceeded to throw half in the face of Lincoln, and the other half in the face of Kimball. Both men were revived, sputtering and shaking their heads to rid themselves of the water.

Bushrod waited a couple of minutes until both captives were awake and somewhat focused. Then he spoke. "I warned you of the consequences and this is just the beginning of what lies in store for greedy men like you who use money and influence to lie, cheat, steal, and even kill to get what they want."

Bushrod paused to let his words soak in.

"I ask you again, Mr. Lincoln, how do you plead to the charges against you?" said Bushrod.

Lincoln was in a state of shock. He looked bewildered, but Bushrod's words cut through his temporary confusion. He looked at his bloody partner and then at Bushrod.

"I plead guilty," he said haltingly. "Please don't scalp me," he begged.

"Explain to the court what you and your partner really did," said a stern Bushrod.

Lincoln paused for a few seconds and then he spoke in halting words about how he and Kimball had learned of the rare earth minerals and brought a team onto the Hayfork Ranch to search for them. They found solid traces, but they led to the small, adjoining ranch belonging to Eldon Olson. They used their ranch foreman to try to buy the ranch. When several attempts failed, they decided to have Olson killed in a staged accident and then bargain with his wife, who was most likely willing to sell the ranch after the death of her husband.

When he had finished talking, Lincoln broke into sobs.

Bushrod hesitated for a bit and then asked another question.

"What did you pay to have Mr. Olson killed in the staged accident?" he asked.

Lincoln looked up at Bushrod. His face revealed a thoroughly beaten and frightened man.

"Five thousand dollars," he finally uttered in a low voice.

"You paid five thousand dollars to have Eldon Olson killed?" said Bushrod with both surprise and anger in his voice.

"Yes, sir," muttered Lincoln, unable to look at Bushrod.

"Then I find you and your partner, Mr. Kimball, guilty of murder," said Bushrod in a loud and stormy voice.

Swifty was leaning forward, his entire focus on the scene in front of him. He had been surprised, but not upset with seeing Chief start to scalp Kimball, but he felt elation in his body over Lincoln's confession. He knew the film of the confession would never survive in a real court of law, but this was good enough for him.

While he was waiting to see what Bushrod did next, Swifty felt a sting in the back of his neck. Within seconds everything seemed to grow black around his field of vision and then everything was black, and he felt himself falling to the ground. Then he felt nothing.

CHAPTER FIFTY-NINE

In his subconscious Swifty heard a female voice calling his name followed by the sound of hard, insistent tapping. His mind felt like it was full of cobwebs and his arms and legs seemed slow to respond to instructions from his brain. Finally, he was able to open his eyes and he began to try to focus.

His brain heard a woman's voice, but he couldn't recognize it, nor could he understand what she was trying to say. Then, gradually, his eyes began to become focused, and he saw the face of his Aunt Judy.

Then he heard her voice calling his name. Her voice sounded like it was coming out of a long tunnel, and then it became louder and more distinct.

"Swifty. Wake up. Wake up. Do you hear me?" she implored. Swifty looked up at her and saw tears in her eyes. He shook his head like he was trying to eliminate cobwebs in his brain. Then his head seemed to clear, and he slowly sat up on the front seat of his truck. His aunt was leaning into the truck, trying to shake him awake.

It took a few more minutes before he could speak in sentences, but he finally managed to tell his aunt he was all right.

"What happened?" asked his frightened aunt.

"I got drugged and knocked out," said Swifty as he rubbed the sides of his head and tried to get his bearings.

"Who did that to you?" she asked.

"I'm not sure," Swifty replied.

"Why would someone do this to you?" his aunt asked.

"I have no idea," replied Swifty.

"We need to get you inside and get some hot coffee in you," said Aunt Judy.

"Let me get up," said a still unsteady Swifty.

Swifty tried to sit up using his arms and hands. He failed the first time and after resting for a few seconds, he managed to get himself upright on the second try. After resting again for a bit, he managed to turn his body toward the open door and slowly swing his feet outside the truck door. With his aunt's help, Swifty slid down to the ground. He had to use his hands and arms to grip the sides of the truck to pull himself upright and stand on solid ground.

Aunt Judy took his arm and put it around her shoulders, and she helped him walk and limp towards the entrance to her store. Once inside, she guided him to a straight wooden chair. With her help he managed to get himself seated. When he tried to turn to face his aunt, he almost slid off the chair and onto the floor.

"Take it easy, Swifty. Try to do everything slowly and carefully," said his aunt.

"I'm trying, but my body seems to think my mind is stupid," replied Swifty. After a minute, Swifty tried again and managed to turn his body in the chair so he could face his aunt. He looked up, but his aunt was gone.

She reappeared in a minute with a cup of hot, black

coffee in her hand. "Drink this," she said. She handed the cup to Swifty, and she held his hand as he lifted the cup to his mouth with an unsteady motion. Swifty felt the hot liquid in his mouth as he sipped the coffee and after a moment, he sipped some more. In a few minutes he had finished the coffee and his aunt had refilled his cup. He drank the second cup much more quickly and with a much steadier hand.

After fifteen minutes and three cups of hot coffee, Swifty felt stronger, steadier, and more in control of his body. When his aunt offered him a fourth cup of coffee, he held up his hand and said, "I've had enough for now. Thank you, Aunt Judy. I think you just saved my life."

"I hardly think coffee saved your life, Swifty," said his aunt with a laugh. "What in the world happened to you?"

Swifty looked up to respond to his aunt's question when he noticed his reflection in the mirror hanging on the wall behind the old counter. "What the hell?" he said.

"What's wrong?" asked Aunt Judy.

"My clothes, what happened to my clothes?" exclaimed Swifty.

His aunt looked at him like he was demented. "You have clothes," she said. "You're wearing them."

"I mean the clothes I was wearing at Legend Rock," said Swifty. "I was wearing black combat trousers, shirt and a black ski mask when we left for the park. They're gone, and all I have on is the clothes I was wearing underneath them."

"Let me check in your truck," said Aunt Judy. With that she hurried out of her store and down the old wooden sidewalk to the side of the building where Swifty's truck was parked. She returned a few minutes later. "There's no clothes in your truck," she said. "I even looked in the bed, and it's empty."

Swifty looked up as if he was not believing what he was seeing and hearing. He shook his head and then began slowly processing the facts he could remember and those his aunt had supplied. Time and the coffee he had consumed were finally disbursing the cobwebs that had entangled his brain after being drugged.

"I think I've figured it out," said Swifty to his aunt.

"What happened?" asked Aunt Judy.

Swifty began to explain the plan and then the events of the evening at Legend Rock to his aunt as he recalled them. The more he talked, the stronger his voice got and the brighter the images in his mind became.

"So, after Chief scared Mr. Lincoln and Mr. Kimball and Lincoln confessed to paying to have Eldon killed, someone shot you with this drug gun?" said Aunt Judy.

"That's what had to happen," said Swifty.

"Why would someone on your team drug you?" asked Aunt Judy.

"The only reason I can think of is they wanted me out of what was going to happen next," said Swifty. "The more I think about it, I'm sure it was Bushrod's idea. He didn't want me involved in what they were going to do next?"

"What were they going to do?" asked Aunt Judy.

Swifty paused. He now had a clear picture in his mind of what probably happened after he was drugged and why. He wasn't sure he should share it with his aunt. His Aunt Judy was a good woman, a strong woman and an honest law-abiding woman. What had likely happened to Kimball and Lincoln wasn't something he felt he should share with her.

Finally, he responded to his aunt's question. "I'm not sure," he said. "But whatever it was, I think Bushrod wanted to keep me out of it."

"Why would he do that after all you had done with him?" asked Aunt Judy.

"I think he didn't want me to see or know what was to happen next," said Swifty. "I can't be guilty of a crime I know nothing about."

"If true, it's twisted," said Aunt Judy. "Kind of sweet, but definitely twisted."

"I don't think it's twisted," said Swifty. "Bushrod wanted justice for his son and he knew he'd never get it in the justice system in this country against two rich gay guys."

"What are you going to do?" asked Aunt Judy with a concerned look on her face.

Swifty smiled at his aunt. Other than his mother, Aunt Judy had been the most important woman in his life. She had cared for him like he was her son, not her sister's. She was also a smart and resourceful woman. Most of all, he trusted her.

"I'm going to get something to eat, and then I'm going to see my grandfather and get his side of the story," said Swifty. "Any suggestions?" he said with a smile.

"You little scamp," said his aunt. "I don't have much here other than doughnuts and coffee and you know it."

"Sounds good to me," said Swifty.

His aunt put several doughnuts in a bag and gave him black coffee in a large to go cup. Swifty stood, put the coffee and bag on the table and gave his favorite aunt a big hug. "Thank you for everything Aunt Judy. I'll find a way to repay you for your kindness."

"You'd better," said his aunt with a wry smile on her face.

"I'll be in touch," said Swifty as he walked out the front door of his aunt's store. Five minutes later he was sitting in his truck with the engine running. He checked his phone and his laptop for messages from his grandfather or any of the other old Green Berets. There were none.

He reached under the dash of the truck and opened a secret compartment. He opened it and pulled out a Kimber full size .45 ACP semi-automatic pistol in stainless steel. The gun caught the sunlight and gleamed in his hand. He extracted the gun's ammo magazine and held it up to the light. Eight rounds of deadly hollow point ammunition gleamed in the light. He replaced the magazine in the gun. Then he stuck the pistol in the holster he kept in the console and slipped it over his belt in the small of his back.

"Time to find out the truth," he thought to himself, and he put the truck in gear and headed south, back to Legend Rock.

CHAPTER SIXTY

The drive to Legend Rock took about twenty minutes. Once he had taken the turn to the site, he was quickly in the parking lot. He looked at his watch. It was about ten in the morning. There were two other cars in the lot. Both of them had out-of-state license plates.

Swifty got out of the truck and stood for a minute. He was still a bit woozy. He stood motionless for about two minutes, and then he set out on the path to the site.

When he reached the creek and made his way along the bottom of the cliff, he heard voices. When he turned the corner of the cliff and came within sight of the fire location the previous night, he heard voices and then saw four or five people wandering along the cliff side, looking at the petroglyphs. He walked to the spot where he remembered the fire. There was nothing. There were no ashes, no slightly burned wood, nothing. Just sand.

Swifty got down to his knees and sifted through the sand with his fingers. He came up with a few bits of burned wood. He rose to his feet and walked over to where Chief had cut Kimball's head. Kimball had bled profusely which is usually the case with any kind of head wound. The ground there was bare. There was no sign of disturbance nor any trace of blood. Again, he went to his knees and used his fingers to sift through the sand. This time he found nothing.

Swifty rose to his feet and looked all around him. It was as if last night had never happened. He listened to the chatter of the tourists looking at the petroglyphs for a minute. Then he turned and walked back on the path to his truck.

Forty minutes later he was driving through the tiny downtown of Meeteetse. As he passed his Aunt's store, he thought he needed to do something for her to reward her for her help and her kindness. People like her were as rare as diamonds. He owed her, and he would until he had a chance to repay her in some fashion.

Swifty stopped in Cody and gassed up his truck. He bought a Coke at the gas station and the cold sweet liquid seemed to calm him down. He finished the can and tossed it in a nearby trash can. Soon, he was driving out of Cody and headed for Beartooth Pass and his grandfather's place.

As he drove, he tried to decide how he was going to handle the meeting with his grandfather. He mentally made a list of questions in his mind. He wanted answers, but he also knew who he was dealing with. Bushrod Olson was not someone you could intimidate. If Bushrod didn't feel like answering any questions, there was no doubt he wouldn't.

When Swifty reached the nearly hidden entrance to Bushrod's land, he pulled into the rough road and stopped the truck. He reached behind himself and pulled out his semi-auto .45 ACP Kimber pistol. He ejected the magazine and checked it. Satisfied, he inserted the mag back into his pistol and returned the Kimber to his holster.

He drove to the old gate and stopped the truck. He

shut off the engine and listened for sounds and looked for any signs. Big Dave had taught him. "Look and listen for what don't belong." He heard nor saw anything suspicious. He sniffed the air. There was a trace of woodsmoke, but nothing else.

Satisfied, he got out, opened the gate and then drove through it. Then he got out and closed the gate. The drive to the clearing was short, even though he took it very slowly. When he reached the clearing, he drove halfway to the old ruined cabin and parked the truck. He slipped out of the truck and slowly and quietly closed the door.

He stood silently next to the truck and carefully scanned his surroundings. He could not see, nor hear, nor smell anything out of the ordinary. He could smell a hint of pipe tobacco, but that was it. Satisfied there was no immediate threat, Swifty slowly and carefully made his way under the cammo covering and walked toward the small log cabin Bushrod called home.

When he got close enough, he could see Bushrod sitting on the small porch of the cabin. He was in an old chair, smoking his pipe. Swifty scanned his body for any signs of weapons. The only things he saw was Bushrod's old Winchester model 94 propped up against the cabin wall next to his chair. Alongside Bushrod's chair was an old battered cooler. Unconsciously, Swifty's right hand drifted behind his back to quickly touch the butt of his Kimber.

As Swifty approached the porch, Bushrod nodded at him. Swifty climbed up on the porch and sat on an old empty chair next to his grandfather.

"Glad to see you're all right," said Bushrod with sincerity in his voice.

"I'm still a bit woozy," said Swifty.

"Could you use a beer?" asked Bushrod.

"I believe I could," answered Swifty.

Bushrod reached over and opened the old cooler and produced two cold beers. He tossed one to Swifty who easily snatched it out of the air.

"Reflexes still look good," said Bushrod.

Swifty grinned, in spite of himself.

"So, what really happened last night," said Swifty.

Bushrod took a long sip of cold beer and then sat the can down on the old cooler. Then he looked directly at Swifty. "We both know nothing we got out of those two rich galoots was ever gonna be admissible in any court anywhere in the U.S.," said Bushrod.

"But we filmed it," said Swifty.

"Film wouldn't have been admissible," said Bushrod. "Besides, there weren't no film in the camera. That was just to make you feel better about what was gonna happen," said Bushrod.

"But I saw Doc set it up," protested Swifty.

"You saw Doc set up a camera with no film in it," said Bushrod.

Swifty was silent for a minute as he digested this new information. Then he spoke again.

"Who put me out and why?" he asked his grandfather.

"Doc put you down with a small dose. He slipped behind you while you were engrossed with Chief's performance," said Bushrod.

"Doc?" said Swifty.

"He's the best of us with drugs and we wanted you out, not hurt," said Bushrod. "When we were done there, we loaded you up in your truck and Doc drove you to your Aunt's place in Meeteetse and left you there. We picked up Doc and drove back here. Then we hooked up the horse trailer, loaded the unconscious cowboys into it and drove it to a small empty rest area east of Cody. We unhooked the trailer there and left it."

"With the cowboys locked in it?" asked Swifty.

"The hasp was held in place with a small stick," said Bushrod. One decent push from inside and the tailgate would have fallen to the ground."

There was a pause and silence fell over both men. Swifty knew what he needed to ask, and he was not sure of the best way to do it. Finally, he broke the silence and spoke.

"What happened after I was knocked out?" asked Swifty.

"Justice happened," said Bushrod with a steely grimness in his voice.

"Justice?" asked Swifty.

"Western justice," said Bushrod. "Our ancestors settled this country long before there were any courts, lawyers, judges or law books. When bad things happened, good men got together and took the law into their hands and got justice for the victims of the crime and for their friends, family, and neighbors."

"Can you describe this western justice to me?" asked Swifty.

"Some I can," said Bushrod. "I had you knocked out so you wouldn't be a party to seeing real western justice happen. I didn't want you to be legally culpable in any way. What you didn't witness or take part in can't be tied to you."

Bushrod took another drink of his beer, and then he spoke again. "Me and the boys are old men. We applied western justice to those two murdering rich assholes. They got what they deserved, and justice was served. We all knew we might be caught, tried, and put in prison, but all of us are the end of the trail in our lives. You're not. We didn't want what we did to touch your life in any way."

There was another long silence. Then Swifty spoke.

"What happened to Kimball and Lincoln?' he asked.

"They disappeared," replied Bushrod. "They vanished from the face of the earth. I can guarantee you no trace of those mangy bastards will ever be found. Not in one year, not in ten years, not in a hundred years."

Bushrod paused and looked directly at his grandson.

"I'm lucky to still be alive. I was ready to die thirty years ago, but I didn't. I've spent the past thirty-some years just existing. I wasn't fond of my son Eldon, but he was my son. He didn't deserve to die the way he did. He died alone and in the dark and not knowing why. He deserved vengeance and that need for vengeance gave me purpose. Me, Doc, Duke, and Chief were given a new lease on life, a purpose, a reason to live when you came to me with the story about Eldon's death," said Bushrod. "We all thank you for that. For the four of us to have one last mission with real purpose was important to all of us, especially to me."

Swifty sat quietly in his chair. He wasn't sure of what to say to his grandfather. He looked at Bushrod and saw something he had never seen. Bushrod had real tears in his eyes.

"I think you should go before I say anything more I might regret," said Bushrod. "But I want you to know how proud I am of you. I didn't get the son I wanted, but I sure as hell got the grandson I hoped for. I watched everything you did while you were here. I couldn't be prouder of you."

Swifty rose to his feet. He left his untouched beer on the porch floor. Bushrod extended his right hand and Swifty took it. The handshake evolved into a strong man hug. Swifty felt the strength of his grandfather in the hug. He also felt the old man's love.

Bushrod walked with Swifty to his truck. When they reached the door of the pickup, Bushrod spoke.

"I want you to have something that means a lot to me, and I hope you will think of me every time you look at it," he said. With that said, Bushrod reached into his rear pants pocket and pulled out his old Green Beret and handed it to Swifty.

Swifty took the beret and looked at Bushrod. "Thank you, Grandpa," he said. The two men hugged again and then Swifty climbed into the truck and drove out of the clearing. The last thing he saw in his rear-view mirror was his grandfather, standing in the meadow giving his grandson a farewell salute.

When Swifty reached the highway, he turned his truck toward Cody and stepped on the gas.

CHAPTER SIXTY-ONE

As Swifty entered the outskirts of Cody, he called Kit on his cell phone.

"Hello," said Kit.

"It's me," said Swifty.

"Who's me?" said Kit. "I know a lot of people and most of them I usually hang up on."

"You know damn well who this is," said Swifty.

"Are you my long-lost partner who left me high and dry while our business is knee deep in work we need to get done," asked Kit.

"The one and only," replied Swifty.

"So, when are you gonna grace us with your presence, Mr. Swifty?" asked Kit.

"I'll be heading home tomorrow morning," said Swifty.

"It's about time," said Kit. "I was starting to think you were working for the government instead of having a real job where you have to actually show up and do real work."

Swifty laughed, said good-bye, and then hung up.

When he reached Cody, he pulled off the road and pulled out his phone. He called The Local, the best restaurant in Cody and made reservations for two at seven that evening.

Then he disconnected the phone and pulled back onto the highway.

He drove into Cody and stopped to fill his truck with gas. While he was pumping gas into the truck, he pulled out his phone and called Ann.

"Hello," said Ann.

"Hey, this is me," said Swifty.

"What happened?" she asked.

"I'll tell you in a bit," said Swifty. "How much do I owe you for the tranquilizer guns, the drugs, and for the bike rentals?" he asked.

"Do you still have the guns?" she asked.

"I can get them. They're stashed up at my grandfather's place," replied Swifty.

"I can stop up there and get them. It'd be a good excuse to meet him and see his place," replied Ann.

"Are you sure you're ready to meet the black sheep of my family?" asked Swifty.

"I've already met him. I used to date him in high school," retorted Ann.

Swifty laughed. "You got me again," he said.

"One of many," Ann said.

"How much for the drugs and the bike rental?" asked Swifty.

"How about you stop by and I can give you a total?" Ann said.

"I've got a better idea," said Swifty.

"What's that?' asked Ann warily.

"Dress up in something semi-respectable, and I'll pick you up at 6:45 tonight," said Swifty.

"To go where?" Ann asked.

"I've got reservations for two at The Local at seven tonight," said Swifty.

"Good lord," said Ann. "Let me check out the window to make sure the sky isn't falling."

"I already checked. It ain't," said Swifty. "See you at quarter till seven tonight. Bye"

"I need a drink," said Ann and she hung up.

Swifty grinned and headed for the ranch. As he drove through downtown Cody, he reached into his vest and pulled out his grandfather's Green Beret. Swifty carefully set the beret on the top of the truck's dash, right under the rearview mirror. Satisfied, he hit the accelerator and roared in the direction of his mother's ranch.

THE END

ACKNOWLEDGEMENTS

Writing this story was a personal pleasure for me. Bringing my character Swifty Olson to center stage and telling his story was interesting, fun, and sobering, all at the same time. As I mentioned in the dedication, Swifty is my fictional embodiment of my old friend Gary Carlson. They are both smart, tough, resilient, and fun loving. Both are adventuresome and self-reliant in a rough and tumble world.

I hope you, the reader, enjoyed learning Swifty's story as much as I did in telling it.

This is my ninth novel and the eighth in a series about my main character Carson "Kit" Andrews, although he has just a bit part in this story.

Please feel free to let me know what you thought about the book, both good and bad. As a writer, I learn from criticism as well as compliments. Please send your comments or questions to me at **rwcallis@aol.com**. I look forward to hearing from you.

I wish to thank all the people who helped me in writing this book. First and foremost is my wife Nancy. She is my main proofreader, critic, and supporter. I also received assistance from Mary Marlin, Marcia McHaffie, and my son Steve Tibaldo. All of them read my periodic drafts and provided proofreading and suggestions as well as encouragement. My son Steve provides advice on military issues, including weapons, equipment, and tactics.

All four of them were exceptionally helpful and necessary for me to write this novel. I couldn't have done this without their help. There were also a few others who read parts of the book and gave me honest criticism.

I would also like to thank Judy Vannoy, my cousin, for allowing me to use her name for Swifty's Aunt.

I write because I enjoy writing and creating a story that exists only in my imagination. I like writing about things both historic and real, and let my imagination take it from there.

When people read my stories and enjoy them it gives me a great deal of satisfaction. Thank you for being one of my readers. Kit and Swifty and their friends exist only in my imagination. For me, it is great fun to have them come to life and see what happens.

Made in the USA
Coppell, TX
08 October 2020

39457425R00213